THE MISREAD CITY

THE MISREAD CITY

New Literary Los Angeles

edited by

SCOTT TIMBERG

and

DANA GIOIA

Red Hen Press 🐓 Los Angeles

Cover art "Wake Up, Angeleno!"
Acrylic on Paper; 40" x 26"
Copyright © 2001 by Sandow Birk

Cover photographs
"Huntington Botanical Gardens" Copyright © 2003 by Steven Dewell
"Olympic Blvd" Copyright © 2003 by Steven Dewell
"Venice Beach" Copyright © 2003 by Steven Dewell

Book and cover design by Mark E. Cull

ISBN 1-888996-69-2
Library of Congress Catalog Card Number 2003091193

Printed in Canada

Publication of this volume is made possible in part
through support by the California Arts Council.

Special thanks and acknowledgement is made to John Ebey
whose support made this book possible.

Published by Red Hen Press

First Edition

To Ray Bradbury, whose imagination made Los Angeles universal and to Jack Foley, who keeps the northern half of the state well-versed.

ACKNOWLEDGMENTS

Brendan Bernhard: "Perhaps These Are Not Poetic Times At All: Poetry and Los Angeles at the Millennium." Reprinted with permission from *L.A. Weekly*. Copyright © 1999 *L.A. Weekly*.

Laurel Ann Bogen: "Pygmy Headhunters and Killer Apes, My Lover and Me." Reprinted from *The Burning: New and Selected Poems 1970–1990* (Red Wind Books) by permission of the author. Copyright © 1991 by Laurel Ann Bogen.

Wanda Coleman: "Prisoner of Los Angeles (2)" copyright © 1983 by Wanda Coleman. Reprinted from her collection *Imagoes* by Black Sparrow Books (imprint of David Godine, Publisher, Inc.), with the permission of the author.

Jenny Factor: "Letter from Headquarters" from *Unraveling at the Name*. Copyright © 2002 by Jenny Factor. Reprinted with the permission of Copper Canyon Press, P.O. Box 271, Port Townsend, WA 98368-0271.

David Fine: "Endings and Beginnings: Surviving Apocalypse" from *Imagining Los Angeles: A City in Fiction*. Reprinted with permission of University of New Mexico Press. Copyright © 2000 by University of New Mexico Press.

Kate Gale: "This Side of the Rainbow." Copyright © 2003 by Kate Gale.

Lynell George: "Walter Mosley's Secret Stories: A Ride With a Mystery Writer Who Evokes the Unclichéd." Copyright © 1994 by *Los Angeles Times*. Reprinted with permission.

Peter Gilstrap: "The House That Blacks Built." Reprinted from *New Times* by permission of the author. Copyright © 2002 by Peter Gilstrap.

Dana Gioia: "California Hills in August California Hills in August." Reprinted from *Daily Horoscope* (Graywolf Press) by permission of Dana Gioia. Copyright © 1986 by Dana Gioia.

Laurence Goldstein: "City of Poems: The Lyric Voice in Los Angeles Since 1990." Copyright © 2003 by Laurence Goldstein.

Pico Iyer: "The Mystery of Influence: Why Raymond Chandler persists." Copyright © 2002 by *Harper's Magazine*. All rights reserved. Reproduced from the October issue by special permission.

Ken Kelley: "Playboy Interview: Ray Bradbury." From the Playboy Interview: Ray Bradbury, *Playboy* magazine (May 1996). Copyright © 1996 by Playboy. Reprinted with permission. All rights reserved.

David Kipen: "Auteurism's Great Snow Job." Reprinted with permission from *San Francisco Chronicle*. Copyright © 2001 by *San Francisco Chronicle*.

Ron Koertge: "Sidekicks." Originally appeared in *Life on the Edge of the Continent* (University of Arkansas Press) Reprinted by permission of the author. Copyright © 1997 by Ron Koertge.

Suzanne Lummis: "Shangri-la" is reprinted by permission of the author from *In Danger* (The Roundhouse Press). Copyright © 1999 by Suzanne Lummis.

CONTENTS

PREFACE

The aim of *The Misread City* is simple. We want to provide a range of perspectives on the current state of Los Angeles literary life—not only in fiction and poetry, but also in its general cultural situation. Since the 1930s, Los Angeles has produced an enormous bounty of strong writing—from classic works in one-time lowbrow genres like detective stories and science fiction to ambitious books in the traditional high art modes of fiction, poetry, and memoir. Some of this work came from the sun-dazed perceptions of visiting Easterners and Brits, but increasingly the literature of Los Angeles has been created by native Californians. High or low, native or imported; however, this creative work has often seemed to exist in a critical vacuum. Too rarely, then or now, has there been a forum in which to argue over the merits, discuss the liabilities, or even puzzle out the basic nature of the work. When Southern California's literary life has been discussed, it has too often been by outsiders. Some of them get it; most don't. Los Angeles may dictate the new electronic culture to the rest of the world, but in literature it remains half colonized. Most of the fault has been our own. For all its varied literary accomplishments, Los Angeles has never developed a serious critical milieu. Although this situation may be changing, progress still seems too slow and too tentative.

At least Los Angeles literature has been treated well retrospectively—mostly by academic critics and biographers. Scholars have carefully documented, analyzed, and annotated the achievements of local masters. The great tradition of L.A. crime fiction, which produced Raymond Chandler, James McCain, and Ross Macdonald, has become a certified field of academic study. Nathanael West and F. Scott Fitzgerald are now unassailably canonic figures. Likewise the fascinating story of Southland literary emigres from Aldous Huxley to Christopher Isherwood has been thoroughly treated (though the late Brian Moore's considerable career awaits an adequate assessment). Similarly, the indisputably colorful career of novelist and poet Charles Bukowski, who lived most of his life in Hollywood and San Pedro, has become a local cottage industry. "I Knew Buk" books and essays are everywhere. More recently, even Bukowski's own master, John Fante, has begun to receive his critical due. It should not seem disrespectful to point out that these authors now are all historical figures. Their reputations, which were largely brokered and secured in New York, London, and Europe, are matters of critical record. Where does one read about the new literary Los Angeles?

The editors of this volume are working writers, not academics. While respecting the scholarly enterprise, we are interested in a different sort of cultural venture—something more timely, speculative, and argumentative. We have tried to capture the Southern California of here and now. We want to get at the Los Angeles that came after the gumshoes, the wisecracking Englishmen, after the Boosters, the Beats, and the boozers, after the despairing heroines of Joan Didion and the coked-up rich kids of Bret Easton Ellis. What is literary Los Angeles about now? Do these old templates survive, the way Hawthorne's Puritans still echo through the fiction of New England and Cooper's frontiersmen still stalk the literature of the mountain West? Without ignoring the city's rich past, we have tried to focus on the present— living writers active in the final decade of the last century and the first few years of the new one.

One guiding conviction in assembling *The Misread City* has been that the literary arts have taken their own shape in Southern California. Visiting pundits rarely seem to understand that it is not necessarily a bad thing that Los Angeles literary life differs from that of New York or London. One of the key differences—an animating and enlarging one— is that traditional distinctions between high and low art have blurred here in the world capital of movies, television, pop music, and pulp fiction. For a variety of reasons, genre-writing has flourished in Southern California—perhaps not the least of which has been L.A.'s distance from genteel Eastern literary opinion. Quietly innovative writers like Raymond Chandler and Ross Macdonald have emerged whose work reconceptualized the possibilities of their genres and can bear the scrutiny of careful critical analysis. Any serious assessment of L.A. literature, for instance, must take into account science fiction, not a genre that would play a prominent part in a book on the contemporary Southern novel or New York literary life. Ray Bradbury would not have developed so remarkably anywhere else. Both *Fahrenheit 451* and *Martian Chronicles* can be read as refracted commentaries on California life and culture.

One wonders if some Eastern critics don't see Los Angeles literary life through the lens of *Fahrenheit 451*—envisioning local culture that has not literally outlawed books but ignores them through mass indifference The statistics disprove that claim. Los Angeles is an enormous book market—by some measures the nation's largest. But the city's vast readership and deep literary culture often seem invisible in New York, Boston, or London, because there are so few critical journals, no large body of criticism announcing, analyzing, and explaining the region's literary identity. Beyond the *Los Angeles Times Book Review*, there is nothing in the Southland comparable to the *New Yorker, New York Times, New York Review of Books, New Criterion, Hudson Review*, or *Nation*, actively shaping cultural opinion. Los Angeles has never sustained a significant literary quarterly, and few of the many small (usually short-lived) journals contain significant numbers of essays or reviews. However serious, the *Los Angeles Times Book Review* cannot provide the breadth of coverage needed to chronicle and critique the local literary activity. (No single journal anywhere could.) It is hardly surprising that Los Angeles literary life has remained more private than public.

The Misread City contains many theories of Los Angeles culture, but it offers no unifying abstraction. Our goal was not to be definitive or timeless but rather, to be culturally useful—informed, thoughtful, and contemporary. We hope the book functions like a good museum group show. We have included pieces with which we disagree because they seemed strong and provocative. We have also included articles critical of the L.A. literary scene. Our goal is to celebrate the Southland without becoming blindly uncritical. Although our aims are hardly boosterish—a real critical tradition is something the Southland could surely use—we hope mostly to send readers back to the authors and poets discussed in the book.

Instead of offering a lengthy catalog of writers—and the city is fairly bursting with them, however hard they can sometimes be to detect—we have focused on a handful of authors who have become iconic, created a new, persuasive vision of Los Angeles, one where the city we lived in was still recognizable as through a stained glass. In some cases, they set their vision elsewhere, like Ray Bradbury, whose postwar suburban

Southern California sprouts on the planet Mars. More often, however, their works take place on familiar streets and in nearby towns.

The Misread City is neither comprehensive nor complete. Our omissions are legion, and we could easily have compiled a book twice a large, but we wanted this volume to be compact and accessible. (We encourage readers who spot unforgivable omissions to edit competing anthologies and denounce us heartily in their prefaces.) We would have liked the space to include many more pieces—something about Héctor Tobar, for instance, whose *The Tattooed Soldier* has become for many the last great L.A. novel, or the body of fiction about the movie industry, or the young and emerging authors whose work is just seeing print. We would have liked an essay on the Southland science fiction tradition, which has most recently included writers like Octavia Butler, Steve Erickson, and Harlan Ellison.

A number of things have changed since these pieces, most of them published in the L.A. press, first appeared. The authors and scenes described have changed in subtle and not so subtle ways. One of our contributors has died. The *Los Angeles Times Book Review* has now steered decisively toward writers and topics of Southern California, and its editor, who is criticized in these pages, has become a colleague of one of this book's editors.

The elephant in the room in any discussion of Los Angeles culture is the entertainment industry, especially movies and television. For many people both outside and inside its city limits, mass entertainment is Los Angeles culture. Literature has often had a tough time here—despite talent assembled in some cases by those very industries—for the same reason the novel had such a hard time in nineteenth-century Italy. Opera exerted such power over both artists and audiences that it seems to overwhelm other theatrical and literary forms. And yet masterpieces were written, like Alessandro Manzoni's *I Promessi Sposi* (*The Betrothed*), one of the classics of European realism. (Of course, it was quickly made into an opera by Italy's thriving entertainment industry.) Movies and television get plenty of coverage elsewhere. L.A. fiction and poetry get almost none. We offer no further apologies.

The fate of the written word in Los Angeles is not so dire, though at times it can seem that way. Literary life in Los Angeles often resembles driving down the city's empty boulevards, past blowing newspapers, undistinguished architecture and billboards for the latest TV show or movie. Instead of New York's proud skyscrapers or London's imperial monuments, the lush public spaces of Parisian gardens, Los Angeles can seem like a clutter of mini-malls and nail salons. But few cities can beat L.A. for private, interior spaces, often meticulously curated with great precision and style, and local arts gatherings are full of animated conversation. (Cultural Angelenos know how to dress and throw parties.) Our literary life is the same: It gets better the closer you get. We'd like to give people reason to slow down and look inside.

—*The Editors*

San Narcisco lay further south, near L.A. Like many named places in California, it was less an identifiable city than a group of concepts.

—Thomas Pynchon,
The Crying of Lot 49 (1966)

It is then that I realize that this land deserves something better, in the way of its inhabitants, than the swamis, the realtors, the motion-picture tycoons, the fakirs, the fat widows, the nondescript clerks, the bewildered ex-farmers, the corrupt pension-plan schemers, the tight-fisted 'empire builders,' and all the other curious migratory creatures who have flocked here from the far corners of the earth. For this strip of coast, this tiny region, seems to be looking westward across the Pacific, waiting for the future that one can somehow sense, and feel, and see. Here America will build its great city of the Pacific, the most fantastic city in the world.

—Carey McWilliams,
Southern California:
An Island on the Land (1946)

I

L.A. LITERARY CULTURE TODAY

LIKE ANY PARADISE
Writers in Los Angeles

DAVID L. ULIN

*Los Angeles, give me some of you! Los Angeles come to me
the way I came to you, my feet over your streets, you pretty
town I loved you so much, you sad flower in the sand, you
pretty town.*

—John Fante, *Ask the Dust*

I have a friend who calls Los Angeles the greatest city in the world for
doing literary work. The first time I heard him say that, I had just
given up my Manhattan apartment in preparation for moving to Southern California, and I was looking for any half-baked rationalization to
convince myself I wasn't making a mistake. L.A., my friend assured
me, would be transformative because literature was not its dominant
form of expression; in the shadow of Hollywood, serious writers were
as anonymous as obscene phone callers, and about as relevant to the
culture at large. There was a value to anonymity, he explained when I
responded skeptically, for it allowed authors the space to explore their
imaginations, without having to justify themselves to prying, or even
interested, minds. "You can work in peace," my friend enthused. "No
one's around to bother you. And even if they are, nobody's paying
attention to what you do."

Six years later, I'm convinced that being a writer in Los Angeles is
far more complicated than my friend would have had me believe. What
he left out was the down side, the moment when anonymity, or solitude, yields to loneliness, and the absolute certainty that one is working
in a vacuum from which it is impossible to break free. Not long ago,
another friend went to a party after finishing his first novel and was
approached by a woman who asked what he did. "I'm a writer," he
answered. "I just completed a novel." Were this any other city, that
remark might have been good for a few minutes of conversation, some

small talk about reading and writing, and maybe a whisper of good luck. In Los Angeles, however—at least the way my friend tells it—the woman looked at him for a moment, her eyes as blank as saucers, before asking, "Why?"

Somewhere in the midst of these extremes—between one friend's solitude and another's isolation—lies the experience of most L.A. writers, an experience as fraught with contradictions, with elation and frustration, as that of the city itself. Los Angeles, after all, is a place where myth and reality collide in jarring, unexpected juxtapositions; a literate town (it's the second largest book buying market in the United States) with only a handful of independent bookstores, a community of readers in which print is often seen as obsolete. Although hundreds of writers live here, it still feels astonishing to discover, say, Hubert Selby, Jr. or Mona Simpson quietly at work in our own backyard. Partly, such dislocation is due to L.A.'s notorious distances, the sprawling, sun-stilled emptiness that makes it hard for people to come together, or even see each other, in any meaningful sense. But more to the point is the way this most visual of American cities tends to look askance at anyone who spends too much time tinkering with words. As Raymond Chandler put it in "Writers in Hollywood," an essay published in *The Atlantic Monthly* in November 1945, "[T]he very nicest thing Hollywood can possibly think of to say to a writer is that he is too good to be only a writer."

Chandler, of course, is the patron saint of literary Los Angeles, the man most people think of when asked to name a writer from L.A. Four decades after his death—and nearly sixty years since *The Big Sleep* helped reinvent the detective novel as existential passion play—he continues to speak to us, his gritty vision of the city's dime store dreams and hopeless illusions a stark contrast to the glittering promises of the local publicity machine. His popularity is so pervasive, it's almost impossible to approach his writing on its own terms; the clipped patois and hard-boiled persona of his detective hero Philip Marlowe have become clichés not only of crime fiction, but of American culture itself. In its day, though, Chandler's work was ground-breaking and original, which explains its influence on countless authors in and out of genre, from Ross Macdonald, Walter Mosley, and Michael Connelly (all of whom set their mysteries in L.A.) to Joan Didion, whose atmospheric writings share Chandler's sense of Southern California as an active character, with a life and personality all its own.

Over the years, Chandler has come to be considered definitive, as if before he started writing, no one had ever thought to describe Los Angeles as less like paradise than paradise *lost*. Yet, Chandler's apocalyptic vision is hardly unique; even among his contemporaries, John Fante and Nathanael West were exploring similar territory, and in the decades since, a certain ennui, or alienation, has come to be one of the prevailing literary personalities of L.A. "Where else should they go but California, the land of sunshine and oranges?" West writes at the end of *The Day of the Locust*. "Once there, they discover that sunshine isn't enough. They get tired of oranges, even of avocado pears and passion fruit. Nothing happens. They don't know what to do with their time." For novelist Carolyn See, a lifelong Angeleno, it remains a relevant perspective. "Southern California," she explains, "bespeaks alienation. The west coast is the end of the road for the American Dream. We're up against a blank wall out here, and we can't go any farther. So even if you get what you want, then what? There is no out, you're here. It looks good, but that's it."

See's point is an important one; for like any paradise, Los Angeles holds within it the seeds of its own destruction, and to live and write here is to do a constant dance with disaster and despair. There's something equally lush and decadent about the region's very landscape—from the sickly sweet scent of night-blooming jasmine to the primal beauty of the San Gabriel Mountains, shaped by the earthquakes that will, someday, take the modern city down. See, in fact, ends her novel *Golden Days* with the nuclear holocaust, although she softens Armageddon by choosing to portray not the doomed but those who survive; meanwhile, other writers like Dennis Cooper and Wanda Coleman regularly explore apocalypses of a less universal kind. As novelist and poet Carol Muske Dukes observes in her introduction to *Absolute Disaster*—a recent anthology of L.A. fiction, in which twenty-five writers, including Sandra Tsing Loh, T. Coraghessan Boyle, Harlan Ellison, and Amy Gerstler explore a variety of breakdowns, personal and otherwise—"We are so used to disasters here that we expect disaster, we write it into our stories like fiery *backdrop*." Even the weather, Joan Didion has written,

" . . . is the weather of catastrophe, of apocalypse . . . The city burning is Los Angeles's deepest image of itself."

In recent years, however, L.A. writers have been forced to confront not only the specter of physical calamity, but the sense that the social fabric of the community is coming apart. Throughout the 1990s, Los Angeles has suffered through a seemingly endless procession of earthquakes, floods, and fires, not to mention the collapse of an economy built on military contracts and aerospace; and the 1992 riots, in which former mayor Tom Bradley's notion of the place as a glorious multicultural mosaic was revealed to be just another public relations lie. As recently as 1991, social critic David Rieff could write in *Los Angeles: Capital of the Third World* that "to read the early history of L.A. and then to compare it with the contemporary city was to be constantly reminded of how little had changed"; now, novelists like Bebe Moore Campbell and Gary Phillips map the scattered, racially divided face of post-Rodney King Los Angeles, a territory that the city's founders, with their ideal of a "new Eden for the Saxon homemaker," would have a hard time recognizing as their own. It is as if, in the words of MacArthur award-winning poet, playwright, and performer Luis Alfaro, L.A. has become a collection of "little border towns," where the only thing we have in common is how much we are not alike.

Although it's tempting to read Alfaro's comment as a lament for Los Angeles's disintegration, the paradox is that he doesn't see it that way. "For me," he declares, "L.A. is a great port city. The mix of cultures is really interesting, and since my work is about clashes of some kind—of nationality or sexuality—the possibilities are endless." The sentiment is echoed by Russell Leong, editor of UCLA's *Amerasia Journal*, whose poems and stories occur in the intersections between public and private life. "In my neighborhood, there's a Sikh temple, a Lithuanian church, a Catholic church, a Buddhist temple and a Ukrainian church," Leong says. "Within this framework of coexistence, you can discover a richness you never knew before." In some sense, such developments are a sign that L.A. is becoming more cosmopolitan; we live in a complex society, and it's only fitting for the city to reflect this idea. At the same time, the last few years have brought Southern California face-to-face with its own contradictions, so much so that when a novel like Cynthia Kadohata's *In the Heart of the Valley of Love* evokes a twenty-first century

L.A. deeply divided between rich and poor, it seems less a work of the imagination than an extrapolation of the present, less a matter of speculation than a declaration of what the future holds in store.

If writers like Kadohata, Leong, and Alfaro are representative of Los Angeles's diversity, it has as much to do with their stylistic choices as with what they have to say. Alfaro, for instance, merges aspects of performance art and stand-up comedy to frame his tales of growing gay and Latino in the inner city, while Kadohata adapts many of the textures of science fiction to her literary needs. To a certain extent, there's an element of the postmodern sensibility in this, the late twentieth century concept that all ideas and structures are fair game. Yet more important is the notion that Los Angeles, despite its changes, is still very much a city where anything goes. That may be one of the stereotypes about the place, but it's also L.A.'s most enduring creative tradition, and it helps define a common ground where the work of, say, Chandler and Kadohata can stand side-by-side. Only in Los Angeles, with its emphasis on entertainment, and its distance from—if not outright hostility towards—Eastern intellectual preconceptions, could these writers merge the sensibilities of high and low culture to create an aesthetic uniquely their own.

In the end, it goes back to what my friend first said about writing in Southern California, for if nobody's paying attention, there are no expectations to contend with about what an author should or shouldn't do. Where he went wrong was in thinking that this anonymity had anything to do with Hollywood, which is as little involved with literature in Los Angeles as it would be anywhere else. Rather, the solitude—and yes, the isolation—that defines so many L.A. writers comes from being three thousand miles west of the seat of literary culture, a condition that encourages a certain independence, as well. "People come here," Carolyn See says, "and they're given this incredible freedom to be what they want. That's the main thing about Southern California, the thing that sets it off from the rest of the world. You have a shot at being what you want."

September 1997

Booked Up
The Los Angeles Times Book Review

Scott Timberg

In the nation's most ravenous literary market, the Los Angeles Times Book Review under Steve Wasserman has become brilliant, erudite, and irrelevant.

If you pay attention to books and authors, it was hard to avoid the phenomenon of Dave Eggers and his memoir, *A Heartbreaking Work of Staggering Genius*. The book, about the death of his parents and his flight west to Berkeley, with his eight-year-old brother in tow, came out last year to a storm of attention and marked the emergence, or crystallization, of a new, wildly funny, hyperironic sensibility.

It was easy to see it coming: An excerpt appeared in *The New Yorker* a few weeks before the book's release, along with a photo of the author. Book sales were brisk—more than 200,000 in hardcover—and rights sales even brisker: Eggers won a $1.4 million advance for the paperback rights, and $2 million for the film rights. The characteristically sober *New York Times Book Review* judged *Heartbreaking Work* one of the year's ten notable books in its year-end issue. "Few books irrespective of merit qualify as literary events, in that they infiltrate the culture," author Robert Polito told *Poets and Writers* magazine. "It's been a long time, perhaps as far back as [Thomas Pynchon's] *Gravity's Rainbow*, since I've seen so many people on the subway reading a serious hardcover book and talking about it."

The book's impact, and Eggers' resulting cult, was not confined to New York literati. In Los Angeles, boutique bookstores such as Skylight Books and Dutton's Brentwood sold stratospheric numbers for a literary hardback by a first-time author. The line for the author's UCLA appearance in April was long enough to rival a Friday night at Spaceland.

How did Eggers' book fare in the *Los Angeles Times Book Review*? It got a dismissive one-paragraph capsule. Sunday review sections have to catch thousands of books that come out each year and squeeze them into limited space, so they're bound to miss sometimes. How did the *Times* do with other writers last year? Not so well. Angeleno author Aimee Bender, whose first work was the critically hailed story collection *The Girl in the Flammable Skirt*, published her first novel—and got a couple of paragraphs in a cap mention. *Imagining Los Angeles: The City in Fiction*, by Cal State Long Beach professor David Fine, the first single-authored history of L.A. literature in fifty years, got no mention in the *Book Review* at all. (It was dealt with in *Southern California Living*, in a weekly omnibus review of books about the West.)

A book review can do more than assess novels and biographies. It can chart the course of a culture—the mood swings, the spikes and depressions, the vendettas and rivalries. Because books can be about anything, reviews can stretch out to consider every kind of ideas there are: politics, sex, urban planning, religious zealotry, abstract sculpture. And since fiction and poetry take ideas and refract them symbolically, a review can delve into both our waking life and our hidden depths. In some cases—the Faulkner-era renaissance in the Deep South, Anglo-American modernism after World War I—a review can spark and maintain a political, ethnic, or regional movement. More recently, literary reviews—both newspaper-supported and independent—in New York and London have sustained powerful literary cultures.

Eggers, Bender, and Fine aren't the only glaring omissions from the *Los Angeles Times Book Review*. Other important books from last year, especially fiction and books by and about California, were overlooked. "I think we're in a really unique literary time in Los Angeles," says the typically chipper Kerry Slattery, manager of Skylight Books. "And I don't have that sense when I pick up the *Book Review*."

Many in the literary community don't read the section at all, preferring the *New York Times Book Review*; others put the dull, windy insert aside on Sunday, planning to get back to it, but never return. Still others complain about the difficulty of finding its flimsy twelve pages inside the enormous, coupon-crammed Sunday paper. Such disregard comes just when the *Review* should be thriving. According to an economic census by the U.S. Commerce Department in 1992 (the last date for which data was available), the L.A. metropolitan area was the biggest book market in the country. L.A.'s lead was also reported in an industry journal last spring. Los Angeles, famed for its commercialism and amber waves of chain stores, now holds as many strong independent bookstores as any city in America—Midnight Special, Dutton's, Book Soup, Skylight, and Vroman's, all with active and well-attended reading series.

Since late '96, the *Book Review* has been headed by Steve Wasserman, an erudite and often charming man who burns with a sense of purpose. When he arrived in Los Angeles in late 1996, he announced that the city would finally get the book review it deserved, a review to rival anything in New York. But his tenure so far has not yielded those results. "He's managed to piss off every editor and publisher in New York and L.A.," says a local literary agent. "That's hard to do." Three years ago, Ray Bradbury collected a lifetime achievement award at the *Los Angeles Times'* Festival of Books, and nailed the *Review* for its featherweight size and lack of L.A. focus. Wasserman soon mended the fence with the author, asking him to write and introducing him at the festival two years later. But local literati are still dissatisfied. "The word on Steve, and on the *Review*, has been out for a few years," one L.A. writer says. "What does he have to say in his own defense?"

Walking with Steve Wasserman is like traveling with a statesman. He moves with confidence, marches briskly down halls, always seems to be buttoning the jacket of his double-breasted suit, firing off bon mots as he walks around corners and down stairs. If you love books, and care about ideas, it's hard not to be a little bit charmed by the man. He speaks with great poise and an enormous vocabulary: It's easy to imagine him winning a steady stream of spelling bees as a grade-schooler. He sees himself, in his own words, "as an ambassador from the republic of letters."

"The distinction between high and low culture is ever more porous and without merit," he says. "You can go hear Sheryl Crow at the Pantages and then drop in at the Conga Room to see Ricardo Lemvo and then go see a Peter Sellars production of Mozart at a matinee at the Music Center." Sheryl Crow seems to be for Wasserman what Fleetwood Mac is for Bill Clinton: his way of claiming street credibility. "And very often you encounter some of the same people you saw at those previous events." Not only are the traditional barriers being eroded: L.A., he says, is rethinking itself. It's good for writers, good for painters, good for everyone.

Wasserman, a former political activist, often uses political metaphors. There's a similarity, he says, between his years with the New Left in Berkeley and his tenure as book editor. "To edit a successful literary review in the noisy culture we all live in," he says, "requires skills of organization and a kind of missionary zeal, a certain kind of activism."

He also speaks often about L.A.'s cultural ferment. One of the strongest raps against Wasserman is that he's not an Angeleno—that he's a New Yorker slumming until a job opens at the *New York Review of Books*, aiming the *Review* at his friends back east. But he was raised and educated in California, in Berkeley. Wasserman originally came to L.A. in 1977, just a few years out of Cal, to work as a researcher for *Los Angeles Times* columnist Robert Scheer. By the next year he was deputy editor of the paper's op-ed page at just twenty-six years old. After working for more than a decade in New York publishing—including six years as editorial director of Times Books, a Random House imprint—he came back to L.A. in late 1996.

"I returned to a city in which, despite all the distractions of the infotainment industry, there were more bookstores than at any time in its history," he says over lunch in a Chinatown noodle shop. "It's really quite extraordinary. And this, despite the seductions of the virtual world, the hypnotizing effects of the movie business. Nevertheless people seemed to be at least buying and arguably reading more books than ever before, at least in Los Angeles. How to explain this? A city synonymous in the public mind with making a fetish of the body, being apparently so devoted to living the life of the mind."

Wasserman speaks this way. The interview he gives over lunch is almost identical to the speech he gives a week later to a local publishing group. And why change it? He can be ravishingly witty and articulate. Even one of his detractors concedes, "He speaks in these perfect sentences that seem to have been written by a philosopher."

When Wasserman surveys the city, he speaks about it as if he were Thomas Wolfe on a train ride across the Deep South, proudly intoning the name of every river and mountain range. But Wasserman uses the name of every university and college between La Jolla and Santa Barbara, every library and research institute between Santa Monica and the Huntington, with an almost biblical gravity. He sees cultural tensions like shifting plates under all of it.

"To put it very bluntly," he says, "I think the city is going through a slow motion nervous breakdown, no longer sure of the old verities, questioning the old assumptions that had for so long provided a sense of self. For many decades that dream of endless prosperity, which was seen as synonymous with the California dream, seemed to underpin most of the fantasies that L.A. entertained about itself. That dream has burst. And Los Angeles—like so many of the people who have flooded into her port—is herself engaged with an act of reinvention." He sees "the shedding of a certain comforting provincialism, and the sometimes reluctant embrace of a wily cosmopolitanism."

How does a book section serve a place that's so darned complex and wily? Wasserman could be doing the voice-over for one of those *Los Angeles Times* ads that runs before movies. "I would say that the *Book Review* is a forum for the exploration of the meaning and identity of America. And of course, of California, and then of course of Los Angeles. In its broadest, deepest sense. The ambition is large. It is to look at books as the place to examine where we've been, where we are, where we may be going—both to explore those issues in our imaginative life, i.e., in fiction, and as we explore them in books that are said to be nonfiction." And then he heads off a criticism he has every reason to expect: "I also regard Southern California and the West in general as a place where the local has gone global. We cannot treat the readership as provincial—somehow interested only in themselves. *They are interested in everything.*"

The other criticism he hears most often is that the section is too intellectual. This is the only question about the book section that seems to makes him angry. That sort of thinking, he says, "is the outdated mannerism of people who should more properly be residing in zip codes like 10025 on the Upper West Side of Manhattan, rather than the more catholic and eclectic precincts of a diverse Los Angeles who they pretend to defend but instead demonstrate the most surpassing and dishonorable disrespect for." He sort of squints as he says it. "That kind of comment I regard as *deeply* destructive of the life of the mind, and is the prejudice of the truly provincial."

As Wasserman courses through the halls of the *Los Angeles Times*, on his way to and from lunch, none of his colleagues nods or says hello.

A spirited and wide-ranging book review could surely be put together by people afraid to speak about Wasserman for attribution. People talk especially about his lack of interest in fiction, his indifference to Southern California writers and topics, including Hollywood, and the tedious and academic tone of the *Review*. They say the *Review* is so late getting to major books that they're out of stores, their authors already come and gone, before they've been covered. They say he's transfixed by "idea books" at the expense of all else—as if he were still editing the op-ed page.

Georgia Jones-Davis, who worked at the *Book Review* for thirteen years and left a few months after Wasserman arrived, will speak only sparingly about him. "I think he had in his mind a wonderful vision for a book section. It turned into a brilliant, introverted little gem. But that's the problem; it's not out there for us."

"It's great that someone's providing a forum for long book-related essays but a shame that this particular forum isn't more interesting or fun," says an East Coast book editor. "Something can be smart without being stuffy, and I'm not sure Steve realizes that."

Jack Miles, a former *Los Angeles Times Book Review* editor and a Pulitzer-winning author, puts it this way: "A consensus view of him, that you'd hear from [local literati], for example, is that he has little use for Los Angeles writers and less use for Los Angeles as a place. He's at home in the New York-Washington megalopolis." L.A. author and critic Carolyn See says the *Review* is "like serving partridge for dinner every night. Not everyone likes partridge."

Of course, there are those who think Steve does a great job with his section, against enormous financial odds. Alain de Botton, a young London writer whose most recent book, *The Consolations of Philosophy*, was trashed in the *Review*, says, "He manages to attract world-class writers, chiefly by doing what any great editor must: allowing writers to follow their passions. That way, he gets the best out of them." De Botton commends the section's themed issues—Africa, Mount Everest, media mergers—and overall intellectual seriousness. To Wasserman's admirers, he's a brave experimenter, putting out a cosmopolitan review at a time when

American newspapers are shortening and dumbing-down coverage. They also credit him and his staff with nurturing the Book Fest, which will mark its sixth year this April and is expected to bring roughly three hundred writers and more than 100,000 attendees to its site on the UCLA campus.

Andrea Grossman, who has run the top-shelf Writers Bloc authors series since 1996, praises Wasserman's editorial approach almost without reservation. Wasserman has a whole packet of glowing letters about the section, many from publishers in New York. Raves from authors such as John Irving and Susan Sontag and others of their caliber have run inside the *Review*, drawing charges of both tackiness and conflict of interest. But the New York publishing establishment has ignored the *Review* almost entirely when it comes to putting its money where its mouth is. The lack of ads, of course, means there's less room for book coverage. "If publishers thought that it actually reached readers, they would advertise," says a New York editorial director. "That's their clearest vote."

The Washington Post has sixteen pages in its book review most weeks, the *New York Times*, thirty-six, and in past years the *L.A. Times* has had far more than its current twelve pages. Wasserman hopes the Tribune Company, which purchased the *L.A. Times* last year, will find ways to sell book ads for all of its several papers at once, boosting the earnings of all the sections. Publishing ads are down all over, and many reviews lose money—though not, as Wasserman insists, the *New York Times'*. The editor is undaunted by this economic reality. "My mission is to put out the best tasting wine I can," he says. "It is up to others to sell it, and to market it. What I do know is that tasters from all over the world have tasted the wine I am making, and pronounced it among the finest currently made."

The proof of the wine is, indeed, in the tasting. Wasserman provided *New Times* with nearly seventy issues of the *Book Review*, and a close reading shows that though the practice doesn't live up to the theory, he has chalked up some unqualified successes: He uses writers like California State Librarian Kevin Starr, poet laureate of the suburbs D.J. Waldie, and the critic Benjamin Schwarz, who recently left L.A. to become literary editor of the revitalized *Atlantic Monthly*. Wasserman's prominent reviews of the *Norton Anthology of African American Literature*, a new translation of Stendhal's *The Charterhouse of Parma*, and Leon Wieseltier's *Kaddish* put those books on or near the *L.A. Times*' best-seller list before they hit elsewhere. The *Review*'s use of illustrations from art and photography books—instead of book jackets or author photos—gives the pages a distinct look that recalls London's *Times Literary Supplement.*

But a review is not made or broken by a few critics or stories; it's about daily and weekly choices. And it's these choices that writers and readers often find cryptic. Read a few issues of the *Review* in sequence, and Wasserman's taste seems downright baffling.

Few writers can bring Greece and Rome to life as vividly as Bernard Knox, an emeritus Harvard professor whose essay collection *The Oldest Dead White European Males* could convince a Visigoth to love the classical age. But even Knox can't make the *Barrington Atlas of the Greek and Roman World* sound very interesting. And it's hard to imagine a book review editor with roughly six and a half pages of review space devoting two solid pages—with enormous illustrations—to an obscure atlas that costs more than $300. The January 21 issue was typical in an extreme, almost cartoonish way: More than half the review space was dedicated to books "On Morality and Photojournalism," a topic surely more riveting to reporters and editors than to the general public. The pages remaining were given to the Arthur Schlesinger Jr. memoir that every other American paper reviewed last fall, and to two pages of letters on *Copenhagen*, a provocative play about physicists Werner Heisenberg and Niels Bohr, written by a Londoner, set in Denmark, and not yet staged in L.A. The February 25 issue asked "Is Publishing Dead?" and then devoted all its pages to opinions on the subject, mostly from major New York publishers.

Or how about the full-page reviews of tomes like *Places of Power: The Aesthetics of Technology* (a slim, $60 book from tiny Ventana Editions) in the January 14 issue, or the two pages on "Picturing California's Other Landscape: The Great Central Valley," last February? Or the cover story from last March: *The Alex Studies: Cognitive and Communicative Abilities in Grey Parrots* from Harvard University Press (with the inscrutable headline "Wanna Nut! What Listening to Animals Tells Us About Ourselves")? These books, whatever unexpected pleasures they may offer, sound not just like university courses, but bad ones.

The books the *Times* over-covers would be less maddening if they did not overlook so many things as a result. Wasserman is like a mad architect, out of a film by Werner Herzog, who's asked for a tiny house and designs one with lush, enormous parlors, but no bedroom or kitchen. He falls down especially with fiction, and with books by and about Californians, but there are notable gaps elsewhere. The *New York Times Book Review* made the new Raymond Carver collection its lead fiction piece, explaining that "Carver once had been a writer; now he was a way of writing." What does the *L.A. Times* do with the most influential American short-story writer of the last thirty years? He gets a two hundred-word cap in "Discoveries." Story collections by John Updike—which completes his "Rabbit" series—and Russell Banks—a thick, career-spanning tome by the author of *Affliction* and *The Sweet Hereafter*—also drew capsule reviews.

Wasserman explains that he reviews roughly twice as much nonfiction as fiction (roughly 800 of the former a year, 400 of the latter, out of a pool of roughly 75,000 books published annually), saying that this is the same proportion that publishers release. Strangely, though, Wasserman performs poorly even when covering books that fall within his areas of enthusiasm. *One Market Under God*, a book of left-leaning cultural criticism by Thomas Frank, was released October 17, soon before the author's appearance at Skylight Books. The book section ran a salient piece on Frank's book—three months later, in its January 14 issue. David Brooks' book of cultural criticism, *Bobos in Paradise*, perhaps the most talked about nonfiction book of last year, launched a thousand magazine articles about the mellowing of the counterculture, but wasn't reviewed until July, three months after many of those stories. Cynthia Ozick, one of the nation's leading literary essayists, received an enthusiastic review—in about two hundred words in "Discoveries."

The "Discoveries" column is written by Susan Salter Reynolds, an assistant editor of the *Review* who deals with three, sometimes four books each week. Reynolds surely deserves a medal for assessing so many books so rapidly, in so tight a space. But many of her reviews tend toward the dotty. A critic can dislike, even savage, Eggers or Updike. But some of her pieces read like little more than the workings of literary prejudice—he's too postmodern, he's too Freudian. One local literary figure says that Reynolds gets so many important books because she's the only review contributor who's alert to important and interesting new books. (Besides Wasserman, the *L.A. Times Review* has four editors; the *New York Times Book Review* has, depending how you slice it, about ten, including six preview editors who read everything before assignment.)

Mystery and detective fiction—here in the hometown of Raymond Chandler and James Ellroy—are also underplayed. Wasserman has largely ignored genre fiction of all kinds—there is almost no science fiction coverage, and mystery novels are almost never reviewed in full. Instead, these books—which could add a populist flavor to the *Review*—are mostly confined to an "L.A. Confidential" column written by a retired European history professor. Readers and writers alike find Eugene Weber, late of UCLA, frustrating. "His stuff is just ludicrous," laughs one local mystery writer. "There was a time when he used this eighteenth century phrase, trying to be cute in a nerdy, pretentious way." And despite its title, "L.A. Confidential" does not lean toward Los Angeles.

The *Book Review* also lacks a consistent voice. By all reports, Richard Eder (who did not return a call seeking comment) left the *L.A. Times* because of the precariousness of the Mark Willes/Michael Parks regime. But for more than a decade, Eder's sharp pieces, appearing in the same space each week, helped anchor the section. Similarly, *The Washington Post*—the review praised most frequently by those contacted for this story—has two well-known staff critics: the curmudgeonly Jonathan Yardley, a Pulitzer Prize winner who writes on American topics, and Michael Dirda, also a Pulitzer winner, who writes urbane essays about world literature. Los Angeles has been a vital and diverse literary scene for far longer than sleepy, blue-blazered Washington, and the *Times* out-circulates the *Post*. But you'd never know it looking at the local book sections.

The fact that no statistic or proportions can explain is this: The *L.A. Times Book Review* is boring. Wasserman clearly has good intentions, and sees himself working on the side of the angels. But the *Review* never happens, it never bites, it never sings, it never laughs. What's puzzling is that the critics he cites as his models—Leslie Fiedler, Dwight Macdonald, the early Susan Sontag—are among the most invigorating writers in the language. Pick them up—or Edmund Wilson, or Pauline Kael, or the

New Republic's almost violently intelligent James Wood—and be reminded that criticism can break windows, open minds.

The most common complaint about Wasserman's section is that it's a flimsy edition of the *New York Review of Books*; the highbrow, left-leaning publication founded during 1963's New York newspaper strike. But the *L.A. Times* section duplicates, mostly, only the ponderousness, the occasional pretentiousness, the stuffy, exclusive tone—qualities that have crept into the *New York Review* as it's aged. What makes the *New York Review* at its best so essential is its edge, its sense that ideas matter and are worth fighting over. The famously combative letters page of the *New York Review* is more heated, more exciting, than anything in the entire *L.A. Times Book Review*.

Some say the *Book Review*'s real problem is Wasserman, personally. Others find him fun, or inspiring, or earnestly well-meaning. "There's a kind of weird innocence inside the insidiousness," says a past contributor. "He's so eccentric, he somehow alarms people. It ends up seeming a little scary." Some people point to his tendency for flamboyant dress (his "pimp suit" and Tom Wolfe-dandy outfit), or his habit of dusting his 9,000-book library, naked, late at night. "He's the most pretentious man I've ever met!" says a local literary agent. "Seeing him walk around at the book festival in his white suit! People talk about it for the next year!" But Wasserman—who is friendly and cooperative in person—could be as weird as he wants to be if he put out a lively review.

But the *Review* is not just a dull read here at home: It's the voice of literary L.A. to out-of-towners. Is it any wonder authors often overlook L.A. when touring? Andrea Grossman, of Writers Bloc, says she has to plead to get novelists—from Paul Auster to A.S. Byatt, John LeCarré to Julian Barnes—to come to the biggest book market in the country. "For some reason," says Grossman, "New York has a hard time admitting that there's a vibrant literary culture here. They'll send authors to San Francisco and San Diego, Seattle and Portland. If you yell and scream and beg often enough, the authors, often, will come."

Indeed, New York publishers mention the local media when asked why they're not sending literary authors through town. "If you're touring a literary novel, or a first novel, you'd probably go through San Francisco," says Carol Schneider, executive director of publicity at Random House. "If you have a book about the entertainment industry, or a celebrity, like Jimmy Carter, you'd come to L.A."

The question of the *Book Review* has a renewed urgency. The Tribune Company, which bought the *Times* along with other Times Mirror properties last spring, could consolidate its book sections, the way some chains combine their foreign bureaus. "Even more than movies, a book opens everywhere at the same time," says Miles, the former *Review* editor, "and there's no reason the Tribune Company couldn't create an economy of scale by operating just one book review." The Tribune papers are notorious for their dedication to profit. And the *Times* is looking for an assistant managing editor—called an "arts czar" by some in-house—to remake the arts, features, and book review sections.

Until newspapers are all owned by a single media baron, they need to attend to their local communities, including their literary communities. They also need to be read, and read widely. Wasserman doesn't need to copy the bland, cheerleading tone that is the official voice of *L.A. Times* feature and entertainment writing. Nor should he emulate the corporate anti-intellectualism of Mark Willes, who sold off the Picassos in the *Times* offices because they set, as he put it, an elitist tone.

It would be wonderful, of course, to live in Steve Wasserman's dream of Los Angeles. A place where, to use his Whitman-esque vision of the Festival of Books, people "got up out of their lap pools, came off the beach, got down off their Stairmasters and came out for the written word." On balance, Wasserman is like a benign insane person. It's good that he's crazy for books, and committed to language and ideas. But in the words of a local writer: "His brilliance has sucked the spontaneity and joy out of the section."

Until we have a brisk and engaging book review, L.A. won't get the attention it deserves out of state, nor will it nourish the scene in town. "I wanted a review that would take our readers as adults," Wasserman often says, "and not give them, as is so common in so much of what passes for criticism in America's newspapers, the baby talk they are served up every day." But the reality is that many dedicated readers don't look at it at all, or never bother to fish it out of the belly of the gargantuan Sunday *Times*, or have no real opinion. "A book review section should matter enormously," says David Kipen, the young L.A. native who edits the well-regarded and California-centric book section of the *San Fran-*

cisco Chronicle. "Naturally, mine isn't the most unbiased view you could solicit on the subject, but cripes, I don't want to live anywhere that a book review section doesn't matter deeply."

Fighting over the book section is the first step to a vigorous local literary culture. Reading it—closely, with enthusiasm and investment and curiosity, perhaps even with anger and disagreement—is the next. At this point, for all of Steve Wasserman's noble intentions and mellifluous phrases, we can't even get started.

March 2001

THIS SIDE OF THE RAINBOW
Literary Venues in L.A.

KATE GALE

The Los Angeles literary readings scene is a vast and unchartered sea. Just getting from one reading to another could cost you life and limb, or at least a speeding ticket, on the freeways, not to mention the possibility of getting lost in strange neighborhoods where graffiti decorates palm trees. Then, for the attendee of Los Angeles literary events, there is the dissonance between celebrities and literary authors. You might stop by a bookstore where you heard there's a reading to find it crowded with Shirley MacLaine followers. But, for a serious writer, the most disturbing aspect of the L.A. literary scene is the sense that you are part of an underground culture. The real culture, the real events, are what happen at the surface—the big theaters, movie studios, Hollywood, Oscar night. A poetry reading on Oscar night is bound to be a disaster as Angelenos hunker down in front of their television to tune in to the crowning of kings and queens in the mothership of the City of Angels, Hollywood.

When I moved to Los Angeles in 1987 from Arizona, I immediately set out to become part of the literary scene. I knew one person in town, and he supplied me with the tool absolutely essential to any would be poet in this town—a *Thomas Guide*. I had come from towns where one used maps, but no map would cover the expanses of L.A. The *Thomas Guide* allows people to find their way at something less than light speed across the vast galaxies that make up a city that spreads across valleys, hills and drainage ditches.

The sheer size of Los Angeles has a significant effect on how the literary world organizes itself. San Fernando Valley people must travel that hour to go to Los Angeles for readings unless they wish to attend the chain store readings. There is a reason why independent stores have better readings. Chain store readings often focus on authors who are popular rather than literary, and the readings are usually located in the children's section or the cafe. Both are places where the noise competition can be pretty lively.

Consequently, to attend good readings, one needs to be willing to drive. What this means for the geographically challenged is that there are many great readings one simply won't be able to attend. If you arrive home in say, Santa Monica, and there is an interesting reading going on at the Gene Autry Museum, the first question you ask is one of distance. I've been in my car three hours today. Do I want to sit in traffic another three hours this evening to go to this reading? Many readings will be attended mostly by locals, the author's friends, and the valiant few who were willing to go the distance. One doesn't have the feeling one has in San Francisco or New York that you can quickly get to anywhere else in the city. Los Angeles has its own unique system of arteries connecting it, and the blood from the feet won't reach the brain for hours.

The reading venues cross the city like a web of lights across the broken and fissured sprawl of dwellings and skyscrapers lost in smog. The Los Angeles County Museum of Art, Krueger Art Gallery in Pasadena, Dutton's Brentwood, Beyond Baroque in Venice, Skylight in Los Feliz and Book Soup on Sunset are each an hour's drive, maybe two, depending on traffic, from most of the others. Book Soup, right on Sunset, has limited parking, is in a difficult location and has a small reading space, yet it brings in many people for both famous writers and L.A. writers with loyal followings. The bookstore has a large variety of books, and on most given weekend nights will be well-attended by Hollywood locals out for the evening and in between dinner and theater engagements. The reading room is crowded, but it remains a place where writers will read to as many people as can squeeze into a small room.

Dutton's Brentwood is cherished by locals, but also a haven to writers all over the city. It too, boasts a small reading space; but for the community, the Dutton's bookstores are as much part of the landscape as the Santa Monica pier. The bookstore in Brentwood wanders from one room to another, and the reading room is rather small, but most attendees would rather crowd in to buy books from Doug Dutton than wander into the faceless Barnes & Noble in the mall for a Starbucks and a celebrity reading.

Krueger Art Gallery and Skylight Books: Krueger Art Gallery is a prestigious reading space. Located in Pasadena, it is run by the poet Lisa
Krueger who takes readings seriously. Skylight Books is centrally enough
located on Vermont to bring in people from all over the city. The reading series there is varied with something in every month's calendar to
please everyone, and the bookstore is beautiful and surrounded by res-
taurants making it a fine place for an afternoon's outing. The bookstore
itself has, as one might expect, has skylights, with trees growing out of
the middle of the bookstore. A large crowd can fit comfortably into the
store, and when the reading is over, there's excellent Indian food right
up the street, or Italian if you prefer.

LACMA: One of the best reading series in town, and the most depend-
able for many years was the reading series at Los Angeles County Museum of Art. The poetry curator, Laurel Ann Bogen was deeply knowl-
edgeable about the poetry world, and her readings attracted a diverse
audience. She brought in poets of national reputation like Philip Levine,
Yusef Komunyakaa and Kate Braverman in addition to local poets like
Mark Salerno, Eloise Klein Healy and Richard Garcia. The reading room
was an art space with plenty of light and good acoustics. One felt comfortable, favored, and one received something rare, payment for reading. Regardless of the success of the Writers in Focus Series at LACMA,
someone else at LACMA eventually took over the position of curator,
and it is difficult to see where that series is going.

Another odd point about reading series in Los Angeles: If you call a
bookstore or venue where you read last year, or set up a reading last year,
it is like going to a restaurant hoping to see your favorite waiter. He or
she either got the acting job and are no longer there, or he/she is homeless and are no longer there. When you call back your bookstore, whoever you spoke with last time, is probably no longer there. Like Oz, one
thinks, people come and go so quickly around here.

Beyond Baroque was the first place in L.A. I went to find poets. Down
the San Diego freeway and into the ghost town of Venice, one finds
Beyond Baroque in a white church-like building. There was an open
mike reading once a month which I began attending. Women with long
hair and skirts, vegetarians and vegans, pot smokers and ex-hippies,

crones and lesbians; each stood up and read their poems fiercely, sometimes shaking hammers. All I could think was, "We're not in Massachusetts any more." I had thought of poetry as a deep and scholarly art. This struck me as more like stand-up therapy. However, in the years that have followed, I've attended more readings at Beyond Baroque where some of Los Angeles' best-known poets will read in a black room under a spotlight. Poets like Dorothy Barresi, Lyn Lifshin and Wanda Coleman have graced the stage drawing crowds of admirers, yet the bookstore is small, and for small presses, it is not an easy place to set up readings.

Midnight Special: An easier place to set up readings, and a bookstore I didn't find until some time later was Midnight Special Bookstore; for many years located on the Third Street Promenade in Santa Monica. A different crowd attends readings at Midnight Special, as the promenade is a popular outdoor mall, and the bookstore attracts a variety of people. If you go to Beyond Baroque, that may be all you're doing in the neighborhood, but at Midnight Special you could go shopping, attend a reading and have dinner without paying again to park your car. The cost for a parking space in Los Angeles will exhaust the most thorough poet/ book lover on a tight budget.

Midnight Special is a poet and book lovers' dream, and I confess was my favorite bookstore in the city. Not only did they also carry a wide variety of socially progressive and political books, but they carried a large selection of poetry, and are friendly to small presses. Small presses tend to be completely ignored by the chains, and in Los Angeles, as elsewhere, one must cultivate the local independent bookstores if one doesn't want to end up selling poetry with oranges by the side of the freeway. However, Midnight Special had its share of problems. Hemmed in on either end of the mall by Borders and Barnes and Noble, struggling for existence, they announced that they would have to move at the end of 2002 because of the high rent. It is clear that the two chain bookstores crushed this independent out of this high traffic location. A back room served as a reading room, providing a pleasant space with chairs, a podium and a microphone which doesn't have the noise and disturbance one usually encounters in a chain bookstore where one's poems are competing with the cappuccino maker. The readings at Midnight Special that I have either attended or participated in always have a good crowd, and readers are high quality, serious writers or political activists. One has to hope that this bookstore will re-open elsewhere.

There are more recent series like the Skirball Center where writers like Bret Easton Ellis and Jay McInerny show up. The new series at the Autry is building both audience and reputation with its curator, Larry Jaffe. Top flight writers are reading in our city every week. L.A. is a city, where despite, Hollywood, and the freeways, literature continues to rumble along the pavement or filter through the palm trees depending on your perspective. The oddities of L.A. are the number of schlocky poetry readings thrown in, and the time and distance required to stretch oneself across the web of freeways to attend those good readings. Looking at the *L.A. Weekly* or even the *Los Angeles Times*, one can see listings of important readings going on every day all over town. All you have to do is get in your car, drive one to two hours, get there, pay for parking, find the event, collapse in your chair and you're there, and then after the event, you can drive home, enjoying the fact that you are part of the literary presence in a city where for only gas, four and a half hours of your time, a white knuckle freeway drive and parking frustration, you are part of the small cult who want to read literature, or even read at all, rather than going to the movies.

Speaking of the movies, we might as well discuss the most peculiar element of Los Angeles readings, which struck me upon arrival. From New York, to the Northeast, to Arizona, I had always believed poetry to be a serious pursuit. Los Angeles sees the art differently, not so much as literature, but as performance art. When Philip Levine read at LACMA, he apologized that at his last reading he had been too boring. When one reads in L.A., one is expected to show their early yearnings toward an acting career. Get up on stage and make it happen. People in Los Angeles are accustomed to professional and polished live entertainment—expert stage actors, deft stand-up comedy, dancing naked girls and the like. Literature is expected to compete for attention. I have heard poets read only their funny poems, their sexy poems, their love poems, their incest poems. I have seen writers shed clothes on stage until they're standing in leggings and a tank top. When you read in L.A., if you want to become part of the scene, if you want to keep your audience awake, to dazzle them, you read them breathless poems that undress and bathe them in a sort of eroticism—like their lives are about to change, a shiny car is about to drive up and whisk them to the Oscars.

Poetry in Los Angeles isn't necessarily about craft, it is also about the look and performance of the poet. Some performance poets have written work that lasts. Wanda Coleman is an example of such a poet. A writer whose work has been part of the poetry landscape since the Watts Riots, Coleman has been around L.A. for longer than most. She has memories of conversations with Charles Manson before he landed himself in the slammer, and she was a performance poet, before performance poetry was cool. However, unlike many, Coleman's work has endured to become read, anthologized and performed across the country.

Clearly many poets who are part of the "Slam" poetry movement in Los Angeles, performing at dives and coffee houses, they are just entertaining themselves and their friends, but aren't writing work you'll ever see between covers or find kids reading in fifty years. But they're having a good time anyway, and that's the point. If you missed that, you've missed everything about L.A. Are you having a good time? How do you look these days? If the answer to both questions is, "Smashing!" then what do you have to complain about? Let's focus on that. If you start to wander from reading to reading, pushing your car onward from freeway to freeway, *Thomas Guide* in lap, you will find some serious writers if you look far enough, and in between, you'll see writers searching for that huge place in the sun where someone remembers their name.

April 2003

TRANQUILITY

MARK SALERNO

What good would it do to state
one's regrets. That baleful list.
oh captain, my suntan. My couch
of memory. Sprung June and skeins
of gauzy light. Dusk and longing.
The choked desires of people I
thought I could save. They wore
slacks they wore skirts they wore
hose and silk. Gone now as summer
beyond anyone's care and lost
in the rose light. What's left is
bitter, a world I always hated.

II

L.A. PROSE

Dueling Prophets of Next L.A.

Susan Moffat

Mike Davis sees murky decay, while Kevin Starr embraces shiny optimism. This odd couple of historians is helping to shape the debate over the past – and future – of Southern California.

If the world has come to see Los Angeles as either hell or heaven—as a "Blade Runnerish" swamp of crime, race wars and economic devastation or a dynamic, multicultural cosmopolis—two of the people most responsible are historians Mike Davis and Kevin Starr.

Gangs, toxic waste, racial strife and a Neanderthal middle class fill Davis' *City of Quartz*, a jeremiad on twentieth century Los Angeles history that depicts the city as the ultimate gladiatorial arena of Darwinian capitalism.

Orange blossoms, red-tile bungalows and Pasadena literati abound in Starr's *Material Dreams*, a history of Los Angeles in the 1920s that celebrates the entrepreneurial, Progressive foundations of this "Great Gatsby of American cities."

When the two books came out in 1990, Davis groupies scorned Starr's boosterism as unfashionably chipper. Many Starr fans dismissed Davis as a left-wing lunatic.

Then came the 1992 riots, and both authors were transformed into media stars. Now, as they work the talk show circuit, fill the op-ed pages, guide European documentary-makers around town and teach a new generation of urban planners, these very public men of letters are helping to define not only how Los Angeles will be remembered, but what it will become.

Marxist and Catholic, thin and fat, rebel and defender of civilization, the forty-eight-year-old Davis and the fifty-four-year-old Starr are the odd couple of the booming industry of explaining L.A.

"I don't know that there's been anybody else as important to shaping intellectual perceptions of Los Angeles," said Warren Olney, host of the influential radio show *Which Way L.A.*

Next year, they will refuel debate with new books: a local history of the Great Depression by Starr, and a chronicle of recent riots, quakes and fires by Davis.

If Davis expresses the despair of the working class, while Starr captures its hopes, it is because they know them firsthand. Starr's poor city childhood in San Francisco seems straight out of Dickens, while Davis' youth in what he calls an "Okie suburb" of San Diego could have been invented by Steinbeck.

Starr envisions the ideal Los Angeles as a city dotted with high-rise apartments and bustling with street life, unified by great public edifices near its center. Davis imagines a place not too different from East L.A. at its best: working people hanging out on the front porches of their bungalows, enjoying the local library branch and the corner mural.

Davis' writing focuses on the victims of capitalism. He chronicles the destruction of working class Los Angeles with the closing of the great auto and tire plants south of Downtown, and traces the roots of current gang warfare to the lack of decent paying jobs.

"I remember sitting around in '67, '68," Davis said, "trying to figure out: well, were you gonna be an auto worker, a longshoreman or a trucker? You just sat down and decided. Look, I could end the gang problem in L.A. in five minutes. Just give me 50,000 good jobs that existed here in L.A. in the '60s."

By contrast, Starr mines the history of Los Angeles for nuggets of hope. He reminds readers that violence-torn Venice was once a Utopian village of canals and concert halls; and that Los Angeles, in living memory, enjoyed a first-rate public transportation system.

"I love Los Angeles," said the ever-ebullient Starr. "You banish violent crime from L.A. and you almost have Utopia."

Both men agree that a sprawling morality tale is being played out here, one with consequences for America and the world. For all their differences, Davis and Starr have one agenda in common: the defense of public space and the civic life it represents in a metropolis that is increasingly walling itself off into gated communities and fortress-like patios. Their shared passions for mundane and precious public places such as parks and libraries make the men friendlier toward each other than one might imagine—as do their working-class upbringings.

Childhood Contrasts

Starr grew up in San Francisco as, what today would be called, an "at-risk youth." It was the city and its churches that saved him, he says. He considers his life a testament to the power of cities—so often seen as corrupters of the young but really great ethical classrooms, and networks of religious, civic and educational institutions linked by public transportation.

His Irish-American family had lived in San Francisco for generations. His grandfather was a firefighter in the Great Fire of 1906. His father was a union machinist.

Tragedy struck early. His parents separated when he was three; his mother had a nervous breakdown, his father was disabled by a brain tumor. Starr and his brother spent much of their childhood in a foster home.

The home, the kind of institutional anchor Starr finds so crucial to a civil society, was where the troubled child developed his dedication to social orderliness and a love of teaching. "He was such a good boy," said Sister Mauritia Bleiker, now ninety-four. "He helped me take care of the littler boys."

When he was eleven, Starr and his brother moved back in with their mother. They lived on welfare in the Potrero Hill housing project where O.J. Simpson grew up. Starr hated the projects, but from the top of Potrero Hill he could see downtown San Francisco shining in the distance—"like Oz," an image he would later apply to Los Angeles. He spent his time roaming the city, exploring the libraries and museums, running a paper route in Union Square, and drinking-in the beauty of churches.

By contrast, the architecture of Davis' youth consisted of scattered rural shacks, suburban tract housing and back-yard chicken coops.

His parents hitchhiked to San Diego from Ohio during the Depression. They came with nothing and within a year had a little house on an acre of avocados. "Nobody ever loved Southern California more than my dad did," Davis said.

Born during his parents' stint in Fontana, birthplace of the Hells Angels, he moved with his family to Seattle, where his parents ran a hot-dog stand on Skid Row. The business failed, instilling the roots of Davis' skepticism of "the mythology of messianic entrepreneurialism"— the widely held belief that mom-and-pop business creation is the cure for L.A.'s woes.

"Communities hollowed out by the loss of automobile and aircraft plants," Davis writes, "will not be re-industrialized by more nail parlors, barbecue chicken franchises or greeting card shops."

From Seattle, the Davises moved back to San Diego County, to Bostonia, a dusty hamlet next to El Cajon. Davis' father, a meat cutter, was a good-natured man. Davis seems to have picked up more of his Irish mother's feistiness. When he writes of Mayor Richard Riordan as "a sixty-three-year-old Irish-American robber baron with GOP monogrammed on his Jockey shorts," Davis admits he may be showing his mother's prejudices against "lace curtain" Irish.

(To Starr, the mayor is merely familiar and benign: "Riordan looks like a thousand other freckle-faced guys in rumpled suits at the fortieth reunion of a Jesuit high school.")

Most of Davis' friends—"sons and daughters of the *Grapes of Wrath*"—knew as teenagers what the rest of their lives would look like: They would be truckers or meat cutters or hairdressers. Davis was into drag-racing, stealing cars and being vaguely angry and aimless—"pretty much your average redneck sixteen-year-old," he said.

It is no surprise that the Utopia with which he opens up *City of Quartz* is the quirky, short-lived Llano del Rio commune in the Antelope Valley: socialism with drag strips. Even today, Davis is drawn to inland Southern California and the West: Vernon and Cudahy, Fontana and Ontario, Las Vegas and Butte, Montana.

By contrast, Starr is essentially an urban, coastal Californian. His Los Angeles faces the ocean—a great trading power that willed its port out of a swamp and touts itself as "capital of the Pacific Rim."

To see California clearly, both men had to leave. In the 1960s they headed in wildly different directions, members of profoundly different generations even though close in age. "We were total products of the late '40s, early '50s," said John Stein, a lawyer and Starr's classmate at the Catholic University of San Francisco, from which they graduated in 1962. "We bought everything they told us."

Starr married a doctor's daughter who attended the genteel Catholic women's college next-door. He spent two years in the Army in Germany, then headed to Harvard University for graduate studies in English and American literature.

Davis, meanwhile, was going through the rites of passage of a teenage radical.

At sixteen, while working as a meat cutter, he quit high school to support his family when his father was temporarily disabled by a heart attack. His fate might have been set. But then his cousin, who had married a black man, invited Davis to a civil rights demonstration in 1962.

For "a lost, you know, confused, teenager . . . coming out of the boondocks of eastern San Diego County . . . (the civil rights movement) was an incredibly beautiful, stirring thing to be involved in," Davis said. It made him feel connected to a larger world. By 1964, he was on a Greyhound bus for New York, headquarters of Students for a Democratic Society.

While Starr was tutoring students in a Harvard office he decorated with an American flag and a portrait of radical-buster S.I. Hayakawa, Davis was filling a one hundred-page FBI record, spraying anti-war graffiti on USC frat houses, traveling from Oakland to Texas as an organizer for SDS, and getting married for the first of four times.

While Starr was writing the dissertation that became his acclaimed book *Americans and the California Dream*, Davis was running the Communist Party bookstore in Los Angeles.

For five years, Davis drove trucks across the country. As he delivered tons of Barbies working for a toy wholesaler in Los Angeles, he amassed an intimate knowledge of industrial Los Angeles that serves him well on his now-famous tours, in which he drives busloads of urban planners up the bed of the Los Angeles River and treats European social theorists to the scenic route through Huntington Park.

Davis spent the 1970s and '80s in and out of college and graduate school on union scholarships at UCLA and in exile in Belfast and London, where he was an editor for the New Left Review and for Verso, a leftist book publisher. He penned *Prisoners of the American Dream*, a unionist, anti-Reagan polemic, dense as a Marxist pound cake.

Meanwhile, Starr had left academia for a life as a peripatetic public intellectual. He churned out columns for the San Francisco Examiner. He was city librarian of San Francisco and executive director of the San Francisco Taxicab Assn. He taught college and worked in public relations. He ran unsuccessfully for San Francisco County supervisor and wrote a massive novel.

He joined the elite circles in San Francisco he had admired as a boy—the all-male Bohemian Club and the Olympic Club, whose cathedral-like swimming pool he had first encountered in an eighth-grade swim meet. He was much in demand as a dinner party guest, a rollicking storyteller with a prodigious appetite for good food, wine and intellectual debate.

But by the late 1980s, Starr was disillusioned with what he saw as his economically sleepy and culturally "alternative" city. He wrote a telling op-ed piece for *The Times* in 1986 describing the passing of the flame to Los Angeles as the leading city of California.

When USC offered him a job in 1989, he took it. Starr is that rare being, a native San Franciscan who loves Los Angeles. He seems to see something of the gung-ho spirit of turn-of-the-century San Francisco in the L.A. of today.

In his five years in this city, (where he has always lived Downtown,) Starr has re-created his role as a public man of letters, expounding on politics and gang violence in *Times* opinion pieces, broadcasting his views on public radio, advising Republican Mayor Riordan and recent Democratic gubernatorial candidate Kathleen Brown and lecturing at business luncheons. He is a proud capitalist but excoriates "the Adam Smith gang" who would let the weak perish in the name of free markets, and cites the papal encyclical of 1891—which demands social justice in any economic system—as his standard for judging modern society.

He is completing the next volume in his magisterial history of California, *The Dream Endures: California Through the Great Depression*, and a book about being Catholic in America.

This fall, Starr was appointed state librarian by Gov. Pete Wilson, a move that will take him to Sacramento on a mission he describes as fostering literacy and civic-mindedness, especially among young people as bad off as he once was.

Davis returned to Los Angeles from Europe in 1987, but saw something very different than Starr did. The country, he said, "had changed beyond recognition"—and for the worse. He tried driving a truck again, but the good wages of the early 1970s were gone.

Angry, Davis focused his writing on Los Angeles. Published in London, *City of Quartz* managed to turn local zoning battles into revolutionary high drama and gritty Fontana into a lyrical paradise lost. Then came the riots, which made the book seem eerily prophetic. That turned it into a best-seller with more than 60,000 copies in print—phenomenal for a social history book—and Davis into a hot property.

Davis looks nothing like the promotional photo on his book cover. There, a crew-cut, blue-jeaned hoodlum glares at the camera, simultaneously thuggish and righteous. In person he is unassuming, courteous, even gentle—more mischievous than defiant. The fire-breathing revolutionary, now married with a baby son, a twelve-year-old daughter and a mortgage; he greets a visitor to his Pasadena bungalow with the baby drooling copiously on his shirt.

He still thinks of himself as an activist, not just an auteur. He walks picket lines for restaurant and hotel workers' unions, works with Friends of the L.A. River, deploys local college students on inner-city research projects, nurtures young writers, is researching a book on the Western environment, and lectures at urban issues seminars.

Inevitably, Davis and Starr crossed paths.

Surprising Friendship

They met when they were invited to debate each other a couple of years ago at a Westside public affairs forum. "I came in my usually pugnacious mood," Davis said. "I came to fight him because I thought he was this kind of corporate apologist."

Instead, Davis said, "I found somebody who was just incredibly kind and complimentary to me. Warm-hearted. A lot more liberal than I had suspected. And I was absolutely charmed by Kevin."

They have become fast friends. When it comes down to it, Davis says, "we're just a couple of middle-aged Irish-American guys."

The two came together in Nick Patsaouras' oddball, visionary campaign for mayor last year. The three huddled to create a template for a pedestrian-friendly city united by buses and trains, graced with greenbelts and bustling with urban energy and new jobs.

Patsaouras lost.

There is a pathos to Davis and Starr, old-fashioned idealists both, looking to Teamsters and popes for guidance, refusing to believe their visions are pipe dreams. Both are acutely aware of being part of a generation that enjoyed the incredible opportunities of a California now vanished.

Says Davis: "When I graduated from school in 1964, there was this magnificent education system all for free. And there were plenty of jobs. Well now I look out and it's appalling. All the advantages I had have not been passed on."

One afternoon, the two men take a walk around Los Angeles, Starr's generous middle swelling his seersucker jacket under a red bow tie as he gesticulates toward the wiry Davis. They're not arguing. They're laughing. Commiserating over editors. Exchanging bibliographical tips on their shared hero, the late L.A. chronicler Carey McWilliams. Tugging at each other's sleeves to point out hidden historic treasures. Finishing each other's sentences.

Starr does try to get Davis to see the bright side of things, taking him to the recently restored 1926 Central Library. "Look at the dignity of this!" says Starr, knocking on the beautiful, solid wood carrels—available free, he noted, for any poor kid to use.

Davis allows that the murals and atriums of the library are impressive. "This is great public space," he says. But he cannot help noting the stark contrast with the impoverished county library system.

Davis takes Starr to his Los Angeles. On the way, ever protective of social order, Starr dissuades Davis from making a left turn against a light. They arrive at Belmont Tunnel, the graffiti-encrusted urban ruin at Beverly and Glendale boulevards, a standard stop on Davis' tours.

In the foreground is a weed-filled lot embraced by two thickly spray-painted walls, leading into the black hole that burrows underneath Bunker Hill, designed to serve a subway plan deserted long ago. A colony of homeless that ebbs and flows with the recession inhabits the area. Above the tunnel creeps a bald hill scraped clear years ago of its crumbling Victorian mansions—including the one where Davis and his SDS cohorts lived—in an aborted program of urban renewal.

Spiking up immediately behind the hill are the sparkling skyscrapers of Downtown, symbols, in Davis' view, of the "spatial apartheid" that separates the towers of high finance from the impoverished streets of Skid Row.

Today, as is often the case, a movie crew is filming in the mouth of the tunnel, taking advantage of its picturesque decay and air of impending urban violence.

That this is where Davis often takes visitors disturbs many people. "If you are out there propagating this view of L.A. . . . you won't get social reform. People will leave and you'll get Detroit," says rival L.A. pundit Joel Kotkin.

Starr takes Davis to the Old Plaza, next to Olvera Street, and describes how the power of cities is close to sacred. "The Spanish colonial notion of cities (was) cross-fertilized with Christian thought on the City of God. This (city) is a vehicle for our salvation, not just our religious salvation but our salvation in this world as well—that there be enough work for people, enough to eat, the possibilities of decent family life and education."

Typically, Davis has a more Machiavellian view of the Old Plaza. He believes that the Spanish bureaucracy set up a secular pueblo here with a garrison to counter the growing power of the Franciscan missions nearby.

And yet, Davis' hopes for the city are no less "Oz-like" than Starr's.

"This is crazy," Davis says as they sit outside the Church of Our Lady Queen of Angels across from the Old Plaza, "but I kinda have this idea that what we should be organizing for right now is to end the twentieth century with a World's Fair in L.A.—have a world exposition devoted to the ecologically and humanly sustainable city. And what better place to do it than L.A.—with all of its environmental problems, and maybe do it along the L.A. River and make real environmental restoration. A green city!"

"The potential to be a wonderful and unprecedented kind of civilization," Davis insists, "exists here."

November 1994

"A WORLD GONE WRONG"
L.A. Detectives

PAUL SKENAZY

The L.A. detective story started in San Francisco, though it didn't stay there long. In 1923, Samuel Dashiell Hammett (1894–1961) published his first short story about a nameless detective who was an "operative" of the Continental Detective Agency in *Black Mask*, one of the most famous of what were called "pulp" magazines. The "pulps" got their name from the cheap wood pulp used for the paper—the cheapest that could hold print. They sold for anywhere from a dime to a quarter, to a mass market of readers eager for tales of romance and adventure. It is estimated that by 1935, more than two hundred pulp magazines were being published in the U.S. each month with a readership of nearly twenty-five million.

Black Mask offered a new kind of sleuth: a man as eager to use a gun or fists as his brains; fast-talking and sharp-tongued, unemotional to the point of woodenness, and indifferent to the codes of law, morality, and domestic ethics that had dominated English detective fiction to that time. These men were urban loners: isolates living in small apartments, and almost always self-employed "private eyes." (The term comes from the logo of the Pinkerton Detective Agency, which featured an large open eye and the slogan, "We never sleep.") Narrated in the first person, the tales recounted violent events in a slang that was considered rough and racy, and seemed to echo the language of the 1920s city streets. As Raymond Chandler suggested in his introduction to *The Simple Art of Murder*, their power came from "the smell of fear which these stories managed to generate":

> Most of the plots were rather ordinary and most of the characters rather primitive types of people. . . [who] lived in a world gone wrong. . . . The law was something to be manipulated for profit and power. The streets were dark with something more than night. . . . The . . . demand was for constant action; if you stopped to think you were

lost. When in doubt have a man come through a door with a gun in his hand. This could get to be pretty silly, but somehow it didn't seem to matter.

The hardboiled form mirrored shifts in the nation itself; the 1920 census was the first in which more Americans lived in cities than the countryside. It was also a time when the Puritan codes that had long ruled public life in America had become law—the Eighteenth Amendment banned the sale of liquor from 1920–1933—yet, paradoxically, were losing their force among the masses of young men and women moving to the cities. World War I had just ended, providing license for a decade of political oppression alongside immense prosperity, the acceptance of a gangster community in league with authorities to supply liquor, and a populace whose spendthrift amorality masked a pervasive disillusionment.

Because of Hammett's talents, and his location in San Francisco, this hardboiled genre soon became associated with the west coast. That association was enforced over the next decade as more writers created stories and novels: Erle Stanley Gardner, Paul Cain (Peter Ruric), Raoul Whitfield, Horace McCoy; and, slightly later, Raymond Chandler. It is hard to say what, beyond chance, produced this congregation of talent in California at this moment. Certainly the lure of film writing had something to do with it, and most of the writers besides Hammett located their work in the Los Angeles area. But circumstance enforced form to remarkable advantage in the 1920s and 1930s, until the tough guy genre became a stock-in-trade of California storytelling. On the readership side, the fantasy visions of Hollywood and of Los Angeles as a lush "Garden of Eden" promising perpetual fulfillment, and San Francisco's reputation as an open and corrupt town long since established in Gold Rush days, encouraged an exoticism that filtered into many of these early tales.

The hardboiled detective novel was a hybrid form; it borrowed motifs from both the tradition of the western, and from the naturalistic work of writers like Theodore Dreiser and Frank Norris at the turn of the century. John Cawelti and others have demonstrated the parallels between the tough guy and the classic western hero—the individualistic and idiosyncratic point of view, the pragmatic ethics, bachelorhood and a lack of personal ties, a suspicion of high culture and formal language, the mixture of protective zeal and angry suspicion of women. But this heroism was tested and revised by the urban circumstances which echo naturalism's focus on the city as a moral wasteland. The open landscapes (and sense of potential) of the western have been replaced by cities in decay, and frontier hardihood has given way to stories of blackmail and deception.

Though Hammett is justly famous for the way he established his settings by reference to San Francisco streets, the small towns dotting the coastline, and the winds, rains and fog so characteristic of the area; California was not yet a conditioning agent in his early stories, and most of the characters seem relatively indifferent to the terrain. Hammett himself shifted the location of his fiction frequently in his brief writing career (he published little of significance after 1934), so much of it was not about California; whatever the setting, he focused his tales less on region than on the links between the underworld of crime and civic authority.

Still, his "Continental Op" stories and two novels, *The Dain Curse* (1929) and *The Maltese Falcon* (1930), were so dense with local reference that scholars have located the street corners, bars and apartment houses he referred to. More important than this use of locale, however, was the framework Hammett employed in the two novels, each of which involved the transplantation of European legend into California. In *The Dain Curse*, that legend was a family mythology of evil which made the young Gabrielle Leggett—heir to the Dain "curse"—feel herself doomed to destroy all those around her; she retreats from this fate into addiction and religious fanaticism. The obsession with blood, drugs and spiritualism are emblematic of the haunting power of this irrational European past that she overcomes only with the help of the "Op," who reveals the immediate, local circumstances behind a series of murders that surround her. The Victorian mansions of San Francisco provide a perfect gothic setting for the dark, brooding history that has been imported to California, leaving events in a deceptive fog that becomes the hallmark climate throughout the saga.

The fog as a suggestive trope for the uncertainty of one's moral and ethical perceptions is even more beautifully conceived in *The Maltese Falcon*, arguably Hammett's greatest creation. From the introduction of the detective, Sam Spade, in the very first paragraph as someone who "looked rather pleasantly like a blond satan," Hammett establishes a San Francisco in which deception controls names, identities and most particularly, the fate of a " . . . glorious golden falcon encrusted from head to foot with the finest jewels," originally a gift to the Emperor Charles from the Knights of Rhodes in the sixteenth century (Chapters 1, 8). In his essay "The Writer as Detective Hero," Ross Macdonald suggests that the falcon represents "a lost tradition, the great cultures of the Mediterranean past." It does, if it exists; the problem throughout the story is to find, and possess, the figurine. And therein lies the treasure Hammett contributed to the California detective tradition: the ambiguous relation of a seemingly rich legacy to the shoddier realms of contemporary west coast life. California, then, is the place where old stories, inherited worlds, are reenacted—seldom to one's benefit.

Hammett keeps the significance of the falcon uncertain while insisting on its fetishistic hold on the imagination. The statue that is finally unveiled in the last pages is a fake, a lead imitation; whether an original actually exists remains unclear. The legend itself thus might be historically false, but the obsession isn't. In this way the falcon becomes a brilliant device for revealing characters whose lives take on clarity and meaning from the quest. It is Spade's job to maintain his skepticism in the face of the falcon's value, and before the alternative temptations offered by the beautiful but deceitful woman who first hires him.

Hammett established the basic structures of the hardboiled novel— the serial detective, the focus on blackmail, the concentration on warfare within families, the revelations about political corruption. The moral geography of the landscape in Hammett's fiction became more explicit in the work of Raymond Chandler and Ross Macdonald: the pervasive fog and rains a sign of disillusion and ambiguity, California an outpost at the edge of the new world and a proving ground for the faiths of the old. Hammett's books revealed the fragility of all institutional links and assurances, from family to friendship, love to religion. In a world where the public laws and life provided no guidance, and lost their magical status as a 'natural' form of values, morality was revealed as not so much unstable as culturally constructed. As Raymond Chandler noted in his essay "The Simple Art of Murder":

Hammett took murder out of the Venetian vase and dropped it into the alley. . . . He wrote . . . for people with a sharp aggressive attitude to life. They were not afraid of the seamy side of things; they lived there. Violence did not dismay them; it was right down their street. Hammett gave murder back to the kind of people who commit it for reasons, not just to provide a corpse; and with the means at hand. . . . He put these people down on paper as they were, and he made them talk and think in the language they customarily used for these purposes.

Perhaps most important was Hammett's contribution to the image of the detective as a morally ambiguous hero. In the "Introduction" he wrote to the Modern Library edition of *The Maltese Falcon*, Hammett described Spade as " . . . a hard and shifty fellow, able to take care of himself in any situation, able to get the best of anybody he comes in contact with" (pp. viii–ix). In his ethics, the detective courted nihilism, but he maintained himself through the ceremonies and securities provided by work: detection as a profession. He was a middle-man, a messenger and guide able to enter the homes of the wealthy and talk the talk of the poor, at home with the tactics of the police and the greed of the gangster. But he remained a contradictory and solitary man. Single, poor, disengaged, lonely but proud of, or in, his isolation, he had few outward loyalties. After he rescued Gabrielle Leggett in *The Dain Curse*, her infatuation with the "Op" gave way to a recognition that he was a " . . . monster. A nice one, an especially nice one to have around when you're in trouble, but a monster just the same, without any human foolishness like love in him." (Chapter 22)

Along with this, the detective was, indeed, a "private eye": a man able to see through the world's self-deceptions. As the moral center of these fictions, the detective echoed the transcendental "eye/I" of Emerson: the individual attuned to the emblematic significance of life's "clues." This private moral perception allowed the detective to resist the prescriptions and codes of others, and instead reconstitute the world in his own terms. Thus, perhaps foremost, the detective was a storyteller; someone who deconstructs the stories of others and then rebuilds them, rearranging the seemingly random events that have occurred during the

novel into a coherent, or at least cohesive, corrective narrative that reca-
pitulates what happens in a more plausible way.

Though Erle Stanley Gardner and others had been contributing stories to *Black Mask* from the 1920s on, the detective and crime tales
only became a staple of the Los Angeles area in the 1930s, and reflected a Depression world, where Hollywood glamour and wealth
appeared alongside poverty, and the enormous growth of Los Angeles
created a complex landscape of a centerless city encroaching on the
vast surrounding mountains, arid land and orchards. In the years from
1920 to 1960, while the population of San Francisco increased by
about 30 percent, Los Angeles changed from a city of almost 570,000
to one of nearly two and a half million residents—a nearly 500 percent increase. (In the 1920s alone, the population of Los Angeles increased by more than 100,000 people a year.)

This meant that Los Angeles was a city with a past; swamped by
recent growth, with citizens whose sensibilities were nurtured elsewhere
(primarily in the Midwest). The migrants were a group seeking a new
beginning at continent's end, attracted by a combination of setting and
weather, mystique and the promise of jobs.

The most famous of the Los Angeles thrillers concern this newly
arrived population. James M. Cain's *The Postman Always Rings Twice*
(1934), for example, takes advantage of the geographic and psychological freedom of car and highway in everything from the setting at a gas
station to the violence that occurs along deserted mountain and coastal
roads. It is a fierce little saga of two down-and-out drifters whose passion for each other reawakens their passion for life. That new life is
bought, however, through another man's death, and this paradox dooms
their ambitions as it liberates their desires.

Cain's novel set the stage for a tradition of stories that suggested
California's seductive capacity to undermine the conventional social com-
pacts of marriage and family in the name of feeling: Cain's own *Double
Indemnity* (1936), the *noir* movement in film, and the detective tales of
writers like Raymond Chandler (1888–1959) and Ross Macdonald
(1915–1983). By the time Joan Didion comes along in the late 1960s
(in her essay, "Some Dreamers of the Golden Dream") to write about a
woman who has burned her husband to death (in his car), she can ref-

erence this tradition as a symbolic cultural shorthand, and explain the end of an affair as like " . . . the novels of James M. Cain, the movies of the late 1930's, all the dreams in which violence and threats and blackmail are made to seem commonplaces of middle-class life." By then, she realizes, "The dream was teaching the dreamers how to live" (17). Mythology now gives form to social practice, and these couples and lovers—all of whom came to the state from somewhere else seeking a new start—are quite literally acting "by the book."

Like Hammett, Chandler and Macdonald were California migrants. Hammett was from Baltimore; Chandler, though born in Chicago, was raised in England; Macdonald, born in San Jose, California, moved to Canada as a child and only returned after World War II. Chandler and Macdonald modified their own experiences to create a mythology of migratory culture in the period from 1930–1970. Their characters come to California from the Midwest. What they leave behind, however—a murky event, a crime, a submerged memory—relentlessly stalks them. Their new lives erupt when these sinful or illegal, unlawful or just shameful past moments threaten to emerge, linking who they are pretending to be to who they once were.

Chandler's and Macdonald's mysteries, then, were always double stories in which two places and two times converged. California became the field on which the past asserted its claims in the present. These hard-boiled narratives portray a culture that dreams of new beginnings but is, despite itself, taught the lessons of continuity and history; there is no clean slate to civilization. The people who imagine California as a panacea, a resurrection, find they cannot obliterate the past. Instead, they are forced to confront, sometimes even celebrate and embrace, their criminal history as their own, in the form of blackmail, reenactments of earlier crimes, or other historical visitations. The detective functions as an intermediary, even medium, who joins past to present.

Hired to rescue his clients, the detective's deeper, more essential job was to discover the ties binding one life and place to others—time represented by geography. Los Angeles was portrayed as an atomized world filled with permanent transients. Neighbors knew each other only to peek or gossip. Respectability had replaced morality, envy substituted for desire. Blackmail—getting the lowdown on someone else—was the new form of intimacy. The detective's job was to penetrate the social fragmentation and reveal the interconnections of personal fear and public violence and greed. The detective proved a singular figure, able to face up to the truths he discovered and force others to do the same.

With his bicultural early life as a poor American child educated in England where he was dependent upon well-to-do British relatives, Raymond Chandler's (1888–1959) was a sensibility divided between two centuries and nurtured by two worlds. It was that paradoxical position, both within and outside of the Southern California he chronicled, devoted to American slang and educated in Edwardian usage, that gives the peculiar feel to his writing. His ambition to "raise" the detective form and to see himself as an artist, along with his deep loyalty to the often graceless world of Los Angeles, make for a complex and shifting series of recreations of Southern California. Detective Philip Marlowe's sometimes tender, sometimes acerbic, always watchful voice proves a perfect vehicle for Chandler's own mixtures of pride in, and contempt for, Los Angeles and for the combination of metaphoric abandon and realistic density that is Chandler's trademark.

The central problem in a Chandler story, as in all mysteries, is that nothing is as it seems. But Chandler's bravura is to add a compensatory pleasure: nothing is ever just what it seems but always suggests something more, something else. Even as Chandler presents the stark, demeaning aspects of his time, he frames his accounts by invoking the chivalric traditions of the past, and playfully overasserts his scenes with extravagant similes. His books bear sorrowful titles like *Farewell, My Lovely* (1940) and *The Long Goodbye* (1953), and feature characters with names like Grayle, Quest, and Knightly. The opening of Chandler's first novel, *The Big Sleep* (1939), sets the stage for this romantic fanfare, as we meet Marlowe below a stained-glass panel in which a "knight in dark armor" struggles in vain to rescue a lady tied to a tree. Later in the story, Marlowe looks at the chess board in his apartment and compares the rules that govern the game with the more human, less functional, laws governing his own moves: "Knights had no meaning in this game. It wasn't a game for knights." (Chapters 1, 24)

This grafting of old traditions to new circumstances is echoed by Chandler's plots, which are constructed as quests: an aging patriarch seeks a missing man who once kept him company, an ex-convict searches for his true love though he hasn't seen her for years, a woman arrives in town to find her sister. These quests, however, replace medieval fulfillment with contemporary perversity; the woman wants to profit from her sibling's fame, the true love is the one who turned her lover over to the police, the missing man was shot by the patriarch's daughter. In the process of discovering these truths, Marlowe unveils the Los Angeles where glamour preys on social inequities, police departments cater to the monied, and the aristocratic families of the community have decayed into flamboyant clans greedy for power and addicted to gambling and dope. Marlowe's voice turns melancholy as he contemplates the fate of his home town in *The Little Sister* (1949): "I used to like this town. . . . Los Angeles was just a big, dry sunny place with ugly homes and no style, but good-hearted and peaceful." Now, he says, what once might have become "the Athens of America" resembles "a neon-lighted slum, a big hardboiled city with no more personality than a paper cup." (Chapter 26)

Chandler's chronicles of this transformation are fragmentary but definitive. His skill is in the individual scene; even his best works like *The Big Sleep* and *Farewell, My Lovely* never achieve the pacing or formal narrative solidity of *The Maltese Falcon*. But his novels possess a literary density absent from Hammett. Prone to splenetic fits on the one hand and sentimentality on the other, at his best Chandler had a feel for loneliness, and a flair for language, that he expended for the lowliest and most troubled of his creations. Spotlighting dank rooms and dead-end lives, Chandler took full advantage of the detective story's insistent focus on the seemingly mundane and overlooked to call our attention to the unobserved oddities and casual interactions of the culture. J. B. Priestley perhaps sums up Chandler's achievement best: "[Chandler] reduces the bright California scene to an empty despair, dead bottles and a heap of cigarette butts under the meaningless neon lights. . . . and suggests, to my mind, almost better than anybody else the failure of a life that is somehow short of a dimension."

Chandler achieves this recreation through Marlowe, a self-proclaimed "shop-soiled Galahad." In his dissertation on the hard-boiled detective tradition, Robert Parker noticed that in California detective fiction, "the crime is the occasion of the story, but the subject of the story is not the detection, but the detective" (p. 8). In "The Simple Art of Murder" Chandler made rather heady claims for his detective as a redemptive agent in a dangerous world: " . . . down these mean streets a man must go who is not himself mean, who is neither tarnished nor afraid." Marlowe struggles to achieve this level of heroism—what in *The High Window* he calls " . . . the justice we dream of but don't find"; in the process, he becomes a modern incarnation of male principles stymied by his own ideals as much as the scene around him, able to report it all in the most expansive of contemporary California dialects.

Ross Macdonald (1915–1983) saw himself as the inheritor of this distinct, and distinctly California, tradition; he borrowed his hero's name (Lew Archer) from a Hammett novel, and his own early writing style from Chandler. He moved Archer about 120 miles up the coast from Los Angeles to a small, wealthy town he called Santa Teresa (modeled after Santa Barbara). From his first novel, published in 1944, until *The Blue Hammer*, which appeared in 1976, his books and essays bear the suggestive richness (and at times, marring self-consciousness) of his own struggles to reclaim California as a homeland and to integrate the multiple dimensions of his background; he admits that popular fiction affords him "a mask for autobiography." Each of the eighteen novels in his Lew Archer series (begun with *The Moving Target*, 1949) presents a narrative reenactment of the past—frequently a moment associated with the first years of World War II—as a way to chronicle the woes of the late 1940s, 1950s, and 1960s.

Macdonald's distinction was to court a middle ground of craft— more carefully constructed and balanced narratives than Chandler if less fierce and intense in their verbal range; a more sentimental attachment of detective and world than Hammett. Issues of political corruption that preoccupy Hammett and Chandler gradually give way to a growing interest in adolescent culture in books like *The Zebra-Striped Hearse* (1962). Chandler's focus on the decayed stature of wealthy aristocratic families becomes in Macdonald a psychoanalytic analysis of the nuclear family. Divorced, educated and remorseful, Archer increasingly becomes a surrogate parent, even amateur therapist, to a wayward and maimed adolescent; and his first person narrative role shifts from cultural guide to function as what Macdonald calls the "mind" of the novel.

Perhaps most important, Macdonald extended the form's attention to the landscape as a moral register of human foible. The tension of constructed world and wild terrain that one saw as early as James M. Cain is transformed in Macdonald into a complex exploration of how legacies of personal deceit and denial parallel and encourage environmental misuse. In an early novel exploring family legacies, for example, Macdonald images the past as a skeleton buried beneath the floorboards of a house; in *The Underground Man* (1971), the metaphor of a hidden former life has been expanded into an emblem of the human abuse of nature: a car buried in a forest clearing is uncovered amid a destructive fire which wipes out immense swatches of the wilderness.

The alternative voices that have emerged since 1970 have all taken their cue from Hammett, Chandler and Macdonald, as well as some of the more subversive and brooding thriller writers who focused on the mind and heart of the criminal and outcast. Certainly the most eccentric is James Ellroy (Lee Earle Ellroy, 1948–). Born in Los Angeles, he moved to the El Monte area of the city with his mother when his parents divorced in 1954. In 1958, his mother was brutally murdered (a still unsolved crime Ellroy wrote about in *My Dark Places* [1996]). He grew up with his father, who, he has commented in interviews, piqued his interest in crime with Jack Webb's *The Badge*, a history of the LAPD. It was in *The Badge* that he first read about the Black Dahlia case that has obsessed him ever since: the murder of starlet Elizabeth Short, who was found mutilated and naked, her body in two halves. Psychologically, Short's murder seems to have merged with his mother's death for the boy, so he had nightmares about Short; visited her grave, felt later that he had actually known her. Expelled from a largely Jewish high school for Nazi comments (and shoplifting and porno magazines, among other things), he joined the army, until he managed to get himself dishonorably discharged after three months. He lived a street life for most of the next years, in and out of jail for theft; spending nights in parks and abandoned apartments, addicted to peeping and women's underwear, and to alcohol, speed, and Benzedex (a sinus inhaler). Schizophrenic and habitually ill, Ellroy finally sobered up through AA and started working as a caddie while he wrote his first crime story, *Brown's Requiem*, which was published in 1981. A flood of work followed: *Clan-*

destine (1982), *Blood on the Moon* (1983), *Because the Night* (1984), *Suicide Hill* (1986), *Killer on the Road* (*Silent Terror*) (1986), and his *L.A. Quartet*: *Black Dahlia* (1987), *The Big Nowhere* (1988), *L.A. Confidential* (1990), and *White Jazz* (1992). Other novels have appeared since, at a slower pace, and less focused on and in Los Angeles, including *American Tabloid* (1995), which many consider Ellroy's best work to date, and its sequel, *The Cold Six Thousand* (2001), which comprise the first two of what Ellroy refers to as his *Underworld USA* trilogy.

It is the *L.A. Quartet* that has made Ellroy the iconic, if also frequently abhorred, poet of post-war L.A., the self-proclaimed 'Demon Dog' of American crime fiction. Ellroy's L.A. is a split-screen image that crosses childhood years of true crime and hard-boiled reading with Ellroy's own life of addicted, petty crime street life, and then mates these with his twin obsessions: his mother's murder and the Black Dahlia mutilation and killing. The result is a vision of the city between 1947 and 1959 as bereft of moral yardsticks, a world of serial killings, sex crimes, serial killings, corruption, and bizarre obsessions. Ellroy layers his plots, twisting multiple lives into a web of interconnections that suggest less a conspiracy than a mad, irreparable tangle of demented, doomed desires. On the surface, in his language, Ellroy creates opuses that reek of racism, homophobia, sexual addiction and a fascination with power and violence. At the same time, this texture of raw, crude experience, delivered in a staccato style that drives a reader relentlessly from one incident to the next, can also be read as an indictment of the world it mirrors. Ellroy has frequently registered his distaste for the Chandler loner, the good man pacing through the 'mean streets,' because of the moral self-pity he finds encompassed in this vision of individualism, rebellion and redemption. Instead he offers an interest in what he calls "the toadies in the system," proposing to create the "secret history" of the culture through fierce if sympathetic portraits of the leg-breakers, the prostitutes, the con men, the corrupt cops and the losers.

"I am the laureate of bad men," Ellroy declared in one interview. There is little to distinguish hero and villain in Ellroy. His trademark storytelling is a mad rap: a raging chorus of voices offering an avalanche of events at an unremitting pace. Mind and heart are gone, idea has been converted to action, dialogue substitutes for description and thought. The inter-changes emerge in a clipped, shorthand echo of street slang. It's difficult to find prose that's harder, scenes seedier, people more desperate or a city more pervasively on the make. Ellroy taunts and seduces his reader, implicating them in the muck through their engagement with the psychosexual violence that he proffers; you feel both dirty and guilty for your reading pleasure. The only discernible note of warmth is an infrequent but unmistakable nostalgia for a tattered ideal that mixes with the gritty violence, the fractured bits of conversation, and the mock news headlines that litter Ellroy's pages. History in these works is less remembered than viscerally represented in a cacophony of desperation. It is through such intensity that Ellroy has provided glimpses into the dark side of L.A. in the late 1940s and 1950s. Still, it's hard to separate the prurience from the historical concern: Is Ellroy playing reporter and moralist, or simply succumbing himself to the indecencies of his role as voyeur, in his unabashed delight with lurid plots, his stylized characterizations, and his anxious effort to reproduce the mangy undertow of a graceless world of grime?

Most of the California mysteries of recent years have been more overt than Ellroy in their homage to the Hammett tradition, maintaining the urban focus, the explorations of social inequity, the tension of institution and individual; and the role of the detective as a mediator and social conscience able to cross cultural boundaries, enact his private code of humane justice, and provide a narrative that will reconstitute a sense of time and order. With the introduction of detective characters from previously disenfranchised groups in the U.S., the male posturing and muscle-flexing, and the homophobia and misogyny, so frequent in both Hammett and Chandler have been mocked and undermined. The very best of these works, by men like Joseph Hansen and Walter Mosley in particular, have subverted such presumptions as they have confirmed the resilience of the form itself.

The earliest of these challenges was made by Joseph Hansen (1923–) in his Dave Brandstetter series about a gay insurance investigator, which began with *Fadeout* (1970). After a long apprenticeship publishing gay novels under a pseudonym to a largely gay audience, and the rejection of his first detective novel by a host of New York publishers, it took two years for Hansen to find a mainstream publisher willing to back *Fadeout* (and another ten before his works started to appear in paperback). From the first Hansen created a hero, and series, that challenged traditional generic codes. Dave Brandstetter is, quite comfortably, gay-strong, easy in his sexuality, as tender as tough. Unlike the Hammett and Chandler private eye known best for his inscrutable isolation, Hansen devoted good portions of each novel to Brandstetter's private life. In *Fadeout*, for example, he is just returning to work after weeks of remorseful mourning for his lover of twenty years who died of cancer, and he has two other extended relationships that carry through the rest of the series. And, again in contrast to the often agelessness of the macho, heterosexual heroic tradition, Brandstetter is in his mid-forties in *Fadeout*, and grows older to match the publication dates of each successive novel, until he confronts his own mortality head-on in *A Country of Old Men* (1991), the twelfth and last book in the series.

As Hansen commented in an essay, "Matters Grave and Gay":

> I made [Brandstetter's] ongoing life story a factor in each of the novels. Too many detective heroes have no life apart from the case on which they're working. This is traditional but not credible. I . . . figured readers would identify with a protagonist who ages, loses friends, relatives, lovers to death and common alienation, meets new people, changes living quarters, quits his job to go to work for himself, begins to think about retiring, even at last is forced to buy a gun, much as he hates them. . . . Looked at from this angle, the series becomes one long novel about Dave Brandstetter.

Issues of intimacy, time, and vulnerability are at the heart of Hansen's tales, providing Brandstetter a perspective unique in the hard-boiled tradition, where a narrowly defined form of masculinity turned plots on claims of control, power, and violence. With Brandstetter, most of the violence is offstage: brief, understated or implied, often reported. The focus on family and childrearing remains, but seen from a gay perspective. There are long-term marriages, but there are others that give the lie to heterosexual domestic mythologies—Brandstetter's father, for example, marries nine times.

As Hansen also noted in "Matters Grave and Gay," " . . . homosexuality serves mystery writers as shorthand for all that is repulsive in human form" (pp. 117–18). Hansen's ambition was to create a gay hero who was, instead, " . . . a decent, upright, caring kind of man." Gay and lesbian life appear in all of the mysteries, in a multiplicity of forms benign and daring, out and closeted, criminal and victimized, offering a multiplicity that the detective genre had, summarily, reduced to mockery and stereotype. What characterizes the approach to sexuality most is the very ordinariness, the flat-voiced refusal of melodrama, with which Hansen introduces his stories. But the consequence of Hansen's gay point of view is to upend all our cultural presumptions. In *Skinflick* (1979), a transvestite named Randy Van explains that he worries about sweating too much because it makes his "identity run" (Ch. 16). And it is just this ability to make identity into a source of mystery and confusion—sometimes comic, sometimes threatening—that Hansen offers his readers.

In *Fadeout*, for example, we have a traditional California story of a presumed accidental death in a car accident when an auto is found in an arroyo below Fox Olson's house. But Olson's body is never found, and Brandstetter doubts that the man is dead, despite the reassurances of Olson's wife and grown daughter. The investigation reveals Olson as someone who, after frustrated years as an unpublished writer, becomes famous as an affable, folksy guitar-playing singer and storyteller on the local radio station. The books he's written earlier that failed all seemed to lack something, we're told; that 'something' turns out to be the love he has for a male he went to art school with. When the two men rediscover each other, Olson begins to write something that focuses on his homosexuality—a manuscript those who know him want to burn and obliterate. The long-absent lover offers a telling observation: "Suppose Dostoevsky had never mentioned his epilepsy, his compulsive gambling. How far would he have gotten?" (Ch. 18)

It's fair I think to suggest this as Hansen's own declaration of independence as a novelist. Each of the novels in the Brandstetter series turns on issues of secrecy and deception—a theme common to detective fiction but one with particular power for the gay and lesbian community at this moment in history, in the years after Stonewall. As R. D. Zimmerman, another gay detective writer noted, "The dynamics [of] being gay feed into the layers of truth in a mystery. I know how to lie very well. I lied to myself, I lied to my family, I lied to everyone around me. I know the layers of secrets. That's what a mystery's about: sifting through the layers to get to the fundamental [truth]." As author Michael Nava noted, declaring his own debt to Hansen, "He used the mystery to actually explore what it meant to be gay. In the classic American mystery, the private investigator is an outsider who's generally viewed [as] fairly disreputable by the people who hire him. So if you are in fact an outsider because you're gay or a woman or African-American, it's a very interesting vehicle to explore the whole issue of being on the fringe."

Michael Nava's (1954–) seven mysteries feature Henry Rios, a criminal lawyer based primarily in Los Angeles. Gay, Chicano, San Francisco public defender turned L.A. defense attorney, Rios has provided a vantage for Nava to comment on the shifting experiences of living in California in the last two decades of the century. Like Hansen, Nava juxtaposes Rios' personal life with the investigations so the lawyer-detective is always implicated in the crimes he struggles to solve. Along the way, from *Little Death* (1986) to *Rag and Bone* (2001), Rios has dealt with alcoholism, the death of his partner to AIDS (in *The Death of Friends* (1996), certainly the most poignant of the novels), a childhood of abuse that has left him estranged from his sister (once a nun, now a lesbian professor in Oakland), the unexpected discovery of a nephew, and a heart attack. And he has solved crimes that mix in enough political and social activism to remind us that American-style detective stories began as tales written about, and for, an audience of lowlifes, riffraff, the poor and barely literate. Nava has created his own version of Los Angeles, a mythological region, as he notes in an interview with Katherine Forrest, where the landscape is filled with "cinematic images" that live in uncomfortable intimacy with the reality of a city which " . . . probably contains the most diverse population of any American city or for that matter any city anywhere. . . . It's a city where the crassest materialism lives side by side with the most sublime spiritual seeking. To write about Los Angeles is to write about life itself."

Among women writers, the most popular and consistently interesting has been Sue Grafton (1940–), known for her alphabet series (*A is for*

Alibi, B is for Burglar, and so on) about Kinsey Millhone. Though Grafton admits that she "chose the classic private eye genre because I like playing hardball with the boys," and Millhone has had her shootouts and fistfights over the years, the emphasis in these books is on location, character, and social mores. *A is for Alibi* (1982) sets the retrospective tone in the opening paragraph: "My name is Kinsey Millhone. I'm a private investigator, licensed by the state of California. . . . The day before yesterday I killed someone and the fact weighs heavily on my mind. . . . Aside from the hazards of my profession, my life has always been ordinary, uneventful, and good. Killing someone feels odd to me and I haven't quite sorted it through." Events haunt Millhone as they don't seem to her male predecessors, and the recounting is shaded by this tone of self-scrutiny.

Millhone is a straightforward, wise-cracking twice-divorced woman in her thirties (she is aging slowly, about a year every two or three novels) who prefers wine to hard liquor, friendships to one-night love affairs. She maintains a strong, local identification with her neighborhood world; runs every morning, lives in a converted garage behind the house of a retired baker, takes her food and drink business to Rosie's bar down the street. She willingly admits to "the latent felon in me," and quickly becomes implicated in the cases she solves—frequently crimes committed years before. Her attempts to piece together a narrative out of the scraps of truth embedded in the lies invariably lead to some invasion of her own world: her home is destroyed, her car wrecked, she discovers unknown relatives.

Kinsey Millhone legitimizes herself by pointing to her investigator's license; Ezekial "Easy" Rawlins, the African-American hero of Walter Mosley's (1952–) series on South Central Los Angeles, doesn't have a license and wouldn't qualify for one. A professional without portfolio, Rawlins' legitimacy is his status in the neighborhood as a black homeowner and working stiff. In *White Butterfly* (1992), he describes himself as " . . . a confidential agent who represented people when the law broke down." His career begins haphazardly in the first pages of Mosley's first novel, *Devil in a Blue Dress* (1990), which reads like a recapitulation of the opening of Chandler's *Farewell, My Lovely* fifty years before. A white man enters a bar frequented only by blacks. But this time, instead of viewing the scene through Marlowe, we see the white invasion through Rawlins' black sensibility as he sits over a drink; out of work, short on money, and ready for whatever comes along.

Mosley both confirms the traditional form of the hardboiled novel and reverses its valence. Like Chandler and Macdonald, Mosley's hero guides us through distinct and mutually exclusive worlds. South Central is like a foreign country, an internal colony of white America, complete with its own language, codes of conduct, and frontier. Easy is hired by whites to ferret out information closed to them by race. But what he discovers, and how he uses his knowledge, is always colored by his sympathies with the blacks who are his neighbors and friends.

We're never far from the pressures of power wielded with vain, unquestioning confidence by a white world that hasn't yet learned to doubt its privileged superiority. A biracial woman is dangerous to her lover because of his political ambitions, the death of three black women is ignored until the white daughter of a prominent citizen dies in similar circumstances, a family can't admit a longstanding affair between a rich white man and his black servant. Easy is caught in the middle, anxious to help others while struggling to protect what little he has.

Like his predecessors too, Mosley's novels are stories of two times and places; as Mosley himself put it in an interview with Jean Nathan: "The books are about black migration from the Deep South to Los Angeles, and this blue-collar existentialist hero moving through time from the middle of the century to the present." Mosley reconstructs the consequences of those migrations: the achievements of so many blacks and the disintegration of a whole way of life as the initial dreams of a better time wane. As he records these lives in *Black Betty*: "There was no logic to the layout of the city. And there were more people every day. Sharecroppers and starlets, migrant Mexicans and insurance salesmen, come to pick over the money tree for a few years before they went back home. But they never went home. The money slipped through their fingers and the easy life weighed them down." (Chapter 9)

It is Mosley's ambition to suggest the forgotten historical legacy of these unrecognized lives. Each novel drops us back into a lost time: 1948 in *Blue Dress*, 1953 in *A Red Death* (1991), 1956 in *Butterfly*, 1961 in *Black Betty* (1994), 1963 in *The Little Yellow Dog* (1996), the mid-1960s in *Bad Boy Brawley Brown* (2002). It is like a high-speed slide show of African-American life. We watch the neighborhoods change, watch the kids grow older, watch the racism remain—upfront, overt, unapologetic. Easy serves as historian and citizen, his accounts of others emblematic samplings of the cultural tale, his own life no less representative. He ages from book to book; by *Black Betty* he is a man of forty. He worries about his mortgage, gets in trouble with the IRS, saves money, buys property, marries. He adopts two children, fathers one, watches as his wife leaves him. He coexists with a neighborhood of cronies: his violent but loyal buddy Mouse; Quentin Naylor, the black cop with his polite speech patterns trying to make things work from the inside; the conniving Mofass, who runs Easy's businesses. Easy's role as detective fades imperceptibly into his role as an adoptive father; as he nurtures his abused and silent child, Jesus, back to health and voice, he also gives expression to the silenced culture.

Conscious of his own role from the first, Easy takes comfort in his position; as he describes it in *Devil in a Blue Dress*: "Behind my friendly talk, I was working to find something. Nobody knew what I was up to, and that made me sort of invisible; people thought that they saw me but what they really saw was an illusion of me, something that wasn't real" (Chapter 18). Invoking the ghost of Ralph Ellison's *Invisible Man*, Mosley points out how detection, like race, can create a shifty security in the blind assumptions of others and creates one more spin on the ghostly spirit of the mysterious detective.

Asked in an interview with Jim Impoco why he thinks Los Angeles has become such a significant location for detective fiction, Walter Mosley suggested that it was because " . . . it's impossible to know L.A. It's an extremely diffuse and diverse city. . . . It's a place of hiding. To be able to know a place, it has to at least in some ways want to be known. And L.A. just doesn't want to be known. L.A. is a big secret, which is why it's so good for the genre." If this is true, it's fair to say that the real mystery in these detective fictions is a quest for place, an effort to discover this hidden center that makes Los Angeles seem, somehow, both representative and distinct, a glimpse of the future and a warning of the impending apocalypse. The California detective story has helped expose, if never quite revealed, the hidden life of Los Angeles and, by extension, the Pacific coast—a place people come to,

Mosley goes on to say, " . . . with the hope of building not only a new life but a new self." The form has been flexible enough to incorporate a range of voices and faces yet preserve its essential thrust, in which the vernacular uncovering of a world of secrets provides what Ross Macdonald calls a " . . . passport to democracy and freedom."

As Nava and Mosley remind us, the detective form has long insisted, and continues to insist, that we recognize those we would condemn as our kin: that rich and poor, insiders and out, have more to do with each other than either group finds it comfortable to admit. Dealing in their different ways with issues of displacement, greed, and disillusionment, these mystery writers have reinvented the genre as they have shaped their talents to its requirements. The tough guy tale that began as popular fiction has now, with the publication of Dashiell Hammett's and Raymond Chandler's work as part of the Library of America, entered the literary pantheon. Hardboiled California has become a staple of the imagination.

April 2003

ENDINGS AND BEGINNINGS
Surviving Apocalypse

DAVID FINE

Whatever else California was, good or bad, it was charged with human hope. It was linked imaginatively with the most compelling of American myths, the pursuit of happiness. When the intensity of expectation was thwarted or only partially fulfilled . . . it could backfire into restlessness and bitterness . . . As a hope in defiance of facts, as a longing which could ennoble and encourage but which could turn and devour itself, the symbolic value of California endured . . . a legacy of the Gold Rush.

—Kevin Starr,
Americans and the California Dream, 1860–1915

Finally, it was the city that held us, the city they said had no center, that all of us had come to from all over America because this was the place to find dreams and pleasure and love.

—Carolyn See, *Golden Days*

L.A.'s fine in the long run . . . you get to choose who you want to be and how you want to live.

—Ann Goode in Alan Rudolph's Film, *Welcome to L.A.*

I

In *The Ecology of Fear*, Mike Davis reports that "at least 138 novels and films since 1909" deal with the destruction of the city. The destroying agents have been both natural and man-made (or the two in conjunction): earthquake, fire, and flood, atomic attack, extraterrestrial or other-race invasion (the former often as metonymic displacement of the latter). The destruction of Los Angeles by atomic or nuclear explosion dominates Davis's taxonomy (forty-nine times), followed by earthquake (28), and then alien hordes and monsters. What is more significant than the frequency of the city's imagined destruction, though, according to Davis, is "the pleasure such apocalypses provide to readers and movie audiences." The entire world, he says, "seems to be rooting for L.A. to slide into the Pacific or to be swallowed up by the San Andreas Fault." In citing dozens of novels and films over the past ninety years that "celebrate" the city's destruction, he reminds us of how long the template for urban disaster has been in place in fiction and film about Los Angeles; apocalyptic renderings have been there almost as long as there have been novels about Los Angeles.

Many of these literary acts of destruction, he claims persuasively, have been generated by racial anxieties in California: white fear of darker-skinned people. His initiating example is Homer Lea's hysterical racist novel about the Japanese invasion and occupation of California, *The Valor of Ignorance* (1909). Lea's work, he indicates, is the beginning of a long line of xenophobic fictions, couched often enough in Bible Belt fundamentalist, kooky religious, or Aryan supremacist terms. Outside the realm of fiction, Los Angeles has had a long xenophobic prophet-of-doom tradition. An early-twentieth-century exemplar was the Reverend "Fighting" Bob Schuler, the target of whose rantings was Los Angeles as city of sin (leveled largely at the predominantly Jewish film industry but also at Catholics and at big business) that would suffer the Almighty's wrath in apocalyptic destruction. More recently, there has been the American Nazi, Andrew Macdonald, who wrote *The Turner Diaries* (1978), an ugly futuristic fantasy based on a purportedly "real" diary kept by a martyr to the white cause, about Aryan soldiers, survivalists, fighting a guerilla war in Los Angeles to rid the city of Jews and blacks.

While Anglo-Saxon racism has been a significant presence in doomsday renderings of Los Angeles, xenophobic literature is far from a local phenomenon. Davis documents the national strain, but he may be overstating his case by locating the racial ground so prominently in Los Angeles. Contemporary racism may well be linked to local fears about the surge of immigrants into the city in the last few decades, but xenophobia has been a common enough response in all immigrant cities. American literature from the middle of the nineteenth to the early twentieth century—a period coinciding with massive waves of European immigration; the first from northern and western Europe, the second from southern and eastern Europe—is replete with sometimes hysterical expressions of literary nativism. Anti-Semitic, anti-Catholic, and anti-"yellow horde" fiction has a long national history. Los Angeles is not exceptional here, although alien/other-race invasion renderings take on an added dimension when applied to a booster city, promoted in the early days to prospective migrants both as a white Protestant enclave (the future home, as Lummis put it, of the "Saxon homemaker") and as the place of the miraculous cure—a marketing strategy that drew a considerable number of sick and infirm migrant s and encouraged as well as a local susceptibility to healers, psychics, medical quacks, and doomsday prophets.

Disaster fiction in Los Angeles goes beyond the invasion mode, though, and there are a number of reasons—and not all of them racial—for apocalyptic fiction's taking sturdy root in Los Angeles. For one thing, although doomsday literature was not invented in Los Angeles but migrated west (in stages, as an urban form, from London through New York and Chicago), it established itself in a city that was positioned literally at the edge of the continent, a place where an unstable physical geography collided with an unstable human geography of displaced migrants and inflated expectation. Since the 1920s Los Angeles offered itself to novelists as the locus of uprooted Midwesterners looking for the quick fix. Among them were religious fundamentalists, desperate health seekers, and movieland castoffs adrift in a place where, their own dreams betrayed, they read the daily headlines of violent crime, municipal and corporate corruption, and Hollywood scandal, all of which fed a loathing for the city that deceived them. "Corn-belt fundamentalism," Davis writes, "with its traditional yeoman antipathy to the 'evil city,' collided head-on with the libertine culture of the Hollywood movie colony in an urban *kulturkamph*. Each side would resort to doomsday imagery to damn and excoriate the other."

Hollywood movies have been complicit with fiction in these disaster imaginings. The old booster city was the site of Armageddon in films ranging from the 1953 *War of the Worlds* (where the space invaders migrate to Los Angeles) to *Earthquake* (1974, inspired by the 1971 quake and featuring some theater seats that vibrated), *Blade Runner* (1982, with its replicants running wild among the vaguely Asian proletarian hordes), and *Escape from L.A.* (1997, with its largely Hispanic island-city concentration camp of misfits, loonies, and subversives). In Ridley Scott's dystopian *Blade Runner*, the twenty-first century city is run by genetic engineers operating from the top of a towering pyramid (analog to Fritz Lang's mise-en-scène for *Metropolis*) while the masses crowd the derelict streets below under a persistent mist of acid rain. In Scott's scenario (based on a Philip Dick story set in San Francisco, not Los Angeles) even the violated or disfigured woman, so prominent in noir fiction and film, shows up: the beautiful heroine Rachel is not human at all but a replicant, a genetically engineered project. Joel Coen and Ethan Coen's Nathanael West send-up, *Barton Fink*, similarly, fuses the victimized woman theme with a Hollywood disaster scenario. Fink, a New York playwright who wants only to write "the theater of the common man" (An Arthur Miller or perhaps Clifford Odets stand-in?) is shanghaied, like Carl Van Vechten's Spider Boy, in a Hollywood inhabited by the usual Jewish producer and publicity man stereotypes. But also in residence is a William Faulkner look-alike named Bill Maher, an alcoholic, cynical self-destructive screenwriter who refuses to stay sober in Hollywood. When Maher's beautiful mistress turns up with a slashed throat in Fink's hotel room bed next to a typewriter with blank pages in its roller, the point seems to be that the beautiful, violated woman is metaphor, or metonymy, for Fink's creative impotence in Hollywood. What follows is the surrealistic blitz (with its Salvador Dali-like images of dripping wallpaper and melting walls), a hotel fire (echo of the "Burning of Los Angeles" canvas in West's novel) and the demonic laughter of Fink's neighbor, the good-natured Ben Meadows, a closeted serial killer (played with manic charm by John Goodman). The Coen brothers are playing here with a number of themes that have been around for a long time in local fiction.

As Los Angeles emerged as America's most conspicuous city-film, media, and pop music capital; nerve center of its war and space industries; and troublesome zone of so many unassimilated, ghettoized immigrants (legal and illegal) who constitute cities within the city—it became the most conspicuous national site for disaster scenarios on screen and in print. The metropolitan city that Davis claims has "500 gated subdivisions, 2,000 street gangs, 4,000 mini-malls, 20,000 sweatshops, and 10,000 homeless residents" (354) has become target, repository, and scapegoat for national foreboding; the place where the worst fears about the future could be placed. The destruction of Los Angeles by bomb, earthquake, fire, riot, or tsunami operates as a recurring metaphor for anxieties about the fate and future of the nation.

Geographic determinism, which Davis acknowledges but downplays, makes the city both an obvious and inevitable choice for doomsday renderings. The land itself, lying on a major fault line, given to periodic quakes as well as annual cycles of fire, flood and mudslide, offers itself to such dark visions. The hot, dry Santa Ana winds, meanwhile, product of the confluence of desert, mountain, and coastal basin, not only contribute to the annual (fall) fires in the hills and mountains, but inflame the nerves of local residents as well, intensifying the dark imaginings.

The eco-disaster in Los Angeles fiction characteristically works in conjunction with human failure, serving in some of the novels as a kind of cosmic wake-up call to the man's destructive interventions on the fragile landscape. This theme of nature's response to man's greed is prominent in Ross Macdonald's crime fiction. Even earlier, in Myron Brinig's *The Flutter of an Eyelid* (1933), the "Big One" comes as the answer of an angry God to Southern California Babylon, dumping the whole coast, "swiftly, relentlessly, into the Pacific Ocean," a prophesy that anticipates Curt Gentry's 1986 scenario in *The Last Days of the Late Great State of California* and John Carpenter's 1996 film *Escape from L.A.*

Even when not envisioned as the site of apocalypse, the constructed Los Angeles has been the recurring locus of the violent ending. That hard-boiled, brutal fiction has taken so strong a hold in a region so given to hyper-inflated dreaming should be no surprise, even if we omit geographic determinism from the equation. From the 1920s to the present, the dominant theme in Los Angeles fiction has been the betrayal of hope and the collapse of dreams. Writing against the optimistic booster literature produced just before and after the turn of the century, the city's novelists constructed a counter-fable about loss. The principal local genres—the hard-boiled crime story, the tough-guy detective tale, and the Hollywood novel, as well as recent ethnic fiction—each in its way, envisioned the city as the place where dreams come from earthquake, nuclear bomb, or fiery conflagration; comes most often, as I have indicated in earlier chapters, as fatal automobile accident, murder, or suicide.

If, though, the major body of Los Angeles fiction has pointed to violent endings, there has been in the last few decades (since the 1960s) something of a countertrend in several recent survivor's tale novels, which take for their subjects not only disaster but also the coping with disaster—the living through, surviving and enduring disaster. The city might offer the prospect of doom, but in some contemporary works, urban disaster has provided the occasion for reaffirmation of self in the capacity to endure. The pace of endings thus can become the place of beginnings—at least as some recent writers have asserted. Over against the ironic pseudo-affirmation of Alison Lurie's *The Nowhere City*, or the dark, nihilistic vision of Joan Didion's *Play it as It Lays*, there have been novels, a significant number of them written by women, about people who find as they come to the end of the line and continent reasons for going on, mandates to affirm the demands of self, community, and spirit. Novels like Christopher Isherwood's *A Single Man* (1964), Kate Braverman's *Palm Latitudes* (1998), Cynthia Kadohata's *In the Heart of the Valley of Love* (1992), and most strikingly, Carolyn See's *Golden Days* (1987) and *Making History* (1991) are such works. They do not represent a cyclic return to the old booster optimism, the pendulum swung back. Far from it. But they do offer affirmations of the strength of the human spirit in the face of millennial, doom-saying and ecological and man-made disaster.

II

In three significant novels featuring Mexican-Americans in present-day Los Angeles—Kate Braverman's *Palm Latitudes*, John Rechy's *The Miraculous Day of Amalia Gomez* (1991) and T. Coraghessan Boyle's *Tortilla Curtain* (1995)—disaster is not rendered as sudden destruction but is woven into the fabric of everyday living as their characters strive to endure poverty, prejudice and marginalization. Rechy, who is part Chicano, focuses his novel on a single day in the life of a Mexican-American woman. It is a day of reckoning for her, a day that begins with her seeing a white cross flash in the sky and ends with her assault by a thief who puts a gun to her head and, just before dying from a police bullet, begs Amalia to bless him. Scattered through the day are the painful memories that she has carried to this present: he discovery that the man she has been living with has been sexually assaulting her daughter, that her younger son has become a homosexual prostitute and that her firstborn son has committed suicide (or has been killed by guards) in prison. Against such a horrific past, the extraordinary conclusion, played against blinding lights from cameras, police spotlights, and pistol shots, makes it "the miraculous day," the day that will vie her the strength and faith to survive.

Boyle's bicultural novel pits an Anglo couple, Delaney and Kyra Mossbacher—he an environmental writer and amateur naturalist, she a successful real estate agent—against an alter ego Mexican couple, Candida and Ameriga Rincon, illegal immigrants who are holed up in the canyon behind the Mossbacher's Topanga Canyon house. While the Mexican couple fights off starvation and flooding in the canyon, their Anglo counterparts, "white flight" migrants to the rustic, "good life" California neighborhood, live behind high walls in a gated tract called Arroyo Blanco (i.e., White Canyon). The entire novel is about walls, fences, and dangerous crossings—from the coyote-led Mexican border crossing of the Rincons to their crossing, or penetrating, the walls of the guarded white world. From its opening pages, where a freak accident links the two couples, to their proximity as "neighbors"—the couples occupying opposite sides of the wall that separates safe suburbia from dangerous wilderness (haves from have-nots)—the novel advances, satirically and comically, the story of cultural misunderstanding and Anglo terror as Delaney Mossbacher's liberal, leanings are put to the test. His dilemma: how to square these leanings with the perceived threat to the world he has built posed by homeless Mexicans in his backyard.

Braverman's more sustained narrative, *Palm Latitudes*, is the most interesting and ambitious of these recent novels about Mexican-American survival. Braverman's expansive, feminist Chicana novel, borrowing in its treatment the Latin American magic realism of Márquez and Fuentes, traces the personal histories, the stories of three Mexican-American women: Marta Ortega, born in Los Angeles of a Spanish father and Indian mother (and occupying the same house on Flores Street in the Echo Park area for more than half a century); Gloria Hernandez, her neighbor, an immigrant and abused housewife; and Francesca Ramos, La Puta de la Luna (Whore of the Moon), who winds up a streetwalker in Echo Parka after being abandoned by a rich Mexican lover. Each, as she tells her story, emerges less as a character than as a voice, a lyrical assertion of female qualities (linked to the lunar, nonlinear, the tropical zones, and the Spanish language) and an outcry against male qualities (linked to *machismo*, the linear city, and the English language).

Throughout the novel Braverman sets what she calls the "personal geography" of the woman against the "angles and linear evolution" of the city. Personal geography is linked to neighborhood geography, to the streets surrounding Echo Park, which stands initially as a kind of free zone existing in opposition to the sharp angles of the postmodern Anglo city. It is represented as a multiethnic enclave of people with a "mixture of blood and gods and alphabets." Echo Park, lying east of Hollywood, west of downtown, beneath the hills that rise above Sunset Boulevard, and just below the Chavez Ravine barrio that was razed to make way for Dodger Stadium, has been central to the history of Los Angeles. Although this history is not part of Braverman's fictional province, it was the site of the city's first local oil boom (Doheney's strike in 1892) and a few decades later the location of Aimee Semple McPherson's Angelus Temple, which has been in continuous operation since the twenties. For Braverman, the palm-lined park with its lake at the center is the nexus of the city, the site of silent communication among the three women, and a place where messages are implicit in natural things, in "letters strewn in leaves, sentences strung between branches."

The natural world is the domain of Marta, a semi-mystical woman whose life is devoted to planting and nurturing flowers, digging, as we see her first from Gloria's eyes, down to "the submerged regions beneath the surface . . . as if she expected to uncover the pulse of the universe. "Martha has magically transformed her landscape of poverty into a lush garden and endangered by two husbands, two luxuriant, eccentric daughters (Angelina and Orqueidia—Angel and Orchid); perverted extensions of her love for beauty. She has created them as rare, exotic plants. Like their mother, they are unable to sustain marriages (which mean linearity and regularity), but unlike the plans of their mother's garden, they become rootless wanderers, constantly transplanting themselves in the search for a perfect life, the perfect man, the perfect wardrobe, returning home (their high heels sinking into Marta's garden) when things don't work out.

Generational conflict here is a sign of urban transformation from neighborhood and community to postmodern fragmentation and instability. The high-heeled, footloose daughters of a deeply rooted Echo Park at its epicenter. The neighborhood stability that has sustained Marta collapses. Flores Street experiences a series of human and environmental disasters: the woman across the street has murdered her husband; the sun is a ball of fire, and Santa Ana winds rip up Marta's plants and spew dust over everything; the gay couple next-door, her only friends, one dying of AIDS, move away; and a tree mysteriously uproots itself, defying gravity by rising from the ground, an act, Marta concludes, of suicide. Marta, who reads events cosmically, senses that the apocalypse has come, "less startling and durable than predicted. Perhaps Flores Street was mere living on in altered form, ash after the conflagration, ash waiting for the sea breeze to take the dust they had become into the air, into oblivion, nothingness" (275). In her vision there are no endings; nothing dies, but everything alters. Nurtured herself by the plants she has nurtured, she knows, mystically, the permanence and numinous quality of all natural forms. Her voice is transcendent, optimistic, resilient. She will endure, go on in an altered state, living, finally, on a bench in Echo Park, where Francesca, La Puta, nearby, leans against a palm tree, waiting for customers.

Braverman's three Latina women, whether they survive or fail in the doomed city, represent alternative versions of Chicana life in contemporary Los Angeles. Despite the flaws of the book—and sometimes over-wrought prose (a too-self-conscious striving for "high style") and igno-rant, unfeeling *machos*; the only sympathetic males are the Anglo gay couple)—the novel is an important achievement.

III

Four novels from the 1960s and just after—Isherwood's *A Single Man*, Lurie's *The Nowhere City*, Pynchon's *The Crying of Lot 49*, and Didion's *Play It as it Lays*—each dealing with an Anglo protagonist, converge on the gesture of the newcomer, the migrant, to lay claim to the city, to know it and find in it a sense of place, perhaps a home. The four writers were themselves migrants. Isherwood, though, was no newcomer to the city where he wrote his novel, having, like his countryman Aldous Huxley, spent his half of his life in Southern California. He left England in the mid-1930s, lived in Berlin for four years, then settled in Los Angeles in 1939, at the age of thirty-five, just at the time his Berlin stories (*Goodbye to Berlin*) were appearing—stories that made him a literary celebrity and became the basis for the John Van Driven play, *I Am a Camera* (in 1951), and later the stage musical *Cabaret*. In Los Angeles he lived on the coast in Santa Monica, worked periodically as a screenwriter, taught college, and was a member of the Vendanta Society in Hollywood. Lurie, born in Chicago and living in upstate New York, spent little time in Los Angeles—enough, though, to gather material for her Los Angeles sat-ire, a book that can be read, depending on who reads it, as either hate mail or an ironic love letter to the city. Pynchon, who lives in New York, and whose superb essay on the 1965 riots has been cited in an earlier chapter, tells the story in *The Crying of Lot 49* of a woman seeking to know a city that remains cryptic, encoded, and ultimately unknowable. Didion, a native of Sacramento and a University of California, Berke-ley, graduate, lived for a time in Los Angeles with her husband, John Gregory Dunne, where she produced among other works, the splendid essays collected in *Slouching Towards Bethlehem* and *The White Album*.

Isherwood's *A Single Man* represents a single day in the life of a single man—a fifty-eight-year-old gay British expatriate, a professor of English at a local state college who lives at the beach (a cottage in

Santa Monica Canyon) and travels cross town to his teaching job. The single day is the scaffolding for the novel, providing as it does for Rechy in *The Miraculous Day of Amalia Gomez*, the structure that supports the narrator's meditations on life, death and loss, rendered in interior monologues, daydreams and conversation. The events of the day—a class taught, a hospital visit to a dying friend, a drive into the hills, a midnight swim in the Pacific—function both as trigger and counterpoint to George's reflections. Throughout the day he is tormented by a sense of loss—the loss of his youth and vitality, the loss of a simpler, more bucolic city he remembers before the postwar development mania (the same loss Marta Ortega in *Palm Latitudes* feels in the angular city), and the loss he most sorely feels, that of his lover, Jim, who has died in a car crash.

The landscape both shapes and takes on the colors of George's moods; smog blankets the San Gabriel Mountains and high-rise developments line the freeways. In a reminiscent mood he returns on his way home from the college, to the Santa Monica Mountains where he used to hike with Jim, finding, in place of the primitive nature he enjoyed, heavy traffic on mountain roads and shoddy housing tracts clogging Mulholland Drive. Looking down into the valley from the crest on Mulholland (like Philip Marlowe looking down from Guy Sternwood's patio to the ruined landscape below), he reflects like a biblical prophet on the city's doom engendered by man's greed. If Cuban missiles haven't brought on the Armageddon, he muses, runaway suburbanization will. The developers have "eaten up wide pastures and ranchlands and the last stretches of orange grove; sucked out the surrounding lakes and sapped the forest of the high mountains . . . no need for rockets to wreck it . . . or a huge earthquake to crack it off and dump it in the Pacific. It will die of over-extension." For the aging, over-refined Englishman, carrying his memories of Cotswold villages, the ravaging of the Southern California landscape is the analog to the apocalypse.

Significantly, the novel he teaches that day is Huxley's Hollywood fantasy, *After Many a Summer Dies the Swan*, about a man who lives in an ersatz medieval castle, owns a celebrity, Forest Lawn-like cemetery, and seeks obsessively the secret to eternal life. His students, though, haven't read the book, so he tells them with a good deal of wit and charm the myth of Tithonus. George knows, of course, that he can have neither eternal life nor youth, but in bed that night, having been put there by his young student Kenny Potts after their drunken late-night swim in the Pacific, he realizes that life is far from over, that he is alive *now* and this will have to do. Speaking to himself in the third person, as if the self is a character he has created, he asks: *"But George is getting old. Won't it soon be too late?"* And answers: "Never use those words to George. He won't listen . . . Damn the future. . . . George clings only to Now. It is Now that he must find another Jim. Now that he must love. Now that he must live . . ." (154). Small affirmation, perhaps, but still affirmation; and one that is in keeping with the California life that George has chosen. He will neither retire, go back to England, nor give up his beach house; he may even find an end to his loneliness and grief. This belief in the possibilities of the renewal of self in a place where friends are dying or dead, in a landscape perched at the edge of the ocean—up against hills capable of crushing him in an earthquake, or bursting into flame, or pouring down tsunamis of mud—is enough for him to go on. Like Marta, the aging Chicana in Braverman's novel, George is rooted to a landscape, a home territory in an unstable land that offers both terror and beauty.

Alison Lurie's double-edged satire on the Westside hip people, *The Nowhere City*, plays the belief in personal regeneration as comic irony. The decision of her migrant heroine, Katherine Cattleman, to remain in a live-for-the-now, live-for-the-moment sixties Los Angeles is not the purposeful existential choice of self-reflective and fully aware character (Isherwood's George) but that of a woman for whom going Californian means a good guru, a new wardrobe, new makeup, and a commitment to self-makeover. You can take Los Angeles on its own terms, as Katherine does, or leave it and go back East, as her husband Paul does. The chief irony of the novel is that Paul is a historian, a bookish, Harvard-trained scholar who has been hired to Los Angeles to write the history of a Santa Monica research firm (perhaps the Rand Corporation) only to find that the firm has no interest whatever in history; it simply likes the idea of having a historian on its staff. Near the end of the novel Paul writes a letter to a New England friend:

The basic thing about L.A., he explained, was that it lacked the dimension of time. As Katherine had first pointed out to him, there were no seasons there, no days of the week, no night and day; beyond that there was (or was supposed to be) no youth or age. But worst, and most frightening, there was no past or future—only an eternal dizzying present. In effect the city had banned historians as Plato had poets from his Republic.

At this point, Paul is ready to go home, having had his early-on fling with the 1960s "L.A. Woman," Ceci, the sexually uninhibited, liberated female (who keeps the lights on during sex, not like Katherine), waitress by night, abstract expressionist painter by day. Katherine's early days, meanwhile, have been marked by continuous misery, migraines, and a distinct hatred for the hedonistic city.

The Cattlemans live in a West Los Angeles bungalow in a neighborhood called Vista Garden—with no vista and no garden. Lurie, following the line laid out by West, play on the architectural masquerades—an initial source of fascination for Paul and of contempt for Katherine (who has kept her New England heirlooms in storage). The stucco houses come in "ice cream" colors, and the whole neighborhood, in which houses are constantly being razed and rebuilt, has the appearance of a movie set. Houses look like pagodas and gas stations, and gas stations look like lighthouses. A drive-in milk bar is topped by a giant plaster cow. Katherine tells a friend that coming in from the airport she passed a twenty-foot-high revolving cement donut. Like the enormous hole in the donut, Los Angeles is for her a huge advertisement for nothing.

The newly arrived Katherine is registering on the early pages of the novel the familiar, and properly Bostonian, derision for the centerless, seemingly improvised and instant city with its masquerade architecture, its plaster cows and donuts hovering above the traffic. It is the same kind of architectural derision that West's New England artist Tod Hackett expressed in *The Day of the Locust* a quarter of a century earlier. Gauging and deriding, the built landscape of the city by eastern canons of taste has been a standard, and long-clichéd feature in the city's ongoing fictional representation. The real issue is that Los Angeles, as one critic put it, belongs "to an entirely different urban code." One can't assess the West Coast city in the language of urbanism learned in the East.

For Lurie, though, as East Coast writer, decoding Los Angeles entails the piling of one, then another image of urban disarray into a mountain of chaos. She does this largely through comic incongruities: smog against palm trees, flowers so big as to appear artificial, a French chateau crawling along a street on the back of a truck, crowds at the beach almost naked against Merry Christmas signs, store windows decorated with painted snow and icicles, and sunbathers lounging beside empty swimming pools. Glory Green, the Hollywood starlet, lives in a house in the Hollywood Hills that contains a ten-foot artificial Christmas tree sprayed "pale pinkish blonde" to match her hair. A prowler lurks the grounds, then runs off in terror when he sees her face caked with cosmetic mud and her hair wrapped in toilet paper.

All of this is funny, if not new (not, that is, since West), and all of it preamble to Katherine's own heady conversation from contemptuous outsider to celebratory insider, from headachy recluse to chic new age woman. She goes native with a vengeance. The conversion comes about after a liberating affair with her psychiatrist, Isadore Einman—a hip Beverly Hills avatar of the Ever-present Now. Nothing really counts in Los Angeles, neither the past nor the future, he tells her, so no one can do anything. "If there's no schedule, then you are free to work out your own schedule. A place like this, Los Angeles, actually it's a great opportunity" (173). To be appreciated, the novel insinuates through its guru figure, Los Angeles must be decoupled both from a sense of history and an ordered sense of place, notions that derive from the East.

In the key conversion scene, Katharine, fresh from sex with Iz, stops in an upscale Beverly Hills boutique and tries on tight yellow Capri pants and a pink top. Wearing sunglasses, she approaches the mirror; what she thinks is another customer coming up behind her is actually her won reflection. She has been, she believes, transformed, made new. At the end of the novel, a disgruntled Paul, who has had enough of hedonism in the anti-historical city, leaves for Boston to look for a job. On his return to retrieve Katherine, he meets her at a Hollywood party (celebrating the reunion of Iz and his mistress, the starlet Glory Green), spotting her in the crowd wearing her yellow pants. Her hair has been dyed ash blond. She tells him she has decided to stay. "You know what's the matter with you, Paul," she admonishes. "You're always thinking about what happened before now or what might possibly happen some time later. You're squeezed between the past and the future; you're not living." (318)

So much for history. So much for the angst of Isherwood's George, who cannot and will not let go of the past. Playing against one of the dominant themes in Los Angeles fiction—the inescapability of history—Lurie offers the quick fix to historical conditioning. One wonders whether to take Lurie's novel as unadulterated satire by an eastern writer who truly hated Los Angeles—and loved to hate it, the way Woody Allen hates it—or a quasi-feminist tract about a woman who comes out from under the domination of an over-intellectualizing, patronizing nerd of a husband (albeit capable of his own California fling). Lurie has it both ways, and that is the point of the novel.

Pynchon's postmodernist take on the woman's search for meaning of Los Angeles, *The Crying of Lot 49*, could not in tone, structure, and yet in offering the city as a network of signs, or free-roaming signifiers that elude meaning, Pynchon's book has an odd connection to Lurie's, which offers a catalog of visual images that bear no relation to Katherine's Bostonian sense of reality (sunbathing beside an empty swimming pool, for instance). With Pynchon, though, the broad satirical stroke gives way to an involuted, labyrinthine comedy resting on the border between insanity (paranoia and delusion in a world of self-referential signs) and conspiracy (the possibility that the signs *do* point to threatening realities outside the self). The city, called by Pynchon "San Narciso," is an arena of signs that point both inward, narcissistically, to the self and outward to a mysterious other world, a world beneath the "real" world, that Oedipa Maas (her name suggesting her role as seeker) has to penetrate. She has come to the city as executrix of the will of a mysterious billionaire financier/developer, Pierce Inverarity, her onetime lover. Inverarity has transformed the city into an industrial and technological behemoth. His legacy is not only Los Angeles (which suggests he is something of a latter-day Harrison Gray Otis, Harry Chandler or perhaps Howard Hughes), but America itself. Oedipa's quest is to understand what he has built and bequeathed, with "his need to possess, to alter the land, to bring new skylines, personally antagonisms, growth rates into being."

Oedipa, who sees the city for the first time from the freeway and pictures it as printed circuit (unreadable, though offering the promise of communication), stays in a motel called Echo Court. Everything in the novel bounces back on itself, bringing to mind what Inverarity had once told her: "Keep it bouncing, that's the secret, keep it bouncing" (134). At the end of the novel, Oedipa Maas, as urban detective, has come to the end of the line. The quest for answers leads her to the very edge of the ocean, where so many Los Angeles characters have come to the end. A dead telephone in her hand, she stands "between the public telephone booth and the rented car, in the night, her isolation complete, and tried to face toward the sea. But she had lost her bearings." (134)

No character in Los Angeles fiction, though, has lost her bearings the way Maria Wyeth has in Didion's *Play It as It Lays*. Everything has come to nothing for her. Narrated essentially as a memory piece by Maria from a mental hospital in Nevada following her breakdown, the novel is a "white book" with more white space than print—eighty-seven chapters, some only a paragraph, in 218 pages—the typographical equivalent to the fragmentation, the discontinuity, of her life. A sometime Hollywood actress, sometime model, she is separated from her director husband and her brain-damaged daughter, forced by her husband, Carter, into having an abortion, and witness—one could say accomplice—to the suicide of a friend, an alcoholic, homosexual producer named BZ who dies in her arms. After his death she says to herself: "I know what 'nothing' means, and keep on playing. Why BZ would say, Why not, I say." Nothing matters—including survival or suicide—in this novel that goes beyond existentialism into pure nihilism.

Maria's life has been reduced to pointless rounds of barbiturate-laced sexual encounters, movement across freeways with no destination, nightmares of stopped-up plumbing, and television news bytes of children found in abandoned refrigerators, houses sliding into canyons, and evangelists preaching that eight million people will perish in an earthquake on a Friday afternoon in March. Her only moments of solace come in daydreams about herself. Carter, and their daughter, Kate, restored to a happy family. She takes to the freeway driving as ritual, a way of playing it as it lays. Habitually, she gets on the freeway at ten in the morning, crisscrossing the concrete landscape, carrying her lunch so she won't have to stop, and making complicated lane changes in a futile effort to give her life some meaning.

Once she was on the freeway and had maneuvered her way to a fast lane she turned on the radio at high volume and she drove. She drove the San Diego to the Harbor, the Harbor up to the Hollywood, the Hollywood to the Golden State, the Santa Monica, the Santa Ana, the Pasadena, the Ventura. . . . Again and again, she returned to an intricate stretch just south of the interchange where successful passage from the Hollywood onto the Harbor required a diagonal move across four lanes of traffic. On the afternoon she finally did it without once braking or once losing the beat on the radio she was exhilarated, and that night she slept dreamlessly. (14)

Elsewhere, in the essay collection *The White Album*, Didion has written of freeway driving as a form of "secular communication"—the only one we have, she says—requiring "total surrender, a concentration so intense as to seem a kind of narcosis, a rapture f the freeway." In this rapture "the mind goes free. The rhythm takes over. . . . The exhilaration is in doing it." For Maria the ability to cross four lanes of traffic without braking or missing a beat on the radio constitutes a victory. The past is blotted out and the future holds nothing; the freeway, as present encounter, is all there is, offering the paradox of endless mobility without destination. This is the only ground to "play it as it lays." The freeway is an environment, a place, not a passage to somewhere. Reyner Banham, the British architectural critic who spent time in Los Angeles in the 1960s, named the freeway as one of the distinct zones of the city: "Autopia" is one of the four ecologies in his *Los Angeles: The Architecture of Four Ecologies*. The freeway, he wrote, is "a single comprehensive place, a coherent state of mind, a complete way of life, the fourth ecology of the Angeleno."

Much of the action—such as it is—in Didion's novel takes place not on the urban freeway but on the highway between Los Angeles and Silver Wells, Nevada, where Maria was born. The town she remembers is gone, like everything else. It has become, appropriate to her state of mind, a nuclear test site. The desert is a wasteland littered with ghost towns, cinderblock motels, gas stations, trailer courts, abandoned talc mines, Pentecostal churches, beer bars, and an occasional hot spring. From the early booster celebrants of the rejuvenating power of the Mojave through Norman Mailer's desert as fun zone for a bored Hollywood crowd to Didion's wasteland, the California desert has gone from a potent symbol of regeneration to one of utter ruin.

In *The Nowhere City* and *Play it as It Lays*, Alison Lurie and Joan Didion offer opposing fictional versions of the destiny of the 1960s Los Angeles woman. For Lurie's Katherine Cattleman, Los Angeles winds up ironically as the place of new beginnings, a future weary from the strictures of New England; for Didion's Maria Wyeth, the city marks the end of the line. What both women share, though, is the need for erasure of the past. Katherine, the New England migrant, after an initial period of misery in the "dizzying present" of Los Angeles, gleefully joins the Westside Now Generation, leaving behind both history and husband; Paul, the professional historian, returns to Boston, where, presumably, history counts. Maria Wyeth, the Los Angeles woman bereft of husband, daughter, and career, and haunted by the past, suffers misery that no new wardrobe will assuage. There is no new California beginning for her, only the hope of getting by each day by finding ways to ease the pain of memory. Driving the freeways without destination, as ritual exercise, is one way of regaining some control. In one sense she is a reincarnation of James M. Cain's Mildred Pierce, for whom fast driving across the Southern California landscape provided a sense of control over one's life, but Mildred was always heading somewhere—toward a future destination she believed could be reached. Maria Wyeth's aimless movement across the freeways suggests a closer parallel to Gloria Beatty's movement across the dance floor in Horace McCoy's *They Shoot Horses, Don't They?* It is movement, Gloria knows with painful existential awareness, that is only a round of endless motion without progress; one ends up in the same place, but exhausted.

IV

Mobility, geographic and social, has always been one of the great enticements of Los Angeles, the city promoted from the beginning as the locus of regeneration and self-transformation. Beginning with Paul Cain, James M. Cain, and Horace McCoy in the 1930s and extending to the 1960s and 1970s of Thomas Pynchon and Joan Didion, though, Los Angeles fiction has undermined this faith in progress, mobility, and regeneration; the California highway ends up as a cul-de-sac, turning back on itself, offering only the illusion of a future. In Cynthia Kadohata's *In the Heart of the Valley of Love* and two recent novels by the Los Angeles-born Carolyn See, *Golden Days* and *Making History*, each the tale of a survivor, the story gets turned around again. Kadohata's and See's female protagonists move in, and across, a landscape of disaster in which they manage to find not only courage and hope but even occasion for celebration.

Kadohata's novel is set in a postapocalyptic Los Angeles of 2052. the city has not dropped into the ocean or become an island as it did in Brinig's *The Flutter of an Eyelid* or the film *Escape from L.A.*, but while not literally cut off from the continent, it may as well have been. After the apocalypse, it has become an unreal city, a nightmare zone of mob violence, roving gangs, police brutality, and rigid class polarization. The rich minority live in "Richtown" on the Westside, and the masses of poor survivors are scattered about the inner city. Air pollution has made the stars invisible, and rationed gas is obtainable only by black-marketed "creds." The novel is both a post-apocalyptic imagining of the city and a projection into the future of present-day Los Angeles, a heightened vision of late-twentieth-century reality.

There is little conventional "plot" in the novel, which is constructed as a series of scenes and episodes that appear randomly ordered, suggesting fragmentation, disjunction, and the reduction of life to the diurnal—the day-by-day battle just to survive in an urban wasteland of homelessness, inexplicable arrests, and marauding, well-armed gangs. While the young female narrator, Francie, has wildly mixed ethnic parentage—Japanese, Chinese, and black—race conflict plays little part in the book, which was published, coincidentally, on the eve of the 1992 Watts riots. Warfare is class based; the déclassé warring masses are of all races. Francie at nineteen, forced to leave her aunt's home after her aunt's lover has been arrested, gets involved with a college newspaper, hanging out with a crowd of former gang members, outcasts, an editor who is dying of cancer, and the man who is to become her lover, Mark. With Mark's love, though, and an occasional blue sky, Francie experiences joy. Los Angeles is "surprising and violent but full of hidden savage beauties." With love comes the will to accept and cope. The novel ends with Francie and Mark hiding in an arroyo from armed marauders. It is not a happy or redemptive ending; they know nothing will change. But the doomed city is also "the valley of love," and this must be enough. In this oddly, perhaps ambivalently, affirmative novel we are left with Francie's final judgment: "Los Angeles was the only home either of us had ever known, and maybe this would be the only love we would ever know. For these reasons, I knew I would never leave Los Angeles. I could not." (225)

The same conviction that affirmation can grow out of catastrophe—indeed that the value of life an love are *born* of tragedy and loss—is the central theme in See's recent "yea-saying" novels, *Golden Days* and *Making History*, the first her apocalyptic stop-worrying-and-enjoy-the-bomb novel, the second, and stronger of the two, the story of a family's grappling with catastrophe and finding through it a path to illumination, insight, and reintegration. Both are about white and affluent people living in the hills and canyons at the very edge of the continent (Topanga Canyon in *Golden Days* and Pacific Palisades in *Making History*)—the ambiguous coastal zone that represents both the locus of the California "good life" up against nature and the place of violent endings for so many Los Angeles protagonists since Cain and McCoy. Buoyed by love, friendship, and family, See's characters find at the edge the strength to go beyond tragedy, beyond last acts into new beginnings.

On one level *Golden Days* is a feminist, men-and-their-missiles, bomb-as-phallus novel about an impending and finally arriving nuclear doomsday on the Southern California coast and on another the tale of willed affirmation of life lived on the edge of doom. See's protagonist, Edith Langley, repeatedly invokes the spirit of Ronald Reagan, Caspar Weinberger, and Alexander Haig as the wielders of male power that will bring on the apocalypse. Offered as a "domestic" equivalent to the phallocentric political power the president and his men have, Edith tells the story, as exemplum, of a single day in the life of an "ordinary" man, a day in which he betrays both his wife and his mistress. Beyond the radical feminist positioning of its narrator, the novel is a celebration of life in a city where survival depends on the art of improvisation. For Edith improvisation goes well. Like See herself, Edith is a product of Los Angeles. She returns to the city in 1980, a twice-divorced single mother without apparent skills, and settles in a rented cottage in Topanga

Canyon. The postmodern city she finds is one where people no longer "make" anything. Instead they make themselves:

> . . . there were few what you'd call *businesses*. No raincoat makers. No soup manufacturers. Yes, there were sweatshops in downtown L.A. And I remember a ceramics factory out in Glendale, but they soon went out of business. What you really have out here is the *intangible*. When you drove you saw buildings, often windowless. They were either cable television stations or movie studios . . . or death factories where they made missiles, or think tanks where they thought them up. . . . I ended up doing something, it seems to me, everyone in Los Angeles did then: I made myself up half hour by half hour.

Golden Days is about Edith's making herself up in Los Angeles, becoming in turn a gem expert, a financial columnist and consultant, and owner of the Third Women's Bank. Two relationships are central to her transformation—with Lorna, her friend from L.A. State College in the fifties, and with Skip, a financial consultant and Pacific Rim investor, who becomes her live-in companion and lover. Lorna, several-times-divorced woman, is a disciple of the San Francisco-based prophet Lion Boyce (who operates EST-like "seminars" catering to yuppies with his you-can-do-anything-you-want message), who becomes herself, in this version of Southern California makeovers; a prophetess and healer, an new age Sister Aimee without Christianity. As celebrity performer she preaches the California gospel of living in the Now and living bravely in the face of doomsday fear (the fear of the bomb, that is, which hovers over the entire novel). Calling herself Lorna Villanelle, she manages to perform some miraculous healings that the skeptical Edith, until her own conversion, dismisses as pure illusion.

When the holocaust comes, Edith and Skip, fortified by love and their advocacy of Lorna's living-in-the-Now philosophy, decide not to flee Topanga Canyon, the place where they feel so rooted. Together with Edith's daughter and a few friends, they make their pilgrimage on foot to the ocean where they form a community with other survivors who have refused to leave. The ocean, symbolic site of California endings, is also, in Edith's revelatory vision, the place of beginnings. That they are alive—and alive to sensations of joy—is the miracle with which the novel closes: "There will be those who say the end came. . . . But I say there was a race of hardy laughers, mystics, crazies, who knew their real homes, or who had been drawn to this gold coast for years, and they lived through the destroying light, and on, into Light ages." (195–96)

Such are the "golden days" of the title, a title not without irony. Heightening the irony is the snobbish and condescending tone of Edith, who reveals only contempt for the "stupid ones," the inlanders who don't make their final, brave stand on the beach and who can't spend their final days before the evacuation dining with the right people at Spago. It remains for the superior people—Edith, her daughter, Skip, some of their neighbors—to survive the holocaust and rebuild society on a matriarchal, pacifist, eco-sensitive model.

See's next and more satisfying realized novel, *Making History*, also deals with a family living through disaster: here not nuclear holocaust, but the devastating trauma of successive, fatal automobile accidents along the coast, one killing a boy named Robin, the boyfriend of Jerry Bridge's stepdaughter Whitney, the second killing both Whitney and her infant stepbrother, Josh. It is a case of history repeating itself—like Cain's postman ringing twice—the second time with devastating effect on Jerry Bridges and his wife, Wynn. The coastal highway crash has, since the time of Cain and Chandler, been a recurring metaphor for Southern California endings; See is tapping into a long tradition of writing about the city. Even when it has not been the site of a fatal accident, the highway at the edge of the continent has repeatedly been appropriated as an image that evokes the sense of being at the end of the line, as for instance in Didion's *Play It as It Lays* and Pynchon's *The Crying of Lot 49*. In *Making History*, though, See complicates the metaphoric use of the coastal highway: it is the site both of the disastrous ending and the potential new beginning. Disaster becomes the *occasion* for Jerry and Wynn Bridges to learn the lesson of living fully in the present, just as the nuclear disaster furnishes Edith Langley with the mystical illumination of her "golden days."

See reworks some of the material of the earlier novel in *Making History*, but she reworks it into a richer, more deeply felt, and complex narrative (told by at least a dozen alternating voices). The similarities between the two suggest the earlier novel as preparation for the latter.

Jerry Bridges, the Pacific Rim financier-developer is a more fully developed Skip from *Golden Days*, and Thea, the psychic, functions much the way the prophet Lorna Villanelle does in the earlier novel: spiritual guide and mystical presence who awakens the characters to an affirmation of life lived in the present. While Thea has little direct contact with the Bridges family (a chance meeting with Jerry halfway up Ayers Rock in Australia, a single consultation with daughter Whitney), her presence hovers over the novel, as does that of the dead boy Robin, whose voice from beyond the grave, as cosmic utterance, frames the novel.

The novel also scales down the anti-male tone of *Golden Days* Edith Langley in the earlier novel would have, before meeting Skip, imagined finding a good man not hard but impossible. She puts the destruction of the world clearly on men's shoulders—not only those of the cold warrior triumvirate of Reagan, Weinberger and Haig, but *all* men. The struggling single mom rages about male destructiveness on levels both local and global: penis as missile and premature ejaculation as the sexual equivalent to nuclear betrayal. In an interview after the later novel, *Making History*, came out, See said the new book is "both a love letter and apology to the 97 percent of the men who *don't* intend to blow up the world."

Making History's Jeff Bridges, like Skip in *Golden Days*, has no intention of blowing up the world—not making it "better" by pouring billions of dollars into investments into Asia, reshaping the Far East into the image of America. As consummate postmodern, Pacific Rim-oriented California capitalist, Jerry is both an idealist and materialist, democrat and empire builder, a man who equates Asian investment with the perfection of the world. He is the New World explore, his reach extending beyond the well-traveled territories of Japan, Australia, and Hong Kong to newer frontiers for development like Papua New Guinea, Indonesia, and Irian Jaya: "If the worlds across the sea were inchoate, unformed, then *fix* them." The resulting New Asia would be like America, but better, "not just a hotel or a factory, but a twenty-first century city-state. . . . a new world—and a better one." This is one way of making history—taking the plunge into the future, taking risks, extending the boundaries of self, going west to appropriate the East.

In the life-affirming finale, narrated by the dead Robin from high above the scene, we view Jerry Bridges's drive home to Pacific Palisades through a heavy rain along Pacific Coast Highway—the highway he had avoided since the accident that killed his son and stepdaughter. Unable to pull off the freeway in the heavy traffic to take the Lincoln Avenue off-ramp and avoid the highway, he finds himself, tears in his eyes, near the site of the accident.

> He thought, in anguish, that it was just as well. He couldn't avoid driving over where Whitney and Josh had died forever. Pull off the scab again! Pull I off! The torn flesh was there, the gaping wound was there. Nothing could cover it. Nothing ever could. (269–70)

While Jerry drives the last few miles home, the narrator cuts to Wynn, who gets up for the first time from the bed where she has lain since the accident. She "splashed cold water on her face and combed her hair. And went down to the den with Tina, the first time she'd done that in months. And turned on the light" (275). Both Wynn and Jerry are making the first, tentative steps toward healing, allowing the prophetess Thea's advocacy of the value of the present moment to enter their lives. Robin's playful voice, meanwhile, reiterates the lesson, channeling it down from the high above the canyon to Jerry through "some left over Indians [he conjures] from the dark canyon": "This is a beautiful world just the way it is, they breathed, waving their waterproof baskets. Don't worry too much about it. You don't have to fix it up *too* much" (274–75). Jerry's vision had been precisely that: to fix the world, to make it perfect; random violence has taught him it can never be that. He knows, too, that he can, like Wynn, begin the task of healing the soul and celebrating what he does have in the present-day. See's multivocal narrative, renders in voices speaking from this and the other side of the grave, indicates a world of interconnected human relationships that transcend the global, neo-colonial ventures that Jerry Bridges has so obsessively pursued.

V

See's *Golden Days* and *Making History*, together with Braverman's *Palm Latitudes* and Kadohata's *In the Heart of the Valley of Love*, can be read as works that synthesize the dialectical opposition that has shaped writing about Los Angeles since the beginning: the boosted and bloated place of new beginnings and the fated site of disastrous endings, America's Utopia and Dystopia. The protagonists of the Los Angeles novel have been for the most part migrants, men and women who have come to the city seeking freedom, opportunity, and the fresh start in a region at continent's edge, where one's past is presumed to be irrelevant and every day is a first day. From America's beginning, mobility has been inscribed in the national myth as the analog to freedom; the open road has been the signifier of selfhood—self-discovery, self-renewal and regeneration. But the burden of the greater number of Los Angeles novels has been to reveal that movement into and through the deceptively open, fluid landscape at the end of the land doesn't easily translate into freedom and that history, what one has brought to the present from another place, is an inescapable condition of the present.

The Southern California highway as cul-de-sac has, as I have indicated in various places, been a recurring image. The 1930s protagonists of James M. Cain, George Hallas, and Horace McCoy—and a generation later, Joan Didion—find that at land's end movement—on the highway or dance floor—is circular and aimless. At the end of the continent, one runs out of room. The vision is claustrophobic. Raymond Chandler's and Ross Macdonald's criminals have fled the scenes of their crimes and moved, as migrants, into high-walled sanctuaries in the hills or against the ocean, only to have their sanctuaries invaded by the detective who knows, and discloses, their histories, destroying their escape routes. The Hollywood protagonists of Nathanael West, Budd Schulberg, F. Scott Fitzgerald, and Aldous Huxley, similarly, learn that the road comes to an end. The culturally diverse voices of such writers as Walter Mosley, Luis Valdez, John Rechy, Cynthia Kodohata, Kate Braverman, and Carolyn See, however, suggest that there may be heretofore unseen streets that lead into the city, to neighborhoods that survive because they are sustained by a sense of community and connection.

Such writers have carried a sense of the city of disaster into the urban present but portray in their works characters who discover the courage, the resilience, to go on. In Carolyn See's fiction the apocalyptic event becomes the opportunity for a new beginning, the occasion for discovering and celebrating life in the present. Edith Langley, in

See's *Golden Days*, returns to Los Angeles in a battered Volkswagen, two kids in the back, and learns that surviving, succeeding, and celebrating mean making your life up, "half hour by half hour." Jerry Bridges, in *Making History*, has crated his perfect Pacific Palisades life—perfect house against the ocean, perfect wife, perfect children—but time, history, and chance intrude on the future-oriented Pacific Rim financier's life in the form of the fatal car crash at the continent's rim—an event that returns her novel, in one sense at least, to James M. Cain's 1930s fables. Jerry and Wynn Bridges must remake their lives in the aftermath of tragic knowledge. Acknowledging and coming to terms with time and history is one of the essential themes in Los Angeles fiction, and See's *Making History* is one of its essential contemporary accounts. The city built by its founders on the promise of a utopian future took its essential literary identity in the decades since the 1930s—in hard-boiled crime and tough-guy detective stories, Hollywood novels, and apocalyptic fictions—as the place resting dangerously on the edge of the continent, the place that forces one to look back to sources and origins.

August 2000

THE HOUSE THAT BLACKS BUILT

THE FORTY-YEAR SAGA OF HOLLOWAY HOUSE,
ICEBERG SLIM, AND HOW A SMALL L.A. PUBLISHER HAS
SURVIVED AS THE VOICE OF THE BLACK STREET EXPERIENCE.

PETER GILSTRAP

*How can you, my Nigger Son, find your identity, articulate
your experiences, in an order of words? Language. Which was
created and conceived by a people who did not even know of
your black existence or Earthly presence?*
—Robert H. deCoy, *The Nigger Bible*

Down on Melrose Avenue near Crescent Heights, in the heart of an
area where people on the street look like they've stepped out of fashion
catalogues and things in stores cost way too much money, there is a
house.

It's been there for a long time, going unnoticed by those on the way
to Fred Segal, yet the characters that live there have been known world-
wide for decades, albeit in certain circles. Folks with names like Whoreson, Daddy Cool, Earl the Black Pearl, The Great Lawd Buddha, Slaugh-
ter, Sugar Man, the Goddess, Phala and Ophelia. They exist in a world
of pimps and whores and crime and struggle and survival, a world that
spins within the walls of a publishing company called Holloway House.

On the vast map of publishing, Holloway is a small dot at best. Yet
for nearly four decades, the business has churned out hundreds of titles,
sold millions of copies, and carved out a loyal readership for its authors,
many of whom have been with the company for most of their professional lives—or until their natural lives ended.

There are many things that make Holloway unique—not the least
of which is the fact that it has survived this long—but most of all it is
this: For virtually all of its life, the company has published books by
black authors for a black audience. That may not sound like such a big

deal now, but bear in mind that back when New York publishers scoffed if the name on the cover wasn't Haley or Ellison or Baldwin, Holloway was happily printing black authors and selling millions of their books in towns that still had drinking fountains marked "Colored."

Yet these are not volumes that are looked upon as great literature. They are not works of layered academic depth, delving into socio-political realms of thought relating to the African-American experience. They are not books that, until fairly recently anyway, have been available wherever finer publications are sold. Though in recent years Holloway material has arrived in chain stores like Barnes and Noble and Borders, in the past you'd likely find the paperbacks for sale at airports, on newsstands, and in liquor stores.

The Holloway catalogue is built on stories written from a street perspective in the unadulterated language of the street; not for nothing does the house call itself the "World's Largest Publisher of Black Experience Paperback Books."

As Odie Hawkins, a mainstay Holloway author for almost thirty years, says, "The black experience is about the ghetto and roaches, the African-American experience is about something else. . . . Many, many African-Americans have never had the black experience. They think they have, but many have never had an urban ghetto experience. They'd be as horrified by it as any middle-class white would be. And I don't know of very many people who have written about it from the inside."

Though Holloway has a Black American Series on the imprint Melrose Square—a collection of sixty biographical titles on personalities like Zora Neale Hurston, B.B. King, Elijah Muhammad and Oprah Winfrey—as well as studious tomes on subjects ranging from *The Book of the Navajo* to *How to Win At Craps,* the backbone of the catalogue is black fiction.

The authors Donald Goines, Hawkins, Joe Nazel, and most notably, Iceberg Slim, have created an awesome canon of gritty work from the underbelly of the black street perspective, work that is honest and raw and utterly intoxicating. According to Holloway, Slim alone has sold more than six million books—making him one of the biggest-selling black American authors in history—and his legendary first work, *Pimp: The Story of My Life,* has been translated into French, Spanish, Italian, Dutch, Swedish and Greek.

Over the years Hollywood has come calling at Holloway; in 1973 Slim's *Trick Baby* was made into a film starring Kiel Martin and Ted Lange, who would go on to tend bar aboard the *Love Boat.* Currently two of Donald Goines' books, *Black Gangster* and *Daddy Cool,* are under option, as is Slim's *Mama Black Widow. Pimp* seems the most likely candidate coming to a theater near you; Fine Line Pictures has commissioned a screenplay with Quincy Jones attached as producer, and Ice Cube is set to play the man from whom he took the first half of his name.

But whether or not any of these films will end up on the big screen is anybody's guess. It would be a nice boost for sales, of course, but Holloway has always ridden along on its own unique inertia, supplying what its readers want.

"It is this kind of survivor," says David Streitfeld, book reviewer for *The Washington Post.* "It's real unusual for a small niche publisher like this to be successful for forty years. The unique thing about them is that when they started, they did provide an outlet for black writers and for reading about black life. The New York publishers—the white publishers—would publish at most one work of fiction a year by a black writer, so Holloway House really was filling a need then. There was a market out there.

"It's survived when there was hardly any interest in black writing at all from the New York publishing world, and then, in the 1970s when there was a huge boom [from New York] and when there was a huge drought in the late '70s and early-to-mid-'80s, it survived. The amount of material by black writers coming out of New York publishing has ebbed and flowed at least twice, yet Holloway has remained alive."

In 1959, around the time that future author Iceberg Slim was doing a ten-month stretch in solitary at the Cook County House of Corrections for having escaped years earlier "like a wisp of smoke," there was nothing called Holloway House. There were, however, two skin magazines that had existed for three years, *Adam and Knight,* put out by Knight Publishing, helmed by Bently Morris and Ralph Weinstock, who died a few years ago. By today's standards, their "mags" were about as racy as a copy of *Watchtower,* and *Adam* even published fiction between the photographs of the coy, teasing lovelies. (Years later, an unknown named Stephen King had one of his first stories in the publication.)

Morris and Weinstock—yes, both white men—took offices on Holloway Street in 1959, borrowed the name, and began to supplement their nudie material with books. Today, CEO Morris is still in charge of the privately held company.

"One of the first books we put out was *The Trial of Adolph Eichmann*," recalls Morris. "And we put out the first paperback book on the life of Ernest Hemingway in 1960."

In addition to *Eichmann* and *Hemingway*, Holloway also offered the reading public pulp bios on Hollywood heavyweights such as Jayne Mansfield and Daryl Zanuck.

In 1965, Holloway moved to its present location at 8060 Melrose Avenue, back when the stretch was nothing special. Morris bought the building and a warehouse a few blocks away on Melrose Place, back when Heather Locklear was nothing special.

In 1968, the house put out *To Kill A Black Man* by Louis E. Lomax, a serious comparison study on the goals, achievements and shortcomings of Malcolm X and Martin Luther King Jr. The book did well—and still sells 20,000 copies a year according to Morris—but was a far cry from what was right around the urban corner.

In '69, Holloway released *Pimp*, edited by Milton Van Sickle, a former metallurgist, Great Lakes oar boat deckhand and electroplater who was with Holloway from '65 to '69.

"I read *Pimp* and told my bosses it was the best book we ever published," says the retired editor. "*Pimp* was what started it, then Robert deCoy came in with *The Nigger Bible*, and they asked me to read it and see if it was worth publishing. I told my boss just the title alone would sell it—which it did."

At this point, Holloway had stumbled onto a hungry market and an empty niche. "A couple of the editors that we had here went into South Central and went into the Watts Workshop and so on and tried to solicit writers," Morris offers. Holloway has had "several" black editors, by the way. "We were the only ones out there encouraging young black writers, and we didn't want them to write about the valley of the dolls, and we didn't want them to write about their trips abroad. We wanted their experiences."

And that's what they got. Enter Odie Hawkins in 1971 with his book *Ghetto Sketches*.

"It was a black ghetto version of *Under Milkwood* by Dylan Thomas," explains Hawkins of the work that, unlike sixteen of his other books, is no longer in print. "I took a neighborhood on the west side of Chicago and wrote my way up one side of the street and down the other."

Hawkins came to Los Angeles in 1965, attended the Watts Writers Workshop, and was working on screenplays when he became aware of Holloway, as did many others, through *Pimp*.

"When I read the book I realized I had some material that was very much like that. Not from the pimp perspective, but what it was like growing up on the west side of Chicago. Slim jumped into a place that was vacant, and Holloway House had enough vision to say that there must be a market out there, because there are people living that lifestyle who read. . . . I've told Bently [Morris] to his face, you're an exploitative bastard, but at least you had enough sense to be ahead of the game."

Holloway was, first and foremost, out to make a profit, but if it could champion unsung black writers along the way, well, it was all good.

"That was the coup, that was the cream on the soufflé, if you will," admits Morris. "In the beginning, we had literary fantasies of trying to enter the publishing community with some kind of force, but it was very difficult for us. Then when we started publishing black material and we felt the derivative benefit, the entire staff felt it. You don't go around thinking 'I'm contributing to society,' but the by-products gave everybody an enormous lift. And we were kind of unique—we were alone."

"Holloway was an outlet for a particular kind of book," offers Hawkins, who has written on subjects from ghetto hell to love stories to the life of an African-American in Ghana, where he lived in the early '90s.

"I don't want to start sounding off about publishing houses, especially black publishing houses, but they're very academic and very partial to people who are writing about things in the way they can relate to them. If you put a college professor as the CEO of a black publishing company, he's going to look at things from a very middle-class perspective. And that's one of the uphill battles some of us have had; they don't want to publish things from what they call 'the street.' If you read Toni Morrison's books—some of them I just can't read. It's just layers and layers of language, and a whole lot of it has to do with us, but not at the level that I relate to.

"I've had the experience half a dozen times of talking to a very nice, middle-class black publisher who said, 'Well, in order for us to publish your book, you'll have to clean up the language, you'll have to do this, do that.' Holloway House never made those conditions."

Along with Hawkins' *Ghetto Sketches*, 1971 also saw Goines' first book, *Dopefiend: The Story of a Black Junkie*. Like Slim and Hawkins, he knew from which he wrote. Goines served in the Air Force during the Korean War and returned a seventeen-year-old junkie. He dabbled in various nefarious careers—pimp, armed robber, bootlegger, card shark—and by the time he wrote his first book, his record included fifteen arrests and seven jail sentences. While in jail he read *Pimp*, and four weeks later he typed "The End" on *Whoreson: The Story of a Ghetto Pimp*, later to be published by Holloway in '72.

Goines published sixteen books with Holloway—*Black Gangster* and *White Man's Justice, Black Man's Grief* are standouts. In October of 1974, while sitting at his typewriter at home in Detroit, he and his wife Shirley were shot by two white men who were never caught.

By the early '70s, Holloway was a house with its own special family of talent, the books were selling, and no other house wanted to touch the stuff. The authors were bringing the world of the streets to the people who knew from streets, but the man leading the charge was Iceberg Slim.

Known only to a stable of hookers, certain members of the law enforcement community, and a few street associates before 1969, Iceberg Slim would become a star via *Pimp*.

"Dawn was breaking as the big Hog scooted through the streets. My five whores were chattering like drunk magpies. I smelled the stink that only a street whore has after a long, busy night. The inside of my nose was raw. It happens when you're a pig for snorting cocaine."

—Iceberg Slim, *Pimp*

Pimp was the first of seven books that would chronicle Slim's life in a world decent folk may loath to tread but love to read about.

"Bob was an incredible human being," says Morris, who green-lighted the manuscript before handing it to Van Sickle. "I think he had an IQ of 165. He was charismatic, articulate, charming, vain, an imposing figure, 6 feet 2 inches, and dressed immaculately. Had he not moved in that particular genre, he could have been anything he wanted. An outstanding politician, a major civic servant, just anything he wanted. He had enormous stature, didn't use expletives, had incredible depth, and yet there was nothing ostentatious about the guy."

The Chicago-born Slim, who died in L.A. in 1992 at age seventy-three, started pimping when he was eighteen. He attended Tuskegee Institute in the mid-1930s for a short period, ironically at the same time as Ralph Ellison. Though he was a self-taught writer, the man had a gift for getting the words down on the page and making them do his bidding.

Iceberg also possessed deep and vast conversational skills. Here Slim describes his pimp lifestyle in an early '70s interview with *The Washington Post*:

"Ressin' and dressin'. I just rested and dressed. And petted my dog and ate chocolates and slept on satin sheets. And went to the penitentiary periodically, I might add."

Slim also offered his thoughts in *Pimp* on how the "principles of good pimping apply to all man-and-woman relationships.

"What I was saying was that the pimp overtly and almost without inhibition, denigrates and despoils the sexual object. His mauling of the sexual object is perhaps a more severe version of what happens in conventional relationships. For instance, in so-called 'square' sexual bouts, the woman winds up, of course, flat on her back in a submissive position. If a man is aware of what sexual button to push to enhance a woman's gratification, he will bite her with the proper degree of ferocity. If he inflicted that kind of punishment on her when she was not in a state of rapture, she would resent it. . . . The kiss-kick ritual is at the very root of the pimp's sexuality.

"My theory is that some quantum of pimp in every man would perhaps enhance his approach to women, because I think it's a truism that women gravitate to a man who can at least flash transient evidence of heelism."

Find a shrink who could argue that. Odie Hawkins heard soliloquies like that many a time, in person. When he was coming up on Chicago's west side, he knew Iceberg Slim as a neighborhood character.

"I lived at 38th and Lake Park when I was twelve, fourteen. It was a red-light district, and Slim was just simply one of several pimps," Hawkins says. "I lived in a building called the Almo Hotel. Picture the hotels on Figueroa Street, four flights, and we lived on the third floor. The first and second floor were transient, it was where the girls turned tricks, and Iceberg Slim was one of the people who came in. At that point, he wasn't a major league pimp—he didn't have nine girls; he had maybe three or four.

"He was a great, great talker, a very intelligent man," recalls Hawkins. "He and another pimp named Big Al used to have philosophical talks sitting on the front steps of the building. I was twelve—fourteen, and I looked at him in the same way that a lot of the major-league crack dealers right now are big to the kids. They got big cars, they wear a lot of gold, and they seem to be able to do what they want to do. Iceberg Slim had a certain kind of status because he was a very sharp dresser, he drove a big car, and he seemed to be someone you should look up to. When he came out to L.A., to the in community the guy was sort of a surprise because *Pimp* wasn't the best-written book in the world, but he was telling something about a world that most people have no knowledge of at all."

According to Morris, *Pimp* "didn't catch on right off the bat. We tried to advertise in *The New York Times*, and they wouldn't accept it because of the title. We raised havoc, but we didn't get anywhere. Here we were, a small niche publisher stuck on the West Coast in the colonies of the United States—and the venerable *New York Times*, no way were they going to kowtow to us."

Slim made an appearance on a popular local talk show hosted by the late Joe Pyne; that did the trick.

"He just created a revolution locally," says Morris. "Every bookstore in the city was calling us." That and a lot of word of mouth provided the catalyst for the ascension of *Pimp*. God knows the reviews, rave or otherwise, weren't flowing in.

"Paperbacks essentially do not garner any review acceptability," explains Morris. "But we did get a lot of press in the black community, and we did get stories in *The Washington Post* and the *Detroit Free Press*, but not book reviews. They did it because it was a sensational story talking about a subculture."

With the book catching on, Slim put his verbal skills to work, lecturing about his life and wicked ways and lessons learned on the college circuit where Morris says the author "was mobbed" at each appearance.

Beyond the period hip cache that Slim embodied, his crushed velvet voice and mellifluous phrasing were hypnotic tools. In the mid-'70s, the author released *Reflections*, an album of spoken word basted over a lazy last call jazz background. (It was reissued on the Infinite Zero Archive label in 1994.) On the cut, "The Fall," Slim lays it down:

"Now some of you guys might be surprised at what I'm about to say, and say, 'Who is this lame, who says he knows the game, and where did he learn to play?' Well, I'd like to tell, of how I fell, and the trick fate played on me. So gather 'round, and I'll write down, and unravel my pedigree."

"Slim used to tell them, 'There are three ways to get out of the ghetto: 1) dead in a basket, 2) in handcuffs, 3) with a college degree,' " Morris says. It's a bit ironic that the reformed ex-pimp was telling this to kids who were already in college, but that was where he captured some degree of a white audience. In fact, Slim's books were included in a Rogue Literature course at Harvard University.

Though he thought of his pimping years and later literary success as a stab at white oppression, and greatly admired Huey Newton and the Black Panthers (this was the period when *Pimp* was on the shelves with *The Autobiography of Malcolm X* and Eldridge Cleaver's *Soul On Ice*), the extremist Panther crowd saw him as a black man exploiting his race for the white dollar.

But if *Pimp* makes it to movie theaters, a new generation of potential Slim fans will be turned onto the master, generating plenty of white and black dollars.

"To me, he's probably one of the best American authors there ever was," says Bruce Rubenstein, who co-wrote the screenplay with Rob Weiss. "I just think the guy is just such an incredible, original writer; he's like Bukowski. When I read Pimp, I was just so enthralled by the book, I just couldn't put it down. It's brutal, brutal stuff, but it's got poetry, you know?"

According to Rubenstein, the film won't be updated with current street phrases, nor will it fall into the tired "Blaxploitation" slot.

"I think that's why so many studios were afraid of it," he says. "The language is so hard, the messages are hard, they're real. We tried to stay really close to the book, we really tried to capture Iceberg Slim's voice. What separates it from Blaxploitation is that Robert Beck was a brilliant guy, a profound guy, and he kind of reinvented the language. We were really trying to transcend the hip-hop thing, because a lot of the guys who were interested in doing the project initially wanted to change all the dialogue to hip-hop, and we were pretty dead against that. It's a biopic, it's a really dark, interesting look at the life."

For his square readers, Slim thought to include a glossary in the back of *Pimp*:

Breaking Luck: A whore's first trick of working day.
Circus Love: To run the gamut of the sexual perversions.
Horns: Ears.
Mitt Man: A hustler who uses religion and prophecy to con his victims, usually the victims are women.
Yeasting: To build up or exaggerate.

Slim has been gone for four years now, the street world he knew has been gone for longer than that, but his work continues to flourish. This from the last page of *The Naked Soul* of Iceberg Slim:

There is solace and joy in my determination to build instead of destroy during the sunrises left to me. I feel such pride at my survival, for the miracle is that I am not a marooned wreck on some gibbering mental reef. I am gratified to be alive at this time and place in the history of the black people's struggle. What a joyously painful transport it is to be part of that struggle, to be a besieged black man, an embattled nigger, in racist America.

Today the Holloway House building on Melrose stands out like a completely healthy thumb. The four-story office building across the street from Pacific Bell is bland, an excellent example of late '50s generic architecture.

The elevator opens on the third floor onto a small lobby that looks like a set from *The Bob Newhart Show*. Friendly Renee (receptionist for eight years) sits at a desk with an intercom system that only recently was upgraded from the one they'd had since the 1960s. The modular plastic chairs are upholstered in Day-Glo tones. Paintings that scream "The Seventies" hang a bit crooked on a wall made of inexpensive wood paneling; most were originally used as illustrations in *Adam* and *Knight*.

Down the Holloway halls where twenty or so people are employed (there are five or six more in the warehouse on Melrose Place), it seems as though nothing has been changed—not a file cabinet, not a desk—for several decades. But there's a feeling that this is not because of any financial hardship, it's just part of the Holloway aesthetic.

"We're doing OK," says Bently Morris, who is tight-lipped when it comes to questions concerning money. "We're doing fine, we pay our bills. We've been here almost forty years. We literally do what we want to do. We're not a fashionable house."

Raymond Friday Locke is senior editor these days. After stints at a history magazine called *Mankind* and *The Hollywood Reporter*, he's come and gone at Holloway three times since 1984. The affable, easygoing Locke has authored thirteen books, including *The Book of the Navajo* for Holloway in 1976, which is now in its fifth pressing. Of money matters, he says, "I've been around here for years, and I don't know. Obviously there were times when we had a lot more help. Five years ago, there were five [editors; he's on his own at the moment, aided by two readers], and we were doing at least four books a month. We did six last year, we used to do around twenty-four or twenty-eight. But I think it's always made money.

"It's a very small house, smaller than since I've known about the place. I think when Ralph Weinstock died—he was senior editor—it appears to me that Morris seriously thought of selling it. The money is there, but I think we're going through a period of Morris deciding what to do with the company."

Locke feels one of the main elements that has kept Holloway alive and publishing over the decades is simply the availability of the books.

"Bently Morris has always had a very close working deal with independent distributors," he says. "There were seven hundred in 1990, now they're down to about one hundred, because we're doing a lot with chain stores, where we used to do very little. I think it was his ability to get the books into newsstands and liquor stores; he always had this marvelous relationship with them where the books would get out to where the audience was."

Locke also says that while Holloway pays standard royalties (and by all accounts is honest and on time), it offers the "lowest advances of anyone."

It helps the coffers that under the Holloway umbrella is Players International Publications, which has put out *Players* magazine for twenty-five years, and the venerable Knight Publishing, which offers up gay and straight delicacies such as the *Adam Film World Guide XXX Movie Illustrated* and *Porn Stars*.

Besides the works of Slim, Hawkins, Goines, and Nazel, Locke points out that in this decade the house has published what he feels are worthy, non-street "genre" books.

"The Donald Goines, Iceberg Slim era had passed, and we were looking to do new things, find a lot of young writers. In '91 we did Lorri Hewett's *Coming of Age*. She wrote it when she was a freshman in college at Emory University [in Atlanta], it's a wonderful book. And Nora DeLoach wrote some excellent mysteries—*Mama Stands Accused, Mama Saves A Victim*. She's now signed to Bantam."

Yet Holloway still gets plenty of manuscripts the old fashioned way, from unknowns whose only representation is the U.S. Postal Service.

"We get a lot in the mail," says Locke. "Most of them aren't any good. We still get people who try to write like Donald Goines, particularly. Just recently, I've gotten three novels written in Spanish. Every now and then we do a book that's not a black book."

It is no longer such an uphill struggle for a black writer to get into print. Where Holloway was once pretty much a black author's only hope, the big guns in the east are moving in.

"Now there's a lot of competition," affirms Locke. "Penguin started publishing their imprint Plume, doing some very good books that normally we would have done, and Berkeley's doing a lot of black books.

We have a deal with Bantam—they're bringing out Slim in [new up-graded] paperbacks."

"I could find you twenty-five books of fiction by black men published by mainstream houses in the past year," states the *Post's* David Streitfeld. "They publish what they think people will want to read, and a lot of material by black men has been published—fiction and nonfiction—in the last three to four years.

"Admittedly, a lot of the fiction is by women," continues Streitfeld. "The argument before Terry MacMillan was that no one bought this material—blacks didn't read—so we're not going to publish any books for blacks. . . . The publishers would publish gritty tales like Goines if they thought people wanted to read them, but I'm not sure there's a wider market than what Holloway House is doing with either a black or white readership. In a way they're lucky; no one wants their niche."

What will be the fate of Holloway? The books still sell, particularly in Europe in recent years, and potential film projects are sure to raise the visibility of the little house stuck on the West Coast of the colonies of the United States. Perhaps the company will grow and enter another heyday, perhaps Morris will step out and sell the place off. Or maybe it will continue to do what it has done for so long—simply survive.

"Frankly, I don't really love Holloway House, but at least it's the best game on the West Coast," says Odie Hawkins. "I know that on the East Coast there are several black publishing companies, but in the whole mix, Holloway House is head and shoulders above all of them. At the same time, it's so low profile you don't even know about it."

October 1998

III

L.A. POETRY

PERHAPS THESE ARE NOT POETIC TIMES AT ALL
Poetry and Los Angeles at the Millennium

BRENDAN BERNHARD

Poets can be divided into two categories: those who fall about laughing when the subject of book sales is broached; and those who, brows furrowed, earnestly assure you that more and more people are becoming interested in poetry. My own preference, I'll admit, is for poets in the first category—gallows humor is always bracing. Once upon a time, to write a poem was to try, against all odds, to outwit the vast indifference of eternity: to set down in a few lines words that would be read hundreds of years after they were written. The vast indifference of eternity is now the least of a poet's problems. What bothers poets today is the vast indifference of the present.

"Poetry is the soul of a culture, man," I was told by a Los Angeles poet named Eric Priestley. If that is true—and it may not be, obviously—then this is a culture that steers well clear of its soul. Poetry matters remarkably little to us, either on a daily level or on a symbolic, even sentimental, level. No one talks about it, and no one quotes it. No one even seems to feel nostalgic about it. Yet somehow it lives on. Proudly, even defiantly. "After all," wrote W.H. Auden in 1964, explaining the situation from the poet's point of view,

> . . . it's rather a privilege
>   amid the affluent traffic
> to serve this unpopular art which cannot be turned into
>   background noise for study
> or hung as a status trophy by rising executives,
>   cannot be "done" like Venice
> or abridged like Tolstoy, but stubbornly still insists upon
>   being read or ignored . . .

The case for poetry was made even more urgently by William Carlos Williams:

> My heart rouses
> thinking to bring you news
> of something
> that concerns you
> and concerns many men. Look at
> what passes for the new.
> You will not find it there but in
> despised poems.
> It is difficult
> to get the news from poems
> yet men die miserably every day
> for lack
> of what is found there.

And so, some forty years after those lines were written, here we are, dying miserably in affluent traffic jams with cell phones glued to our ears. If poetry felt pretty small-time in Williams' day, it feels positively microscopic now. Yet even in the crush of rush-hour traffic, poetry rears its graying head. In April (poetry month), a group called "Poets Anonymous" launched a billboard campaign throughout the city. The idea seemed to be that, instead of staring at the latest ads, weary drivers would enjoy contemplating a few lines of poetry in extremely large, commuter-friendly type. Most of the stuff was pretty lame, barely preferable to the sales pitches that surrounded it, but one poem-fragment (by Nikki Giovanni) came close to articulating why an anonymous group of poets might feel desperate enough to put poems on billboards in the first place:

> perhaps these are not poetic
> times
> at all

Perhaps not. The two things that seem to excite Americans right now are toilet humor and technology. Poetry, on the other hand, seems quaint;

like starting a civil war or planting your own cabbage. The Serbs like poetry, and look what we did to them—we bombed them back to the Renaissance, where poetry belongs. "I try not to read poetry, not even dead people's poetry," I was told by Christopher Knight, the *L.A. Times'* art critic. "It's hard to explain why. I find something embarrassing about poetry. It's such a weird, atavistic thing to do."

But what does it mean to say that these are not "poetic times?" What would poetic times consist of? Endless bloodshed, as in Homer? Kings and queens, as in Shakespeare? The New York art world, as in Ashbery and O'Hara? It's hard to say—in fact, the term is probably meaningless, since people have produced great poetry under almost all imaginable conditions. Even in Stalinist Russia, when poets were persecuted and imprisoned, poetry thrived.

Still, even if it's impossible to define what a poetic time might consist of, you have only to turn on your television, or stare into the nobody-home shades of the person in the tank-like vehicle next to you, to sense what an *un*poetic time looks like. It looks, surely, like a time in which human beings are being slowly buried under an avalanche of marketing and media. When one thinks of contemporary poetry, particularly in L.A., what comes to mind is not poetry so much as the ad campaign for ABC created by the copywriters at Chiat/Day in Venice. It's those ultrahip scribblers, after all, whose brief, carefully worded messages we're always reading. These, you might say, are the lyric poems of the age. "My, what big pupils you have," they taunt from benches and bus shelters and billboards all over the city. In a better world, the copywriters at Chiat/Day would be imprisoned, or force-marched up to the Getty and made to stare at travertine marble until they went blind; but they, not poets, are the contemporary wordsmiths whose work actually influences people.

But so what? If these are not poetic times, a growing number of people will turn to poetry for precisely that reason. Poets in the second category may have a point: More poetry is being published than ever before, and according to certain critics who are paid to read it, the best of it is as good as anything in our literature. It may even be that we are living through a golden age of poetry and just don't appreciate it. As Randall Jarrell observed, in a golden age people complain that everything looks yellow. (Of course, he hadn't seen the ABC ads.)

"What's remarkable is the terrific poetry being written at every level," I was told by David St. John; arguably the city's most lauded poet. (He is also one of the few to have a major publisher—HarperCollins.) We were sitting in a café near his home in Venice, and St. John, a smart, friendly, articulate man with a true Californian's ease of manner, was warming to his theme. "You can go often to a reading by a group of people you've never heard of and be stunned by how well-written and gorgeous the poems are. I've been surprised in this city by the levels of the writing. The audience for poetry in L.A. is tremendously sophisticated, probably more sophisticated than anywhere in the country except New York. The audience in L.A. happily engages itself with poets from Charles Bernstein to Charles Wright. They're happy to hear these poets of radically differing aesthetics, and to appreciate them with equal fervor."

"I see what you're talking about with regard to readings," I told St. John, "but what I don't see is people talking about poetry in everyday conversation, and I never see anyone reading poetry. Poets just don't seem to come up."

"It's the culture," St. John answered sadly. "Anyone who's lived in Europe knows the place of poetry in the culture. I've lived in Rome and I've lived in Paris. You open up a daily newspaper in Italy, and there's an article by Moravia, or Eco, on a *movie*, or a local arts show. You have distinguished writers talking about the culture in newspapers!"

"Whereas here we farm all that out to specialists."

"Absolutely. And it seems to generate a kind of isolation of the arts—poetry, music, ballet, opera. They have their audiences, very strong audiences, but they remain circumscribed. And I think it's because the figures who are important to those arts aren't brought into the larger cultural conversation."

"When people talk about there being a revival, are they talking about poetry in terms of performance?"

"No. I think the audience is there not only for the readings, but for the books. And I'll tell you why I think it is. I think it's because the official language of the culture, the language of the nightly news, the language of newspapers, the language that surrounds people in their daily lives, becomes so self-evidently empty to everyone that, instinctively, people have gone looking for language being used with any kind of integrity whatsoever. They *know* that language can connect to ideas and human emotions, but it's not around them, they don't see it anywhere."

Not everyone has as sanguine a view as St. John. Dana Gioia is a poet who grew up in Hawthorne. His essay, "Can Poetry Matter?," which was first published in the *Atlantic Monthly* in 1991, got people talking about poetry in greater numbers than anyone could have imagined possible. (The *Atlantic* received an enormous amount of reader response for the article. This suggests that although people may not read poetry very much anymore, they are aware of the fact and want to know why.) "There is a huge renaissance of poetry activity in L.A.," Gioia told me over the phone from his home in Northern California, "but there are no governing standards. You can't have great literature without great standards, and no one wants to hear this, especially in L.A. There's a real mistaken impression that more art is better art, whereas in fact lots of bad poetry will deaden the appetite for good poetry."

"Are there any good poets in L.A. I probably wouldn't have heard about?" I asked.

Gioia thought for a moment and then said: "As a matter of fact, there's a woman named Leslie Monsour. Do you know her?"

"I don't."

"Hold on a second," Gioia said, putting down the phone. A minute later he was back. "She sent me a little chapbook of poems, and it's really good. She seems emblematic of the situation in L.A. A person of genuine talent, and more importantly, of that dogged self-critical capability that is so important to a poet, but which in L.A. has had no soil to take root in. Her work is compressed, formal, with an ironic turn to it. There's a poem of hers called 'Parking Lot,' which you might like."

Gioia then proceeded to read the poem to me over the phone. He read the lines slowly, clearly, to make them easier to follow.

> It's true that billboard silhouettes and power
> Lines rebuke dusk's fair and fragile fire,
> As those who go on living have to prowl
> And watch for someone leaving down each aisle.
> While this takes place, a tender moon dips toward
> The peach and blood horizon, pale, ignored.

I try to memorize impermanence:
The strange, alarming beauty of the sky,
The white moon's path, the twilight's deep, blue eye.
I want to stay till everything makes sense.
But oily-footed pigeons flap and chase—
A red Camaro flushes them apart,
Pulling up and waiting for my space;
It glistens, mean and earthly, like a heart.

"Now that," said Gioia after he had read the poem out, "strikes me as a pretty good poem about a parking lot."

It struck me the same way. I'd been reading a fair amount of L.A. poetry—in fact, for a few weeks I was probably reading more poetry written by Angelenos than anyone else in the city, though I was constantly berating myself for not reading more, because it wasn't even a fraction of what was out there—and this particular poem was the first I'd come across that struck me as a truly memorable expression of the city. Not that it was perfect. It got off to a decidedly shaky start, with half rhymes that should really have been full rhymes and a slight obscurity of meaning, but when the moon appeared on that "peach and blood" horizon, the poem took off.

We ask both very little and a great deal of poets. All we ask of them, really, is that, once in a while, they string together a few good lines—but they do have to be good. And if they manage to produce a handful of great poems, even good ones, we can forgive them their less successful efforts. In the last nine and a half lines of her poem, Monsour had won me over. "I try to memorize impermanence"— how many times had I tried to do that? Staring at the beauty of the city, trying to imprint it on my mind like a photograph? With its oily-footed pigeons, glistening red Camaro and insistent sense of pressure— someone always behind you, cursing you, waiting for you to *move*— "Parking Lot" struck me as a topnotch bit of contemporary urban poetry encased in that mustiest of forms: a sonnet. It was nowhere to be found, however, in what was effectively the city's telephone directory for poets: *Grand Passion: The Poetry of Los Angeles and Beyond*, an anthology with more than its share of mediocre doodling. Monsour, I later learned, had submitted some of her poems, including "Parking Lot," to the editors, but had been turned down.

"It was the parking lot at the corner of Ventura Boulevard and Laurel Canyon in Studio City," Monsour told me when I met her over lunch at Farmers Market. "It's a heavily used parking lot, because there's a Vons there, a Sav-On, a video-rental place, a Gap, 31 Flavors, Kinko's—there's just about everything there, and people are crawling all over each other so they can park and do their errands."

"So your epiphany was rudely interrupted."

"Well, if someone's waiting for you to clear out of your parking spot because they need the space and you just sit there, they do start to wonder what the hell you're doing. So even if you're noticing the sunset and going into a reverie about an aspect of Earth's beauty, you can't be oblivious, because parking spots are in demand."

"Perhaps you should have called the poem 'In Demand.' "

"Actually, I chose 'Parking Lot' because 'lot' has other meanings. 'Lot' can mean your lot in life, or your lot in the cemetery, and it's kind of like the whole system of population control, you have to get out sometimes to make room for others. The engine in the car is the heart beating, a new life waiting to take another heart's place."

"Was it really a Camaro?"

"No. I chose a Camaro because it fit the meter and the mood, and because someone in a Camaro strikes me as a person who might be impatient for you to get out of your parking space. At least you'd be aware of this big engine rumbling, waiting for you to leave. I was thinking of it as a muscle car with hotheaded youth at the wheel."

Monsour is in her forties, a smallish woman with pale skin, thick reddish-brown hair, and sleepy, heavy-lidded eyes. She has published two chapbooks, and was recently selected by the venerable *Poetry* magazine as a featured poet, an honor Monsour characterized as the poetry world's equivalent of "playmate of the month." Partly because she married and had children, Monsour got off to a relatively slow start as a poet. She spent a lot of time in poetry workshops—as most aspiring poets do—where free verse was king, and rhyme and meter long-vanquished enemies, and the technical side of the art was discussed only in the vaguest terms. What is a poem? "Well," a poet-teacher might answer if given a truth serum, "it's whatever makes *you*, the customer, feel good." (Poets have to look after the bottom line, too.) The workshops she attended, Monsour has said, "were like music classes where no one knew how to read music; we listened as we hummed our tunes, and we talked about the way they sounded, and the way they made us feel. But we skipped the basic, important questions of key signature and beats per measure."

In 1987, Monsour took a class at UCLA Extension with a poet named Timothy Steele, a leading member of a group known as the "New Formalists." Steele, a strict rhyme-and-meter man with a disarmingly gentle manner, soon had the erstwhile free-versers whipped into soldierly shape. Metaphorically speaking, they learned how to polish their shoes, oil their guns, press their trousers and make their beds. Instead of ignoring tradition, they saluted it. Monsour found she enjoyed being in the ranks of the New Formalists and finally began to write the kinds of poems she had always hoped to write. In this, her experience was similar to that of Vikram Seth, the Anglo-Indian novelist who studied informally under Steele when both were graduate students at Stanford in the late 1970s. Seth went on to write *The Golden Gate*, a best-selling "novel" about San Francisco yuppies, written entirely in rhymed sonnets. (The book is dedicated to Steele.) Seth, who told me that Steele is "one of the great poets in the language," has credited his friend with teaching him to look at poetry "not simply as an indulgence, as a letting off of passionate steam, but [as] an attempt to crystallize experience, to make from it memorable communication."

If the choice is between passionate steam and crystallized experience, the average L.A. poet is probably more interested in steam. Writing poetry is seen as a therapeutic act, not just by amateurs but sometimes also by professionals. "It's like therapy for me," Eric Priestley said one afternoon as we stood on a rundown stretch of Western Avenue, outside the office where he does his writing. Then, screwing up his face into a parody of Anthony Hopkins' in *The Silence of the Lambs*, he launched into a hilarious imitation of Hannibal Lecter mocking our earnest belief in the socially redeeming value of "therapy." I took this to mean that, even if he did often write poetry partly for therapeutic reasons—and what poet doesn't?—Priestley was well aware that the relief a poet might feel after writing a poem did not guarantee the quality of the final product.

Nonetheless, the idea of poetry as therapy, of poetry as confession, of poetry as an airing of "my" feelings, may well be what attracts most of the small number of readers who are still attracted to it. What many people are looking for is not art so much as authenticity, confession, identity. "Who the hell cares about Anne Sexton's grandmother?" Auden snapped after hearing the American poet read aloud one of her "confessional" poems. The answer, of course, is that lots of people do. Like Sylvia Plath, Sexton is seen as a "feminist" poet, and this easy-to-understand label wins her readers and gives politically minded teachers a platform from which to teach her. Being an unpopular art, poetry is especially vulnerable to politicization, if only because labeling someone a "feminist" poet automatically adds political significance (feminism) to something people secretly believe to have no significance whatsoever: poetry. Ours is a highly utilitarian culture, and poetry is the least utilitarian art form imaginable. Even in the dullest museum, you can at least look for someone to pick up.

Being black, Eric Priestley is automatically labeled an "African-American poet," a label he resents. "Poetry, real poetry, transcends ethnicity," he told me. "It's a universal language like mathematics"—a remark paradoxically borne out by the fact that translations of poets like Neruda and Rilke and Kahlil Gibran seem to sell far more in the States than those of homegrown poets like Dickinson or Frost. Still, even if he wanted to, it was obvious Priestley couldn't escape the label. Though we started off talking about poetry, within minutes we were talking about race—a subject that had not come up during my conversations with white poets.

"One of the things you have to realize, man, is that Los Angeles is probably one of the most segregated cities in the world outside South Africa. God, man, it's incredible . . ." Priestley said, and one had only to glance at the dusty, bare-bones neighborhood we were talking in to realize the lived reality behind that observation. Nonetheless, in a poem simply entitled "L.A.," he offered up a wildly juicy hymn to the city in which English and Spanish trade lines:

> The last time I saw L.A.
>   she was singing los corridos
>   muy pulcra mas penachos rojos
>   enferno many feathers mezclarando

all mixed up in el pelo
  crooked justice angel hair . . .
   she was mucha salsa con chile
    smoking fumas by the minute
 giving birth to little ashes
  pimienta pepper sangre blood
   & dripping jalapeños . . .

Even better, perhaps, was the superb "Nobody Dies," as rousing a poem about the failure to rouse the dead as one can imagine reading:

 wake up brother & tell us
  when you died
 did your synapses fail to pass acetylcholine
  to the next nerve juncture on that day
 hangman's knot crimped your sphincter & turned your
  bowels to water in the bigots' clay?
 did they whip your head till it flayed in the maw?
  was it the wrong place wrong time?
  did they smoke your hood?
 were they yoking you to the bone raw?
  did you take your sappin' good?
   wake up brother!
  tell us how you died!

Of all the poets I met, Priestley was probably the most fun to talk to. But talking to him was also confusing. One moment he'd rail against the "effete snobbery" of the "Yale and Harvard" crew, the next he'd make fun of "freestyle" rappers who thought they'd invented free verse. He believed young poets should practice writing in meter, but seemed uneasy with the idea that that might entail spending a lot of time analyzing poems already written in meter. He complained that he'd never been invited to read at UCLA, but then added that he'd been on a panel at UCLA during a Festival of Books. In a way, he seemed trapped. Cut off from the white world, estranged from his own neighborhood. And as with a lot of poets, his biggest problem was that he was practicing an art form that most people knew little about.

"To converse and have discourse about these things between you and I, half of the people in my neighborhood, man, they would have walked out of this room," he told me at one point. "They wouldn't know what the hell y'all talking about. Who is *Pound?* Who is *Eliot?* That's a problem. That's a serious problem. And it has to do with education."

"And if we'd been talking about Duke Ellington or Charlie Parker, same problem?"

"Same problem. If you're talking about Dr. Dre or Tupac Shakur, they know about those people."

"Or Robert Johnson and Bessie Smith?"

Priestley waved an arm in disgust. "Oh, man, please. I started quoting Melvin Tolson one day, this guy says, 'Who's that you're talking about?' I said, 'That's one of the most celebrated poets of the Harlem Renaissance.' Even the advanced kids today, they wouldn't know Tolson."

Perhaps that was why, these days, Priestley was writing a lot more prose than poetry. A founding member of the Watts Writers Workshop, he had already published one novel (*Raw Dog*), and had written several more, along with a screenplay version to accompany each one. For Priestley, I suspected, poetry was a luxury—or perhaps it really was a form of therapy after all. The day we spoke, he was wearing a cap with the words FINAL DRAFT printed on it. He'd gotten it for free with his screenwriter's computer program.

The one really famous poet L.A. has produced is the late Charles Bukowski, and he has plenty of followers. Timothy Steele is not one of them. Steele, Vikram Seth's mentor-pal at Stanford and now a professor of English at Cal State L.A., is exactly the kind of poet Bukowski derided in his poem "The Replacements":

> Jack London drinking his life away while
> writing of strange and heroic men.
> Eugene O'Neill drinking himself oblivious
> while writing his dark and poetic
> works.
> now our moderns
> lecture at universities

> in tie and suit,
> the little boys soberly studious,
> the little girls with glazed eyes
> looking
> up,
> the lawns so green, the books so dull,
> the life so dying of
> thirst.

Like a lot of Bukowski's poems, this one is as easy to read as an article in *USA Today*, and rather more appealing. Critics like Harold Bloom like to point out that, to be good, a poem must reward repeated re-readings; what they sometimes forget is that, to be read, a poem must also reward a *single* reading. This Bukowski's poems do. And if there isn't much to be gleaned from a second reading, well, you can always turn the page and go on to the next poem. Bukowski wrote a lot of them.

The problem is that single readings aren't what they used to be: These days, a poem's lucky to get a single skimming. We read like people with a train to catch. Perhaps this is why most people now think of poetry as a kind of performance art, something to be listened to in a club rather than read on a sofa. Even poets rarely ask if you've "read" a poet anymore; they ask if you've *seen* him.

When I mentioned Bukowski to Steele, he made a wry face and told me that, as a judge for a book contest, he'd once read a volume of Bukowski's called *The Roominghouse Madrigals*. The memory made him smile. "After reading a lot of obscure poetry," he told me, "there was a certain charm about Bukowski which is—this isn't fair, but . . ." (Steele started to laugh) " 'I get up in the morning/it's ten o'clock,/baby, let's get a beer'—you know, you could understand it." Still laughing, Steele then quoted a statement by Coleridge about poetry broadening our sympathies and told me how, after reading Bukowski's roominghouse poems, in which cockroaches were constantly being urinated on and stepped on and generally made to go SPLAT about once every three lines, he began to feel quite sympathetic toward the little creatures.

"Obviously you think Bukowski's been a fairly disastrous influence on young poets," I suggested when Steele had stopped laughing. "But he does seem to touch people."

"Yeah, and I think it's partly because they don't think of the art, they think of the artist, or the image of the artist, so they're drawn to him for that reason in part. He's a kind of rebel, and in that sense, I think you're much better off taking a pop star, because heaven knows, Lennon-McCartney and Dylan write in meter, so you at least get something of the art from them."

Though he has lived here since the late 1970s, Steele is not well-known in L.A., where his advocacy of metrics goes against the grain. ("Well, bully for you, Mr. Steele" was one poet's response when I showed him a poem by Steele.) A youthful-looking fifty, he has published three books of poetry and two books of criticism. To me, his poetry can seem both contemporary and slightly antiquated, as in the following epigram (an antique form in itself) called "A Million Laughs," which might have been written about Robin Williams:

> No one can out-lampoon, -joke, -quip, or -pun you,
> But the funnier you get the more we shun you.
> The moral, sir? He who possesses wit
> Should also have the sense to ration it.

One of the things you notice about "formal" poetry of this kind is that it's easier to memorize and quote. Lines pair off into couplets or cluster together in quatrains or sestets, and stick more easily in the mind. A point Steele likes to make, when the discussion turns to formalism, is that rhyme and meter are inherently pleasurable. "I think if people do discover the joys of working with meter, the negative press that it so often gets—that it's a straitjacket, that it constrains feeling and emotion horribly—when they see that that isn't the case at all, they get very excited about it. And also it introduces into writing a kind of hedonistic element in the very best sense. Leslie [Monsour] took to it like a duck to water. Something had been missing, she had been looking for something, and that was what it was."

Steele, as a reading of his criticism reveals, is a scholar as well as a poet in a city in which self-expression for its own sake is valued much more highly than erudition. This was a point made to me by Samuel Maio, whose book *The Burning of Los Angeles* (1996) is one of the more ambitious attempts to capture the city in verse. (He now lives in Northern California.) "If you read all those dusty books by poets like Auden and Hardy and Eliot," Maio told me, "you weren't cool. That's how I felt. I really sensed an anti-intellectualism. A lot of it, bizarrely, comes from those poets who have found their way into teaching positions. Somehow, their idea is, 'I'm not really a teacher, man, I'm a poet,' and to reinforce their identity as poets they're consciously anti-intellectual."

Steele wears his learning lightly, but he does wear it. In one of his most moving poems ("Sapphics Against Anger"), he writes:

> Angered, may I be near a glass of water;
> May my first impulse be to think of Silence,
> Its deities (who are they? do, in fact, they
> Exist? etc.).
>
> May I recall what Aristotle says of
> The subject: to give vent to rage is not to
> Release it but to be increasingly prone
> To its incursions.
>
> May I imagine being in the *Inferno*,
> Hearing it asked: "Virgilio mio, who's
> That sulking with Achilles there?" and hearing
> Virgil say: "Dante,
>
> That fellow, at the slightest provocation,
> Slammed phone receivers down, and waved his arms like
> A madman. What Attila did to Europe,
> What Genghis Khan did
>
> To Asia, that poor dope did to his marriage . . .

As poetry goes, this is on the academic side. Obviously, the poet is well-versed in the classics of Western Lit, and his poem is written in a form that dates back a mere twenty-six centuries to the ancient-Greek poet Sappho. (Each stanza is made up of three lines of eleven syllables, followed by a fourth line of five syllables, so that each verse ends with a kind of "dying fall.") The language is quiet, unflashy, but also terrifically controlled and subtly melodious. In what comes close to being a credo, a kind of secular prayer, Steele continues his poem by stating why all that learning might be useful:

> . . . May I, that is, put learning to good purpose,
> Mindful that melancholy is a sin, though
> Stylish at present.
>
> Better than rage is the post-dinner quiet,
> The sink's warm turbulence, the streaming platters,
> The suds rehearsing down the drain in spirals
> In the last rinsing.
>
> For what is, after all, the good life save that
> Conducted thoughtfully, and what is passion
> If not the holiest of powers, sustaining
> Only if mastered.

Does it matter if people in L.A. read L.A.'s poets? Not really. What matters is that people read poetry—then they might read L.A.'s poets as well. Or so I told myself after coming to the conclusion that although I liked certain poems by all the poets mentioned here, as well as by poets not mentioned here, such as Suzanne Lummis, Harryette Mullen, James Ragan, Amy Gerstler, Charles Webb, Steve Kowit, Ellyn Maybe and others (there may be a shortage of poetry readers in L.A., but there's no shortage of poets), I had come across only a handful of poems whose absence from my life might, occasionally, produce a small twinge of regret.

While I was reading L.A.'s poets, I was also re-reading some poems by Philip Larkin, a morbid, depressive and reactionary English poet who, oddly enough, gets a favorable mention in the afterword to *Grand Passion*. (He's best-known for his poem "This Be the Verse," which begins: "They fuck you up, your mum and dad,/They may not mean to but they do./They fill you with the faults they had/And add some extra, just for you.") One poem in particular ("The Trees") had been holding my attention. In form and subject matter it was about as traditional as you could get, but "avant-garde" poems are now about as traditional as you can get also. It doesn't matter anymore how poems are written; it just matters that they're good.

> The trees are coming into leaf
> Like something almost being said;
> The recent buds relax and spread,
> Their greenness is a kind of grief.
>
> Is it that they are born again
> And we grow old? No, they die too.
> Their yearly trick of looking new
> Is written down in rings of grain.
>
> Yet still the unresting castles thresh
> In fullgrown thickness every May.
> Last year is dead, they seem to say,
> Begin afresh, afresh, afresh.

"The Trees" is dated June 2, 1967, nineteen days before the official opening of the Summer of Love. Larkin, a librarian who looked like a potato with glasses, no doubt found the Summer of Love to be as loveless as all the other summers. ("Too often summer days appear/Emblems of perfect happiness/I can't confront," he once wrote, not exactly what girls grooving on Hendrix and the Stones wanted to hear.) But whereas Hendrix and the Stones now look painfully dated when they're taken out for a sentimental airing on VH1, "The Trees" remains as far beyond the reach of fashion as the day it was published.

Still, reading that last stanza, I heard the trees saying something else. Though it threw the meter off slightly, in my head the poem closed like this:

> Yet still the unresting castles thresh
> In fullgrown thickness every May.
> *Poetry* is dead, they seem to say,
> Begin afresh, afresh, afresh.

But how, except in a poem, could you say something so perfectly?

Poetry Anyone?

Who reads poetry anymore? Does anyone? The *Weekly* asked various intellectual types—people who do, presumably, read a lot of *something*—if poetry gets a look-in. Here's what they had to say:

David Wilson, director, Museum of Jurassic Technology: I don't read poetry very much anymore, even though I was pretty interested in it at an earlier point in my life. In my case, I think the reason is I have less time to read in general; I find myself working until I collapse. I miss it. It's an experience unlike others, not one you can replace with other things. I've actually tried to get back into it, made a point of finding poets I thought I might be interested in, but I've just never engaged with it again in the way I did once.

Arianna Huffington, author, political commentator: I love reading poetry. I still read Greek poets like Seferis and Cavafy—"Waiting for the Barbarians" is one of my favorite poems, and "Those people were a kind of solution" is one of my favorite lines. I also love Rumi. Right now that's the book I'm reading. I love Wordsworth, too, and a lot of the English poets, probably because I lived in England.

I have never discussed poetry with anyone in Los Angeles until [this phone call]. It doesn't mean that people don't love it, because people don't know that I love it—it just hasn't come up. It came up much more when I lived in London. People talked about poetry a lot more in London, and they also quoted much more, not just poetry, but literature in general. They did it in an unselfconscious way, as part of the things they carried with them. When I was in England I read a lot of W.H. Auden and Christopher Fry. There's a great poem of Fry's called "A Sleep of Prisoners." I particularly remember the last stanza:

> It takes so many thousand years to wake,
> But will you wake for pity's sake?

Just recently I was writing a column on Hillary Clinton's listening tour in New York, and I happened to have been reading a poem by Rumi where he talks about "longing for your listening silence." I didn't quote it, though, because it would have seemed so entirely affected. You really cannot quote poetry in an American newspaper column without seeming affected.

Oliver Stone, film director (message delivered via an assistant): I do read poetry when I can. Tennyson's "Ulysses" is one of my favorites—always has been.

John Rechy, novelist: I read contemporary poetry infrequently. I do very often re-read classical poetry, and in my courses I often refer to Pope, the Metaphysical poets, then moving to modern times, T.S. Eliot, Hart Crane, James Thompson. I've pulled away from poetry, because it seems to be lacking in what I consider the language of poetry, which is passion. I think an alienation has been created, and some tight groups of poets seem to have developed a private language that shuts me out. They've become citizens of their own country, as it were, and because I deal with words and the exactitude of words, when I find that an intelligent man—i.e., myself [laughs]—isn't connecting, I refuse to blame myself!

Octavia Butler, novelist: I don't read a lot of it. My favorite right now, because it relates to some stuff I'm writing, is Gwendolyn Brooks. I guess what I like about poetry when I read it is that it says so much with so few words and says it so well.

There's one poem by Brooks I've been reading to groups when I speak, which is about the loneliness of being God. I'll read some of it aloud for you. It begins, "It must be lonely to be God,/Nobody loves the master, no," and after saying why it might be lonely to be God, it ends:

> Perhaps—who knows?—He tires of looking down.
> Those eyes are never lifted, never straight.
> Perhaps He tires of being great,
> In solitude, without a hand to hold.

Jon Wiener, historian: At the moment, I read some of the poetry in *The New Yorker*, I read poems by friends, and I occasionally go to readings by my friends, though rarely. Sometimes I also read the poems in *The Nation*, though I'd emphasize the "sometimes."

My friends don't read poetry. The only people who read poetry are poets, but you don't need me to tell you that. *The New Yorker* is the main place that I have any contact with the world of poetry, and sometimes there's wonderful stuff in *The New Yorker* and I read it and enjoy it and don't think about it very much afterwards. It's just pleasure.

Russell Jacoby, author (The Last Intellectuals): I couldn't add to Dana Gioia's article in the *Atlantic Monthly* ["Can Poetry Matter?"]. Only very sporadically do I read poetry. I don't think I have anything to offer you.

Christian Darren, screenwriter: I read probably 100 percent more poetry in my twenties than I do now in my thirties, which is indicative of how people are romantic in their twenties and pragmatic in their thirties. I once read a lot of romantic poetry, which I cribbed and sent on to various loves of mine as if I'd written it myself. I don't know anyone who reads poetry or mentions it. I'd have to say that poetry, especially if you're dealing within the narrow parameters of the film community, is far from the reality of what people are looking for. Even novels are far afield unless they have a concrete hook, so poetry is several steps beyond that.

Glenn Goldman, owner, Book Soup: We turn over the poetry section once every ten months, which is very slow. The section's intensively stocked for the level of sales. It's more of a commitment on the part of the bookstore than something designed to generate sales. I have read poetry over time, but not particularly recently. I was a big fan of Yeats and Wallace Stevens, but I pretty much exhausted that. I'd say contemporary poetry is outside my field of interest at the moment. That's not to say that if someone interesting was brought to my attention I wouldn't pick him up, but at the moment I'm not reading anyone.

The poetry I see falls more or less into two camps. One is the camp that sits at home and is self-taught, and the other is the people in academia who are writing for their colleagues. I think a lot of the stuff that's in the first camp is very personal in many respects and hard to sell to the public, and the stuff in the second camp is very esoteric and difficult for the public to understand.

Our best-selling book of poetry for the first six months of the year is *The Captain's Verses* by Pablo Neruda, which sold fifty-two copies. That's followed by the paperback edition of Ted Hughes' *Birthday Letters*, which only sold fourteen copies. After that is a new edition of Borges' *Selected Poems*, then Rimbaud's *Complete Works*, *The Rubáiyat of Omar Khayyám*, Henry Rollins, *Twenty Love Poems* (Neruda again), something by Fernando Pessoa, then a gift edition of the Neruda, then another Neruda, and Rilke's *Selected Poems*.

Doug Dutton, owner, Dutton's Brentwood Bookstore: Our sales figures for poetry have gone up appreciably over the last three years. I don't know what the reason for it is. Is it *Il Postino*? Did that capture the popular imagination? Is it because there are a lot of readings around town that weren't here before? There does seem to be a legitimate poetry phenomenon. Why it is beats the hell out of me. Must be the millennium.

Callie Khourie, screenwriter: I've been to a few poetry readings, which I always enjoy more than I think I'm going to before I go. I read Emily Dickinson and Rilke, and the *Spoon River Anthology* and stuff like that, just whatever I come across or what somebody turns me on to. A lot of the new poetry I read [is] in various literary digests, like *The Paris Review* or *Nimrod*, and we actually get a magazine called *Writers & Poets*, so I read a lot of it in there.

It's so hard to talk about poetry, because I so rarely do it. It's not like reading a book or seeing a film, which is a more communal thing. I read it, I think about it, and I forget about it. But I don't really talk about it. Louise Glück's *House on the Marshland* is a fantastic book. Oh, and of course Auden's poems blow my mind. I would find it almost impossible to pick one poem by him, because for me, each one is such an emotional experience. I also like to read Rimbaud in the bathtub. My copy is completely mildewed from sitting by the bathtub.

Michael Silverblatt, host of KCRW's Bookworm: [The reason people aren't interested in poetry] is a very simple one, and it's so sad it's almost unbearable to think about. Randall Jarrell said in *A Sad Heart at the Supermarket* that in the hornbook of his grandmother, the children's primer for elementary school contained selections from the Bible, Shakespeare, *The Pilgrim's Progress*, all kinds of things. If you've grown up with this being how you were taught to read, it's always in your life. Children were once regularly taught to read things that would take them till they were adults to understand, and it would put them in touch with the traditions of their language. We don't have that in America, you see, and we haven't had it for years. We once did. My mother, a working woman all her life, remembers her high school Latin. And what she was reading in Latin was not "See Dick run." She was reading things she only began to understand when she was an adult. And she learned all this in a public school, and as a daughter of parents who didn't speak English. Most Americans have never been put in the presence of the greatnesses of our own language in any sense—not multicultural, not classical, not dead-white-male. In fact, if you think about it, most of us grew up reading books not written by an author but by a committee whose sole concern was that you learned to read, not that you enjoy reading.

In my neighborhood, the guys who deliver pizza come from all over the world, and they tell me that America is the first country they've been to where the houses are not full of books. That's what they tell me when they see all the books I have lying around.

Michael Tolkin, novelist, director and screenwriter: I do read a lot of poetry. I try to keep in mind Edmund Wilson's dictum that you should read something luminous every night. I'm not that adventurous when it comes to single volumes by new poets. I like the anthologies, like *The Best American Poetry*, because then someone else has done the work of discovering people for me. Generally I go for the warhorses: Williams, Stevens, Frost, though the Frost I like is the manic-depressive swamp Yankee, not the kindly farmer. I don't know or read any contemporary L.A. poets. I'll read whoever gets published in *The New Yorker* or the *London Review of Books* or whatever intellectual journals have poetry in them. I don't know what it is about poetry, but I like it. I like geniuses. In collected works, I'm drawn to the last fifteen pages or so. I like seeing what people wrote before they died.

September 1999

CITY OF POEMS
The Lyric Voice in Los Angeles Since 1990

LAURENCE GOLDSTEIN

"yes, it's insanity
writing poetry in Los Angeles"
  —Wanda Coleman,
  "The Lady in the Red Veiled Hat"
  Mercurochrome

As I grew up in Los Angeles during the late 1950s and early 1960s, reading the master poems of modern American literature and wondering why there seemed to be no remarkable poets in *my* city, I chafed under the sense of cultural inferiority passed from one literary person to another in the Southland like some swamp fever on the lowest slopes of Parnassus. Further north Robinson Jeffers was writing his last poems in Tor House, and the Beat poets had made San Francisco *the* City of Art in my envious imagination. An anthology called *Poetry Los Angeles* (London: Villiers Publications, 1958) informed me that verse was being committed in my precincts, but nothing in the book seemed remotely like a masterpiece, and almost none of it tried to make anything of California as a subject. Who in greater Los Angeles would read this imported book anyway? Randall Jarrell wrote in a letter of 1954 from Laguna Beach, "This is certainly an uncultivated part of the World—you get the impression that the inhabitants, at breakfast, spell out *Little Nancy* with their fingers and their reading for the day is done." That is snob wit, but it was true that neither Laguna Beach nor my hometown of Culver City featured a venue for new books, and you could travel through a decade's worth of social occasions without hearing a reference to *Lord Weary's Castle*, or any volume by Randall Jarrell.

Los Angeles poetry was written by a small number of talented people, and consumed by the same group, which clustered around the magazine they published, *Coastlines*, and recreated the camaraderie and fissures of the national poetry scene. Ann Stanford has remained my personal favorite of this group, which also included Josephine Ain, Sanora Babb, Alvaro Cordona-Hine, James Boyer May, Bert Meyers, William Pillin, and Mel Weisbrud. This was the saving remnant that made visiting poets feel at home, but one senses that the hothouse atmosphere made most of them sweat uncomfortably. Charles Gullans cast a cold eye upon them in "Cocktails," which they graciously published in the final issue of *Coastlines* (1964):

> The dead who jam the broad forecourts of hell,
> Know just as much and gossip just as well.
> But here they stand, appallingly alive.
> They live because you live. They batten, thrive
> On your hard substance and identity.
> They are the emptiness that you will be
> When they suck dry the meaning of your name.
> And never doubt they can, they made this game—
> The fool, the tool, the boor, the arrogant bores,
> This editor, that critic, and these whores.

In 1964 Randall Jarrell was writing nostalgically in "Thinking of the Lost World" about the golden years of his childhood spent in Los Angeles, and might have savored this poem for its disdain of literary coteries, none of which, he finally and desperately realized, had brought him as much happiness as the remarkable sunshine of Hollywood and "Mama's dark blue Buick" and the playful illusions of the movies. But he never took an interest in poetry written in Los Angeles, nor did any of his fellow poets and critics for the influential Southern and Northeastern quarterlies.

Even more than in most American cities, poetry in Los Angeles struggles for recognition under the omnipresent shadow of the mass media, and especially the ubiquity of the visual and performing arts. Movies and television are the native flowers of the Southland, and their enormous cultural presence has always pushed less popular arts to the margins of public attention. As Nathanael West warned in his prophetic novel of 1939, *The Day of the Locust*, the free-standing works of an individual creative vision have no chance of distracting the general public from the more facile and widely-distributed products fabricated in the dream factories, which now include not only the movies of West's day, but television and recording studios, and the small and larger venues for theater, song, and spectacle. If poetry in Los Angeles looks healthier these days, it is in part thanks to the poetry readings and poetry slams at coffee houses and nightclubs, and to the 'zines that broadcast, through giveaway weekly pulps and the Internet, news from the Muse to the counterculture. It's still an underground and minority art, but at least its practitioners are more numerous than the insular elite of Gullans's cocktail circuit.

My intention in this essay is to focus on some exemplary volumes of poetry emerging from Los Angeles, beginning with three seminal books from the year 1990. It is painful to draw the line at that year because it eliminates from discussion some of my favorite poems about the city. I never hear of an earthquake without recalling Henri Coulette's chilling couplets in "Quake": "The swimming pools of Eden suddenly are empty. / Bertolt Brecht's spectacles lie splintered on the floor, // For all the world is made of glass and makes to break, / And shines like stars without a heaven, and makes to cut." And Mark Jarman not only wrote the quintessential surfing poems in *Far and Away* (1985), but helped later poets see how the diverse communities, like an archipelago, cohere thanks to the freeways that bring, say, residents of Pasadena and other inland spots so swiftly to the beach towns. "The Supremes" is my favorite from this volume, with its artful juxtaposition of the Motown girl group and the Pacific swells, "little more than embellishments: / lathework and spun glass, / gray-green with cold, but flawless." And Garrett Hongo, also writing in the reminiscent mode, set down in "The Underworld," from *The River of Heaven* (1988), the most gorgeous evocation of the movie palace—"L.A.'s old Orpheum, / a once lavish Fox now gone to skinflicks, horror fests and community matinees"—in contemporary literature, the verbal equivalent of David Lynch's camera eye in *Mulholland Drive*.

But 1990, for good and ill, is where we begin. Charles Gullans's *Letter from Los Angeles* (John Daniel and Company, 1990), is a more forgiving poetry from the author of "Cocktails." The title poem, which opens the volume, evokes the semi-tropical languor of the city, its warm winds and scent of orange and lime, and its ubiquitous flowers, all enumerated as a type of paradise. But the poem has a characteristic turn in which Gullans steps back from the enchantment of a landscape too sensuous and innocent for human comfort. The "one concern" of the Pacific Ocean, he says in another poem, is "with today." Nature has no memory, but the poet is a postlapsarian in his obsession with the sad lessons of the historical and personal past. Gullans cannot pretend to merge his consciousness with an Edenic bower of bliss, however much he yearns for its easy pleasures. Stated in such a formulaic fashion, the attitude sounds more puritanical than Gullans will be in the ensuing poems. As we proceed through the book, though, the "Letter" proves useful for the clear limits it sets to the poet's genuine enthusiasm for a city that, like New Orleans, might as well be named the Big Easy. Faced with its voluptuous abundance and its tendency to erase the past in the spirit of continuous self-invention, the poet defines himself by what he can do without.

Or what he must do without. As an aging scholar, Gullans of necessity looks upon the culture no less than the nature in Los Angeles as lacking the nourishing spirit of history, of human record:

> I'm home and finding the Los Angeles
> Nobody loves where everybody lives,
> The concrete miles that crouch beneath Bel Air
> And Brentwood to the sea, if living is the word
> For bare accommodation in these rooms
> With nothing that we do not bring to them.
> In the impersonal we make some life
> With a few sticks and rags, a bed, a chair,
> Some pottery, some pictures, and the phone.
> No attics and no basement, thus, no past;
> No history, therefore no legacy.

The austerity of these decasyllabics—their refusal to render for us inventive figures of speech, daring prosodic variations, tone-shifts, or allusions—offers us the sober pleasure of an observant sensibility reporting experience of one portion of the great city. Because Los Angeles has no commitment to the historical, the poet must be an almanac and emblem of history-making, rescuing his own life from the poverty implied by this stance through a series of meditations on the folkways he finds too attractive to resist.

Gullans's "take" on Los Angeles tends to be through its nightlife, especially its bars. Speaking of an earlier volume, Robert von Hallberg, in *American Poetry and Culture, 1945–1980*, remarks that "Along with Edgar Bowers and Turner Cassity, Gullans helped [the] traveler's theme, the degradation of eros, to evolve into a sub-genre, the barroom poem of jaundiced courting." The rhetorical danger in such a subgenre is that the poet will too easily succumb to the cynicism and world-mockery of the intellectual on a barstool, the chief failing of the city's most (in)famous poet, Charles Bukowski. When Gullans's poems decline to this tone, their plain style can sound like whining:

> We live forever in the midden heap
> Of old emotions, where our history
> Has its own tedium and tawdriness . . .

> or

> It is the maimed who come here.
> Widowed, divorced, or unattached, the lost,
> The lonely, the deserted. Time at the local
> Is less a pleasure than a way of life . . .

The author gains some points for not neglecting to say the obvious, but no poet can afford to dwell very long at this level of discourse. What makes Gullans's work significant and satisfying is his relentless self-analysis. As one of the barflies he speaks with authority of "The old corruptions of the blood and brain" that make of his alienation a general human condition. Like the John Wilkes he praises, he has "an aristocrat's disdain / Of canting ethics," and registers his sexual adventures and misadventures with candor and precision. These episodes move the lyric action into a domestic space, the real paradise of the book-lined study, the dining room where the congeniality of guests can be fully enjoyed, and the bedroom where "Eros the Terrible" can bring to quotidian life his ecstatic power. Gullans is representative of many Los Angeles poets who prefer the personal or private realms, the communion of bed and board, shut against the influences of the sprawling public arena.

Gullans undertook a rhetorical withdrawal from the postcard landscapes of Los Angeles because he saw the city, in a Jonsonian and/or Baudelairean manner, as a kind of Babylon, a movable temptation he yielded to even as he remained a conscience within its precincts. In this sense his poems remind me of some of the city's moral fiction, such as Evelyn Waugh's *The Loved One,* Christopher Isherwood's *A Single Man,* and Joan Didion's *Play It As It Lays.* In his best poem, "Calvin at the Casino," Gullans brilliantly figures our spiritual risk as flawed citizens seeking a meaning to life beyond the senses by the conceit of a Las Vegas gambling hall. That kind of judgmental distance, enacted in the heroic couplets he uses to frame his terse abstractions from the sloppiness of our everyday chatter, belongs to the moralist who has chosen, or settled for, the stoical pleasures appropriate to his age and profession. In poems he wrote up till his death in 1994, he charted his pleasures in the city as evidence of his damnation. "We dwell here in God's darkness," he wrote. "Let it be."

Wanda Coleman lives in an entirely different Los Angeles of the imagination from Gullans. This African-American poet identifies Watts as her locale, and her poetics derives from the Beat prosody of dynamic oral performance. (She has issued several spoken work recordings, including a solo CD, "High Priestess of Word.") Her poems move us around the city excursively; we visit parking lots, beaches, go-go joints, fast-food shops, freeways, jails, liquor stores, and streets in every part of the metropolis. Coleman is staking out as her psychic territory "that bitch, mother America" whom she has internalized and complains about like an angry Whitman drifting through an abundance just out of reach. An applicant to the literary elite community, she collected 4500 rejection slips, she says, before her work achieved a measure of recognition not only in California but throughout the country. (She received the Lenore Marshall Poetry Prize in 1999 and has enjoyed National Endowment for the Arts and Guggenheim fellowships) The "essential" Wanda Coleman can best be sampled in her volume of 1990, *African Sleeping Sickness: Stories & Poems* (Black Sparrow Press).

Coleman's comic way of dramatizing her encounter with the poetry community is to fantasize a Hollywood life for herself, not as a star but as a degraded victim dwelling on the underside of glamour:

> on the boulevard i watch the blind tap out courage
> behind my shades i too am numbed by neon and am
> hustling ass for that pimp, success

Hollywood and Watts become the nearly allegorical poles of her experience, and "Hollywood" is less a geographical district than a state of being that includes the academy, the elite literary world, the spots of privilege and power in which her presence is suspect. Drug-running and prostitution are the metaphors for mobility between the realms of Watts and Hollywood, and she is never certain when her warm reception in the tonier parts of the city is just the "Niggah-of-the-Minute syndrome" and when she has been welcomed for her authentic achievement. So, as renegade writer and as citizen she wanders the city writing the chronicle of her dailiness.

The typical Wanda Coleman poem features herself as the main character, dressed in black leather jacket or dashiki to take on the wolfish world with a reciprocal toughness, or undressed and indulging in sexual pleasures. But she chooses to open the title section of *African Sleeping Sickness* with a poem in which her persona is retracted. This is "Black Madonna":

> screaming legions/her children chase her down shame street
> they stone her lover into flight. they violate all
> sanctuaries. there is no place for her to hide. fouled/her
> breath is foul, her hole is foul, her soot skin ashen with
> filth—pustules and granulating sores. biblically speaking,
> she writhes in manifest pain/forsaken. plagued. the screaming
> legions of her children tear at her breasts and partake of her
> flesh. they slit her consciousness that she may never sleep.
> she of the night of nights. she conceived without vaginal
> birth/without woman. unclean. she—the victim of victims
>
> *father, the crucifixion did not take*

A book centered in Watts that begins with screaming children and a female vagrant makes an obvious critique of social injustice, and poems that follow extend that critique into multitudinous lives of the ghetto. But Coleman does something else in this snapshot of a street scene; she rages against the human condition that turns a well-meaning woman into a victim not only of her sexual activity but of the plagues of heaven. It is the message of African-American spirituals that Jesus died to redeem mankind, but the rage of so many poet-prophets has been that *"the crucifixion did not take,"* that this fallen world remains a place of inexplicable suffering where mother Jerusalem wanders in filth and physical pain bemoaning the fate of her children. By means of such allusions Coleman gives depth and texture to the everyday urban landscape. The violence of her verbs, the ugliness of her imagery, the crammed and cramped rhythms of her prosody, enforce this visionary world upon her readers, making them responsible for picking up where messianic promises left off.

The plagued figure of the Black Madonna prefigures many poems in which "the virus" takes over Los Angeles, killing the poet's friends in Watts and Hollywood alike. The sinister agent of AIDS changes everything in Coleman's world, especially sexuality which is no longer an innocent pleasure or a commercial transaction but a harrowing and dangerous contact event like a mugging. More elegiac than her previous or subsequent volumes, *African Sleeping Sickness* remembers the prematurely dead:

> memories of the neo-uranian poet who
> spent a good deal of time on venus but favored
> the rigidity of self-reflection. he died lusting
> for that too fleet decade of polymorphism unleashed
>
> "you don't know what a time that was for men"

Whoever she is referring to in this poem, it is impossible not to think of Paul Monette in reading such lines. Monette's volume of 1988, *Love Alone: Eighteen Elegies for Rog* bristles with some of the same anger as Coleman's as it chronicles the gay life celebrated by Charles Gullans, but changed utterly from the older poet's innocent loveplay. In Monette's poems the landscape of Los Angeles, washed clean by the sea breezes, manifests the most degraded form of cultural memory: "I open / the door to the morning and half the city's / Capri and half Buchenwald."

As her view of Los Angeles has matured, Coleman's verse has become more elliptical, dreamlike, philosophical. The "virus" serves as one more symbolic figure for the violence against humanity enacted in Los Angeles, raising fundamental questions not entirely predicated on class and race. "They say Hatred drives a hard bargain / but he sold us out cheap," she writes in an early poem. Yet her civic indignation rises spiritedly in poems like "South Central Los Angeles Deathtrip 1982," from *Mercurochrome* (2001). Thinking, no doubt, of the cult volume *Wisconsin Death Trip*, Michael Lesy's 1973 collage volume of photographs and commentary about the morbid lives and gruesome deaths in a small town in Wisconsin during the latter part of the nineteenth century, Coleman presents a sequence of portraits of dead black men and women victimized by the Los Angeles police force:

> jes another X marking it
>
> dangling gold chains & pinky rings
> nineteen, done in black leather & defiance
> teeth white as halogen lamps, skin dark as a threat
>
> they spotted him taking in the night
> made for the roust
> arrested him on "suspicon of"
> they say he became violent
> they say he became combative in the rear seat of
> that sleek zebra maria. they say
> it took a chokehold to restrain him
> and then they say he died of asphyxiation
> on the spot

We are accustomed to hearing about the criminal history of Los Angeles in films, like *Chinatown* and *Boyz N the Hood*, or fiction, like John Gregory Dunne's *True Confessions*, or theater, like Luis Valdez's *Zoot Suit*, but poetry generally eschews the documentation of specific incidents that engender significant changes in urban history. Poems like these are a minority in Coleman's oeuvre; she focuses more on the personal than the communal, but they mark her determination to be that citizen-prosecutor or "unacknowledged legislator" Shelley praises as the essence of poetic power.

Coleman says at one point, "all I want to write about is me / no one else is doing it." The attention-getting aspects of her poems are obvious: they shout, they tell jokes and funny anecdotes, they perform dizzying feats of syntactical contortion. But they are not personal in the sense that confessional poetry is personal. Coleman creates a folkloric "I," a figure who is sometimes a "haint," a mere camera eye, and sometimes a scatological presence of mythic proportions. Like other Los Angeles poets published by Black Sparrow Press—Charles Bukowski and Diane Wakoski come to mind—she is prolific, indeed *driven* in her need to recapitulate the terms of her experience in a free-verse style ingratiating enough to secure a large audience. Such ambition has its problematics: a felt doggedness in the daily composition, a sense of strain in trying to make the commonplace remarkable, a tarting-up of language to do the work of sustained imaginative effort. Coleman, like Bukowski, likes to write fiction as well, and some of her poems are just shards of storytelling in a prosaic tempo. But at her best she shows us her city and her sensibility with splendid precision and good humor.

Amy Gerstler's volume *Bitter Angel* is the third volume from 1990 I wish to discuss. Her case is a paradoxical one. When this volume won the National Book Critics Circle Award she became the darling of workshops and magazines, widely discussed not only as a quintessentially postmodern poet—Jorie Graham's claim on the book jacket of *Bitter Angel*—but also as a quintessentially Los Angeles poet. And yet there is not a single Southern California place name or location in the poems, nor in her subsequent volumes *Nerve Storm* (1993) and *Crown of Weeds* (1997). How can this be? The situation compels us to think more deeply about how a writer represents region in her work. As we have seen in Gullans and Coleman, there is the straightforward manner of setting the poems in a recognizable spot that becomes an agent in the narrative adventures of the "I." This might be called the Whitmanian method, as when the Bard of Manhattan sets us down on the Brooklyn Ferry or before a Broadway parade. But there is also the strategy of Emily Dickinson who "sees New Englandly," as she claims, not because she describes Amherst with topographical accuracy but because she looks at universals like trains or hummingbirds with a peculiar angle of vision derived from the spirit of place. Reconstructing that spirit of place can be immensely difficult. It's not enough to point to her Puritan legacy, and that of Emerson and other Transcendentalists; we also have to immerse ourselves in her day-to-day reading, her walks, her avocations, the sermons she heard and the paintings she admired. Likewise Amy Gerstler's poems have archaeological strata that need to be uncovered before the actualities of her local culture become visible.

In her poems there are plenty of cues and clues to help the perplexed. The Southern California inflection in these poems may be easier to spot if we begin with an example. Here is the whole of a prose poem, "Slowly I Open My Eyes," which has the subtitle, *gangster soliloquy*:

> While the city sleeps there's this blast of silence that follows the whine of daylight: a defeat that wraps around buildings like a python, or one of those blue sheets they bundle corpses up in. *Wanna go for an ambulance ride?* Fragments of the sordid and the quote unquote normal vie for my attention. Hacking coughs and seductive yoo-hoos dangle in the 3 a.m. air. Up on this roof, I smoke cigarettes and wait. I feel like god up here. No kidding. Jerusalem Slim on his final night in the garden. Mr. X, Dr. No, The Invisible Man. All the same guy, different movies. It's a city of delinquents: my disciples. Maybe some bum down below finds one of my stubbed out butts and is delighted. Everybody's looking for something to inhale and something else to empty into. The whole city reels and twinkles at my feet, but the stars aren't impressed. They see it every night. The eighty-year-old elevator operator downstairs snores like he's trying to suck up the Hudson. Humans act as if they're going to stick around forever, but nobody ever does. That's what cracks me up.

The poem reminds me of "Invitation to a Gunfighter" in *African Sleeping Sickness*. In that poem Wanda Coleman addresses Durango, a black outlaw in the Wild West, and tells him his time is over, the townspeople have tired of his act, and it's "time to take that long technicolor ride //

before they ambush you in the saddle / and leave you face up in the sun." That is, the romance of Black Power has now receded so far into the distance that our public memory of it is like a movie—Huey Newton the likely star—and has ended the way all violent flicks always end, with the community terminating the unwanted intruder. In Gerstler's poem the romance of the doomed gangster is given just as fragmentarily, with the eloquence artists have gladly lavished on the stylish type of the gangster. "The real city," Robert Warshow noted in *The Immediate Experience*, "produces only criminals; the imaginary city produces the gangster." Gerstler's gunfighter speaks as if he had read Warshow's classic essay on "The Gangster as Tragic Hero," and perhaps watched Warren Beatty play-acting "Bugsy" Siegel as well.

Her gangster is aware of himself as imaginary, an inventor of identity for himself. His possibilities are chosen from the movies: Mr. X, Dr. No, the Invisible Man, and also Christ, whom he drolly calls Jerusalem Slim, another "delinquent" who met a violent end for offending the local constabulary. The gangster feels like god because he's on top of a skyscraper, like James Cagney in *White Heat*: "Top of the world, Ma!" But the triumph is meaningless because the city is nothing more than a shell, a sign of defeat, the figure of his impending doom. The city is something he empties himself into, as sexually into his moll; he's like a gun whose purpose is to empty itself into other people, good and bad alike. And so he aimlessly fills himself with the movie stories that glorify his brief moment, an arrogant fiction reproached by the heavenly stars which have seen it all a million times before. In another poem, "Astronomy," Gerstler ponders the harmony of the spheres, and just thinking of their immortality "will still elicit tears, as in / 'A sigh is still a sigh . . . ,' a line from / the song 'As Time Goes By.' "

That song, of course, is known to everyone as the signature tune of *Casablanca*, another movie about gangsters in an "imaginary" city. The point I am making is that Gerstler's postmodernism is nourished by the movies, and more generally by the popular culture that threatens to make all private acts of imagination adapt to its dominant formulas. The anxiety about authenticity in our time has found its most pervasive metaphor in the way popular culture involves itself in our everyday consciousness, and Los Angeles has since the beginnings of the film industry been the favored site for the epoch-making shift in self-realization.

Though all poetry undertakes to investigate such fictions as they render speaker and reader imaginary, one would expect Los Angeles poetry to be especially alert to such transformations, just as the Los Angeles/Hollywood novel, from *The Day of the Locust* and Isherwood's *Prater Violet* to Carolyn See's *Making History*, has anatomized the same desolation and self-fashioning that Gerstler evokes in her gangster's monologue.

In a sense, then, Los Angeles is less a place on a map than "Psychotown," to cite the title of a poem in *Crown of Weeds*. "I lived in this region all / my formative years," Gerstler writes, in the assumed voice of a haunted maiden. Psychotown is a mindscape rather than a landscape, a place where repressed desires become manifest: "We recover our / submerged selves here. One soul-chomping / goblin after another is hauled up from / our depths." Can one read the poem without thinking of Hitchcock's trend-setting film *Psycho*, which enacts the schizoid condition she describes in the poem? To live and write in Los Angeles may entail the acting out of an obsession, a possession, if only as a warning to fellow citizens about their susceptibility to violent impulses.

Finding more illustrations of this tendency toward the fantastic and delusional in Los Angeles poetry would not be difficult; they are abundant, perhaps overabundant. I will cite two. One is Charles Harper Webb's poems in which he uses a Hollywood motif to probe the causes and purposes of his everyday behavior. In "Fantasy Girl" and "Marilyn's Machine," from *Reading the Water* (Northeastern University Press, 1997), the Romantic Image of perfect erotic fulfillment from an ideal female is evoked, savored, and then deconstructed. The dream factory can drive you to your doom, as it does the gangster in Gerstler's poem, and so it must be resisted night and day as a condition of making a truce with the pathological power of the city. Turning away from the overheated imagery of Bruce Willis and Jane March, in the movie *Color of Night*, Webb seeks out his wife as a salvational reality principle:

You hit rewind, pop out the tape, then plod
    to bed and let your wife, with no gaffer to backlight a transparent
gown or bounce diamond-glitter off her eyes, with no director
to coax out each breathy line, with no shadowy, hellish past—

only the usual dark and tortured human history—to heat her kiss,
with only her arms, that would have pulled out of their sockets
if she'd dangled like Jane, to draw you back into her body,
back into this flawed and precious life.

The second example is James Harms, who in *The Joy Addict* (Carnegie Mellon University Press, 1998) writes poems about a variety of Southern California personalities and landscapes, including Newport Beach, the foothills and canyons of Los Angeles, the Roxy on Sunset Boulevard, the Ocean Park of Richard Diebenkorn, and the joys of surfing "east of Avalon," and who in *Quarters* (Carnegie Mellon University Press, 2001) offers one of the most charming of narratives in the Hollywood style, even with an improbable Hollywood happy ending. Having reminded us in his poem "Gridlock" that the essence of life in Los Angeles is the existential act of driving, or rather the frustration of *trying* to drive on the so-called freeways, Harms relates a fantasy situation in "Fable" in which the speaker seeks a parking place close to the beach where he intends to do some surfing. He finds the perfect spot but has no change for the meter. While vainly asking passers-by for help, he stops to aid an old woman who has lost her breath in the street; at the end of the poem, as the meter maid makes her relentless way toward his car, the old woman, now visible in the second storey of her apartment across from the speaker, waves the boy into her driveway as a reward for his good deed. In the ruthless world of Los Angeles, the moral is: not only should you *always* carry a bag of quarters, but you should heed the wisdom of fairy tales and the fable of the Good Samaritan.

As immigration has made Los Angeles more cosmopolitan and multicultural in the 1990s and afterward, new myths and tropes have become commonplace in the poetry of the city. In fact, Los Angeles has always been a place occupied by diasporas from different parts of the nation and the world, half nostalgic for the place they abandoned but also joyful about the mild weather, the tolerance of different lifestyles, the distractions and glamour of Hollywood, the easy access to the Pacific Ocean, the desert, and the mountains. And, though Los Angeles suffered a Depression and recessions along with the rest of the country, there has always been a fundamental level of prosperity in this last frontier of the American Dream. The poets most sensitive to the upside and downside of this mentality have been the ethnic groups increasingly visible in the everyday life of the city, no longer confined to ghettos (Watts, Chinatown) but uneasy about the social dynamics of a city with such a long history of genteel and not-so-genteel racism and prejudice. Books of the 1990s which insist on an ethnic perspective emerge from a recent tradition of widely read volumes from and about other parts of the United States: Rita Dove, *Thomas and Beulah*; Cathy Song, *Picture Bride*; Gary Soto, *The Elements of San Joaquin*, Linda Hogan, *The Savings*, and many other chronicles of biculturalism and biconsciousness. Aimed at a large audience, such books usually offer a simplicity of versification: short lines, plain diction, plenty of narrative exposition.

Juan Delgado is an exemplary figure in this new poetics, as evidenced in his two volumes, *Green Web* (University of Georgia Press, 1994) and *El Campo* (Capra Press, 1998). In both books Delgado, a professor at California State University, San Bernardino, tells the fundamental story of his community: the migration toward El Norte from Mexico. As with the authors discussed above, Delgado is not concerned with Los Angeles as an actual location to be articulated precinct by precinct into a demographic whole. Rather, Los Angeles is only one of many way stations or destinations looming before the "wetbacks" (Delgado leaves out the quotation marks, but I cannot) as they cross the border, often guided by a "coyote" who may play the trickster and abandon them, and make their uncertain and fearful way toward a better life. An early poem in *Green Web*, "He Took Her Away," puts it plainly:

> Through a car door bound
> from swinging open by rope,
> Mother saw an oil-soaked road
> streaming backwards to Mexico.
> Father had broken his promise,
> was taking her to America.

The mother's dispossession and unhappy backward looks (she is compared to Lot's wife) anticipates problems of settlement in the new territory. In other poems Delgado describes the difficulty of finding work, overt racial prejudice, and the way technology erases natural features in the world of the gringo. (For example, the monstrous leaf-blower of "Poor Harold's Luck.") Delgado maps out the grievances and remorse of the new settlers, often in their voices rather than his own, in order to create an alien realm of which Los Angeles is merely a portion.

When Delgado recommends a lifestyle of being "in transition, always," one can see that he harbors mixed feelings about his fate, much like Richard Rodriguez, whose autobiographical prose on this subject has made him the spokesman for the displaced Chicano/a. But if one bonds to the freeway as the spirit of emancipation in the Land of Liberty, is one defying the civilization to the north, or is one submitting to its fundamental spirit? Even when the poet considers sexual attraction, in "Flavio's New Home," he puts it this way:

> How the freeway's ivy clings
> and when I am thinking of you,
> I am drawn to the fast lane,
> the way it curls, spirals and bridges,
> always leading back to itself
> like a sacred serpent swallowing its tail.
> All the way the arrows and green signs,
> fluorescent, assure me of name and mile.

Set against poems that record visits to the timeless villages of Mexico, these all-American hymns to the fast lane and the virtues of keeping on the Open Road, mark Delgado's sense of self-transformation into a citizen who has successfully followed the vectors of historical necessity up the coast to a place that is not Westwood, Santa Monica, or Van Nuys, but "el campo" where "campesinos" can pause, like the migrants of *The Grapes of Wrath*, and test the new land for its hospitality.

"It's in the hunger that we know who we are," writes Amy Uyematsu in her poem "Belly Breaths" from *Nights of Fire, Nights of Rain* (Story Line Press, 1998). Not in the nourishment, but in the hunger. There is first of all the hunger to stay alive in an environment of maximum danger. In the poem "Summons" she surveys the perils of Los Angeles, or any of the "burning cities" of modern America: "pay attention to all the warnings / don't go to bed with open windows / inhale in half breaths / consider sex with new lovers / a dangerous political act." And most of all there is the terror of random drive-by shootings, an apt metaphor for all the contingencies of life in a city prey to "catastrophe":

> we know what it feels like to wait
> for that random bullet
> aimed into the crowd for the sheer pleasure
> and power of its anonymity

In Uyematsu's poetry we come the closest to the apocalyptic vision of Nathanael West's *The Day of the Locust,* in which the painter Tod Hackett labors over a giant canvas depicting "The Burning of Los Angeles." On one level this burning, an apt figure for a desert community vulnerable to forest fires, is the "burning burning burning burning" of T. S. Eliot's wasteland—the "burning" of passion, desire, sin, vice, corruption. On a more political level, as in Uyematsu's poem "The Ten Million Flames of Los Angeles," it is the burning of Watts in 1965 and 1992, the burning of crosses on the lawns of minorities (I witnessed these cross-burnings in the Baldwin Hills as a boy in Culver City). She declares herself a witness to the moral degradation of the city, an angry prophet of worse infernos to come, the fire next time.

Now that people of Asian descent compose more than 10 percent of the population of California, their voices are likely to attract more listeners, and some of what they say will not be welcome in the genteel parts of the city. Uyematsu, as a Japanese-American, unsurprisingly carries the memory of Manzanar (where her parents were incarcerated) and Heart Mountain into the poems, and offers herself as a figure of the vindictive alien, the Other:

> you see us invading without firing a shot—
> Japanese businessmen zeroing in on downtown Los Angeles,
> Korean shopkeepers spreading along Olympic & Western,
> Chinese immigrants pushing you out of Monterey Park,
> running for Mayor, sneaking past the once untouchable
> borders of lily-white San Marino,
> Pilipino families buying West Valley tract homes. . .
> young Asian hoodlums topping the evening news,
> broadcast by Tritia Toyota and Connie Chung look-alikes.

If Juan Delgado preserves the victim's-eye view of immigration and suggests the pains of not belonging to an established order of things, Uyematsu has a triumphalist rhetoric, though one that can collapse in other poems from a righteous anger to self-pity, especially when she considers how people she has loved (children, lovers) have migrated from her own household. If she can think nostalgically about going to see Toshiro Mifune films at the Toho LaBrea in her youth, and how she savored the film fantasy of the powerful warrior, the irresistible Asian, she does not succumb to the blandishments of the cinema but looks around her at all the "mixed" neighborhoods, at the "proud / pachuco tradition," the Jews, Native Americans, Blacks, and celebrates the diversity of the city.

Back in 1971 William Irwin Thompson noted in *At the Edge of History* that "In Los Angeles it is much harder to distinguish between personal fantasy and social reality because the realization of fantasy is one of [the city's] dominant cultural traits." If we now feel so much more dubious about the binary distinction of "personal fantasy" and "social reality" it is in part because Los Angeles, as a metaphor for the media culture, has triumphed in just the ways that Thompson predicted it would. Social reality of all kinds now stands revealed as a tangled mass of myths and illusions, many of them recognizable as Hollywood formulas. This fact has not made it easier for Los Angeles poets, who may feel that they are living in an atmosphere doubly rarefied by the surreal tradition of their native milieu. Los Angeles poets can remind one of Thomas Pynchon's heroine Oedpia Maas, in *The Crying of Lot 49*, searching the ruins of Los Angeles culture for some system of communication or structural coherence and coming up, as Amy Gerstler does with Perry Mason novels or Amy Uyematsu does with samurai films, with imaginary signs as the crucial elements of a meaningful code. The movie theater and the cave of the living room encircling the television and computer are dream hotels whose presence informs poetic reverie in ways that make even the most playful of readers uneasy about the contemporary moment.

There is more to Los Angeles than these poets have revealed, but they show that poetry continues its ceaseless enterprise of imagining into life even the most complex of subjects, not as local color or regionalism but as part of the national project of naming and claiming the whole of America as our nineteenth century sages, from the Founders through Whitman, programmed us to do. The dozens of ethnic identities in Los Angeles have helped provide a counterweight to the force of virtual reality and a homogenized mass identity, but they too draw upon and engender mythologies as powerful as the engines of immigration itself. Poems are sources of fantasy, as movies are, but they are also grit in the gears of dream machines, "reality checks" that broaden the identity of Los Angeles as a contested site in American culture. We've all had a century-long laugh at the burlesques of Los Angeles in the media—lotus land, locust land, or Woody Allen's "Munchkin land" in *Annie Hall*. Now it's time to remember that Karl Shapiro called Hollywood "a possibly proud Florence" back in 1941, and that even earlier Vachel Lindsay was proclaiming Los Angeles as the site of a renaissance of wonder. As the poets of Los Angeles gradually rescue their city from the mortmain of stereotype and situate it, newly-discovered, in our consciousness, we may find it as familiar, and as strange, as our own transfigured neighborhoods.

March 2003

ON BEING A CALIFORNIA POET

DANA GIOIA

A California poet almost inevitably feels the competing claims of language and experience. Here on the western edge of North America, we speak a European language that was transported centuries ago to a new continent. English is a northern tongue—born originally of Anglo-Saxon, Norman French, and Norse. However rich its vocabulary with later overlays of Latin, Greek, and Italian, this island tongue was shaped in other latitudes. By the time it had moved westward to the Pacific, Spanish was already rooted in California among the state's indigenous languages. New places and unfamiliar things had already been named, and those names have endured. This situation presents the poet with a paradox. Although English is our language, it remains at some deep level slightly foreign to our environment—like an immigrant grandparent whose words and concepts don't entirely fit the New World.

I am a Latin without a drop of British blood in my veins, but English is my tongue. It belongs to me as much as to any member of the House of Lords. The classics of English—Shakespeare, Milton, Pope, Keats, and Tennyson—are my classics. The myths and images of its literature are native to my imagination. And yet this rich literary past often stands at one remove from the experiential reality of the West. Our seasons, climate, landscape, natural life, and history are alien to the worldviews of both England and New England. There were no ranches or redwoods, abalone or adobe, in the Old World or the East. Spanish—not French—colors our regional accent. The world looks and feels different in California from the way it does in Massachusetts or Manchester—not only the natural landscape but also the urban one. Our towns are named Sacramento and Santa Rosa, not Coventry or New Haven. There is no use listening for a nightingale in the scrub oaks and chaparral.

Although the seasonal imagery of British poetry—so carefully developed over centuries from close observation of nature—has both beauty and resonance to a Californian, it seems hardly less fantastic than the wizards, fairies, and dragons who also inhabit those literary landscapes. To us, England is as exotic as Ilium or Cathay. Summers here are brown and dry, winters green and mild, and every month finds something blooming. The reality of California doesn't fit the poetic archetypes of the English tradition. Our history has no knights or kings, princesses or peers. We can muster a few broken conquistadors, but it was an army of indefatigable Franciscans who claimed California for their invisible, celestial empire. Wandering through a vast, unarticulated landscape, they christened the rivers, mountains, harbors, and settlements after Catholic saints until they had exhausted the roll call of heaven. Then they borrowed Spanish words—descriptions, nicknames, and even jokes—or adapted Indian terms to complete the mission. San Pedro, Sausalito, La Mirada, El Segundo, Shasta, Cotati, Topanga and Soledad are not places one would find in Wordsworth or even Whitman. Our challenge is not only to find the right words to describe our experience but also to discover the right images, myths, and characters. We describe a reality that has never been fully captured in English. Yet the earlier traditions of English help clarify what it is we might say. California poetry is our conversation between the past and present out of which we articulate ourselves.

I was born and raised in Hawthorne, California, a tough working-class town in Southwest Los Angeles. Hawthorne was also my mother's hometown. Her Mestizo father had fled his reservation in New Mexico to settle on the West Coast. My father's family had immigrated from Sicily at the turn of the century and gradually made their way west. Surrounded by Italian-speaking relations, I grew up in a neighborhood populated mostly by Mexicans and Dust Bowl Okies. I attended Catholic schools at a time when Latin was still a living ritual language. I went to Junipero Serra High School, a Catholic boys school run by the French Marianist order—many of whom were Hawaiian, Chinese or Mexican. The school was located in Gardena, which then contained the largest Japanese population in America—a city in which Buddhist temples outnumbered mainstream Protestant churches. Having experienced this extraordinary linguistic and cultural milieu, I have never given credence to Easterners who prattle about the intellectual vacuity of Southern California. My childhood was a rich mixture of European, Latino, Indian, Asian and North American culture in which everything from Hollywood to the Vatican, Buddha to the Beach Boys had its place.

My adult life has comprised equal parts of wanderlust and home-sickness. The first journey, from Los Angeles to Stanford, still feels like the farthest since I was leaving the world of the working-class and im-migrant family for parts unknown. Since then I have lived in Vienna, Boston, Rome, Minneapolis and New York, but I always called myself a Californian. And I always knew I would return. In 1977 my girlfriend and I went to New York, planning to stay two years. We married, had children, and eventually remained there for nearly two decades. It was an exhilarating and rewarding place, but it was never truly home. In 1996 we returned to live in rural Sonoma County. It is too easy in our society for an artist to become rootless, but I believe that it is essential for some writers to maintain their regional affinities. To speak from a particular place and time is not provincialism but part of a writer's iden-tity. It is my pleasure and my challenge to speak from California.

June 2002

CALIFORNIA HILLS IN AUGUST

DANA GIOIA

I can imagine someone who found
these fields unbearable, who climbed
the hillside in the heat, cursing the dust,
cracking the brittle weeds underfoot,
wishing a few more trees for shade.

An Easterner especially, who would scorn
the meagerness of summer, the dry
twisted shapes of black elm,
scrub oak, and chaparral, a landscape
August has already drained of green

One who would hurry over the clinging
thistle, foxtail, golden poppy,
knowing everything was just a weed,
unable to conceive that these trees
and sparse brown bushes were alive.

And hate the bright stillness of the noon
without wind, without motion,
the only other living thing
a hawk, hungry for prey, suspended
in the blinding, sunlit blue.

And yet how gentle it seems to someone
raised in a landscape short of rain –
the skyline of a hill broken by no more
trees than one can count, the grass,
the empty sky, the wish for water.

A Gallery of Southland Poets

PYGMY HEADHUNTERS AND KILLER APES, MY LOVER AND ME

LAUREL ANN BOGEN

Pygmy headhunters and killer apes play basketball at the Y. The killer apes win but the pigmy headhunters are not sore losers. They take the basketball home and boil it in your cast iron pot.

Hair. Lots of hair. Hairy devils those pygmy headhunters and killer apes. Vidal Sassoon chewed on this dilemma for awhile.

Pygmy headhunters and killer apes had flannel cakes at Musso and Franks. They were very hungry and ate three helpings each. But they wondered about the flesh beneath my flannel.

Pygmy headhunters and killer apes were homesick for Africa. They watched Make Mine Malt-o-meal on TV. They especially liked the part where John saved the world with gruel. It reminded everyone of home and they all had a good cry.

A cup of coffee is an honest thing. More honest than I am now. Its velocity in my veins throbs with need. I need to tell you this. You make my head hurt like sutures. You make this silly fist a killer.

Bone, hair, water, food. It is morning again. Last night the jungle used my fractured jaws to spear a message. Pigmy headhunters dance while killer apes beat their chest forget about you forget about you forget about you.

PRISONERS OF LOS ANGELES

WANDA COLEMAN

in cold gray morning
comes the forlorn honk of workbound traffic
i wake to the video news report

the world is going off

rising, i struggle free of the quilt
& wet dreams of my lover dispel
leave me moist and wanting

in the bathroom
i rinse away illusions, brush my teeth and
unbraid my hair
there's the children to wake
breakfast to conjure
the job
the day laid out before me
the cold corpse of an endless grind

so this is it, i say to the enigma in the mirror
this is your lot/assignment/relegation
this is your city

i find my way to the picture window
my eyes capture the purple reach of hollywood's hills
the gold eye of sun mounting the east
the gray anguished arms of avenue

I will never leave here

LETTER FROM HEADQUARTERS

JENNY FACTOR

What a day! The rat maze was lively. One girl
Got fired and two others bought a new car
On the Net. By 6 PM, my desk had its usual

Three paper cups with old tea bags and a soda can,
And an ether trail of guilty Web trips to procrastination.
Horoscopes, numerology. Today, I ran your numbers next to mine.

Casual games. They tell nothing personal. Only seem
Personal. A wish list. Or a mirror. Offers or dreams.
At lunch, out on the last manicured patch of green,

I faced a hillside rough with California chaparral:
Yucca, those burnt-out mountain candles, a gray thatch
On their giddy stalks where once they were white with bells,

Seized by ridiculous blossoming. A jester's rd
Riding the spiny back of a hedgehog, its nose in the sand.
Now they are the shell of what they were. Dead–

They seem dead. Posts sticking up like markers
On a lightning-leveled field. They will bloom again
In spring (I have seen it before). Back upstairs,

I returned to the fluorescent sunrise of my desk,
Where I clicked and moved yellow trains of text
Across my screen. It's been so many weeks

Since someone touched me that when
Sun Lee laid a job bag by my hand,
That moment her forearm brushed my skin

Brought brandy to my cheeks
And lips before I returned to the tall singleness of my stem.
Most days, I like these solitary weeks.

The intimate corners of my intimate bed. Sundown
In a house with candles. My own hands
On my own breasts. My spirit nobody's but my own.

My thoughts, ditto. My spaces, self-arranged.
In this decade I will not share with anyone
But my son. How I have changed,

As I open the door on a dark room with no one there,
To wooden train tracks on the floor,
Last night's Batman mug on the stairs.

Wanting mostly to stay warm
On nights I dream of a woman tangled in my hair,
Or my own hand reaching in a burrow, finding shy life inside of fur.

Sometimes, my ex brings our son to my apartment door
And asks whether I would like something casual
All night. And I say, "No." Thinking to stay reliable for–

For what? For whom? Here the weather is implacable.
Yours waxes and wanes like a moon.
I do not want something casual

With you. But for five weeks, your dawn messages in my ether
Have made the sun rise, and I jump out of bed
And into my day's solitary adventure

With your voice riding shotgun at my side.
After work today, I stepped off the edge of grass
Up the dusty slope where beige lizards hide

In tiny holes, where the cactus are anchored like thumbs
Among the spicy sage and desert paintbrush,
Inside the brown-green tangle of shrubs.

And sure I could make some comparison
Between blooming yucca and hope. But I believe
It is a cycle, and I question

The urge to deliver, every few years,
The baby of oneself whole to new home.
I am *so certain* I ought to live alone. But over

And over, I have taken the long road to the obvious.
I want to call this new way what it is:
How I am finding in sand, in dust

Enough for bloom, enough for sustenance.

SIDEKICKS

RON KOERTGE

They were never handsome and often came
with a hormone imbalance manifested by corpulence,
a yodel of a voice, or ears big as kidneys.

But each was brave. More than once a sidekick
has thrown himself in front of our hero to receive
the bullet or blow meant for that perfect
face and body.

Thankfully heroes never die and leave the sidekick
alone. We would not stand for it. Gabby or Pat,
Poncho or Andy remind us of the part of ourselves
that is painfully eager to please, always wants a hug,
and never gets enough.

Who could go to that funeral and watch the best
of ourselves lowered into the ground while the rest
just sat there, tears pouring off that enormous nose?

SHANGRI-LA

SUZANNE LUMMIS

*In New York they think all of California is like
L.A. and they think everyone in L.A. has a
maid. And they don't believe you if you try
to tell them.*

Radio talk show caller

It's true, here we are all blonde,
even in the dark, on Mondays
or in slow traffic.

Even in our off-guard moments,
startled by a passer-by,
we are young.

Here we are all privileged,
even in our sleep. At night
the maids hover like sweetly

tranquilized angels over
the glazed or enameled surface
of things, purring *clean clean* . . .

It's all true. We girls sip lemon-lime through a straw,
make love, Revlon our nails.
We take our long sleek legs out for a walk,
let them catch light.

When someone snaps, "Get real!"
it hurts us, real pain like we've seen
in the news. So we throw beach robes

over our tans, and cruise down the boulevard
tossing Lifesavers into our mouths,
car radios singing *am*.

New York, is it true
that in the rest of the world it is winter?

Our state is a mosaic of blue pools,
even the Mojave, and the palm trees
line up straight to the Sierra Nevadas,
And the surf comes down slow like
Delirious laundry, even near Fresno.

New York, is it true that great cold
makes the bones ache as if broken?

We're sorry we can't be reached
by plane or bus, sorry one can't pull
Even the tiniest thing out of a dream.
We're like the landscape inside
a plastic dome filled with water.

But turn us over, then upright.
See?
No snow falls.

SAFFRON

DAVID ST. JOHN

Even the thin tube of Spanish saffron
Sitting on the spice rack above the butcher block
Cooking table seems to glow with the worth
Of at least its weight in gold & today
At the beach a dozen Buddhist monks in golden
Robes stepped out of three limousines
To walk their Holy One out along the dunes

To the water's flayed edge where the sand burned
With a light one could only call in its reddish
Mustard radiance the essence of saffron
& what I remember most of the scene as
The Holy One knelt down to touch those waves
Was his sudden laughter & his joy & that
Billowing burnt lemon light opening across the sky

FAE

TIMOTHY STEELE

I bring Fae flowers. When I cross the street,
She meets and gives me lemons from her tree.
As if competitors in a Grand Prix,
The cars that speed past threaten to defeat
The sharing of our gardens and our labors.
Their automotive moral seems to be
That hell-for-leather traffic makes good neighbors.

Ten years a widow, standing at her gate,
She speaks of friends, her cat's trip to the vet,
A grandchild's struggle with the alphabet.
I conversationally reciprocate
What talk of work at school, not deep, not meaty.
Before I leave we study and regret
Her alley's newest samples of graffiti.

Then back across with caution: to enjoy
Fae's lemons, its essential I survive
Lemons that fellow Angelenos drive.
She's eighty-two; at forty, I'm a boy
She waves goodbye to me with her bouquet
This place was beanfields back in '35
When she moved with her husband to L.A.

THE TEN MILLION FLAMES OF LOS ANGELES
—a New Year's poem, 1994

AMY UYEMATSU

I've always been afraid of death by fire,
I am eight or nine when I see the remnants of a cross
burning n the Jacobs' front lawn,
seventeen when Watts explodes in '65
forty-four when Watts blazes again in 1992.
For days the sky scatters soot and ash which cling to my skin,
The smell of burning metal everywhere. And I recall
James Baldwin's warning about the fire next time.

> *Fires keep burning in my city of the angels,*
> *from South Central to Hollywood,*
> *burn, baby, burn.*

In '93 LA's Santana winds incinerate Laguna and Malibu.
Once the firestorm begins, wind and heat regenerate
on their own, unleashing a fury so unforgiving
it must be a warning from the gods.

> *Fires keep burning in my city of the angels,*
> *from South Central to Hollywood,*
> *burn, LA, burn.*

Everybody says we're all going to hell.
No home safe
from any tagger, gangster, carjacker, neighbor.
LA gets meaner by the minute
as we turn our backs
on another generation of young men,
become too used to this condition

of children killing children
I wonder who to fear more.

Fires keep burning in my city of the angels,
But I hear someone whisper,
"Mi angelita, come closer."

Though I ready myself for the near conflagration,
I feel myself giving in to something I can't name.
I smile more at strangers, leave big tips to waitresses,
laugh when I'm stuck on the freeway, content
just listening to B.B. King's "Why I sing the Blues."

"Mi angelita, come closer."

I'm starting to believe in a flame
Which tries to breathe in each of us
I see young Chicanos fasting one more day
in a hunger strike for education,
read about gang members preaching peace in the 'hood,
hear Reginald Denny forgive the men
who nearly beat him to death
I look at people I know, as if for the first time,
Sure that some are angels. I like the unlikeliness
of this unhandsome crew–the men losing their hair,
Needing a shave, those with dark shining
eyes, and the grey-haired woman, rage
and grace in each sturdy step.
What is this fire I feel, this fire which breathes freely
inside without burning them alive

Fires keep burning in my city of angels,
But someone calls to me,
"Angelira, do not run from the flame."

ENGLISH CON SALSA

GINA VALDÉS

Welcome ESL 100, English Surely Latinized
inglés con chile y cilantro, English as American
as Benito Juárez. Welcome, muchachos from Xochicalco,
learn the language of dólares and dolores, of kings
and queens, of Donald Duck and Batman. Holy Toluca!
In four months you'll be speaking like George Washington,
in four weeks you can ask, More coffee? in two months
you can say, May I take your order? In one year you
can ask for a raise, cool as the Tuxpan River.

Welcome, muchachas from Teocaltiche, in this class
we speak English refrito, English con sal y limón,
English thick as mango juice, English poured from
a clay jug, English tuned like a requinto from Uruapan,
English lighted by Oaxacan dawns, English spiked
with mezcal from Mitla, English with a red cactus
flower blooming in its heart.

Welcome, welcome, amigos del sur, bring your Zapotec
tongues, your Nahuatl tones, your patience of pyramids,
your red suns and golden moons, your guardian angels,
your duendes, your patron saints, Santa Tristeza,
Santa Alegría, Santo Todolopuede. We will sprinkle
holy water on pronouns, make the sign of the cross
on past participles, jump like fish from Lake Pátzcuaro
on gerunds, pour tequila from Jalisco on future perfects,
say shoes and shit, grab a cool verb and a pollo loco
and dance on the walls like chapulines.

When a teacher from La Jolla or a cowboy from Santee
asks you, Do you speak English? You'll answer, Sí, yes,
simón, of course, I love English!

And you'll hum
A Mixtec chant that touches la tierra and the heavens.

DEATH COMES TO THE BABY BOOM

CHARLES HARPER WEBB

Fire drills didn't get us ready, or bomb shelters,
or *Dracula Has Risen from the Grave.*
        Not even
Vietnam prepared us for the ice-cream truck

jingling "Stars and Stripes Forever" as Death waves
        pink Torpedos, exploding Eskimo
            Pies. Death comes
to us with a gray beard, leading a horse for picture-

taking. "Who is this clown–Gabby Hayes?" Bill quips,
        and feels a vein in his head blow. Death comes
            to us
as a new black-and-white TV. We watched Pinky

Lee clutch his chest and fall, gasping "Help me,"
        to fifteen million kids. Still, we're amazed
            when Death–looking
like Howdy Doody, Phineas T. Bluster,

Princes Summer-Fall-Winter-Spring delivers milk
        laced with arsenic to our front door. Our friends
            scare us:
Clare's breasts, Harold's belly, Bobby's hair.

We dodge mirrors, skittish as vampires. Bad-thought
        alarm! Call 911 to report an Unsettling
            Thing! Death comes
As the Gillette Fight of the Week Turn it on;

162

Sugar Ray's bony fist floor us; razors slit
        our jugulars and writs. Death comes humming,
             "Bryl Cream,
a little dab'll do ya." Death uses

Wild Root Cream Oil, Charlie. Death vows, "Some day,
        Alice–Pow! Right to the moon!" Death comes
             as a Dumbo
pen, blacking our teeth. Death comes as a brain-

eating Davy Crockett hat. Death comes as Elvis,
        crooning "Heart-Failure Hotel," "Hound Dog"
             ripping our throats,
hit 45s screaming like Dad's circular saw.

Death comes to us as a Mark Wilson Magic Set.
        Climb in the box; you won't climb out. Death comes
             as a black
hula hoop. Slip it over your head ; you disappear.

Escaping from Autopia

Chryss Yost

but even leaving, longing to be back,
to do again what I did yesterday–
I, Miss Highway, I couldn't drive off track

or crash. I joined the candy-coated pack
to follow yellow lines and concrete, gray
but even. Leaving. Longing to be back

beyond those lines, in other lines. Like smack
these flashback rides, E-ticket crack: You pay
you have to stay. I couldn't drive off track,

or spin to face my enemies' attack.
The road signs told me "NOW LEAVING L.A."
but even leaving, longing to be back

to go again. I knew I had a knack
for getting there and going. Child's play,
And anyway, I couldn't drive off track,

once safety-strapped onto that strip of black.
I couldn't lose or get lost on the way,
but even leaving, longing to be back
and be okay. I couldn't drive off track.

IV

THE WORD RESONATES

AMERICAN IDOLS

JOHN POWERS

A few weeks after the death of John Cassavetes in 1989, I was out drinking with an Australian documentarian who toasted the late filmmaker for never selling out. "Say what you will about him," Dennis bellowed, "you have to admit that he stayed the distance."

I thought of these words as I read *Waiting Period*, the new book by the seventy-four-year-old, L.A.-based novelist Hubert Selby Jr., who shares Cassavetes' cussed insistence on grappling with human passions in a way that most people find weird, even scary. Although you wouldn't know it from the press coverage (for instance, David Ebershoff's clueless review in last Sunday's *L.A. Times*), Selby is a major American author who has produced at least two novels of indisputable greatness—*Last Exit to Brooklyn* and *The Room*—and would, in a just world, be reckoned superior to such sleek literary politicians as John Updike or faux renegades as William Burroughs, the Deepak Chopra of junkie-lifestyle hipsterism.

Selby has always had a gift for making you feel the envies, lusts, murderous rages and devouring melancholies that boil beneath the surface of daily life. This takes a bleakly funny form in *Waiting Period*, a warped tale of justice whose antihero Jack begins the book by deciding to shoot himself, but during the waiting period for getting his gun, decides it would be wiser to poison those who've made the world so miserable. And so he starts doing just that, while we follow his every thought in a claustrophobic interior monologue occasionally punctuated by a second voice (God's? Satan's? Selby's?) that appears to endorse his lethal antics. By the time Jack goes after a white-racist murderer, we can't quite tell whether we're supposed to think this liberal vigilante is crazy or distributing an Old Testament form of moral retribution. What carries us along is Selby's style, whose supremely modern rhythms perfectly capture the eddies of a man's innermost thoughts and call forth echoes of urban masters from Dostoyevsky to Celine and Jim Thompson. It's the voice of the outsider who's attuned to everything the official culture won't say, or maybe *can't* say, about who we actually are.

While Selby's work doesn't sell in great numbers, he has always remained faithful to his way of seeing, which is another way of saying that he has integrity. Ever since the Romantics, Western culture has celebrated artists for pursuing their own unique visions, especially if it meant living free of ordinary society. Naturally, this didn't mean that writers or painters had to forgo all interest in fame or comfort (nobody expected Picasso to stay in a garret once his paintings started to sell) or that the culture business wasn't dominated by money. But celebrity and riches weren't essential to the bohemian ideal, the belief that it's honorable to spend your whole life making art, even if your paintings never sell, editors hate your poems or you tread the boards for years without ever being discovered by a big producer.

Not so long ago, there was grandeur in such a life, and the grandeur lay in the fact that it had no guarantees or safety nets—you could wind up at sixty, broke and unknown, having spent a lifetime working at jobs far beneath your capabilities. It's easy to picture a Godard who never got to make *Breathless*, a Bukowski never taken to Musso's by Sean and Madonna.

But ideas of the artist are hardly immutable, and we now live in a culture that shows very little respect for those who don't make it. A TV exec recently told me, "If a show's not a hit, it's nothing." And what's spooky is that the same attitude now dominates our society. *New York* magazine's Michael Wolff recently noted that the Manhattan elite has turned on longtime favorite Woody Allen, not simply because his movies have slipped and his social life is unsavory, but because he's entered an embarrassing state of "hitlessness." Things are even worse for those who were never hot. To use the sneering term of *American Idol*'s despised judge Simon Cowell, our culture now sees them as "losers."

Meanwhile, of course, the media relentlessly promote the "winners." Magazines keep churning out Power Lists (*Entertainment Weekly*'s recent "It" list anointed such titans as Lara Flynn Boyle), there's no escaping the articles about eighteen-year-old novelist Nick McDonell, who's just published a Manhattan knockoff of *Less Than Zero*, and every paper in America has urged us to read Alice Sebold's *The Lovely Bones* (my wife did, and liked it fine). A couple of Sundays ago, the *L.A. Times* ran a big article on novelist Michael Chabon's dealings with Hollywood, which sounded pretty darn pleasant: Why, the dude's getting six-figure options on short stories he hasn't even written yet.

Now, Chabon's a genuine literary talent, so I don't begrudge him the money (okay, maybe a little), but what made the story depressing was its fixation on his paychecks. Unlike earlier generations of writers in Hollywood who savaged the industry because they were ashamed to be hooked on its money, Chabon had nothing but good things to say about his dealings with Scott Rudin, even praising the "fruitful" notes that the thuggish but sensitive producer made on his scripts. (God, I'd love to see those.)

Then again, how could we expect otherwise? Selling out has become the national ethic. Presidents auction off nights in the Lincoln Bedroom or hit up drug companies for contributions right after proposing policies favorable to those very corporations. CEOs lie to inflate stock values so they can make a killing by selling off their own shares at artificial highs. Fabulously rich filmmakers like Spielberg stick product placements into "personal" movies, journalists like Andrew Sullivan cheerfully appear in Gap ads, *The Best Damn Sports Show Period* lets advertisers come up with skits and segments. You might chart our culture's changes by measuring the distance between Herman Melville writing *Moby Dick*, a viciously panned novel that anatomized the dark whorls of the American psyche, and his distant relative Moby, who uses that white whale's name to trademark the music that he instantly sells to commercials.

I remember my disillusionment when Lou Reed and Miles Davis first turned up on TV pitching motorcycles—it felt like a betrayal of some grand idea—but those born after 1970 would probably think me naive. They were raised to see such behavior as a necessary part of the gig: It's advertising, cross-promotion, *branding*. In fact, the moralistic phrase "selling out" barely makes sense in a society in which almost everyone is implicated with corporations and media (I myself worked happily for several years at *Vogue*), a society in which agonized shrieks of despair can quickly be turned into corporate product—and mansions for the shriekers. This isn't to say that every artist is eagerly grabbing at the golden ring (I haven't yet seen Thomas Pynchon flaunting his American Express card) or that it's become impossible to create good art: Moby's done some terrific songs. But our familiar ideas of the rebel and sellout no longer mean what they once did. The romantic era of the artist-as-outsider is over, a brief historical glitch in the long, complicated history of patronage. This is the age of the artist-entrepreneur.

As we try to figure out what exactly this might mean (do you enjoy David Byrne's music for Windows XP?) and get used to a society that increasingly respects only winners, I keep thinking about all the un-known artists out there who continue to pursue dreams colored with romantic idealism. L.A. is filled with writers, actors, musicians, paint-ers, comedians, performance artists, photographers and filmmakers, and we all know gifted, hard-working souls who never made it because they're unlucky, lacked connections, grew self-destructive, came along too early or too late, had slightly the wrong face, didn't know how to play the game or had just enough talent to make trying an inner necessity but not enough to make them great (the universe can be cruel this way). In these days when Adam Sandler tops *Forbes'* star-power rankings, we should be saluting the heroism of the men and women who spend long years waiting tables or riding buses in pursuit of some grander dream. In such devotion, there is no little nobility.

Speaking of which, I met Selby once, nearly a decade ago, when I drove him to a studio to do an interview for a documentary. Although he's known for his writing's dark intensity, he was all decency, warmth and intelligence. The crew declared him a Wise Man and I understood why he'd become one of L.A.'s best-loved literary figures among the kind of readers who'd never crack open an issue of *The New Yorker*. He was the kind of man who appealed to real outlaws and bohemians—ringe artists, actors strung out on drugs or their own craziness, rock & rollers who believe that the point of life is to give a rebel yell.

What I remember most clearly was the eagerness with which he accepted his small honorarium (he was obviously broke) and the worn look of his small apartment. I drove off stunned and ashamed that one of our greatest novelists should, in his 60s, have to live so humbly. I haven't seen him since, but I'm told he still lives in that apartment, still needs money and still keeps on writing. He's staying the distance.

July 2002

LITERARY RADIO

MARCOS M. VILLATORO

Los Angeles, many told me, is the place where no one reads. This I learned in the first few days of moving here in 1998. No one reads books, not like they do in that other city—you know. The Mecca of Publishing. The tabernacle of world lit. Here, we do movies. We read contracts, we write (or sign) deals. We spread ourselves across the broad screen. You're a writer? they said to me. Well son, you've come to the wrong place.

In my first few weeks here, my second novel was published. A local gentleman by the name of Marc Cooper invited me on his show at the KPFK Pacifica Radio studios. You know Marc. Only one of the most articulate journalists of our day; the English translator for Chile's president Salvador Allende in the 1970's, and now writer for the *Nation*. The guy who wrote the seminal memoir *Pinochet and Me*. That Marc. Marc and I had a fine chat on the radio about my book and the purpose of literature in contemporary society.

A few months later, Marc asked if I'd like to interview other authors for the radio. That sounded like fun. So I started driving across the illiterate tundra of my new home town to discuss literature with novelists and poets with books coming out. Many were from out of town and had drivers who escorted them from their hotel to the station; others simply drove to North Hollywood after dropping their daughter off to soccer practice.

A year later the interviews morphed into a Regular Scheduled Program. We called it *Shelf Life: Books from the Edge of the Shelf.* It plays weekly in southern California on Mondays at two in the afternoon.

It wasn't long before I started receiving phone calls from—yes, you guessed it—New York. Publicists, to be specific. Publicists who had heard of a new radio book show in Southern California. Publicists who understood that Angelenos buy more books then do New Yorkers in any given year. They knew that a good 150,000 of those book buyers were trapped on the 405 or the 110 at around two o'clock on Mondays.

Because let's face it: people who listen to public radio? They're the same people who claim Dutton's Brentwood Books or Vroman's as their favorite hangout.

For me, playing host to the radio show, it's been great fun. The guest writers also seem to enjoy themselves. Many times they're nervous, sitting in the coffee room at the station, waiting their turn. They're afraid of that first prologue of a question, "Now, Ms. Smiley, I've not gotten a chance to look at your novel *Horse Heaven*, so tell us about it. Is it about horses? Or religion?" At *Shelf Life*, their host is a fellow writer who has as part of his vocation the necessity of reading, so he's perused the book at hand with a writer's eye.

At first I thought my being a novelist would have been a hindrance, as writers are a competitive, butt-sniffing breed. Yet the very opposite has proven true: they learn of my own background behind the typewriter and thus relax behind the microphone, with that familiar "You understand my loneliness!" flashing across their faces.

So for twenty-seven and one half minutes we talk about their book, the craft of writing, the development of their characters, their struggle over plot. We talk mysteries, historical fictions, political novels. Michael Ondaatje discusses the art of film editing for *The English Patient*. Gioconda Belli talks about the Nicaraguan Revolution. Jeffrey Eugenides takes on a hermaphrodite.

In its first year, *Shelf Life* has found a growing audience. I judge this from the emails I receive after each Monday broadcast: the usual "Really interesting interview today" or "what was that writer's name again?" It's not a deluge of emails, but a trickle that's grown larger through the months. And I don't fool myself: my show is but one of a legion of shows in Los Angeles. For this town relies upon radio to make it through the day. How many hours do we sit in traffic, making our way from Long Beach to the Valley, working through the expanding and contracting snake of cars on the 405? For many of us, radio gets us there and back.

We have a lot to choose from. In the public radio arena, there are Larry Mantle and his two-hour morning show, Kitty Feldy and her afternoon hour and a half (both on KPCC). Switch to KCRW, you'll hear Warren Olney on *To the Point* and *Which Way L.A.?*, two of the smartest talk shows I've ever tuned in to (Warren has the gift of Bob Edwards:

questions so sharp you could cut paper with them, and an ability to make guests get to the point quickly. Each time I hear his "All right," I know the interview will move on in a timely manner). We've got Tavis Smiley, Neil Conan, Terry Gross, all NPR hosts.

Then, when you want to get *really* radical, you move the dial over to the figurative left a notch or two and tune into KPFK, 90.7 FM. Pacifica Radio. So dependent on listeners that it's perpetually poor, so free of ads and corporate funding and that it sometimes seems on the verge of ceasing to broadcast, the outspoken KPFK is public radio with an attitude.

And KPFK is where I've hung up a shingle for my little book show. At two o'clock every Monday, I do nothing more than join the constant conversation that happens throughout southern California—doing my part to keep the driving public informed, entertained, and hopefully pulling into their driveway safely.

This town doesn't just listen to radio. It *needs* radio to survive. To make it to work and back. To keep in touch with local communities and the globe. Public radio in Los Angeles does what any story sets out to do: teaches us and delights us. There are call-in shows, where we carefully cradle our cell phones to our necks and give our opinion on gay parents adopting and whether or not the Valley should secede. For those who are book readers, it's my pleasure to be a part of this large conversation through *Shelf Life*.

I'm not blind to the fact that if you throw a stick out your window here, you'll hit an actor in the head. Hollywood does run this town, just as German-based multi-billion-dollar corporations have bought up all the publishers in New York (Just wanting to be clear: wouldn't want to have you think that the New York *editors* run the literary show!). Yet there's something energetic about being a secondary character in the L.A. entertainment world: you've got to work at it to make your presence known. And if *Shelf Life* plays a tiny role in displaying the world of writers and readers in Southern California, as well as keeping in touch with everyone driving home, that's just fine with me.

January 2003

Auteurism's Great Snow Job

JUST IN TIME FOR THIS SPRING'S IMPENDING STRIKE, A LOOK AT
ELEVEN SCREENWRITERS YOU SHOULD KNOW—AND WHY YOU DON'T

David Kipen

I. Misdirection

To enter a parallel universe, just dial (323) 782–4591. A blithe male
voice speaks the titles of half a dozen or so current movies, the dates
and times they will screen at a certain private auditorium in Beverly
Hills, and finally the names of the filmmakers responsible. The titles
are largely familiar. The names, to any but the most idiosyncratic
cinephile, are not. In recent years, the recording might have alerted
callers to showtimes for Robert Rodat's *Saving Private Ryan*, say, or
Frederic Raphael's *Eyes Wide Shut*.

Has there been some mistake? Didn't Spielberg direct *Private Ryan*?
Didn't Kubrick direct *Eyes Wide Shut*?

Yes. As a matter of fact, they did. They just didn't write them. And
to the Writer's Guild of America's Film Society—if to practically no one
else in the film-going world—directing isn't everything. As for whether
there's been some mistake, in fact there has, and too many people have
been making it for far too long. It's called the auteur theory.

As developed by Francois Truffaut and other mid-century French
film critics who would soon become directors, and later refined and
popularized in America chiefly by Andrew Sarris; the theory would have
us believe that directors are the principal authors of their films. Further-
more, its adherents contend that the best directors are those whose personalities—despite the interference of studios, producers and other presumed philistines—assert themselves recognizably from film to film.

Alfred Hitchcock, for example, belongs in what Sarris dubbed the
auteurist "pantheon" because his films betray consistent preoccupations;
in his case, largely with themes of guilt, paranoia and mistaken identity.
Only a wiseacre would dare suggest that the surest way into the pan-

174

theon therefore is to make the same picture over and over. John Huston, meanwhile, never made the same movie twice; and therefore stands outside the pantheon as either a weak auteur or—it gets a little hazy here—no auteur at all.

The auteur theory has hardly stood unchallenged all these years. Critics came out of the woodwork to attack Sarris after the 1963 detonation of his original grenade in the spring issue of *Film Culture*, and later after his taxonomy of directorial gods and demigods appeared between covers in 1968 as *The American Cinema*. The redoubtable Pauline Kael—who has exerted as great an influence over the breezy, visceral style of contemporary film criticism as Sarris has over its auteurist substance—slugged back in 1971 with "Raising Kane," her book-length argument that Orson Welles hijacked most of the glory for *Citizen Kane* from its true auteur: screenwriter Herman Mankiewicz.

Then, in 1975, along came the only counterpuncher who ever really laid a glove on the auteurists. That's the year Richard Corliss published *Talking Pictures*, which survives—out of print, at least—as film criticism's greatest untaken turnoff. He constructed his own revisionist pantheon, and peopled it with favored screenwriters who had been locked out of Sarris' earlier shrine. For example, instead of Josef Von Sternberg (*Underworld*), Howard Hawks (*Scarface*) and Ernst Lubitsch (*Design for Living*), Corliss elevated Ben Hecht, the man who wrote all three pictures. Then he went looking for what themes each canonized screenwriter's filmography had in common.

II. Corliss Was Careless

There was just one problem: It didn't take. There are several possible reasons for this. First—and Corliss saw this one coming a mile away—there's the confounding question of credit. Never mind who's the auteur of a film; it's hard enough to figure out who's the author of the damn screenplay. Between source material and shared credits and adaptation credits and story credits and uncredited rewrites and on-set improvisation, how's anybody supposed to give credit where credit is due?

By scholarship, that's how. By sifting the drafts and interviewing the principals and recognizing their styles—in short, by doing the kind of old-fashioned spadework that requires too much patience for most film scholars or too much time for most well-meaning daily reviewers. It's far easier just to assign credit for a film to its director. This shortcut will usually be either wrong or, at best, incomplete, but it sure is quick.

Leaving aside the problems of imprecision and multiplicity in screenwriting credits, Corliss sabotaged his own campaign in at least three ways. First, he invited Sarris to write the introduction to his book. His nemesis obliged with an essay so sportingly self-deprecating that Corliss' manifesto wound up sounding reductionist by comparison. Like Mark Antony, Sarris pronounced his old NYU student Corliss an honorable man. The hint was not lost on the auteurist establishment Corliss had attacked, who, like good Roman legionnaires, promptly buried him for it.

More important, Corliss slighted contemporary film by reserving only half a dozen or so of the thirty-five niches in his pantheon for active screenwriters. As critical practice, this was unimpeachable. (Just as the dead outnumber the living, so it is with monographs about them, and rightly so.)

But as public relations, omitting all but a few working scenarists proved disastrous. Without much in the way of new work coming from his mostly deceased or retired pantheon, how could Corliss hope to be proven right or wrong, or to be argued about long enough for his ideas to gain purchase on the movie-going imagination?

By contrast, Sarris had evaluated more than a hundred directors in *The American Cinema*, many of them just starting out. He included two appendices totaling more than one hundred pages, supplying needed chronologies and credits to a generation of fledgling auteurists. Too often Sarris predicted greatness for the mediocre and mediocrity for the great, but to an entire generation of cinephiles, no night at the movies felt complete until they'd come home and compared their opinions of the director with his. People admired Corliss, but they rifled Sarris, absolutely dog-eared him.

Last but by no means least, Corliss was careless: He forgot to coin a catchy name for his theory. Whatever its failings as doctrine, auteurism represented a masterstroke of nomenclature. Suddenly, a generation of film geeks could now impress not only girls but also themselves by dropping a little French into the conversation. Next to the worldly wise weltschmerz of the "politique des auteurs," Corliss' "theory of screen-writers" sounded like a homework assignment.

III. The Schreiberite Heresy

So, if not "a theory of screenwriters," then what? Escriteurism? No, too derivative. To go with another French locution would be tantamount to surrender. Scenarism? Somehow it lacks that exoticism that only a foreign language can confer. But if not French, what?

Yiddish, of course. What language could better christen a script-based theory of film criticism than the mother tongue for many of America's first screenwriters, a language as intrinsically funny as French is highfalutin'? It naturally follows that the rightful name for this new heresy can only be the Schreiber Theory.

But is it too late for a late-blooming schreiber theory to supplant the hardy, non-native auteurist spore? Not by a long shot. The auteur theory is shakier than ever, thanks to a combination of bad late-career movies by some hitherto-promising pantheon candidates, an involuntary lack of productivity from others, and the generalized jejune awfulness of what passes for the American cinema in an increasingly globalized market.

The last-named factor doesn't bode much better for a screenwriter-centered movie universe than for a director-centered one. But it's still possible to concoct a long list of several active screenwriters who have more recognizable signatures and better batting averages than most auteurs. Indeed, the trick has proved to be keeping the list to manageable proportions.

What follows is a list of eleven reliably gifted contemporary screenwriters. Used right, it could help condition filmgoers to recognize and look for screenwriters' names—the way they already do for directors'.

IV. Eleven Good Writers

To qualify for inclusion among the eleven, writers had to meet three criteria. First, each should have at least one credit in the past decade. No sense duplicating Corliss' tactical miscalculation by shortchanging the current scene. In fact, many of the screenwriters below have movies opening in the new year. Some of these movies will most assuredly stink, thereby jeopardizing their writer's standing in the new pantheon. If too many stink, the new pantheon itself may topple. But if enough shine, or at least fail in interesting ways, they should reinforce the case for a writer-centered cosmology.

Second, look in vain for any writer-directors here. This condition is not imposed to impugn the frequently ambitious work coming from Cameron Crowe, Robert Towne, Ron Shelton or their like.

Instead, it's intended to throw a little overdue limelight on those writers who don't direct—who may, in some cases, be constitutionally maladapted to direct. Many writers tend, after all, to be solitary sorts, little given to the persuasive gregariousness a director needs. A good director—and make no mistake, a good screenwriter wants a good director, just as a good writer wants a good editor—excels at telling people what to do. A good writer feels more comfortable telling fictional characters what to do, and even they don't always listen.

Finally, everybody listed below has at least two movies to his credit. This stipulation leaves out terrific screenwriters like Charlie Kaufman—the credit for his genreless wonder *Being John Malkovich* all went to its director, Spike Jonze. Kaufman has two promising movies in the pipeline: *Human Nature*, a love triangle involving two primatologists and a man raised as an ape; and *Adaptation*, a puckishly titled reworking of Susan Orlean's book *The Orchid Thief*, to be directed by Jonze. Once these pictures come out, Kaufman's stock may soar or drop, but at the moment—for reasons better taken up shortly—he and other one-offs will have to wait.

Why eleven? First, because ten's not enough. Second, because ten hasn't exactly been the luckiest number for Hollywood screenwriters; the last man to draw up a list of ten screenwriters was Martin Dies of the House Un-American Activities Committee. And finally, because Mel Brooks had his numbers wrong in 1978, but his heart was in the right place. "Anybody can direct," he told *The New Yorker* that year. "There are only eleven good writers."

The List: Paul Attanasio: A former film critic for *The Washington Post*, Attanasio's credits include *Quiz Show*, *Donnie Brasco* and a stillunfilmed biopic of Lindbergh. The figure in the carpet here may be a preoccupation with ideas of assimilation, as with the narc Brasco's infiltration of a Mob family, or contestant Mark Van Doren's attempt to transcend his WASP caste and ingratiate himself into American mass culture.

Ted Tally: Author of the great play *Terra Nova* (about the practical Norseman Roald Amundsen's defeat of doomed, chivalrous English-man Robert Falcon Scott in the race for the South Pole), Tally's credits include *The Silence of the Lambs* and *All the Pretty Horses*. All three de-scribe a kind of Gotterdammerung, a twilight not of gods, but of god-like men and the passing of their courtly ways. These include the cow-boy way, the Victorian way and even the Lecter way, according to which a serial killer's victims are not brutally slaughtered, but sautéed.

Susannah Grant: A list truly reflecting the lopsided demographics of today's successful screenwriters should probably have half a woman on it, but Grant has distinguished herself lately with credits including *Ever After* and *Erin Brockovich*. Their shared-meaning element—as Webster's puts it when differentiating similar but not identical words—is not just the presence of strong, underestimated women, but of men in deus ex machina roles—Leonardo da Vinci in the first case, that biker/homebody in the second.

Frederic Raphael: Also an accomplished novelist and classicist, Raphael's several pre-*Eyes Wide Shut* credits include *Darling, Two for the Road* and the nonpareil British miniseries *The Glittering Prizes*. Our foremost romantic coroner, Raphael frequently tends to concern him-self with the decay of love—usually over an extended or fractured time scheme, preferably among the rich, and frequently marked by a sting-ing facility of language in both monologue and dialogue.

William Goldman: An atrophied novelist and screenwriting's frankest, funniest interpreter to the wider world, Goldman's credits in-clude *Butch Cassidy and the Sundance Kid* and *Marathon Man*, from his novel. Both pictures, and several of his other works, are about running away—Butch and the Kid from the Superposse to Bolivia, Babe Levy from a bunch of Nazis to the doorstep of anyone who'll let him in.

David Webb Peoples: A former film and sound editor, Peoples' credits include *Blade Runner* and *Unforgiven*. Both films follow laconic, vio-lent, disillusioned men who take on a dirty job, meet up with an innocent—a doe-eyed secretary, an aspiring gunfighter—and survive a horrific trial to win a measure of redemption.

William Broyles Jr.: A former editor at *Texas Monthly* and *Newsweek* and writer-producer for "*China Beach*," Broyles' credits include *Apollo 13*, *Cast Away* and the forthcoming remake of *Planet of the Apes*. Even the most dedicated auteurist would have to concede the motivic consistency of these pictures, all variations on the theme of exile and return.

Jean-Claude Carriere: Surely the only screenwriter to have worked with Luis Bunuel, Milos Forman, Volker Schlondorff, Andrzej Wajda, Philip Kaufman, Peter Brook and Louis Malle (directors all, but not a stiff in the bunch), Carriere's many credits include *The Tin Drum*, *Danton* and *The Unbearable Lightness of Being*. Carriere habitually treats the plight of the individual trapped by an oppressive, claustrophobic state—perhaps not surprising in the work of a diagnosed agoraphobe.

Neal Jimenez: A graduate of the UCLA screenwriting department (whose graduates, correlated against their cross-town rivals from USC, would offer still another way to re-sort recent film history for further study), Jimenez's credits include *River's Edge* and *The Waterdance*. In both examples, characters confront the inexplicable—the motiveless murder of a teenager by her boyfriend, the sudden paralysis of a paraplegic—and have dispiriting, unromantic sex before attaining some measure of compromised grace.

Eric Roth: Every great critical superstructure has at least one inexplicable exception. For auteurism, it's how a competent journeyman like Michael Curtiz could have made *Casablanca*. (When we consider that Julius and Philip Epstein and Howard Koch wrote it, things become a skootch more explicable.) For the schreiber theory, it's how a thoughtful screenwriter like Eric Roth, with intelligent scripts including *Forrest Gump* and *The Insider* to his credit, could ever have written *The Concorde: Airport '79*. The former pair both explore the problematic idea of trust—a corporation's trust in an employee, a whistle-blower's trust in a journalist, a simpleton's trust in the world's goodwill. Probably the Concorde passengers trusted the pilot, too.

Aaron Sorkin: For Sorkin, as for Attanasio, Broyles, Larry Gelbart (M*A*S*H), Joss Whedon (*Buffy the Vampire Slayer*) and so many others, the siren song of television's bigger paychecks and (relatively) smaller hassles with directors has proven hard to resist. Sorkin's credits include *The American President* and the adaptation of his play *A Few Good Men*, plus the television series *Sports Night* and *The West Wing*. Linking them all is a weakness for snappy byplay straight out of Ben Hecht, and a tendency to dramatize the writing process onscreen. His principal achievements to date, all enjoyable in varying degrees, are two movies about writing legal briefs and legislation, respectively, and two network series about writing sports news and political speeches. Now that's consistency.

There now, that drove a nice stake through the heart of auteurism, didn't it? No?

No. Of course not. What we have here is at best a hasty prolegomenon to any further writer-centered film criticism—hamstrung by what looks, in retrospect, like a partiality to white males that surpasses even that of the major studios whose work the list disproportionately favors. The roster completely ignores source material and collaborators, as well as dozens of films by the anointed eleven that don't fit their supposed signatures nearly as well as those it cites do. It also downplays most of their bad movies, and totally discounts the very real possibility that their distinctive signatures have emerged, not because they reflect the artists' inmost predilections, but because their employers typecast them and wouldn't let them do much else.

Now, what dubious French-derived school of film criticism does that remind us of? Hands?

You get the point. But director-centered and writer-centered film criticism are far from equally worthless. For a better idea of why, it may help to take a brief look at auteurism's secret idiot brother: management consulting.

Along about mid-century, America's managers looked around and noticed that their employees were doing all the work, while they were merely getting rich. All they had to show for everybody else's elbow grease was money and guilt. To massage their money, they devised tax shelters; to massage their guilt, an entire pseudoscience grew up around the motivation of other people—many of whom were already fully motivated by pride in workmanship, or by the need to provide for their families. The myth of the master manager was born.

The parallel to film directing isn't exactly opaque here. Every member of the filmmaking team—from the writer to the author of the source material, to the actors, to the director of photography, to the gaffer—has a story about seeing his own work attributed to someone else, usually the director, in a review. Perhaps only the director has no experience of this.

It's the classic worker's complaint: I did all this work, and my manager took the credit for it. Directors and managers alike live in fear of hearing the question, "Yes, but what exactly do you do?" So much so, in fact, that they've devised two separate answers for it. Their public answer is, more or less, "Delegate." Their private answer is, of course, "Everything."

V. Auteurism in Theory and Practice

Auteurism (like the schreiber theory) can really only be practiced in one way. A critic sees the films, looks up or compiles a filmmaker's filmography, and stares at it until patterns begin to emerge. Hardly anyone ever remarks on this low-tech methodology, but there's really no other way. That's how Truffaut must've done it, that's how Sarris must've done it, that's surely how Corliss did it, and that's by God how anybody else fool enough will do it, too.

Seen from the perspective of how auteurists actually work, we begin to see what so many of them have against versatility. It makes their job harder. What do Huston's *The African Queen* and *The Asphalt Jungle* have in common? Stare some more. Well, what do they? Tired yet? OK, come back to that one. Now, what do Hitchcock's *The Man Who Knew Too Much* (1935) and *The Man Who Knew Too Much* (1956) have in common? Of course! They were both directed by an auteur.

Stare at anything long enough, including clouds, stucco ceilings and John Huston's filmography, and patterns will begin to emerge. First thought, best thought—especially on deadline. Newspaper criticism may actually be the last vestige of automatic writing since the heyday of the surrealists. This isn't meant to invalidate all biographical criticism—the presumption that there's something to be gained by studying works of art by the same person together, rather than separately—just to humble those who would elevate it to the status of a manifesto.

Lost in most discussion of biographical criticism is what effect it has on those living artists it enthrones. Say you're Ted Tally, drunk with power now at having made the cut into the hallowed eleven. Hey, you say, damn if my work isn't marked by undercurrents of the Gotterdammerung. But what do you do next? Do you start sniffing around for a Wagner adaptation to take on? Or do you risk throwing those pigeonholing critics a curve, and do an original about the *The Twilight of the Mortals*, or *The Surprising Comeback of the Gods*?

VI. Open Letter to a Closed Shop

The schreiber theory can only ever be a subspecies of chaos theory—which doesn't make it unworkable, just more reliant on fuzzy logic than most intellectuals were ready to sound when Corliss first pointed the way in 1975. The smartest people in Hollywood generally agree that the auteur theory is arrant hogwash. Unfortunately, the smartest people in Hollywood are the screenwriters, who have even less power than esteem, and too often less self-esteem than either.

This year will test just how much power the writers of film and television really have, as their current contract runs out on May 1. That's May Day which, coincidentally, is what the film industry is already quietly screaming. No writers, no movies.

If prior years are any indication, there will indeed be a writers' strike this year, and it will not end soon. By contrast, directors' strikes can usually be measured in hours, after which interval the studios tend to cave and give the DGA everything the writers got and more—yet another sore point in the perpetual war between the canvas chairs and the swivel chairs.

Beyond the usual monetary negotiations over residuals in foreign, cable, satellite and even Internet markets, some of the WGA contract debate has thus far focused on the so-called possessory credit. This is the notorious "A film by" credit, which at best duplicates the director's credit, but at worst awards sole authorship of a film to a director-for-hire, who may have had nothing to do with it other than to call action and cut.

Almost all directors do more, of course, but none of them does it alone. Nevertheless, the possessory credit remains a cornerstone of the

DGA contract, and naturally the writers want it out. Such writer-directors as Phil Alden Robinson (*Field of Dreams*) have even tried to set a good example by voluntarily forgoing the possessory credit, even though they seem more entitled to it than most.

Other non-fiduciary issues in the contract talks include free rewrites—which some directors, producers and studios persist in expecting almost as a kind of conjugal right—and the right to attend rehearsals and shooting if the director has no objection. Yes, the writers' role in Hollywood has come to this: He currently lacks the right even to accept an invitation to the sound stage, and is in essence negotiating merely for the privilege of being kicked out should a director countermand such an invitation.

The writer's enforced absence is what accounts for those unforgivable, increasingly common moments in movies when an actor mispronounces words or phrases that his character would know as well as his or her own name. Would Kelly Preston, playing a reporter in *For Love of the Game*, ever have been allowed to refer to her "city editor," rather than her "city editor," if the woman who wrote the line had been present to help her? This wouldn't have usurped the director's responsibility for coaching a performance. It would merely have spared Preston the ridicule she widely suffered at the hands of newspaper reviewers who know all too well what a city editor is.

Thalberg said it succinctly in 1939: "The writer is the most important person in Hollywood, but we must never tell the sons of bitches." The wonder of it is, the sons of bitches have always known. They just kept it to themselves, or grumbled about it only in like-minded company.

Of course, if screenwriters are finally serious about overthrowing auteurist rule, they can start by not climbing all over themselves—and sometimes each other—to become directors. How is anybody supposed to respect a profession that everybody's forever stampeding to get out of, or at least trying to parlay into a dual career? Plus, it doesn't always work. The WGA rolls are littered with the stunted careers of those who have tried to bust out of the writers' ghetto and failed. They get into it principally to protect their scripts—"I only direct in self-defense," Brooks once said—but usually, one of several things befalls such would-be hyphenates:

One, they fail and can't regain their footing as screenwriters. Two, they neither fail nor succeed, but merely grow old waiting for a green light, like Richard Carstone in *Bleak House*, wasting away while suing for his legacy. Three, some succeed as directors, but—seduced by the prestige, happy to delegate such bothersome chores to underlings— they never write again. Or four, a happy remnant succeed as writer- directors, inflame the dreams of their fellow scribes and, like Towne, maybe even find time to write and direct a movie every five or six years. By contrast, with little aspiration to direct, Hecht's contemporary Jules Furthman—admittedly, under a more prolific system—helped write more than a hundred pictures.

VII. Twilight of the Auteurists

It would be nice to find a smoking gun, some canceled check in the Director's Guild archives made out by old DGA president Cecil B. DeMille to Andrew Sarris with a memo line reading "vast auteurist con- spiracy—PAID." But that's not going to happen. (Might make a nice maguffin for a Hollywood thriller, though.)

No, the auteurs trumped the schreibers through an honest but shabby confluence of directorial ego, writerly insecurity, shrewder collective bar- gaining, studio favoritism and critical laziness. The success of the auteur theory is the product of countless collaborators—just like the good movies it purports to explain, and the bad ones it labors to explain away.

In the French Resistance, of course, collaborators were shot; in Hol- lywood, the worst they can expect is a stab in the back. Between now and May Day, the backs of erstwhile collaborators—writers, studios, directors watching nervously from the sidelines—will be stabbed, scratched, and closely watched. Logs will be rolled and chips bargained. If the anticipated work stoppage comes to pass, we'll all have plenty of time to brush up on our old movies on video. Yesteryear's masterpieces should hold up to fresh scrutiny just fine. But can we say the same about our assumptions as to who made them?

April 2001

HIGH-TONE TALK

SCOTT TIMBERG

*Can LACMA's Paul Holdengräber, disciple of a long-dead
German intellectual, inject the spirit of haute culture into
this determinedly pop-art town?*

To optimists, the city has become an enormous radio: voices everywhere,
speaking, echoing, reflecting on matters cultural and civic. Of course,
you have to know where to look, when to listen, in this city of vast
distances and discontinuous neighborhoods. But series at bookstores,
universities, museums—not to mention smart talk shows on public radio, ideal for commuters stranded in cars—have never been more plen-
tiful in Los Angeles. The city, some say, is experiencing a renaissance of
talk. Think intellectuals and artists are gentle people? The Los Angeles
County Museum of Art, not long ago, became the site of a conversation
about art that turned ugly. The scene was a panel about Made in California, the museum's unconventional survey of the Golden State's visual
art and pop imagery over the last one hundred years, which engulfed
nearly the entire museum during its five-month run, was heavily attended by the public and roundly assaulted in the press. For the panel,
seven art professionals—scholars, curators, an art critic and an artist—
got together to offer attack, defense or postmortem.

The discussion almost immediately turned diffuse and frustrating:
To an onlooker, it was like watching seven different conversations in
seven different rooms. The speakers came down along predictable lines,
with the academics offering cheerily "inclusive" points of view, a *New
York Times* critic defending (sometimes eloquently) traditional standards
and a self-described Chicano artist hinting that the notion of quality
was code for elitist racism. The debate circled central points it never
fully engaged. In the audience, anger rose like smoke.

When it came to the question-and-answer period, many in the crowd
forgot Made in California and simply insulted the panelists. One ques-

tioner, asked to keep her query "pointed," insisted that there were no rules forbidding her opinion, which was far from congratulatory. UC Irvine professor Jon Wiener stood up and denounced the panelists' discussion as "pedestrian." The more criticism, the more the audience cheered and egged the assailants on. At event's end, as attendees and participants filed out to a friendly cocktail reception on the patio of the LACMA West building, it was clear that the discussion had gone nowhere and shed light on nothing.

"I think it was a disaster," says Paul Holdengräber, the impresario behind the evening. "A real disaster—but from the hundreds of messages we're getting, and from the fact that internally, within the museum, people are talking, the fact that it did happen was really important."

Holdengräber, who is the head of the Institute for Art and Culture, which sponsored the event, aims to offer "rigorous and lively debate" through his more-or-less monthly series at the museum, but he admits that this one delivered neither rigor nor liveliness. "I've gotten so many comments from people saying it was one of the best conversations they've heard," he says. "And I feel very sorry for these people. Like it's really too bad: 'I'm so sorry, what can I do to help?' "

Holdengräber, a pan-European educated in Paris and at Princeton, a self-described "linguistic monster," wants to get people thinking, speaking, engaging with high culture. He wants to reawaken the childlike sense of wonder, to sharpen minds without the usual academic pomposity. "The only way I remained awake," he says of his years in academia, "was by looking at other people fall asleep—that movement of the head that we can identify. And I do not particularly care for the lecture hall."

Despite Holdengräber's tangible goals, not everything he tries works out: An event last October with the intentionally tacky title "The Healing Power of Art" involved Russian satirists Komar and Melamid and comic writer Dave Eggers. The evening was intended to make arts mavens look at their own conformity and pious assumptions. To many who attended, though, the event was pointless and inane, lacking the spirit of laughter it promised. Holdengräber calls the appearance by abstract painter R.B. Kitaj, speaking about Van Gogh, "the Kitaj disaster" for its enormous preshow mess: 1,200 people showing up for an event that could only hold half that many, with actor Michael York holding a sign identifying himself, as if he were trying to jump a red velvet rope on Sunset. (The Institute has since begun a reservation policy.) But none of these events got as completely muddled as the Made in California panel—which left many in the audience as frustrated as did the LACMA exhibit itself. "You have to know how to fail brilliantly," Holdengräber says with an accent almost comically European. "And I did so just magnificently."

Fail or not, Holdengräber has put together the city's most in-demand intellectual series, one that books up as quickly as a Springsteen concert. "Paul is one of the great mad hatters of Los Angeles," says Michael Silverblatt, host of KCRW's literary interview show Bookworm. "His way with an event is to leave it free to succeed or fail. This is a great virtue. Usually you go to an event, and you know exactly how it will turn out. There's no excitement. Paul's things are exciting in mysterious ways. At the beginning of the series you didn't know if you were going to get in. There was an enormous sense of anticipation. He's an intellectual who wants to be a sideshow barker, or a sideshow barker who wants to be an intellectual."

Holdengräber has directed LACMA's Institute—a two-person team, plus a host of volunteers, that orchestrates the speaking series as well as internal museum events—for just over two years. In that time, he's brought Susan Sontag to discuss her novel In America, director Tim Robbins to interview lefty oral historian Studs Terkel and polymath memoirist Richard Rodriguez (Days of Obligation) to interview himself. ("He paced back and forth," Rodriguez recalls of his host, "like I was the pregnant wife and I was delivering.") He's hosted Jamaica Kincaid discussing Thomas Jefferson's relationship with his African slave, and writer Pico Iyer recounting the week he spent living at LAX as a metaphor for the human condition. Beat poet Lawrence Ferlinghetti appeared and drew a crowd of 2,000, way more than will fit into LACMA's Bing Auditorium. In March, painter David Hockney, discussing his discovery that painters as far back as the Renaissance used optical devices to aid their work, drew an enormous crowd as well. Coming up on May 31, jazz photographer William Claxton is scheduled. At each event, Holdengräber moderates as much as he thinks necessary. Though he constantly riffs on his favorite poets and philosophers, Holdengräber comes across like a big kid full of enthusiasm—a twelve-year-old on a sugar high—instead of a stodgy academic. He speaks six languages, four of them well, and slips from one to another to find the root word for whatever he's discussing. "What I like about him is that he's quite mad," says Rodriguez. "He's one of the very few people I know in the whole world who's in love with ideas, in love with language. And you can tell—it spills out of his mouth. It's wonderful to be with someone like that, impossible to love them, because they're always talking, they never shut up. But it's wonderful. He's sort of the last European in America."

Holdengräber is fond of saying that institute is a verb and not a noun, and that his goal is "to initiate, to instigate and, yes, to irritate!" He wants to leave his audiences with one impression: "Thinking is a pleasure."

He lived up to his ambitions not too long ago with a lively, illuminating evening around conductor Esa-Pekka Salonen and opera director Peter Sellars. The trio discussed the legacy of composer Igor Stravinsky: to Salonen, the artist of the century; to Sellars, a self-promoting monster who "looked through the trash and found God." The conversation, both high-minded and colloquial, managed to speak to many issues—the city's impact on artists, the rootlessness of modernism, fascism and folk culture, and, most memorably, exile. Holdengräber's genius was mostly to lie low and let the high-cheekboned conductor and the spike-haired director go at it. "Everybody there could take something from the evening," Holdengräber said later, "without it becoming populist, banalized, dumbed down."

It's evenings like this, and evenings like the angry and unfocussed Made in California panel, that show the difference between Holdengräber's efforts and a conventional speaking series. Like the guests he favors—Iyer, Rodriguez, Salonen—he's an exile, a polymath, someone who combines his backgrounds and travels in a way more fruitful, more provocative, than the usual multicultural clichés. "My motto," he says, "is rigorous and playful debate. Both of them can go together marvelously." Or, it turns out, terribly.

"People," he's fond of saying, "are hungry for substance." The Institute fills a vacuum, he says, satisfies a hunger. But to some Angelenos, the city's awash in public conversation—from Andrea Grossman's Writers Bloc series to readings at bookstores to lectures at UCLA and USC and the Getty. Ralph Tornberg, the philanthropist who sponsors the

Institute, also helps fund series at two other museums. And besides all the private salons cropping up in the lavish homes of rich Westsiders, the city hosts groups like the Los Angeles Institute for the Humanities, whose members, including *L.A. Times* book editor Steve Wasserman, author Susan Faludi and poet-playwright Luis Alfaro, gather for monthly discussions. But there's no series as well-known or as longstanding as the program at New York's 92nd Street Y.

What's unique about Holdengräber's program—besides the heat it's generated around town—is its wide-ranging eclecticism and mix of high-tone discussion with a rare accessibility. The series is free, and while it helps to be on the Institute's mailing or email list, anyone who calls during the appointed reservation hour can get in, LACMA member or no. (The number to call for information, or to be added to the mailing list, is 323–857–6088; for reservations it's 877–522–6225.)

Iyer credits Holdengräber with splicing different traditions together in a way that duplicates L.A.'s wild diversity. "We're used to thinking of intellectuals, especially from the East Coast and Europe, as dour, skulking, downturned figures," he says. "And some people think of excitement as a sign of folly. But Paul, to a rare and heroic degree, manages to combine high spirits with high intellect, and to flood the book-lined study with light and spirit."

Author Carolyn See says he's gracious and charming and has a "civilizing influence." And Douglas Messerli, publisher of Sun and Moon Books, considers Holdengräber, and others like him, important to the city's evolution. "There's not quite a vacuum, but there's been a real lack of discourse. Sometimes when there is exchange people are baffled. I remember going to dinner parties when I first moved here, and if you had a spirited discussion, people were frightened."

Dissenters concede that Holdengräber is smart, and charming, but also sycophantic, covering his subjects in endless and rambling flattery. "In eighteenth century English literature there were these characters who were really well-versed in current chitchat," says one Angeleno, calling Holdengräber a creature of affectation and pretension. Others suspect him of fraudulence, wondering about the Austrian accent on this Texas native, this intellectual Barnum who seems to come alive around famous people. What's in it for Paul Holdengräber? they ask.

Holdengräber learned to argue almost before he learned to talk. "I grew up in a family where arguing was part of what you did," he says of his childhood in Mexico City, Switzerland, Vienna, Düsseldorf and Brussels. "We spoke about everything. Everything was an object of discussion and debate and difference of some kind." Holdengräber's parents were Viennese Jews who fled the Nazis in the late '30s, leaving Austria for Haiti, where they met as members of a small community of exiles. His father, a vegetable farmer and later a textile merchant, was an especially strong intellectual influence on Holdengräber, who was born in Houston. By the time he was four, they had left for Mexico. "Whenever we were having lunch and something came up that I didn't know he would say, 'Look it up!' When I was growing up, eight and nine, I had to write reports for him on books I read. I had to underline every word I didn't know. And that would make me go to the dictionary." Holdengräber and his father, he says, have been engaged in a vigorous but good-natured struggle all their lives. "When I was ten years old," he says, "my father thought I was already late because I had not read the complete works of Goethe."

Holdengräber went to college in Louvain, Belgium, where he was taught by pugnacious Jesuits, then to graduate school in Paris, where he studied with Michel Foucault and Roland Barthes—for better or worse, two of the most influential intellectuals of the last forty years. After taking a doctorate in comparative literature at Princeton in 1993, he taught at Williams College in western Massachusetts, a pretty place that lacked the grit and friction he wanted. Academia fostered an environment "that put boundaries on the imagination . . . where you write an article for forty-two people," he recalls. "My appetites are greater." By 1995 he was a postdoctoral fellow ("a jolly good fellow" is the phrase he can't resist using) at the Getty; he worked, over the year following, at the Getty Research Institute. In 1997 he came to LACMA to assist Stephanie Barron, chief curator of modern and contemporary exhibitions.

With Barron, he helped moderate some of the early elaborate planning meetings for Made in California, and moonlighted in the graduate school at Claremont College, teaching cultural studies. A few months later, he took the Institute—an idea already hatched by museum director Andrea Rich, but barely—and ran with it. The first event he orchestrated was anthologist Jerome Rothenberg performing prose poems by Picasso. "It's not as if we had a program in place and the Institute led a national search for someone to head it," says Barron. "The Institute took off in a way beyond anyone's expectations." Holdengräber's energetic, chaotic temperament and programming are not typical of the museum staff, Barron admits. "There are people who like it, and people who prefer that things be a little more planned out," she says. "You couldn't run an entire institution this way."

At the end of the Made in California panel, a local art critic came up to Holdengräber to tell him it was one of the worst things he had ever witnessed. "It was nearly as bad as the show," the critic said. Recalls Holdengräber: "And I wanted to talk to him about it, and he left! If you have grievances, express them!" Can conversations make a difference? Some come and go with no record or impact. Some become venerable institutions, like the series at the 92nd Street Y. Still others, like Socrates' often drunken discourses about sex and politics, alter the whole course of a civilization.

"I'm always surprised that Los Angeles doesn't have more forums like this," says Richard Rodriguez of Holdengräber's efforts. "It is clearly one of the great cultural capitals of the world, yet my sense as a Northern Californian is how little conversation at the civic level is happening in Southern California. And that means magazines, newspapers, television shows. Here you are, the pop media capital of the world, yet there is this kind of silence. So my sense of Paul from the beginning was that he wanted to get Los Angeles to focus on conversation."

Holdengräber is not the first Southlander to try to bring disparate members together for a dialogue about the city and its direction. In 1929, when Los Angeles had recently passed San Francisco in population and was beginning to feel its oats as an intellectual capital, a few dubious experimenters launched a journal called Opinion. From left to right, from anarchist to aesthete, the group centered around a charismatic poet and bookstore owner named Jacob Zeitlin. "Had satyrs been permitted in ancient Israel," Kevin Starr writes in Material Dreams, an L.A. history that documents the circle, "they would have resembled this small, dark, curly-haired, hawk-nose sensualist hierophant."

Though Zeitlin's journal folded—Opinion's editors, reputedly, had too many opinions—it helped instigate a movement of culturally ambitious men striving to build a regional culture outside the movie industry. With a zeal for book collecting developing in this still-provincial city, Zeitlin's bohemian group, along with others like the California Art Club, began to lay down an intellectual infrastructure for the city. Zeitlin, writer Carey McWilliams and others helped bring serious authors and serious classical music to the city, and began important modern art and photography collections. They also took the direction of their city personally— in marked contrast to the reckless boosterism and development being urged by the *L.A. Times*.

Like Zeitlin, who hitchhiked from Texas to California, hoping to bring Chicago-style literary populism to Los Angeles, Holdengräber aims to conjure the spirit of 1890s Vienna in the City of Angels by "bringing the arts to live together again, while at the same time making people less afraid." He's probably never appeared in public without quoting Oscar Wilde: "Either you make the arts popular or you make the people artistic."

Rodriguez thinks such efforts are important, especially in a state fragmented by so many languages, creeds and competing myths. "I think something will come out of California," he says, "beyond the bolshevism of Mike Davis and the despair of Joan Didion. And it will spring in relation to Paul's dream."

Holdengräber's intellectual hero is Walter Benjamin, a German intellectual (1892–1940) whose most famous photo shows him brooding behind an enormous moustache. Holdengräber wrote his doctoral thesis on the scholar; he can barely get through a conversation without quoting him or referring to one of his essays. Though Benjamin is best remembered today for pessimism and nostalgia, for committing suicide at the French border for fear of capture by the Gestapo, he was also a champion walker. (With Charles Baudelaire, he was strolling's poet laureate.) Some of his most famous essays are about the flaneur, a figure of inspired, nineteenth century aimlessness who walked to catch glimpses of passersby and "who demanded elbow room and was unwilling to forgo the life of a gentleman of leisure." The flaneur sought streets full of crowds but uncluttered by horse-drawn carriages. (Around 1840, they were known to take turtles walking along city avenues.) "To endow this crowd with a soul," Benjamin wrote, "is the very special purpose of the flaneur. His encounters with it are the experiences that he does not tire of telling about." A century and a half after the stroller's heyday, Holdengräber is driving down Fairfax Avenue, seeking to recapture the experience of which Benjamin wrote. But there are no crowds, no cobblestoned pavements, no ferries sighing along the Seine; instead of a few carriages, Fairfax is crowded with beat-up Chevys, street construction and SUVs. "Los Angeles is not particularly a city for the flaneur," he says as he cruises past the 99 Cent Store, "because flaneury presupposed rubbing shoulders, catching glances." He refers to a story of Poe's, a poem of Baudelaire's. "And here we are caught up in our cars, our own little universes." A little farther up Fairfax: "The security of this Park LaBrea, of all gated communities, is something I fear, somehow."

Holdengräber's indifference to the automobile goes way back. At sixteen, he hiked 170 miles across the Swiss countryside, and he claims to have walked every street in Paris from one side to the other. "When I was eighteen years old, instead of getting a car I asked my father for ten pairs of shoes, which I got. And I walked. I loved walking. I didn't like cars; I thought they changed people's relationship to the world. I feel lucky to have a father who was fearless about the world. He felt that his son should do what he did, which was hitchhike around the world. So when I was eighteen years old I came to the United States and hitchhiked around twenty-nine states. I was everyone's lost son. It teaches you how to entertain people with stories." An ambulance screams by.

Now he's approaching street construction, and tiring of driving. It clearly doesn't suit him. (He carries a cell phone almost exclusively so he can call his wife, Barbara Wansbrough, a Hollywood set decorator, when he gets lost, which is nearly every time he climbs into a car.) When he first moved to town, he only found his way home to Santa Monica by getting to Sunset and driving west to its end. "Do you know the famous lines of Benjamin's, from Berlin Chronicle, where he says, 'To find oneself in a city is easy—to lose oneself is an art'?"

Holdengräber gets out to walk, but there's no crowd. A few homeless men, a scattering of kids in backpacks getting off from school, but none of the charge, none of the random glances or serendipitous meetings that Holdengräber imagines from Benjamin or Baudelaire. He surveys abandoned side streets; his spirits droop. He drops into a dusty, delightfully obsessive Yiddish record store and comes alive again. "Our compatriot from the art museum!" says the shop's owner, Simon Rutberg, extending his hand. They discuss a Connie Francis version of "Havah Nagila" that Holdengräber wants to buy for his wife.

"I'm trying to get Mel Brooks to the Institute, to the museum," Holdengräber says, spotting one of Brooks' records on the counter. "What, does he paint?" says Rutberg, sweeping his hand over the wall behind him as if holding a dripping roller. "Two coats!"

Despite all its private pleasures, Los Angeles is a city in which the concept of "public" may be as dead as anywhere in the civilized world. Whether it's public spaces, public architecture, public schools or public transportation, Los Angeles keeps to itself, favors the private—especially compared with cities such as London or New York, established in more civic-minded centuries past. What L.A. has always needed is institutions that can knit the private factions together and instill in people a sense of living in a community. It's unlikely that Paul Holdengräber, in a monthly speaking series that accommodates only a few hundred, can pull off such a feat single-handedly. But he's setting a tone that the rest of the city can follow, however hard that may be. "I think sometimes that he doesn't know how rough-and-tumble this place is that we call California," Rodriguez says. "And in that sense how difficult his job is going to be. To get a conversation here is really going to be something. Because we're fragmented—not only physically and geographically, but in the ways we understand each other. For a city that is quite so confusing and confused as L.A., I find his fragmented intelligence to be quite thrilling and appropriate."

Says Silverblatt: "What I would like to see is the museum leave these things completely in Paul's hands. He's got ideas about how to stage an event, but the institution doesn't want anything unpredictable to happen. When you've got a person as inventive as Paul, you should trust him. I wouldn't like him as much if I didn't think him capable of both the wonderful and the terrible."

Holdengräber has bigger plans than the series, though. He'd like to do more events each year, and to bring Hollywood talent like Warren Beatty, Curtis Hanson, Steven Soderbergh and Susan Sarandon out to discuss issues that go beyond their next movies. "I want to connect in a meaningful way with the movie industry," he says. He'd like to become a full-scale public intellectual, to spend more time on the radio and in other media, to host a public television show modeled on National Public Radio's Fresh Air, to put together a mammoth event at the Hollywood Bowl.

In a city full of charlatans and false surfaces, where high culture often seems like an invader from another, older world, Holdengräber is that rarest of things: He is what he claims to be. What he claims to be, though, is a kind of intellectual huckster, a creative anarchist. "You don't get to be P.T. Barnum without the accusations of humbuggery," Silverblatt points out. "Is it a real bearded lady or is it a fake?" Holdengräber doesn't deliver each time out, but he's building an important forum in which people can dream, fight, argue. Says Iyer, "He marries exuberance to sophistication."

Here's Holdengräber, looking forward to an upcoming show: "When the line wraps four times around the Bing and five hundred people are terribly angry, and I get one hundred letters: 'How dare you! I am such and such!' . . ." Holdengräber pauses to laugh. "It's fine. The whole world should have this problem!"

May 2001

THE MYSTERY OF INFLUENCE

WHY RAYMOND CHANDLER PERSISTS WHILE SO MANY
MORE RESPECTED WRITERS ARE FORGOTTON.

PICO IYER

I opened my eyes, in no hurry to wake up. The memory that started off my Sunday was Dona Maura's fingers on the table. I closed my eyes and tried. It was after eleven and I'd slept enough. The light that worked its way through the venetian blinds was weak, almost nonexistent and was accompanied by the sound of rain, which I wasn't sure if I really heard or just imagined . . . The vision that greeted me in the mirror was of a man whose hair and general demeanor recalled one of the Marx Brothers.

This passage from the Brazilian novel *The Silence of the Rain*, by Luiz Alfredo Garcia-Roza, just translated into English, brings with it a kind of déjà vu. Something is being conjured up out of the collective memory—the rain, the loneliness, the restless man alone—that feels as familiar, the worldly-wise narrator would no doubt say, as a hangover on a Sunday morning. Inspector Espinosa writes with a Parker pen that "dated back to the war—the second, naturally"; he envies the "cops in American movies." When he gets home at night there's no wife, or even dog, to greet him, just an answering machine; for breakfast he munches on leftover cheese, and admits, "It wasn't brunch at the Plaza, but it would do." When the narrative switches to the third person and we see the inspector from outside wandering, as often as not, from a local McDonald's to the Forensic Institute, it is to find that he "walked across the weight room like a priest walking through a nudist colony."

That simile is the tip-off: here is none other than Philip Marlowe, the iconic gumshoe patented by Raymond Chandler, translated into modern-day Rio and outfitted with a few local mannerisms and a new name. It is not entirely surprising to find Marlowe walking the sun-bleached, crime-riddled streets of Rio. Of all the great figures of the

197

American Century, he seems one of the most durable, in part because he travels so widely and so well. Hakuri Murakami, who has quietly revolutionized Japanese literature with his everyday mysteries of identity and disappearance (who am I, and what happened to that memory—that girl—that was here a moment ago?), began his career by translating Chandler, among others, into kanji and katakana script. Fay Weldon, in her recent autobiography, confesses to growing up on Chandler at her Scottish-inflected school in New Zealand. Many of the most distinctive writers to have come from Los Angeles in recent years, from Ross Macdonald and Walter Mosley to Kem Nunn and even Bret Easton Ellis (those coyotes howling in the hills), could never have written without Chandler's shadow by their side. And his list of admirers extends to even more unexpected places—W.H. Auden, Somerset Maugham, and now Garcia-Roza. "I opened a beer and waited for the three beeps from the microwave," says Inspector Espinosa, and we are instantly on familiar ground again.

Influence is a curious thing, as the Everyman's Library release of the first complete collection of Chandler's short stories (and its simultaneous release of two omnibus editions of his novels) underlines. There is, after all, no anniversary to celebrate, no ostensible reason why Chandler should be brought before the public eye again (none of his seven novels has ever been out of print). Yet he seems as central to us today as the Nobel Prize-winning poet born in the same year as he was, who likewise commuted between the English and the American ways of seeing things to suggest a modern fracture, T.S. Eliot. Dreiser, Lewis, Upton Sinclair are all more warmly received into the canon, yet none of them gave us a voice, a presence—a moral stance, really—as easy to recognize as hard to forget as Raymond Chandler did.

Even fewer American writers of the past century gave us a location (in Chandler's case, Los Angeles) that casts such a mythic spell. L.A., in Chandler's fiction, is not only a femme fatale but a shorthand for illusion; Hollywood comes to seem an allegorical zone in which nobody is what he seems (not even the straight-talking detective), morality itself is in turnaround, and the self is undergoing its ninth rewrite, being worked on by other hands. Even those who have never head of Marlowe recognize, almost instinctively, the setting in which we most often find him: the rain-washed streets, broken neon flickering above the empty hotel, the darkened room. Chandler's favored locales have become as familiar as the souls who inhabit them, the dangerous blondes circling around a loner who hides his soft heart behind quick quips and a hopeful bravado.

One way to explain Chandler's continued hold on us is to point out that hew was among the first writers lucky enough to begin creating novels just as the movies were asserting their force as the mass art form of the American moment; like Graham Greene in his way (and more recently, Elmore Leonard), Chandler wrote with the movies and sometimes for them, even when he was only writing novels. Whereas at the novelists of a slightly earlier generation—Faulkner and Fitzgerald, famously—lost their way in trying to become screenwriters, Chandler allowed the movie's sense of story to quicken his prose even as his feel for atmosphere colored the films around him. Six of his works were made into motion pictures, and twice he was nominated for an Academy Award (for *Double Indemnity*, which he wrote with Billy Wilder, and *The Blue Dahlia*, which he adapted from a work in progress). At some level Humphrey Bogart-prep-school dropout turned romantic loner—could never have existed if Chandler had not invented him.

To this day Chandler's stamp is most obvious in the movies, from *Chinatown* to *L.A. Confidential*; when Christopher Nolan, the director of *Memento*, made his first film, *Following*, on a tiny budget in contemporary London, he based his story (a story, as it happens, of a burglar's ruthlessness) on a two-timing blonde who wears her hair lie a forties heroine and a lonely dupe in a small room with a typewriter and a picture of Marilyn Monroe on his wall. Yet there were other writers—James M. Cain, Jim Thompson, and especially Chandler's immediate inspiration, Dashiell Hammett—who gave us the noir voice, too. What is it about Chandler that moved Evelyn Waugh, of all people to refer to him, in the late forties, as "the greatest living American novelist"?

The Everyman's Library stories, a few of them long unavailable and the rest drawn from hard-to-find collections, suggest an answer by showing how Chandler wrote before he was truly Chandlerian. Mostly written in the thirties (the years running up to the publication of his first novel, *The Big Sleep*, in 1939) for such pulp magazines as *Black Mask* and *Dime Detective*, Chandler's earliest warm-up exercises feature a kind of proto—Marlowe known as Mallory, who struggles, of course, to bring justice to an L.A. that probably thought the *Morte d'Arthur* was an Italian joint on Sunset. (Chandler himself was literate enough to recall, no doubt, that the real Sir Thomas Malory, who gave us our sense of high chivalry, was, in William Gass's words, "charged with robbing churches, with extortion, with rape, and jailed nine times by our least numerous count.")

Earlier detective writers such as Hammett, had perfected the story of action; Chandler in some sense extended their work into an entire vision, a *Pilgrim's Progress* through a culture that had never heard of Bunyan. It is no surprise that in the course of his career Marlowe comes to the rescue of a woman called Miss Quest and falls for a cop's daughter called Miss Pride. The very first page of his first novel finds him sidling up to a rich man's mansion and taking note of a stained-glass panel of a knight in dark armor trying to help a naked lady. If he lived in the house, Marlowe thinks, he'd probably be trying to help the knight.

A little of what Chandler brought to the form, then, is reflected just in the way he took the brute monosyllables of Hammett's detective, Sam Spade, and turned them into more flowery and literary-sounding Mallory than Philip Marlowe. Yet in the early stories, Chandler is locked inside a bare-bones formula; trying to embellish it he sounds very much like today's Chandler imitators: "Beautiful hands are as rare as jacaranda trees in bloom, in a city where pretty faces are as common as runs in dollar stockings." Three similes appear in consecutive sentences; adjectives are thrown on as if they were exotic spices.

One unusual aspect of Chandler's literary career is that he published his first story when he was forty-five, his first novel when he was fifty, after a long career as an executive for various oil companies. Thus he and his central character are already bruised and disenchanted when we meet them—yet never without a touch of schoolboy romanticism, and even the hope of something better. Even in his often wooden apprentice exercises Chandler had his hold firmly on the two characters that would distinguish him forever, the knight-errant detective, living alone with his wounds, and the woman, the city that is usually about to bring him down.

Somehow it is always night in Chandler's Los Angeles, and the fog is coming in off the ocean while lights up above, beckoning and half unreal, belong to the houses of the crooked. Chandler's gift always, was to see that the sunshine is the least interesting thing about California; all that is real there happens in the shadows. Darkness, in fact, is what gives dimension to the place, as the bright surfaces of the day are peeled back to reveal something troubled. In books such as *The Little Sister*, Chandler would give us near-perfect Hollywood novels, n which the exotic Mexican beauty turns out to be a gangster's moll from Cleveland, and the movie star comes from Manhattan, Kansas. But all his books, really, are meditations on false fronts and borrowed identities, on a world in which everyone is on the make; Los Angeles is a "paradise of fakers," for which Hollywood is really just a symbol. Chandler located abortionists, dope addicts, and beatniks before the rest of America knew that such characters existed; but deeper than that, he saw how people were beginning to take their cues, their lives, even their sense of themselves, from he unreal characters onscreen. In one of the stories, a man wears a hat "which looked like a reporter's hat in a movie"; ten pages later the lobby of a private club "looked like an MGM set for a night club."

The persistent image for the treacherous allure of California, is, of course, the blonde, not because Chandler was a misogynist but because a beautiful woman was the thing most unsettling to a susceptive man alone—especially a man with a quixotic taste for gallantry. The women in Chandler's fiction make for his detective s much more trouble than the men make from them and there is always the sense—a sense that gives the stories much of their psychological unease—that the man who can handle killers and lowlifes so effectively is undefended, at some level, against women (or, at least, against the softer and more credulous side of him that women arouse). The real action and tension in most of the stories comes from this intricate dance with and around attraction.

Toward the end of his career, Chandler started bringing these themes to the fore, having Marlowe reminisce about the love he has never really gotten over, while the women around him start asking ever more searching and personal questions.

"You in show business?"

"Just the opposite of show business. I'm in the hide-and-seek business."

Yet greater explicitness was unnecessary. The charged space in Chandler's writing is the space, often very small, that separates Marlowe from whatever woman is coming on to him.

Style is the easiest thing to admire about Chandler, of course, and his most famous device, the simile, is a perfect way of catching a world in which everyone is playing at being something else. "The swell," you read of the ocean near San Diego, "is as gentle as an old lady singing hymns," and with that inflection you inhale essence of Chandler. His style (like Hemingway's) is so easy to imitate that it becomes almost impossible to transcend. Yet one thing about Chandler that put him beyond the reach of many of his disciples is that, apart from the smell of the sage and the sound of the ocean in the distance, the red lights disappearing off toward Ventura and the suburban houses with their curtains drawn in midday, what Chandler was really doing was mixing worlds that had seldom heard of one another's existence. "People who spend their money for second-hand sex jags are as nervous as dowagers who can't find he rest room," he writes in *The Big Sleep*, and one realizes how few writers conversant with secondhand sex jags were likely to write about dowagers (or vice versa). Much of the spin of his sentences comes from these unlikely juxtapositions ("Strictly speaking," says a thug in *The Little Sister*, "we don't have to get into no snarling match").

It is easy to forget, amid his California settings, that Chandler was classically educated at an English public school (the same school from which P.G. Wodehouse graduated four years before him), and that, as a faithful son of Anglo-Irish gentry, he fought in the trenches of World War I with the Gordon Highlanders. California has always been best seen by slightly questioning ironists from abroad (such as Chandler's movie colleagues Hitchcock and Wilder), but in Chandler's case there as the particular magic of a world of con men and "demi-virgins" being inspected by someone raised on Euripides and Victorian hymns. The fictional biography has Marlowe born in Santa Rosa and educated at the University of Oregon, but instinct tells us that he is really an English gentleman in mufti set loose on the mean streets of Bugsy Siegel and George Raft.

Chandler had few illusions about England. One of the most intriguing stories in the Everyman's collection is the last in the book, "English Summer," which was never published in his lifetime and was buried, in raw form, in one of his notebooks. One of only two Chandler stories set outside California, it takes place in England, and, moreover, a fragrant, never-never England where the seductions of California are even more chimerical: a woman's hair here is not blonde but "gold," the kind of hair that might belong to "a princess in a remote and bitter tower." (Chandler, one recalls, could even find in Bay City a place called the Tennyson Arms.) Yet for all the glamour of Lady Lakenham and her Elizabethan home, husbands are being knocked of and women are playing on men's weaknesses as expertly as they had in California. "Nasty," the totemic Chandler word that echoes on the second page of his first story, take s on an ever more disquieting nuance, as when the protagonist of "English Summer" puts his arms around a murderer: " 'He was always nasty,' " she says. " 'So I did what I did.' " At times Chandler sounds almost like D.H. Lawrence in his rage at England's proprieties ("so careless, so smooth, so utterly dead inside").

Yet Marlowe never relinquishes something in him of the classic public schoolboy, as anatomized so powerfully by John Le Carré and Graham Greene—romanticizing the women he does not otherwise know what to do with, nursing his pipe and his game of chess, dropping allusions to Eliot and Kierkegaard while thugs cosh him on the head. To the end of his days, Chandler drank the favorite drink of the raj-gin with lime juice—and lived by the code of his school and its famous old boy Ernest Shackleton. When Marlowe finally extends his trust to someone—Terry Lennox, in *The Long Goodbye*—it is largely, we feel, because the otherwise feckless-seeming Terry speaks in an English accent, has perfect manners, and is first seen in a sleek Rolls-Royce (most dangerous of all, Marlowe believes Terry to be a hero from the foxholes of World War II). And one has to recall that when Chandler visualized his books being turned into films, it was not Humphrey Bogart he saw as Philip Marlowe but, incredibly, Cary Grant.

Yet for all the foreign airs and graces combined, uncomfortably, wit a naked hatred of the rich), Chandler knew the inside of the grafter's world as if to the manner born. If you read Kevin Starr's latest volume in his ongoing history of California—*Embattled Dreams*, which covers the forties—you realize that Chandler was making none of his material up. LAPD detectives in the forties really did wear gold rings and shot suspects in the back; Starr reports, and when a body was found in the morning, the apartment of the deceased was sometimes on the market by late afternoon (thanks to cops more eager to secure a real estate agency's commission than to pursue a fleeing murderer.) Murders were so common in 1947 that roughly fifty of them were covered only on the back pages of the *Los Angeles Times* (where they were devoured by, among others, Thomas Mann), and even after the "Black Dahlia" case of the same year—a naked woman found in a car, sawed in half, her nickname taken from Chandler's film of the year before—there was never any shortage of juicy scandal: Walter Wanger, producer of *Joan of Arc*, shot his wife's lover in the scrotum; Robert Mitchum was set up in a marijuana bust.

What Chandler brought to all this was not just a foreign eye and sensibility but, more, an old-fashioned, even outdated moral sense that saw in L.A. a kind of Jacobean wasteland (it is a passing irony that Chandler also happens to be the name of the ruling family of Los Angeles, which, until recently, owned the *Los Angeles Times* and has bestowed upon the city, among other things, the Dorothy Chandler Pavilion). As Jonathan Lethem, who has smuggled some of Chandler into his own postmodern novels, said this summer at a Chandler celebration, the classic detective story presents us with a group of innocents from which we try to pick the guilty party; Chandler's work, by contrast, presents us with a group of guilty souls from whom Marlowe tries (with increasing bitterness) to find an innocent. And whenever he does find someone on whom he can project his hopes, that person turns out to be the most cunning dissembler of all.

Earlier this year *Tricycle*, the Buddhist magazine, ran an article portraying Philip Marlowe as a "true American bodhisattva," a "Zen Peacemaker" seeing through the emptiness of surfaces—California, a perfect image for what the Buddhists might call samsara—one who, holding to no creed, ventures out into the dark to banish illusion. This might sound far-fetched, but it is certainly true that in the Zen temples of Kyoto, near which I live, Chandler is devoured as eager as if he were Suzuki (one American Zen student I know wrote his master's thesis on Chandler's vision); and if this is not how most of us see the shopworn detective, it is, surely, part of how Chandler saw him. "Are you honest?" a woman asks our hero at one point. "Painfully," he answers. "I heard you leveled with the customers," says a client in the late story "The Pencil." "That's why I stay poor," says Marlowe.

Over and over we see Marlowe suffering from his attempts to remain upright in a cit that is all curves. Where a Hercule Poirot or a Sherlock Holmes, say, compels our admiration by brilliantly solving of some kind, Marlowe wins our sympathy by singularly failing to do so. He is always in the dark, at some level, getting the wrong end of the stick. The classic detective invariably gets his man; Marlowe usually fails even to get his woman. It is a measure of the kind of fiction that Chandler was producing; in fact, that the mysteries he contemplates (how can someone possibly betray a friend, and what is the right course of action in a society that's turned upside down?) are the kind that can never be solved.

Thus the very people Marlowe looks down upon from his dark aerie, invariably look down on him—the women because he has no money, the men because he has no clout. One stock scene in almost every Chandler story has someone asking the detective how much he earns, and, when answered honestly ($25 a day, plus expenses), greeting him with an incredulity that borders on contempt. "You're small-time," a hoodlum says to Marlowe in *The Long Goodbye*. "You're a piker, Marlowe. You're a peanut grifter. You're so little it takes a magnifying glass to see you." This strain of abuse continues until, by the final novel, *Playback*, he is being described as a "beat-up California peeper," a "dirty low-down detective," a "small-town nobody." "Well, what do you know?" a woman says when he insists on his honesty. "A dick with scruples." The men he meets hit him on the head, and the women hit him in ways that heave even more lasting injuries.

Psychologists, at this point, could talk of Chandler's own bitterness at being consigned to the small-town nowhere of genre fiction, even as his letters and essays were showing him to be among the most thoughtful American writers of his time; part of his frustration, often, was that he was writing books for readers who had no time for his allusions to Anatole France and *The Brothers Karamazov*, even as the people who might have enjoyed his digressive reflections felt embarrassed about opening books that were said to be crime fiction. If Marlowe's tragedy is to be a man of principle in a city where morality is a dirty word,

Chandler's was to be a figure of high culture (at least as he saw it) in a genre where fanciness was seen as a needless obstacle.

In his movie version of *The Long Goodbye*, from 1973—a film best savored if you assume it has little to do with Chandler—Robert Altman catches something of this sense of being out of time and place by having Elliott Gould, a Bogart of the seventies, drive around post-sixties L.A. in a sleek black roadster from the forties, dressed, almost pathetically, in a dark suit and tie even as the California girls around him are dancing around topless. "What the hell are you from?" a cop asks, Marlowe answers, "A long time ago." When Altman actually has Marlowe turn into a killer at the end; he is, in effect, killing off Marlowe himself, or at least that high heroic Marlowe that Chandler so defended. In the books, after all (on one of the last pages of the last novel), Marlowe walks away from a $5,000 payoff and, when pressed, suggests it be sent to the Police Relief Fund.

John Bayley, in his introduction to the stories, is one of those who disparages Chandler when he becomes serious and reflective, preferring instead the rat-a-tat-tat action of *The Big Sleep*. For those in search of vivid, fast-moving detective stories, rich with the smell of murder and honeysuckle, the early books are indeed the best; but for those of us who read Chandler not because of his plots but in spite of them (when asked by filmmakers shooting *The Big Sleep* to reveal who killed one of the characters, Chandler famously cabled back, "NO IDEA"), his writing is best when it leaves detective fiction behind altogether.

Chandler's culminating work, for this kind of reader, is without question, *The Long Goodbye*, which takes the love affair with Los Angeles to its last bitter gasp and, like the better kind of fiction, leaves us with more questions than it answers; one is more unsettled than satisfied at the book's conclusion. There are almost no one-liners in the book, and very few similes; most of the narrative seems to be moving away from any mystery of the kind that can be "solved." Marlowe dares to make himself vulnerable, even to lay himself on the line, for Terry Lennox, the smooth playboy who at some level represents everything Marlowe longs to be (with his nice manners and his background of heroism), and when Terry is found to have played him, the way everyone else does, there is nowhere for Marlowe to turn. Whatever illusions he kept himself going on before are now exhausted, and the detective-story formula so clearly shown in the early stories is stretched to the point where it snaps. When Marlowe, at the end of the book, takes a woman into his bed, for almost the only time in his career, it feels, in the context of his loneliness, less a triumph than a gesture of defeat.

By the time of the throwaway coda that is his final novel, *Playback*, the spirit of the books has vanished. Many of the story's characters are senior citizens, and, instead of L.A., the detective tools around the affluent San Diego suburbs of La Jolla, as Chandler did in his final years. Neither the author nor his detective even seems to have the strength for any wit—"Down below, the ocean was getting a lapis lazuli blue that somehow failed to remind me of Miss Vermilyea's eyes." As in the later stories, Chandler starts to turn a faintly therapeutic eye on Marlowe, and the fine balance of woundedness and conscience that distinguished him is gone. "Haven't you ever been in love?" a woman asks him, and then, "How can such a hard man be so gentle?" When Marlowe actually finds a virgin in his final published story, twenty eight years old and kind, he turns away from her regretfully. "I've had too many women to deserve one like you." In his final novel he likewise rejects a redhead (and *New Yorker* reader) who invites him to come and escape with her to "one of those tall apartment hoses along the ocean front in Rio" (where, we might imagine Inspector Espinosa lives).

Were Chandler to see how his character has been reborn in such a building (the dust jacket of *The Silence of the Rain* describes Espinosa as a blessed with "the mind of a philosopher, the heart of a romantic, and enough experience to realize that things are not always what they seem"), he might permit himself a smile. And were he to see how his books are being released with such fanfare—Professor Bayley acknowledging that his late wife, Iris Murdoch, was a Chandler aficionado, too—he might feel himself vindicated a little. Yet in his life he ended with a sense of failure. He had used up the form he took on, and there was nothing to put in its place. On the last page of the last novel, Marlowe seems to accept an offer of marriage, and for those of us who have followed him through a quarter of a century, we know the jig is up. A married Marlowe is about as resonant as a Hamlet with two kids and a dog.

October 2002

V

REPRESENTATIVE AUTHORS

WALTER MOSLEY'S SECRET STORIES
A Ride With a Mystery Writer
Who Evokes the Unclichéd

LYNELL GEORGE

Midafternoon, and we are sailing. The wide span of Century Boulevard seems vast in its possibilities, a seductive expanse with room to roam or expand. At quick glimpse, it is sparkling, but a brief pause at a light reveals something quite different-a poorly patched facade, a wall of chain link encircling nothing, rubble from some long-lost decade left to rot or rust.

"Look at these giant streets!" Walter Mosley rides jump seat, taking in L.A. the way many Angelenos do, at forty-five-miles-per, the window raised, studying the blur of color and shapes skidding outside the windshield. We make a left onto Central Avenue, slowing enough to see features on figures sitting in Will Rogers Park. Picnics. A ballgame. Families, black and brown, taking advantage of the sun, the air carrying a cool mist that, with imagination, could conjure the nearby ocean. "These houses are nice—they're little, tiny," he says. "A lot of people come here and say: 'When are we gonna get to the bad community?' " The answer comes in a voice colored the softest shade of irony: "You're in it, brother."

At the tip of 76th Place and Central slumps the shell of a broken and singed mini-mall threatening complete collapse. The All-American Liquor Junior Market's marquee still advertises "Hot dogs $2.50," as if the building is only momentarily darkened, the owner under the weather or off on a brief vacation. And there are survivors—fish markets, a shoeshine parlor-cum-barbershop, a senior citizen center, the Universal Missionary Baptist Church, all grouped around empty lots strewn with trash and weeds.

Mosley grew up here, and he's been mining these broad streets, and their smaller side arteries, for stories for nearly half a dozen years. But at first, he doesn't seem to register the damaged terrain. Or doesn't speak about it. He's busier reconstructing the past, letting the vacant lots spark a fragment of a memory, reading the symbols in piles of wood and iron.

"When I was a kid along (this stretch of Central), there was a White Front, a hardware store, a liquor store, little markets and bars, a shoe store, television repair shops, a whole economic community," he recalls, his voice moving with a bit of a rhythmic lilt. In moments, he erects filling stations in empty lots, replaces the nuclear-age post office with the old Goodyear plant and a parking lot full of gleaming tail fins.

Mosley's measure of fame comes from the detective stories he's astutely woven from that vanished place. His mysteries are period works, spanning 1948–1961 on these streets—Denker and Slauson and hot-lit Central Avenue—where dreams and hard work intersect. And Ezekiel (Easy) Rawlins, his reluctant private eye, navigates the hurdles of this world—the Police Department, the subtleties of discrimination, unabashed racism—with both feet planted firmly on the sidewalks banking these wide boulevards. A protagonist acutely sensitive to the mercurial nature of his world, Easy's not quite a social commentator, nor an island of a private eye like Philip Marlowe. Instead, he's at the center, struggling, hoping to make it through one day into the next.

Easy Rawlins is about to appear on film, played by Denzel Washington, as Carl Franklin (*One False Move*) directs *Devil in a Blue Dress*. *Devil* (1990) and Mosley's third book, *White Butterfly* (1992), were nominated for Edgar awards; *Butterfly* and his second, *A Red Death* (1991), were nominated for Golden Dagger awards (*Butterfly* won). President Bill Clinton has proclaimed Mosley his favorite mystery writer, and his works—which sell well but have not hit the best-seller charts pop-up on college reading lists with increasing frequency, surrounded by the works of Chester Himes, Richard Wright and Ralph Ellison, his most frequently cited literary forebears. The latest Rawlins installment, *Black Betty*, set at the dawn of the '60s, four years before Watts blew, is due next month.

L.A. itself, you could say, comes to Mosley in a dream. He lives in Greenwich Village in New York, estranged from this city for more than a decade—L.A. was a claustrophobic web of the too-familiar and the unattainable, and he had to escape—but he's never stopped feeling the pull of the city's possibilities. It's a somewhat idealized L.A. that Mosley creates in his books, patterned after the close, culturally diverse South Los Angeles community of his youth, not the alienating vastness he felt navigating through the rest of the city. He re-creates that early community, those connections, those voices, with memory, history and the grand stories of his late father, Leroy Mosley. The vision of Los Angeles that persists in his writing is a clever variation on the one he remembers but is worlds apart from the one he confronts on brief visits. Though the city inhabits his heart and head, "I don't get it from L.A.," he says. "I get it from how I stand in relation to L.A."

Writing about Easy, he says, "is in a way reclaiming experience." And in recasting the past, Mosley also lends a sense of clarity to the present—and possibly the future.

It is quintessential Raymond Chandler: "I went on out and Amos had the Caddy there waiting," Chandler's detective Philip Marlowe observes in *The Long Goodbye*. "He drove me back to Hollywood. I offered him a buck but he wouldn't take it. I offered to buy him the poems of T.S. Eliot. He said he already had them."

Amos, Chandler's "middle-aged colored chauffeur," is a shadow figure whom Walter Mosley would eagerly give flesh and form. With lyric grace, Mosley has evoked many of those who passed through in silence, subtly sketching faces and histories for figures that have appeared as ghosts in this genre.

It's 1948 when Easy Rawlins, in Mosley's first installment, is laid off from his aerospace job in Santa Monica. World War II had created a humming assembly line of defense-industry jobs that helped fuel a mass migration west to fill them. But when an exhausted Easy refuses to put in a little overtime after a particularly hard shift, his high-strung boss fires him, leaving Easy in a spot, unsure of how he'll raise his $64 mortgage payment. As he mulls it over in a neighborhood bar owned by an ex-boxer named Joppy, his answer sidles up to him: DeWitt Albright, a white man in a flashing white suit glaringly out of place in these environs, who knows a little too much about Easy's private affairs but offers him fast money to a find a white woman who "has a predilection for the company of Negroes." It's Easy's chance out.

"Working for Joppy's friend was the only way I saw to keep my house. But there was something wrong, I could feel it in my fingertips. DeWitt Albright made me uneasy. . . . I was unhappy about going to meet Mr. Albright because I wasn't used to going into white communities like Santa Monica to conduct business," says Easy, ". . .

but the idea that I'd give him the information he wanted, and that he'd give me enough money to pay the next month's mortgage, made me happy. I was dreaming about the day I'd be able to buy more houses, maybe even a duplex."

Easy is the tangible, full-coverage insurance, the safety net, for his clients, Mosley explains. "The idea about Easy is, who will be there for you when you really need it? And this is not whether you need ten dollars, this is like when you come running and somebody's after you. Easy is not the kind of guy who figures, 'Well if I do this, I'll get killed.' He says: 'I'll do this, and I might get killed but I'm going to do it anyway, because this is where you have to stand up.' "

When Mosley speaks of Easy, it's as if he's relating the escapades of an irascible cousin or the brother with the gold tooth who always gets the barber chair with the best light-a figure he knows inside and out. In the stories, Easy emerges as the sort of black male figure that so much of popular culture has collectively erased from public consciousness or has yet to find a place for at the dinner table. There is a familiarity about him, a human softness that despite the unrelenting violence of his life allows him to be sickened by the sight of a corpse or to open his heart and arms to children, whom he takes in like strays. There are friends to answer to, comeuppance to be paid. He, unlike Chandler's Marlowe, is irrevocably tied to his world, his community, the landscape. "He has a lot of commitments in the world. These people are people he knows and he's responsible for. I don't understand how somebody like Marlowe could live," says Mosley. "He had no friends, no lovers really. No children, no parents, no job. I mean nothing."

Easy's universality, his human side, appealed to Jesse Beaton, who is producing the film version of *Devil in a Blue Dress* with Gary Goetzman; Jonathan Demme and Ed Saxon are executive producers. Browsing at a West Hollywood bookstore, Beaton, who was eager to find another project to tackle after *One False Move*, pulled the book from the mystery shelves a few years back. She was taken by it for a couple of reasons. "There's so little documentation of that period in L.A. We know a lot about Harlem, what a rich, lively, vital world it was. Unfortunately, so much of that (L.A.) world is physically lost. Burned in fires, riots, re-zoned, crashed down, empty lots. Very little of Central Avenue remains. The Dunbar (Hotel) is there, but what was surrounding it is not." On a personal level, she emphasizes, "I was about to lose my house. I thought, in this world we live in, people who feel that they would never have anything in common with someone like Easy Rawlins do. We all are trying to hold on to that bit of the American dream. I felt that whoever you were, you would understand this. I lost my house," she says with a chuckle, "but Easy kept his."

Easy Rawlins has friends to spare, in more than one city. "He sort of represents that mass movement out of the South and into L.A. during the war," says David Fine, editor of the anthology *Los Angeles in Fiction* and professor of English at Cal State Long Beach. "Watts is filled with displaced Southerners. There is this sense in his novels of people living on the edge, being uprooted and displaced. I don't know anybody who writes about South Central that way. He's got a real sense of life lived exposed, raw, right on the edge of existence."

What makes Mosley's work sound authentic to many black readers' ears is that he never uses the shorthand "South-Central" in his writings. He steers clear of sweeping generalizations, working to create an image so clear one can see its pores or recognize the voice in the dark. Many a behatted church lady will be happy to tell you that before the '70s, "L.A. Negroes" lived on the east side or the west side of a city efficiently divided by Central Avenue. "It was wonderful," says Mosley's childhood friend Kirsten Childs, "to see (in Mosley's books) this place that's not a caricature and not smaller than life. Not meaner, not nicer. People live here, grow up and die here. It was like this whole world was created as I remembered it."

Some, like Richard Yarborough, associate professor of English and Afro-American studies at UCLA, compare Mosley's simple yet vivid landscapes to those of filmmaker Charles Burnett, who directed *To Sleep With Anger* and *Killer of Sheep*, both about black life in Los Angeles. Their manner of revealing the unclichéd complexities of life in black L.A. is often elegant, even in its grittiness. Yarborough sees the most striking similarities in the way Burnett's and Mosley's work shows big-city life in the postwar decades merging with the superstitions and pace of the South. And Mosley, he says, "captures the oral tradition right in the movement from the one site where it grew up to the other where it is changing. Easy can speak quote-unquote, conventional English, or he can speak black English. In 'A Red Death,' he is reading about Roman history, yet he has Army experience and is part of the street."

Easy finds his surest footing as a black everyman—someone's father, brother, cousin, lover—with bills to pay, marital problems, feuding friends and an insatiable lust for a life that is seldom anything less than hard. He's not a formal detective with a license, he's a "utility man" who does favors; in his part of town, he knows where to go, what to ask and how to ask it.

"I felt a secret glee when I went into a bar and ordered a beer with money someone else had paid me," Easy confides in *Devil in a Blue Dress*. "I'd ask the bartender his name and talk about anything, but really, behind my friendly talk, I was working to find something. Nobody knew what I was up to, and that made me sort of invisible; people thought that they saw me but what they really saw was an illusion of me, something that wasn't real."

There are many who might lay claim to being Mosley's paradigm for Easy. Neighborhood cronies. Back-room prophets. It's Mosley's father who's most often cited. But, says Mosley's friend Childs, "I know that Easy is based on a lot of different people, but there is a part of Easy that is definitely Walter. This major vulnerability. There were certain things that were letting you see part of Walter's soul, part of Walter's mind."

On one level, a pretty airtight argument can be made that Easy's progenitor, a man whose favorite color is gray, is just as elliptical as the character he so impeccably created. Even though he would furiously argue the point, he, too, could meld with the shadows—if his eyes didn't skitter about so much.

"Easy isn't a shadow," Mosley maintains, and so begins the dance, the teasing smile in his voice. "You know what he's thinking, doing. . . ."

"But the people in his life don't."

"True."

"So wouldn't that make him a shadow?"

"Well . . . not exactly."

The debate is interspersed with a running commentary as we drive through vaguely familiar haunts, but if the conversation veers too close to the territory Mosley chooses not to discuss, he deflects questions with veils of jokes and riddles and anecdotes or turns inquiries inside out. The entire production is performed always with the most elated version of his smile, fully revealing a generous gap separating his front teeth. Shifting characters, maybe slipping into the voice of Easy's best friend Mouse, or giving voice to an anonymous man standing on the corner, Mosley's a mimic at the ready with quick, and many times acerbic, remarks.

"In the '40s, there was a time of great hope in Los Angeles," he says, his eyes lit with the momentum of a story. "It was a big place, it was a countrified place. It was a place where if there was a job, the job was digging ditches, it wasn't somebody saying: 'We're looking for colored people or Japanese people (to dig) ditches.' It was, 'We're looking for people to dig ditches.' So no matter what color you were, you were working there. And if you were a white man and said: 'I'm not working next to that niggah,' they'd say, 'Well, get outta here, because I got twenty niggahs working here and I need to dig my ditches.' There was hope and opportunity. And as L.A. began to redefine that hope, that possibility, the dream lost a lot of its glitter. Even though a lot of the dream came true—a lot of us who came through that time became lawyers and doctors—still, a lot of us are down in the boarded-up 'hood."

At once warm and veiled, there is the public Mosley: the raconteur, the debater, the banterer, the charmer, the wild and wide-eyed eight-year-old; there is a more contained Mosley: the thinker, the analyst, the inquisitor. He's as obsessed with the intricacies of *Married With Children* as by the stories of his orphan father's vagabond youth in Louisiana and Texas. He's a conundrum who pulls from Louis Armstrong and folk singer Mary McCaslin with equal fervor and fascination.

"There is kind of an elusiveness to his soul," says Frederic Tuten, who was Mosley's writing instructor and is now his best friend. "I can't presume to say that I know Walter." This understanding seems only to deepen their connection. "We both have this kind of strange part of us that didn't grow up, so the world is always full of surprises. It's as if the two of us have been condemned to solitary confinement, and when we're let out, we are sort of amazed by what we see."

What passes in Mosley's view this particular afternoon is not the often-resurrected image of a bombed-out war zone, although these communities and their collections of wide boulevards and tree-lined streets are struggling with their wounds.

"It's just a community of scarring," says Mosley. "It started in '65 and (then) just got more and more." We roll along, verbally sifting the remains, wondering about the cause of the damage: urban unrest of '65 or '92? Maybe a neighborhood fire or the earthquake or just plain old garden-variety urban blight?

"There's great wealth in the city, but there is a kind of disintegration going on," he says, still watching, recording the image, possibly filing it away. He readjusts himself in the seat. "You have to understand the character of these people from the inside, not from the outside. I don't know who this fellow is," he says, gesturing toward a stout man in a three-piece suit, glasses, Bible in hand, his black hair powdered with patches of silver. "He's not walking like he's nervous, you know what I mean?"

Mosley believes, as do many African-American educators and pundits, that what rests at the core of this community's unraveling has less to do with absence of monetary riches than it does with historical amnesia. "An identity has been misplaced, and that's one of the things that I'm a very small part of. Everything that happens to black people in America is not talked about. So we lose it. It's not written down." Countering this loss within popular fiction, Mosley suggests, is like chasing a remedy with that proverbial spoonful of sugar. "It's an adventure," he says with a coy laugh, "because most of the things that Easy does are kinda fun."

On this stretch of road, the juxtapositions are jarring—the crumbling detritus of some once-fetching 1940 storefront squats next to a circa-1980 convenience structure of glass and concrete. The ragtag collection plays tricks with time and place.

These darkened doorways inspire brighter memories. "Even though most of those stores were owned by white people, at least there were stores in the community where people could go shopping, where people could get jobs. There was a relationship developing with the community, and that's really what's gone. And that, I think, is analogous to a physical reflection, in a negative sense, (to) the hope that is also gone from the community." His voice goes soft, loses speed. "But a lot of the people are the same. They're still here."

And 76th Place itself pulses on. For ten years, the Mosleys lived here, near Central, in a white wood-frame house edged in green, with a small front porch that provided a perfect stage for stories. Today, it's a street of single-family dwellings, pastel duplexes, rose bushes, birds of paradise exploding askew. A woman, on her knees, polishes the knob of her iron screen door while children, mostly Latino, command the center of the street with balls and bikes.

Near the corner, a large wood-frame court of bungalows painted crisp white, its property line marked off by a tall iron fence, sparks something. Mosley leans forward in his seat to frame the picture better. "Right here is the court—Poinsettia Court—they're all over L.A.," he says, finger jabbing at the glass. "That's where I imagined Easy living."

It all comes back in a flood. An easy smile moves across his sand-colored face and large, sad eyes.

"My father raised me in this neighborhood and he had high hopes for me. It wasn't: 'Walter can get a job at the garage, maybe, if he's lucky.' He was saying, 'My son is going to make it, 'cause I'm going to make something out of my son,' which he did."

What might be absent physically is made up for by what has failed to dissipate spiritually, Mosley notes. "This community is still really kind of wonderful because when you really look directly at people, people are kind of smiling a lot and telling each other stories. (But) it's kind of a funny (feeling). It's not like what I remember physically, but then again, it is what I remember physically."

The unfolding scene plays tricks with one's memory. With the notion of memory itself. Vaguely familiar backdrops, partly familiar players. This lively tree-banked street next to Central Avenue, where life persists despite its new ghost-town feel. Beauty parlors specializing in a "Texas press and curl" and soul food cafes now coexist with *discotecas*, *mariscos* and taco stands. And behind it all, lending a somewhat surreal backdrop, the downtown skyline hovers like Oz.

Down the block a little farther, Mosley points out a house stripped, he says, of its former character. His full lips return to a gentle pout. "That's my house right there, but it's not the same anymore."

This little strip of small homes, duplexes and bungalow courts was, Mosley believes, much more of a neighborhood than could be found elsewhere in the basin. He remembers a community that often disregarded color, religion and ethnicity, possibly important for a child whose father was black and whose mother was white and also Jewish. He grew up relating the struggles of his black forebears to those of his mother's Eastern European lineage. He speaks of fleeting crushes on the Mexican girls who lived nearby and was fascinated by them because they were "so Catholic." This community that "got along" was perhaps a built-in comfort zone for Mosley.

"Everybody knew one another. People are still living there who lived there when I was a little kid, and that's not the way you think of L.A. The real Los Angeles, the Los Angeles I lived in, there was no Hollywood. One thing," says Mosley, his voice drifting like a whisper, "even though you couldn't find a way out, there was a great sense of possibility."

Ella Mosley admits she kept a sentinel's watch on her only child. She and her husband met at a local school (she was an elementary school clerk, he was a plant manager), and Walter Ellis Mosley was born in 1952. "I always worried about him, and you don't want to be that way, but you can't help it," she says. "Walter wanted to walk down the street one time to the store, he was six maybe, he had never done that before. There was nothing that could have happened to him, so we let him, but I'm walking on the other side, trying to keep out of sight."

About the time Walter was ready for junior high, the family moved across town to a comfortable four-plex just off the western stretch of Pico, a new retreat that Leroy Mosley, who collected property as others do stamps, made a hideaway by planting an exotic array of vegetables, fruits and flowers.

Drifting back to his adolescent years, Mosley recalls most clearly the ache at the pit of his lungs from the air that so often smudged the skies ocher. He remembers feeling trapped within the flat, hot vastness.

He read voraciously. "I'm not sure that it was traveling through books. I love to read. I was reading Dickens, Hesse, that kinda brooding youth stuff. I was reading whatever I got introduced to in school that I liked, and stuff my parents had just read. My first favorite book was *Treasure Island*."

His intake later increased to include a steady diet of comic books and paperback sci-fi. Mysteries didn't enter into the picture until his twenties, and the only writing he was flirting with at the time didn't venture further than poetry.

"I was very unhappy," he says. "It seems to me like I wanted something, but the something was intangible; I didn't know how to get it. In L.A., that big middle portion of L.A., people don't walk on the streets, people don't come from the same background or the same area, so your connection with people is very tenuous at best." Once out of his little neighborhood, the connection was gone.

He cut it completely when he decided to attend Goddard, a "radical" arts college in Vermont. "I thought I really had to go someplace where people will be like me. Things that I will say, they will understand." But upon his arrival, Mosley wasn't sure he understood them. "They had a large black population . . . and they were all living in the same dorm, except me. It wasn't that the school wanted them to live there, it was the decision on their part. I thought, 'I'm going to search out a ghetto to live in? Nuh uh.' "

He drifted from one campus to another and from one set of adventures to still others without a goal, with not even the essence of direction. "I think I was informed by like the Kerouac and Ginsberg sensibility, and also by L.A. and the hippie movement," he explains. And what was he studying? Mosley pauses, then lets out an explosion that doubles as a laugh—"Who knows?"

Writing came a little later, like a storm out of nowhere. After receiving a BA in political science from Vermont's Johnson State College in 1977, he met Joy Kellman, a dancer-choreographer, while he was working on a Ph.D at the University of Massachusetts at Amherst. They married in 1988. He'd shown talent as a potter and painter and some aptitude for computers. "I was sitting in a room, and I was working as a consultant programmer. It was a Saturday, and nobody else was there. I was writing programs. I got tired of it, so I started typing on the computer," he says. "I typed: 'On hot sticky days in southern Louisiana, the fire ants swarmed. . . .' I said—'Hey, this is cool. This means I could be a writer.' So I start writing."

In a few months, a manuscript, *Gone Fishin'*, under his belt, he enrolled in a graduate creative writing program at City College of New York. It was 1986. "He was writing these wonderful, beautiful stories," says Mosley's onetime instructor Tuten, author of *Tallien: A Brief Romance*. "The vividness of the characterizations, the very simple, elegant beauty of the prose. And there is a lyricism there that you don't find in much American writing today."

After Mosley had completed his instruction with Tuten and won CCNY's De Jur Award, he asked Tuten to critique a new manuscript. Excited by the power of the work, Tuten took it to his agent, who promised to sell the book—and did, six weeks later.

"He didn't give it to me with that kind of anticipation," Tuten says. Since then Mosley has weathered the blizzard of events, Tuten believes, with ego safely in check. "He's had plenty of occasions to play a big shot. He's never done it with anybody. I can't say that he's humble. He knows the value of this work, but he didn't become a writer to become famous. He didn't become a writer to become a celebrity. That happened, and I've never seen anyone else handle it so well as he."

Walter happy at last? Well, happy would seem a stretch. Contented but busy seems to sum up his demeanor, which at moments makes him appear as if he is leaning on a gilded railing of some grand balcony, watching it all unfold. Lately, his thoughts center more on the final tinkerings on his blues novel, *RL's Dream* (due next year) and testing his chops with a screenplay, his own take on the relatively nascent 'hood-film genre that he's been banging out on his laptop in his Santa Monica hotel room. With all the clamor surrounding him of late, Mosley seems to fly from vague disinterest to a quiet merriment when talk of his success rises in conversation. "He's very controlled," his mother confides later. "But being too controlled is not good. I always thought that his head would get too big, but he is just as easygoing. (He) never lets on that everything is great."

At its downtown source, Pico Boulevard, crowded with life, noisy with enterprise, serves as the vivid bridge, the wide road to the Westside. It's the bridge from Central Avenue to Mosley's teen years, the period in which he planned his grand escape.

"This is so L.A., these palm trees standing here, big wide streets and all these completely innocuous cinder block buildings. It seems like this place where nothing real is going on, which is why you can really write crime fiction about L.A.—because really behind all these things, there is all this weird stuff, and strange people who come from all over the place . . . and you don't know where they went after they left here.

"When you see something like this," he gestures toward the boulevard, "this isn't as real as what's in your head. In your head, you have the details," says Mosley. His gestures are careful, understated. His hands are reserved only for the most dramatic moment in the action, a crescendo. "When I was a kid, and this was before cable, black people got together and told stories. And storytelling is its own fuel. All you have to do is evoke a feeling. Sometimes it's just a word. A sentence."

However, unlike Easy, who has cast his lot with Los Angeles ("He's going to live in his neighborhood. And either he is going to get killed in that neighborhood or he's going to survive in that neighborhood"), Mosley hasn't.

"I wouldn't live in Los Angeles," he says. "The center of Los Angeles, though I am moved by it aesthetically, living in it, I remember being very kind of, I (didn't) know how to get out. There were no walls, but there was great distance."

He's tiring of questions or maybe of just coming up with serious answers to them. The eight-year-old peeks from behind the hedge, the trickster upsetting the balance, toppling the status quo. With a part-dreamy, part-devilish expression inhabiting his eyes, he takes a breather.

Roaming around his hotel-room carpet on stocking feet, he finally pauses to install himself in the love seat, to take advantage of its view of the very edge—the lazy Pacific as it curls and stretches eight stories below. He sits, legs pulled beneath him, dressed entirely, once again, in black: socks, jet shirt tucked into charcoal trousers. His calf-length cashmere coat, which he wears on the dust jacket of *White Butterfly*, and his Kangol hat (one of a pair he and his father purchased in London) are draped across the foot of the bed, suggesting that the pause is only temporary.

Over the course of the week, he's been busy with a varying collection of duties and diversions: lunch with his mother, a visit to his father's grave (he died of lung cancer late last year), a meeting with "the movie people," interviews, more pages filed away on the screenplay and, of course, some time set aside to catch up with his favorite TV family, the Bundy's on *Married With Children*. The room is cluttered with tools of his spare time: a Hilma Wolitzer novel, a copy of Ray Bradbury's *Fahrenheit 451* (for an essay he's working on), a flute and sheet music. His laptop, folded away, rests on the room's only table. His morning writing ritual is a constant. With the jet-lag, it begins at 3:30; he quits at about 10:00.

"A novel, it seems to me, has to be larger than the mind of the writer," he says. The largeness of L.A., though daunting and "stultifying" to a younger Mosley, is now the precise dimension he seeks to replicate in his work. "The novel is based on a plot, and the best way to describe a plot to me is the structure of revelation. If you can hold it all within a small space, a space small enough for you to see and perceive, then you don't have the feeling of revelation, because it's too controlling. What you want is something big, where things surprise you, where things become."

He would like to avoid narrow pigeonholes or empty spokesman roles, despite the expectations of those of any hue.

"Expectations?"

"Well, you know if you're black and you make it, you should want to be helping other black people in ways that most people don't even help their family. And I think a lot of black people feel that responsibility. I know I do," he admits. "But at the same time, it can interfere with your work. People come up to you and say, 'Well, you have to write in African tones, my brother.'

" 'Well, you know, I'm writing the way I write.'

" 'But you see, your mind has been brainwashed by The Man, and you have to return to our true identity.' "

He tends to be more populist and universal in his thinking. "A good novel comes out into the world and grows as people read it. Other people, they see things, learn things, they get a little inkling of something that may make its way into something else (or in the) actions that they take in their own lives. I want black people to have a good time. I mean, I want black people to read the book and say, 'That's my language, that's my life. That's my history. But I want white people to say, 'Boy, you know, I feel just like that!' "

Human struggle, failure, and the occasional reward of good fortune serve as the dramatic and emotional engines for much of Mosley's work. "I'm not really happy," he says, "with political writing as political writing. That kind of sociopolitical writing they do about black life—'The Black Man, blah, blah, blah, and the Black Woman, blah, blah, blah.' And then the white this and Jim Crow and all this other stuff. I mean I like mentioning it, because I think it's a part. But it's such a small part of black life."

"Politics?" I coax him toward elaboration.

"Well, politics is a big part of our life, and so is racism. But most black people are living lives, making love, raising children, listening to music, working hard, saving money, learning new skills in order to survive, watching television, telling jokes, telling stories—so much of life is that. And black life in America is really kind of a celebration. Even when people are really sad," says Mosley, eyes wide, hands painting vast landscapes, portraits, busy triptychs.

"And when they're sad, how do they celebrate it?"

The answer is sly, trademark-simple: "That's the blues."

May 1994

AN OBSESSION WITH COMPULSIONS

SARA SCRIBNER

Modern surrealist Aimee Bender can cut as smoothly as an X-Acto knife when she slices into the minds of her awkwardly obsessive characters. This unflinching newcomer at times seems like a great young hope, a female counterpoint to the David Foster Wallace/Dave Eggers/George Saunders power circle. Swirling fantastical events into ho-hum lives like a mischievous magical realist, she can be deeply seductive and often hilarious. Sometimes, though, you just wish she'd lay off the bag of tricks.

That feeling nags throughout Bender's first novel, *An Invisible Sign of My Own*, (Doubleday) the anticipated follow-up to her surprise short story collection, *The Girl in the Flammable Skirt.* An unexpected hit (from the literary dogtown of Los Angeles, no less), *Girl* opened up a chick-centric world that was contemporary and ruthless but also frank and poetic. Its cast of characters included a grieving librarian who runs a slow sex train in the library's back room and the desperate wife of a war veteran whose husband has returned home without lips.

The stories were Valley Girl Calvino. A fan of the Italian surrealist along with and García Márquez and Hans Christian Andersen, Bender infused a bizarre sense of fun to even the darkest and most desperately absurd situations. The characters were often twisted females in the middle of meltdowns, hanging onto the sheer physicality of bodies and the visceral engagement of sex in order to join life's circus. Sadness commingles with whimsy. Though they never deeply analyzed themselves, her characters' intelligence kept them from letting themselves off the hook when they are being selfish and vain.

Susie, the narrator in "Fell This Girl" is both alien and familiar. She is petty and insecure in a way that's typical of many young women, yet she pushes it all over the top. Just when she's taken the reader's sympathy to the limit, she says something sad and honest. After a one-night stand, she analyzes the way her conquest holds her like he's in love. "The first date, you're sort of a stand-in for whomever he loved last, before he fully realizes you're not her, and so you get all this nice residue emotion." By keeping the terrain recognizable, Bender can fill her stories with the modern-day equivalent of circus freaks doing strange tricks that amuse and dismay.

In contrast to the ribald stories, *Invisible Sign* is an uptight book with its knees clamped shut. It's all about keeping control in a pretty dull little universe. The only relief we get is a dreadlocked little id of a second-grader named Lisa Venus.

The world is a small suburban town with a big ice-blue, architecturally significant hospital (read: death encased in ice) as its only distinguishing centerpiece. The book's narrator is Mona Gray, who is a number-obsessed, twenty-year-old math teacher without a college degree; she got the job because she loves long division. She is also a deeply disturbed single woman who obsessively knocks on wood and has the creepy habit of eating soap after—or in the middle of—a sexual moment.

Intimacy is a big problem for Mona. Describing coming home after her third time with her first and only boyfriend, she says, "I checked my messages to see if anyone had died while I was out in the world having sex."

The central figure in her world is a scarred science colleague determined to crack her neuroses, Mr. Jones. Her family's next-door neighbor, Jones wears a wax number around his neck to express his moods—fifteen is an average day: "Generally he hung steady around fifteen. Only once did I see it go up to thirty-seven."

Somehow, the number obsession and the sex hang-ups are supposed to go hand in hand with Mona's philosophy on quitting—and they all somehow relate to her father's decade-long sickness, which might be real and might be imagined. Trying to fit all of Mona's quirks together is as mind-boggling as advanced algebra, but it's easy to understand why Bender keeps piling on the compulsions. It is in illuminating her characters' oddball behavior that Bender's words shimmer.

"It's a fine art, when you think about it," explains Mona. "To quit well requires an intuitive sense of beauty: you have to feel the moment of turn, right when desire makes an appearance, here is the instant to be severed, whack, this is the moment where quitting is ripe as a peach turning sweet on the vine: snap, the cord is cracked, peach falls to the floor, black and silver with flies."

There are plenty of interludes like this, which make *An Invisible Sign* strange and satisfying reading. But when you get right down to it, the book's town is as familiar as an airtight '50s sitcom, only with weirder characters. Bender's conundrums—staying clean or getting messed up in the world, shunning desire or pulling it close, accepting life's messy possibilities or making your own non-options by quitting—make the love story feel like a screwball comedy. But Claudette Colbert never toted home an axe and fantasized about self-dismemberment.

It makes sense that Bender grew up in Los Angeles (she now lives in West Hollywood): Her stories capture the experience of living in a slightly battered absurdist parade. Bender's fascination with working out deep fantasies in metaphor and movement is no accident: Her father is a psychiatrist and her mother is a dance teacher and choreographer. (She once ran to her father because of her terror of a thunderstorm. He asked her if she was angry at anyone; she was, and was shocked into recognizing the twisted ways of the psyche.)

After graduating from UC San Diego, Bender went to San Francisco and became an elementary school teacher (fodder for a lot of *Invisible Sign*). She'd originally wanted to write plays, but was turned down by all the programs to which she'd applied. Eventually, she headed off to UC Irvine's writing program, where she became friends with another student, Alice Sebold, the author of the fantastically successful *The Lovely Bones*. It was at Irvine that she learned that playing it straight didn't work for her.

In prose, sometimes she doesn't play it straight enough. Bender tries to camouflage her weaknesses with plotting by layering on the psychoses. But Bender's young women, even the multi-inflicted Mona Gray, come across as heroic in a book universe groaning with chronicles about vain, single young women tallying up their daily calorie counts. In the end, this makes the complicated, deeply flawed *Invisible Sign* well worth the trouble.

The world needs a female surrealist. The most famous—Calvino, Barth, and Barthelme—are all male. And Los Angeles deserves a female author too weird for *Oprah*. Bender is not quite ready to take on the heavyweights yet: She has a knack for the quick summation of character in the quirky short story, but can't sustain her magic act for an entire novel. Though she clearly yearns for a little of García Márquez's magic, her stories have no sweep or sense of history and her characters work better as snapshots.

Bender's currently at work on a second novel and another collection of stories. As she develops a novelist's artistic heft, it seems unlikely that the nimble storyteller will survive. Unlike her muscleman from *Girl*, Bender will have a hard time pulling off that balancing act.

August 2000

The Romantic Egotist

Scott Timberg

After decades of being misunderstood, novelist and gay icon John Rechy is fighting back—and making Hollywood take notice.

When most novelists go to parties, they don't have to worry about being threatened, challenged, or decked. But that's the way it was for John Rechy, back in the days when he haunted parties in and around Hollywood.

"At the time, I was very well-known," says the author of *City of Night*, the groundbreaking 1963 chronicle of gay hustling. "Basically, someone would come up and say: 'You think you're really hot shit?' Somebody would get a little tipsy and they'd want to take me on—arm wrestling or something. 'You think you're such a stud.' " One of these challengers was Peter Orlovsky, the Beat poet and Allen Ginsberg's boyfriend, who accosted Rechy at a party in San Francisco's Nob Hill, sizing him up and asking him how much he could bench-press. "And my answer was always the same: 'Look, I don't *care* how strong I am. It's that I *look* like the stronger man.' "

It's a quintessential Rechy response, the dismissive words of a man whose life and career have been devoted to the beauty and mystery of surfaces, artifice, and the power of ego over any and all obstacles. His books have been placed on the short-list of classic Los Angeles novels, alongside Nathanael West's *Day of the Locust* and Raymond Chandler's *The Big Sleep*. Rechy, an El Paso native who moved to the city almost thirty years ago, is a kind of poet laureate of the city.

Rechy has certainly not been idle since *City of Night*'s publication, especially not recently. He's served as a guru to generations of gay men, and his books still excite all kinds of readers, young and old, gay and straight. He's won numerous prizes and became the first novelist to win the PEN/West Lifetime Achievement Award in 1997. His writing workshops, offered through USC's graduate school and privately, are widely acclaimed, and he's taught some of the West Coast's sharpest authors and journalists.

The novelist—whose small stature, impish smile, and barrel chest lend him the bearing of a well-exercised elf—treats writing like a big fight for which he's constantly training. The mixed reviews for his twelfth novel, *The Coming of the Night*, published last summer, have brought him back with both guns blasting. Simultaneously, Rechy and his companion, a major-studio film producer, have been working on the film rights of his books and have several projects in development. Gus Van Sant, the director whose *My Own Private Idaho* alludes to Rechy's angelic street hustlers, has spoken with the two about making a film of *City of Night*. With the April release of a remarkable CD-ROM produced by USC's Annenberg Center, *Mysteries and Desire: Searching the World of John Rechy*, the author's fans will get an "interactive memoir" of his life that will allow them to read old reviews and watch computer-generated gay men cruise in Griffith Park. Whatever the reception for his latest work, Rechy is now more visible than he's been in years.

Rechy himself could be a character in an Evelyn Waugh-style satire about contemporary L.A. A gay bodybuilder of mixed Mexican and Anglo blood, a proud narcissist who's worked hard to keep himself looking twenty years younger than his actual age, a lover of California's light and glamour and movies; Rechy, sixty-five, embodies much of the city's best and worst features. Life, he says, is a performance—if done right, a grand performance.

Rechy still has an enormous following, especially among gay men. But his detractors say he's superficial, a writer of limited gifts coasting on his early successes, a throwback to the gay world of the pre-AIDs '60s and '70s who hasn't matured or adapted. He's both a gay hero and a gay outlaw; and as such, his battles typically begin—rather than end—when a new novel is published.

Not everybody who meets Rechy, truth be told, wants to arm-wrestle him or praise his prose. For years, most of the people he met—the men, at least—wanted to have sex with him. And most of them did. Rechy worked the streets of New York and Los Angeles—Pershing Square, Selma and Hollywood boulevards—from the late '50s to about 1980, as both a hustler (who was paid) and a cruiser (who wasn't). "I remained on the streets longer than anybody in the world," he says, letting out the kind of knowing laugh with which others might recall hard-drinking fraternity days.

Rechy wove his early years on the streets into the novel *City of Night*, which is still considered his greatest achievement. The book began as a breathless letter written to a friend about the sadness and joy of Mardi Gras; when Rechy found the letter, crumpled and unsent, he sent a clean draft to the *Evergreen Review*, where it was printed as a short story alongside Beckett and Kerouac.

The novel, published in 1963 by the maverick Grove Press, became an instant best-seller and, due to its glimpse of the gay demimonde during a far less candid era, a publishing phenomenon. It drew the same kind of breathless, gauntlet-throwing jacket copy as *Naked Lunch* and *Last Exit to Brooklyn*. "Rechy tells the truth and tells us with such passion that we are forced to share in the life it conveys," wrote James Baldwin. *The Washington Post* called the novel "one of the major books to be published since World War II." *City of Night*'s impact went way beyond book review pages: Jim Morrison intoned its title in The Doors' "L.A. Woman," and rocker David Bowie, painter David Hockney, and director Van Sant have all spoken of its inspiration. Van Sant, in fact, says he gave Rechy's book to Keanu Reeves and River Phoenix, his street hustlers from *Private Idaho*. "I gave them both *City of Night* and said: "If you want to know the life of a street hustler, this is the place to start.' Later, I found that Keanu had bought all of John's other books."

But something else happened when the book was published. It began a feud, mostly within the gay intelligentsia, about Rechy's worth as a novelist. Was he a great literary writer or just a hustler who wrote a book? *The New York Review of Books* ran a mocking, dismissive review under the title "Fruit Salad."

The article became a seminal event in Rechy's life and not just for internal reasons: Others followed the *New York Review*'s lead. All over the press, critics speculated that a mere street hustler could not have written a book like this, that it must've been Tennessee Williams or James Baldwin using a nom de plume. Rechy, uninterested in having his private life examined, dropped out of sight; he read, from the safety of Caribbean beaches, about glittery Manhattan and Fire Island parties at which the white-hot young writer John Rechy appeared.

City of Night remains a remarkable and influential novel, and its spontaneous style and powerful rhythms echo Whitman, the Beats, and early Elvis Presley. It also established the pattern that some say Rechy has adhered to too closely in the ensuing four decades. We hear a lot about what happens to this "youngman"—Rechy jammed words together and often shattered syntax—as he roams from city to city, but we never really get to know him. Arthur Little, a professor at UCLA who loves the book, points out: "You spend hundreds of pages with the narrator, but you never know his name. So *City of Night* becomes an elaborate one-night stand." Some of the richness in the book, and in Rechy's later work, comes from its religious imagery. It's got more Catholicism than a Scorsese film—the book is dripping with ritual, holy iconography, a yearning for heaven, and prostitutes who look like "fallen angels." Its first line captures its tone well. "Later I would think of America as one vast City of Night stretching gaudily from Times Square to Hollywood Boulevard—jukebox-winking, rock-n-roll moaning: America at night, fusing its darkcities into the unmistakable shape of loneliness."

The appeal of *City of Night* reached beyond gay men. Henry Turner, a young writer and filmmaker who helps run the Slamdance Film Festival, picked the book up while wandering around Europe years ago and was struck by its emotional directness. "I'm not gay; I didn't read it as a gay book. But *City of Night* seemed to be the most honest expression of the adolescent male experience that I'd ever read." Turner is now one of Rechy's many devoted students. "He talked about narcissism, about being interested in appearance, he talked about the father. The male literary tradition is mostly about *concealing* emotion. It blew my mind—it really blew my mind. There were times when I was yelling out."

Many of Rechy's characters are aloof and withholding, and Rechy's childhood friends say the same about him. He writes of being an isolate who drove wildly into the deserts around El Paso or stretched out on mountains above the city, staring at the Texas sky. But the Rechy now alive and well in a tasteful Mediterranean apartment in Los Feliz is anything but a standoffish brooder. He's a man, instead, of almost incomparable personal charm. A smile seems always to be playing around the corners of his mouth. But he's less cheerful when discussing the reception of his new book.

"I've never doubted my work—never, never doubted my work," he says, leaning forward on his couch toward a table covered with crystal goblets. Others *have* doubted him, though, and he admits that his straight readership has been eroding for years. It's been six months since the release of *The Coming of the Night*, which looks at one sex-drenched day and night in Los Angeles at the dawn of the AIDS epidemic, and he's still angry at *L.A. Times* reviewer Gary Indiana. The gay, often curmudgeonly *The New Yorker* trashed the novel, comparing it to "the middle-to-lowbrow fictions of a Jackie Collins." ("Rechy may be more "shocking' to the still-shockable, but Collins is a lot more fun," he wrote in his front-page review.) Step into Rechy's writing workshop, ask him how he's doing, attend one of his speeches, and he'll unload on Indiana, calling the reviewer—whose name he sometimes pretends to have trouble recalling—a victim of "penis envy."

The games Rechy played with anonymity early in his career have given way to what he calls "a very dignified demand for attention." Besides letters to recalcitrant editors and critics, Rechy is writing an article about *The New York Times'* failure to review the new book. He speculates that he's on a blacklist at *The Times*—"I've been done in by someone in the lower echelons," he announces to a Monday-night class—but the slight is only part of a larger problem. "I really want to get to the damn issue of *the ignoring*. And I also want to deal with the warning that every writer hears—from publishers, editors, and everything—that you do *not* protest. And my question: *Why not?* Why do you have to take shit?" His article, he says, will deal with his many victories—apologies from papers, Web sites, reviewers—even an apology from the poison pen of Gore Vidal.

"My point is: What do I have to lose? Being silent has never been effective for anybody. And I feel writers get maligned that way. We're actually inhibited. "Oh, they'll mistreat you in the next review.' *Bullshit!* At least be heard. I have to uphold my dignity—that's the whole thrust of the thing. So fuck 'em."

As Rechy continues to fight, his novels are drawing attention from Hollywood. For years, he turned down the few offers he got, figuring his stories would be exploited. But his boyfriend, who now owns the rights to the books, has been working to bring them to the attention of directors and movie executives. Rechy has written screenplays for *City of Night*, *The Fourth Angel*, and *Marilyn's Daughter*, and he has several projects in development besides the potential Van Sant film. Rechy and Mexican director Arturo Ripstein, for instance, have scouted locations for a film treatment of the well-received 1991 novel *The Miraculous Day of Amalia Gómez*.

Rechy explains his recent currency in Hollywood: "I'm going to tell you *unabashedly*," he says with a puckish smile. "Because I have *refused* to lay down, I've refused to be knocked down. I'm telling you, I have fought for the kind of respect that I deserve. And I have not quit. I'm still doing it. And I'm seeing the [payoff] now—the Lifetime Achievement Award, the cover of the *L.A. Times Book Review*. And I feel triumphant about this. When I first appeared, I battled that fucking review from *The New York Review of Books*. That son of a *bitch*, man. He wanted a knockout punch—he really wanted to destroy me. And they all followed suit—*The Village Voice*, *The New Yorker*, Richard Gilman. And they were wrong. The Book of the Month Club—"Our readers don't enjoy this sort of stuff'—and then years later they're issuing *City of Night* as one of their books." A pause. "But I feel good about it. It still stings, but in a triumphant way."

Though Rechy gets frustrated when the press fixates on his years on the street, he exudes pride, even nostalgia, when discussing his days and nights hustling. When talking about how the scene changed from the '50s to the '70s, for instance, he becomes a Proust of Pershing Square, wondering if one can recall experience without romanticizing things past.

Rechy's career on the streets began in the mid-'50s. He'd served briefly in Germany during the Korean War, but the Army granted him early release so he could attend Columbia University. He went to New York nearly broke and took a room at a YMCA. There he met a merchant marine who bought him hamburgers and told him how to make fast money hustling. Instead of graduate school, he headed for Times Square.

He writes in an autobiographical essay: "On Times Square, which the merchant marine had told me about—arousing a cacophony of terrified excitement, strange magic—I study other idling youngmen selling their bodies. From them I learn quickly how to stand, look—as if I had *always* known. A middle-aged man approaches and says, 'I'll give you ten dollars and I don't give a damn for you.' " Instead of being insulted, Rechy was gratified. "Two needs of my time then: to be desired powerfully, and not to be expected to care."

Rechy's approach was always the same—to look tough but available, to wait for men to approach, to remain aloof and play dumb, to slip off into alleys and houses for privacy.

Soon after the success of his first books, though, he left the street and moved back to Texas. "I had an idea in El Paso, to open a gym for intellectuals—and I discussed it with an investor." (When asked what he would offer to attract these intellectuals, he responds, laughing, "Myself, as an example.") But this idea, however auspicious, was not to be, because in the early '70s Rechy got a call from a friend at Occidental College asking him to teach. Soon after moving to L.A. and taking up his professorial duties, he started hustling and cruising as well.

The world around him had changed drastically. As the era of Elvis and Little Richard gave way to David Bowie's Ziggy Stardust, the sexual types on the street reflected the evolution. "Earlier, we always had the so-called studs and the queens," says Rechy, who was the former. "And then, when I came back, there were the very androgynous young men. And I suppose that's why I was able to make a comeback, because I was sort of retro." He gives a self-deprecating laugh. "One person said to me: 'I haven't seen one of you in a long time.' "

His confidence was low when he returned to the streets after years of living with his mother in El Paso. "I was actually terrified to go back to the streets. I mean, Goddamn, I wondered if I'd survive." He began to body build with even more fury, to make sure he had the strength to protect himself, and went out after the sun had set so his age wouldn't show. But here, as in everything, his ego buoyed him through. "Word got around that I had once been a famous *model,*" he says, laughing. "This was Santa Monica Boulevard, so this was the *most* they conceive. And they meant a body model, not even a fashion model. There was *awe* around me."

Though part of what sparked his return to hustling was financial, Rechy emphasizes that he went back by choice. That made him even more unusual among his peers on Selma and Santa Monica. "It seemed that in my time there was much more pride about being a hustler. Because now I think it's very, very, very sad—I think a lot of the kids who hustle have to. It's terrible. I believe that young people should choose what they want to be, and if one chooses to be a hustler, fine—but not *have* to be one because there's nothing else. I don't think anybody should be forced to be a doctor, either."

In both the '50s and '70s, while he was developing aspects of his street persona, Rechy worked to cover up the fact that he was a writer or even a reader. Any signs of intellect would scare off his "numbers." Sometimes he'd see his books in the homes of the men who picked him up and keep his mouth shut. Other times, his aesthetic side would take over. He would often begin an evening at the L.A. Public Library, reading Camus or Milton, before heading out to Pershing Square to hustle. One night in San Francisco in the '50s, at a cruising theater on Market Street, Stanley Kubrick's World War II movie *Paths of Glory* came on, and Rechy's eyes were so drawn to the film that he sat down, overpowered, and forgot about sex altogether.

"Once when I was leaving an orgy, someone said, 'Aren't you the author?' And I said, 'No, but I must look like him.' " As he taught at local colleges, it became more difficult for Rechy to stay entirely anonymous. Once, during his stint at UCLA, Rechy was on Santa Monica Boulevard at about 3 a.m., with no shirt and an oiled chest, and a car made a U-turn. Its window came down as it approached. "Good evening, Professor Rechy," a young man said. "Are you out for an evening stroll?"

Could the decades spent hustling have anything to do with Rechy's narcissism? The novelist has no problem admitting so, explaining that his exhibitionism, early feelings of rejection, and love of approval all came together when he was in "that arena." "I felt a rush of desire coming toward me, and I suppose a lot of it had to do with the repression of my childhood, its mixture of Catholicism and restrictions."

In the years after 1977's *The Sexual Outlaw*—a book of almost kaleidoscopic promiscuity, in which male bodies are linked together in combinations that recall human Rube Goldberg machines—Rechy started to worry. Young gay men, he concluded after visits to sex clubs and warehouse orgies in New York, might be going too far. He began to write and speak in tones of caution. "During that time, nobody foresaw AIDS. But a careful reading of my books, especially *Rushes*, will indicate that I was very worried about what was happening, and I became very controversial and unpopular for a time. I was worried that we were moving beyond sex, that it was no longer sex, just sensation, the sensation of pain and humiliation—we were just bludgeoned. I thought it was a dead end." The gay community, he says, treated him like a betrayer.

If Rechy has been targeted, it hasn't been by homophobes but by other gay men. "A faction of gay people," he says, "have been my most vociferous and venomous attackers." The novelist dismisses his negative reviews as the product of hostility and envy, but there are substantial and interesting arguments contained in these pieces.

Alfred Chester's argument in *The New York Review of Books*, in particular, is often overlooked—it's usually described in the press only by its offensive headline, "Fruit Salad," as if it were just a burst of Old World homophobia. Certainly, it's a little bitchy. But one can admire *City of Night* and still have to concede that at least half of what Chester—who was openly gay—said is true and has become even more true of Rechy's recent work. Chester, who died in 1971, argued that the book is unmusical and self-consciously literary ("that disgusting rhetoric that Rechy pours all over everything like jam"), and derivative of half a dozen writers, among them Genet and Capote. But the biggest problem, Chester wrote, came from the narrator, who's a stand-in for Rechy himself. The hustler protagonist offers "absolutely no real, living response" to all the chaos and hedonism, leaving much of the book emotionally dead, and he's just another self-hating gay man who's afraid of commitment. That's not to mention all the "heavy," simplistically Freudian ideas that Rechy serves up alongside the inflated rhetoric.

Indiana's review, similarly, is far more than character assassination. Indiana praises Rechy's early work lavishly before describing the decline marked by *The Coming of the Night*. "Each of Rechy's later books lacks some vital ingredient of his robust early talent; this is puzzling, because what he does well in one book he does badly in the next, and vice versa."

And while Rechy and his fans argue that he's been penalized for being outside the Northeastern literary establishment, it's not only New York critics who are frustrated with his work. Greg Sarris, a UCLA professor and novelist, teaches *The Sexual Outlaw* in a lesbian and gay literature course. "I find the students—lesbian, gay, and straight—dislike it. They feel that he's stereotyping. They feel he's brutal to his fellow man. He puts down S&M, but he's sadistic toward those whom he's supposed to love and support. The women—lesbian or straight—can't believe they have to read such things."

Sarris is disturbed by the arrested adolescence and worship of youth in Rechy's books, and by the novelist's eroticizing of dark, forbidden spaces like back alleys, sending gay men the message that sex is exciting only when it's illicit.

Rechy's main failure, he says, is his inability to grow from an Eldridge Cleaver figure—driven by anger and the energy of protest—to a writer like Toni Morrison, who can look at the contradictions of relationships and the difficulties of outgrowing oppression that has seeped into a minority culture. "Where is something like that in gay literature?" Sarris asks. "Gay writing has to do what African-American literature has done since the '60s. We've been too busy celebrating ourselves. We're still being silly and funny and celebrating the fact that we fuck. Now that we're out, we want to love. Where are the stories of real relationships? In his work, Rechy doesn't see any way that we could be defined by anything but sexuality."

Why do so many of these arguments come from other gay men? Rechy has a theory. "I've said this and it sounds flippant, but a lot of it is actual penis envy. It truly *is*. Look, Gary Indiana is not an attractive gentleman. Alfred Chester was a *monster*. Which is irrelevant. Except, what I represent is a kind of envy to them. It is a curious thing—it finds its parallel in the straight world—that the *desirer* and the *desired* are different entities. The desirer is intelligent, perhaps rich. The desired is just physically attractive. And when the desired become identified as being intelligent, then you have *transgressed*. It's the *Blue Angel* syndrome in heterosexual terms—the blond bimbo."

While Rechy's books are usually, and often enthusiastically, reviewed, and a writer named Charles Casillo is researching a book-length study, there is very little serious critical writing about Rechy's work. Juan Bruce-Novoa, a professor at UC Irvine who has taught an entire class on Rechy's work at a German university, explains why Rechy has been critically ignored outside of gay studies. "People say you can write about anything you want now, but it's not true. John, in his best writing, is telling you to live the way the existentialists told you—a risking of life in every moment. And a lot of people don't like the fact that he urges an outlaw life." His writing, too, has gotten more sexually explicit with almost every book, which scares people off. "He's always trying to go one step further."

The "youngman" of *City of Night*, like most Rechy heroes, launches himself on a quest to substitute sex and pleasure for an infinitely distant heaven and absent God. By book's end, the young hustler realizes he's less young than he was, and no less lonely. He's traveled the country, scoring and getting paid, without allowing anyone to make an impact on him. But in New Orleans, in the book's final pages, he meets "a well-built, masculine man in his early thirties, with uncannily dark eyes, light hair." The two begin a thirty-five-page dialogue on reciprocal love versus fleeting, anonymous sex. In the end, despite pleas from his "intensely, moodily handsome" suitor to settle down, the hustler decides he prefers his freedom.

It's a moment—with its rejection of commitment and embrace of hedonism—that defines virtually all of Rechy's writing, but only partly defines his life.

It was during the first flash of the AIDS epidemic, around 1980, that Rechy met a young man from the Midwest, and they came together after an argument about Buñuel. (The author does not want his companion's name used, though the two are a visible couple.) Then in his mid-forties, Rechy took this opportunity to leave the streets. He now finds himself in an ironic position: the icon of gay promiscuity, who's written novel after novel about the swirling, psychedelic beauty of anonymous sex, creator of characters who fight commitment at every turn, settled down like a suburban dad. The two live in adjacent apartment buildings but—after years of commitment—are looking for a house together.

But while he can't say enough good things about his relationship and endorses the idea of gay marriage, he thinks gay men should fight the now fashionable implication that they need a spouse. "I don't think it's necessary to have a relationship. It's very much like the 'old maid' syndrome, the way a woman would be judged if she wouldn't get married. And the same thing is happening with homosexuals. I think one can live a perfectly decent life by oneself."

Rechy once compared gay men who have sex on the street to Rosa Parks' refusal to sit in the back of the bus, calling both revolutionary acts. He continues to champion gay sexuality.

"When you first discover that you're gay, there's a whole pressure on you to conform," he explains. "And if you pressurize anything, it finds release. We come out of a heterosexual union, so in a sense we're born into the enemy camp. Out of a heterosexual union comes this stranger. *There* begins the outlaw, for God's sake. Not later, on the streets." Add the movies and billboards that beam images of heterosexuality at gay men, combine it with religion, and you've got enough pressure for an explosion, Rechy says. The fierce dedication of gay male sexuality is the result. "It's what we have and it's what we've converted, to our credit, to something very rich—very, *very* rich.

"But let me ask you this, if you knew of a park where very attractive women, not prostitutes, hung out, and sex was easily available, right off the road, in the bushes, or wherever, would you take a peek at that park?" He pauses. "I know a friend whom I met in Griffith Park a long time ago, who said, 'This keeps me from suicide.' And that's one of the themes of *The Coming of the Night*. For a long time sex kept us going."

Rechy has always felt very close to his mother, and when she died in the early '70s, he began an intense period of mourning and drug abuse. He began seeing a psychiatrist but only began to heal when he realized how he'd let his body go, how his face had gotten gaunt. "Well, whatever narcissism may be as an illness," his shrink told him, "it *saved* you."

Narcissism, like Los Angeles, is one of Rechy's great causes; he calls himself "a champion of good narcissism." Pride about one's looks, achievement—they're nothing to be ashamed of. Crafting a novel, a sculpture, is not morally higher than crafting one's body. "I *hate* when it's called a neurosis," he says. "It's a very, very curious thing. If you say that you're a son of a bitch, people consider you saintly and humble. But *somebody else* can say you're a son of a bitch—why should *you*? And if you feel genuinely good about yourself—and you know, I do, it's not a pose; I feel good about my art, about my affections, and my physical being—then I feel qualified to extend myself. And I *like* physicality." He proudly points out that some of his students begin to work out when they take his class. They dress better; they lose weight.

Rechy doesn't hide his love of appearance. At one of his Monday-night classes, he unloads on his favorite punching bag: "If you see Gary Indiana on his Web site and then see me on mine [www.johnrechy.com], you'll see who's jealous of whom, you'll see what it's all about! And he has a very small penis—he really does—very tiny!"

In the Greek myth, Narcissus was a slender, beautiful boy who was pursued by the nymph Echo. Proud and aloof, Narcissus repeatedly rejects Echo's pleas, as he has rejected the adoration of many before her. Stopping by a lake one day to take a drink, his eyes fell on his own reflection, and he froze, in the words of Ovid, "like a fallen garden statue, Gaze fixed on his image in the water . . . Falling deeper and deeper in love with what so many had loved so hopelessly." He turns into the flower narcissus.

Rechy tells a similar, if Freudian, story near the beginning of *City of Night*: "From my father's inexplicable hatred of me and my mother's blind, carnivorous love, I fled to the Mirror. I would stand before it thinking, I have only Me! . . . I became obsessed with age. At seventeen, I dreaded growing old."

But these days, Rechy doesn't have to look into a pond, or a mirror, to see himself—and *his* narcissism hasn't slowed him down. He sees his influence all over—on fashion, rock stars, other authors.

"Believe me, I was a—fuck it if it sounds awful—I was a *pioneer*," he says with a guilty laugh. "I walked through downtown Los Angeles in a genuine motorcycle leather jacket—I still have it, an honest-to-God classic motorcycle jacket—and no shirt. And oh! Wow! Was that startling. And I was the [first] one to brazenly walk down Hollywood Boulevard with no shirt." He speaks of his invention of the scoop shirt—a T-shirt with a stretched-out neckline—and his use of odd capitalization and exclamation points years before Tom Wolfe. "You know that

Tom Waits was influenced by me. Hockney. Bob Dylan called me from San Francisco the night before his motorcycle accident to tell me how much he liked *City of Night.*"

Some of Rechy's students find his narcissism amusing or distracting. But others say that his immense self-regard is an important part of the wisdom he passes down to them. "He has the idea of a writer having a sense of dignity and developing confidence within yourself," says Jocelyn Heaney, an editor at Larry Flynt's *Barely Legal* magazine and an enthusiast of John Cheever's tweed-jacketed short stories. "It might seem kind of silly, but it's about not letting anyone take away your dignity as an artist. It's a great lesson to give your students."

It's a cold December evening when one of Rechy's female students rushes into his Los Feliz apartment, apologizing for showing up a few minutes late for his writing workshop. "Oh, it was worth the wait, darling—and I love your hair windblown like that," he says as she takes her seat beneath an enormous photograph of Garbo. "I tell my students that they'll not only come out better writers," he says, "but they'll look better. *Look* at you all—a couple of you came in looking rather dowdy."

Rechy's writing workshops are an opportunity for the novelist's talent as a showman. He has an instinctive command of the theater, and the inherent comedy, of even this most academic of social gatherings.

Later the same night, he'll ask a student to remove his sweater, knowing that he's wearing a hideous Hawaiian shirt under it, and use the shirt as a running joke throughout the rest of the evening. He does the same with any student who writes a clunky line or phrase—coming back to it repeatedly for laughs. Throughout the evening he goes back and forth between serious literary talk and his campy, one-man show. Another night, he'll ask a woman to stop chewing gum, explaining that it distorts her features.

It would seem like Rechy's emphasis on appearance, and his teasing of students, would leave some feeling bruised. But somehow it works. Says private workshop student Henry Turner: "He compliments the women, and he insults the men. And it's funny. He likes to exercise his sense of timing—he'll say something and leave the punch line half said, and then he'll get back to it, finish it a minute later." "And he times it perfectly," says Nichole Morgan, a young fan of Raymond Carver and Sylvia Plath who studied with Rechy at USC. "He gives his jokes just enough room without letting them get out of hand—but they're a relief from the intensity." Morgan has since followed him into two private workshops and hopes to take more. "He's very perceptive of people's thresholds—he has a sense of who he can jab and who he can't." This said, no man who's averse to helping women off with their jackets or walking female students to their cars should take Rechy's class.

The workshops involve more than sartorial advice. Some courses are built around novels like *Don Quixote* and *Ulysses*, others on what writers can learn from films like *Sunset Boulevard*, *Persona*, and *Gone with the Wind*. (This last is Rechy's favorite, and he once told *The New Orleans Times Picayune*: "The only thing that scares me—and I'm terrified of it—is dying a tacky death. Slipping on a banana peel or something perverse. I want to go out with grandeur, like Melanie in *Gone with the Wind*, and get Max Steiner to do the music.")

Rechy's students speak of the direct and practical impact his classes have had on their writing. Like his many friends, they're remarkably loyal. Unlike famous writers who do little more than lend their name and reputation to their courses, Rechy really puts out for his students, offering remarkably attentive criticism and publishing connections. He's as dedicated and perceptive a teacher as anyone could hope for.

He's taught Kate Braverman (*Small Craft Warnings*), Sandra Tsing Loh (*Depth Takes a Holiday*), Gina Nahai (*Moonlight on the Avenue of Faith*), and a number of journalists, including two upper-level editors at Larry Flynt Publications. "It helped me more than anything I've ever done," says Allan MacDonell, a former *Hustler* executive editor and one of the key players in Flynt's attack on hypocritical politicians. "I've been an editor for a long time, and I've been working on other people's writing for a long time, and he really ups your game." Says Loh, known for her comic one-woman shows: "I found him really incredibly useful and developed a lot of material for *Aliens in America* in his workshop. His sense of language is so precise."

Rechy's relationship to one of his most successful former students shows just how combative—or is it playful?—he really is. Michael Cunningham is the author of 1998's *The Hours*, a meditation on Los Angeles and Virginia Woolf that became both a best-selling novel and winner of the Pulitzer Prize. Rechy treats Cunningham, who studied with him in the late '70s and now lives in New York, as an ungrateful son, someone who disavows all connections to him. "Michael actually *lies*," Rechy accuses, "says he never took a writers' workshop other than Iowa." Rechy talks about Cunningham furtively whispering his thanks—when others were out of sight—at an awards banquet. Last month at UCLA, giving a speech about the Los Angeles literary tradition, Rechy spoke of a novelist—never named—who erased all L.A. ties, even taking his first book out of print so the East Coast literary establishment would not hold his California roots against him. Rechy gets a laugh when he says that this is the first novelist in history to have two first novels. He's talking about Cunningham.

So how does this unappreciative punk respond when asked if he ever knew or studied with John Rechy? Without hesitation: "I don't think I've ever had a teacher who taught me as much before or since." Cunningham goes on and on, talking about Rechy's courtly teaching style, his skill at creating a healthy atmosphere for criticism in the class, and calling him "hugely intelligent, hugely respectful." In other words, he does anything but dodge his associations with the novelist.

When told about Rechy's words for him, Cunningham sounds partly confused, partly hurt, wondering where he might have failed to give credit where it's due. But what about that other matter—burying your L.A. roots? Why is that early book about California, *Golden States*, out of print? The reason, Cunningham says, is simple: It's just not very good.

But he asks, even after hearing about Rechy's frustration with him, "If you speak to John, please give him my love."

There's a curious contradiction to Rechy. He's a man of almost electric intelligence who can discuss Joyce and Stein, Bergman and Buñuel, and serves as literary godfather to some of the nation's best young writers. At the same time, he sometimes produces flat, cartoonish characters and writes interminable descriptions of their physical appearances and work-out routines. These are, for example, some of the first lines from *The Coming of the Night*: "Jesse—the kid—woke with one thought in his mind. Today he would do something wild to celebrate one glorious year of being gay—and it *was* great to be gay and young and good-looking

245

and *hot*. Of course, his designation of 'one year' was not exact. He had been gay from the time he became aware of sex. . . ." Rechy talks about revising his books—even the spontaneous *City of Night*—more than a dozen times, but some of his writing seems dashed off. And his reputation outside the gay world is still unsteady: Rechy concedes he loses readers, gay and straight, when he departs from gay themes, as he has with books like *Our Lady of Babylon*, a novel about wanton women through the ages, and *Marilyn's Daughter*, the imaginary chronicle of Marilyn Monroe's forgotten child. He feels he's been typecast.

Rechy remains a hero to gay men but has publicly denounced the category of gay writer. "I resent the labels. I'm a *writer*. And for a long time I was a gay writer. And I wasn't a Chicano writer, because Goddamnit, you can't be gay and Chicano. No, really, those discussions were held by a gentleman at UCLA. Then I was a Los Angeles writer. Jesus Christ, I'm a *writer* and one of the *best* for God's sake, so I hate the characterizations because they limit the art. That's why I resent it—the ghettoization of literature." He's simply not a joiner. He thrives on exile, exiled even from his own subcultures.

Cunningham, the prodigal son, thinks Rechy's reputation has suffered because gay literature has become its own world away from the mainstream. "I think John is one of the casualties of the ghettoization of gay literature," he says. "I think history, the final arbiter, will vindicate John's work." Its best quality, he says, is its vitality. "Which is part of what turns people off—it's just so juicy and alive and sensual. The work makes people too nervous. There's a long, long history of work that made people uncomfortable, that fifty years later became part of the canon," he says, referring to D.H. Lawrence and Henry Miller.

The novelist sees himself the same way—as someone too dangerous for the mainstream. Rechy is nothing if not competitive—he struck up a rivalry with one of his own characters, trying to outscore the young stud in *Numbers*—and he speaks sometimes as if Rechy the writer were in competition with Rechy the sex icon. Oscar Wilde once said that he poured his talent into his work, but his genius into his life. Rechy would never say the same thing about himself. Part of what makes the John Rechy CD-ROM—which includes interviews, live-action footage, old letters, even the "Fruit Salad" review—so interesting is that it gives his family, his physical style, and his literary battles equal weight with his writing.

"I don't mind saying this: I know what's what," he says. "I'm one of the best of our time, best of my generation. I certainly rank with Norman Mailer. I certainly outshine Philip Roth." Same with Gore Vidal. "I know I rank with them, and that's my rightful place. And not as a gay writer, not as an ex-hustler, not as a sexual outlaw."

When assessed simply as a novelist, though, Rechy's work leaves something to be desired. Some of his books since *City of Night* are strong, some aren't; even that first book has deep flaws alongside its brilliant energy and lyricism. Writers since Whitman have spoken of the need for raw, lived experience—all kinds of it—to power good writing. Rechy has taken this manifesto further than almost any living writer—perhaps too far. While he's certainly been a writer first, his greatest creations are not his novels but his rich personality and his wildly varied, vulnerable, and defiant life itself. If living well is the best revenge, Rechy should be a happy man indeed.

February 2000

SPELLBOUND
Yxta Maya Murray's new novel juggles past and present

ARIEL SWARTLEY

Early in Yxta Maya Murray's third novel, *The Conquest*, is an L.A. scene at once hilariously plausible and utterly scandalous that takes place not in a downtown courtroom or on a Hollywood back lot. It's set instead behind the travertine walls of the city's most luminous monument to civility, the Getty museum. The perpetrators are the sort of characters most often associated with British comedies of manners—historians, curators, conservators. But as Murray tells it, even dedicated preservers of the past find themselves infected by something bubbly and ephemeral in the California air:

> By midnight, the place is jumping. Scholars french-kiss and sip cosmopolitans on neoclassical chaise lounges, or attempt to dance to the low jazz bubbling from a boom box, taking time-outs to peer up at the Rembrandts, Turners, Titians, getting as close to the work as they like. No *whoop whoop* sounds when they get within sixteen inches of the French canvas or the Aztec calendar . . . A month ago a squib of duck liver *did* flop onto the peach satin of a rococo sofa, and last winter a drunk Egyptologist left a light lipstick imprint on a Vermeer when she tried to kiss it . . .

The scene, with its affectionate satire and giddy hyperrealism, is emblematic of Murray's book as a whole. *The Conquest* is a rarity among novels: philosophical and amorous, serious and deliciously entertaining. The book's narrator is thirty-two-year-old Sara Rosario González, a Long Beach native and daughter of Mexican immigrants, who works at the Getty as a rare book restorer. Teresa, her boss and instigator of the gallery romp, is a Boston Brahmin and reigning expert in the field of "faded watered-silk endpapers." Since her recent cancer surgery Teresa can no longer convince herself that mere objects should be treated with the same reverence as human life. "Happiness," she lectures Sara, "does not reside in Gutenberg's ink."

Nevertheless, Sara remains enchanted with thick vellum and crumbling leather, and with the delicate art of "resurrecting and protecting a history not everyone else can see." At times she seems like a woman under a spell. Her passion for manuscripts has already taken a toll on her love life. Intent on her career, she has postponed marriage to her high school sweetheart, Karl, for so long that he has found another woman. She knows that her dead mother, a high-strung skeptic, would berate her for collaborating with institutions that make Mesoamerica's stolen artifacts footnotes to Western imperialism. But Sara likes to think of herself as "a happy spy who lives in the emperor's castle."

What's holding Sara in thrall is one particular manuscript, a folio from sixteenth century Spain. It purports to be the memoir of a young Aztec woman brought to Rome by Cortés as part of a group of jugglers designated as tribute from the New World to the pope. Teresa and other experts have attributed the text—a picaresque tale of sex, adventure, art, and magic—to one Padre de Pasamonte, a monk whose gift for blasphemy and erotic storytelling forced him to flee Spain in 1561. But Sara believes that the narrator—called Helen by her Vatican keepers—is exactly what she claims: a female, brown-skinned native of Tenochtitlan. As she positions the transparent sheets of linen necessary to reconstruct the manuscript, Sara dreams of a greater act of restoration. If she can establish the storyteller's voice as authentic, she will have resurrected a piece of her own vanished history as a woman and as a descendent of ancient civilization—and possibly laid her mother's ghost to rest as well.

Murray grew up in Long Beach and teaches criminal law at Loyola law school. Her two earlier novels established her ear for streetwise Mexican-American voices. *Locas* (1997), which is based in part on her experiences clerking for a trial court judge after graduating from Stanford law school, is set in Echo Park and told from the alternating perspectives of a gang leader's uncertain sister and his aggressive girlfriend. In *What It Takes to Get to Vegas* (1999), Rita Zapata, pigeonholed as a slut before she knows how to kiss, embraces her destiny with stiletto heals and a motormouthed vengeance, sailing after the beautiful, bruised welterweights at the local gym. The book's power lies in its portrayal of adolescence's tightrope dance between assimilation and individuation, which Murray uses as a focus for larger conflicts of growing up Latina.

In *The Conquest*, Helen's manuscript is the novel's tour de force, an imaginative re-creation of Clement VII's Vatican, Titian's salon, and the lost magic of Aztec juggling. But it's Murray's own juggling of sixteenth and twentieth century idioms that buoys the reader from Oceanside fern bars to Venetian canals. The metaphors that she wrings from the tools of bookbinding or the fossils in the Getty walls (cut from the same stone as Saint Peter's) underscore the question that tantalizes both Helen and Sara: What from the past is worth keeping, and how much space should it occupy in any of our lives?

Ask Murray how she came to write *The Conquest* and she mentions her two-year struggle with another novel "that will just remain in a drawer forever," and her subsequent discovery of W.H. Prescott's massive work, *History of the Conquest of Mexico*. In particular she cites a paragraph describing the dancers, buffoons, and jugglers that Cortés carried to Rome after his siege of the Aztec capital. "That's the sort of moment you're waiting for a novelist," she says.

Still, the failed novel and the serendipitous passage weren't the whole story. "Okay," Murray says after a long sigh. "I don't want to sound dramatic, but I had cancer and I thought I was going to die." She was thirty-two when she was diagnosed; she discovered Prescott's history while convalescing. "Reading about these destroyed nations after my surgeries, I just thought, 'I should do something with this because everything disappears.' "

Murray didn't know she would set *The Conquest* at the Getty until she'd written almost half of Helen's tale. She knew she wanted to embed the sixteenth century story in a contemporary context. It was a way "to struggle with a lot of the themes that I found interesting—the visible versus the invisible world, how as a modern person you contend with all of this history that has been destroyed and which is your only legacy." She was also fascinated by an institution she calls "an instant icon for Los Angeles" and "a fabulous, old-fashioned palace."

For the first time Murray is writing fiction in a voice that's close to her own—educated, professional, analytical. Perhaps as a result, her imagination soars in a host of other characters. There's Sara's mother, who "liberates" a Mayan codex from a museum show and holes up with it in her bedroom; there's Padre de Pasamonte's Spanish mistress, a voluminous correspondent and poetry-quoting libertine. There are also the complex, tender-hearted men in Sara's life. Her father, a hardheaded contractor, worries about his daughter's love life like a mother hen; Karl, her sometime fiancé who Murray says is based in part on her own high school boyfriend, is a Marine with a taste for literature, a potential astronaut whose response to history is to look to the stars, black holes and all.

Murray says that while recuperating she was determined to keep a clear memory of her illness, "but I had to let go of it. It's like that with history as well. You want to pay your respects to it and love it. And also make a future." In *The Conquest*, she does both. Past, present, male, female, new world and old, shine like the city lights seen from the Getty's ramparts, all the more brightly as they merge into a single, glittering prize.

November 2002

THE TARNISHED STATE OF T. C. BOYLE

CHRYSS YOST

The master of irony, T. Coraghessan Boyle, lurks against a patio wall, sipping an iced tea: He's a punked-out Willie Wonka, with a wild (if thinning) thatch of mango-tinted hair above dark sunglasses, a sharp nose, and a slightly sinister smile. What Wonka is to candy, Boyle, fifty-three, is to words: an inventive and energetic genius with a devious sense of humor, who enjoys nothing more than setting out an opulent buffet where hypocrites, gluttons, and fools can find their just desserts. A professor at USC, Boyle is the author of *A Friend of the Earth* (set in Santa Ynez), *Riven Rock* (set in Montecito), and *The Road to Wellville*, to name just a few. Boyle is the Candyman, and you, reader, are about to be invited into his factory. Once inside the doors, both language and life are suddenly not so simple.

Boyle has come to discuss his work in a Montecito Mexican café, with Jaguars purring in the parking lot, because his novel *The Tortilla Curtain* has been selected to inaugurate the fledgling "Santa Barbara Reads!" program. Perhaps the most controversial—and certainly the most Californian—of Boyle's novels, *The Tortilla Curtain* first hit the shelves in 1995, just in time to fuel the smoldering Proposition 187 controversy. Supporters of Prop 187 hoped that drying up access to public services would stop the flow of undocumented workers from Mexico. Despite much opposition, Prop 187 was passed by over 60 percent of California voters in 1994.

Set in a state deeply dependent on cheap Mexican labor, *The Tortilla Curtain* remains painfully relevant. Like Prop 187, Boyle's novel has given people plenty to argue about; it's become a popular choice for book clubs and community reading programs well beyond the state's borders.

The book is a smorgasbord of ironies, a novel bound to twist in the gut of the reader. Those hungry for a lite snack of pat solutions, life-affirming morals and happy adventures should seek their chicken soup elsewhere. Like Wonka leading hapless children through room after room of temptations, Boyle doesn't force feed. His characters feel more like caricatures than flesh and blood people, and that's not necessarily a bad thing; at least the reader doesn't feel too bad when the characters fall— as they inevitably will—into one of Boyle's meticulously crafted traps. Like Wonka, Boyle simply watches—occasionally mumbling a dispassionate "Stop. Don't"—as they haplessly plunge toward their doom.

The Tortilla Curtain focuses on two couples: Delaney and Kyra Mossbacher, rich white yuppies living in Topanga Canyon, and Cándido and América Rincón, illegal aliens who have struggled to cross the border to find the American Dream. Their lives first collide quite literally when Delaney hits Cándido with his freshly-waxed Acura, slightly damaging the car's headlight and—as if that weren't enough—seriously injuring Cándido. He suffers through his long recuperation at a makeshift camp hidden in the chaparral while pregnant América struggles to earn enough money for their rice and beans. The contrasts are stark, and occasionally heavy-handed, but they are the contrasts of humanity. Are we doing enough to help immigrants, or too much? What do the haves owe the have-nots, if anything? And who is really responsible for crime in our neighborhoods?

Crime? Up here? Wasn't that what they'd come here to escape? Wasn't that the point of the place? All of a sudden, the gate didn't sound like such a bad idea.

The upstanding, and mostly blond, citizens of Arroyo Blanco Estates are having a homeowner's association meeting, trying to decide whether or not to build a security gate. The competing voices of Arroyo Blanco—which translates to "White Stream"—could be the inner voice of an ever-growing number of communities in Southern California:

> "I can't believe what I'm hearing," the man said, and his long legged wife nuzzled closer to him, her eyes shining with pride and moral authority. "If we'd wanted a gated community we would have moved to Hidden Hills or Westlake, but we didn't. We wanted an open community, freedom to come and go—and not just for those of us privileged enough to be able to live here, but for anyone—any citizen— rich or poor. . . I cut my teeth in the sixties, and it goes against my grain to live in a community that closes its streets to somebody just because they don't have as fancy a car as mine or as big a house."

Californians, of course, don't want to be exclusive. This is the state where we chill at the beach, where we wear flowers in our hair, where nobodies become stars overnight.

California celebrates the made-for-Hollywood romance of Old Spain while the schools struggle to accommodate Spanish-speaking children, welcomes Taco Bell and bans tamale carts. The problems, of course, are not new, and you won't get any easy answers from Boyle.

"I really don't know how I feel about anything," says Boyle, nursing his iced tea, "until I write about it. That's why I write, really. Even then, I don't always know. I want to write in a way that forces people to think things through, from different sides. It may make you sad or angry, but that's the function of art. Good writing has got to be entertaining, and it's got to make you think."

In shining a bright and unflattering light on the things most of us would rather not think about, *The Tortilla Curtain* invites comparison with John Steinbeck's *The Grapes of Wrath*, a book so controversial it was banned in much of the country and burned (twice) in Steinbeck's hometown of Salinas.

The Grapes of Wrath is classic American Dream turned nightmare, and no writer today is better at corrupting a dream than Boyle. While it takes some chutzpah to declare yourself the new Steinbeck, Boyle leaps right in, introducing his book with a quote from *The Grapes of Wrath*: "They ain't human. A human being wouldn't live like they do. A human being couldn't stand it to be so dirty and miserable." Boyle addresses many of Steinbeck's issues from an updated perspective that moves the battleground from the fields of the Central Valley into the suburbs of Southern California, where endless remodeling, landscaping, and housecleaning have created an unquenchable thirst for cheap labor without benefits. As desperate as they are, Cándido and América will be dirtier and more miserable before the story ends. Boyle heaps misfortune after misfortune on them, and yet, like the Joads in Steinbeck's novel, the Rincóns push to survive, even if they have to eat garbage and cats to do it.

Some of the earliest criticism about *The Tortilla Curtain* is probably not surprising: Who the heck does this middle-class white dude think he is to write about this stuff as if he knows about it? What makes him think he can write about being Mexican, let alone an illegal immigrant?

"That's the most racist thing of all." Boyle snorts, obviously still rankled by the accusation. "It's the same old line, that only Mexicans can write about Mexicans, only women can write about women, only dogs can write about dogs. . . where does it stop? I'm a writer. I write about people, all sorts. That's it." He pauses, and asks the waiter for more ice. Sitting on the shady patio of the Café del Sol, Boyle begins to list his critics as if pulling them out of a line-up. "The P.C. nunnery, the politically correct orthodoxy, of course was the worst. The white liberals were upset with me for poking fun, the right was upset because they thought I was soft on immigration . . ." The list goes on. Chicano Studies. Nature writers. Upsetting people is the risk—some might even say the goal—of satire. It is a risk Boyle has taken throughout his career. *The Tortilla Curtain* isn't a comedy with jokes and punch-lines; it is social satire, serving up layers upon layers of hypocrisy.

From the very beginning of his Converse All-star walk toward fame, Boyle's nothing-sacred approach has focused on over-the-top irony, bizarre situations, and outrageous characters. In his first writing class at State University of New York at Potsdam, Boyle wrote "The Foot," an absurdist one-act play in which centers, quite literally, around the foot of a young boy who has been otherwise eaten by an alligator. The boy's parents keep the foot, with its tennis shoe and ragged sock, in a shrine on the coffee table. Boyle soon turned to short stories. As he explained in an interview with George Plimpton in *The Paris Review*, "Plays, after all, involve staging, which involves working with people, something I am incapable of." That may be, but he's never been one to avoid the stage or shun a spotlight.

Called "inventive" and "verbally exuberant" by the *New York Times*, Boyle has also drawn his share of criticism. Bill Mar, writing in the *Boston Globe*, dismissed his *Stories* as "gauche amusement." Mar suggested that "*over the years, Boyle's tales have become more buffoonish. Who cares if a real estate shark is stomped to death by a senile elephant or a mean stock trader is drawn and quartered by the devil?*" Of course, no fan of Boyle's would wish anyone he cared about into a Boyle story anyway, and even the negative reviewers have to admit, as Mar does, that reading Boyle "is like a visit to the funhouse." If you're not in the mood to see your reflection wavering back at you from a distorted mirror, read someone else.

Boyle is no modest ivory-tower intellectual; he has a voracious appetite for attention. "It's why we write: ego. We have something to say and we want people to hear it. I want people to read my work. I love the interviews, the book tours, the readings, all of it." As for being the official, if temporary, author of Santa Barbara: "It's the apotheosis for any writer, isn't it? To have all these people reading and talking about your work?" He loves the idea that people all over town will be able to recognize their fellow *Tortilla* readers by special pins. "Just the idea that people will talk about the book in grocery lines, at the bank. Imagine! Maybe a local bar like Dargan's could host a *Tortilla Curtain* night, like their trivia night? There could be bar fights! Over literature!"

It's easy to picture ringmaster Boyle hosting a "buy a pitcher for lit'ture" night at the local pub. He is a writer who knows the value of self-promotion. Born Thomas John Boyle, and known as "Tom" to his friends, he began publishing as T. Coraghessan (cor-AG-hessan) Boyle, a name so outrageous that *The New Yorker* featured a cartoon showing a woman in a bookstore with the caption: "I'm looking for a book by T. What's-His-Face Boyle." Boyle claims Coraghessan from his mother's side of the family tree and jokes that it is an old Gaelic term meaning, "Take two and call me in the morning."

One of his most autobiographical, and best-known, stories is "Greasy Lake," which opens:

> There was a time when courtesy and winning ways went out of style, when it was good to be bad, when you cultivated decadence like a taste. We were all dangerous characters then. We wore torn-up leather jackets, slouched with toothpicks in our mouths, sniffed glue and ether and what somebody claimed was cocaine. When we wheeled our parents' whining station wagons out onto the street, we left a patch of rubber half a block long. We drank gin and grape juice, Tango, Thunderbird, and Bali Hai. We were bad.

That's Boyle: the typical working-class Irish-Catholic boy gone sour, a crazy punk who once stole a three-foot-tall statue of Jesus and placed it in the road so His outstretched arms were directing traffic. He claimed in one interview that he still refuses to enter a cathedral, even as a tourist. Both his parents were alcoholics, and Boyle shot up, dressed up, and tore up the roads of Peekskill, New York, and generally raised havoc until 1972.

That year, after having spent a few years as a high school teacher, he rode the success of a story called (appropriately) "The OD and Hepatitis Railroad or Bust," right into the graduate program at the prestigious Iowa Writer's Workshop, where he studied with literary greats John Cheever and John Irving. In 1988, his novel *World's End* won the PEN/Faulkner Award and national attention. After earning an M.F.A., then a Ph.D. from Iowa, Boyle was hired by the University of Southern California, where he is now a tenured professor. When asked about USC's reputation as a school for privileged white kids, and how that might have influenced him in writing *The Tortilla Curtain*, Boyle points out "In sheer numbers, not percentage but sheer numbers, there are more international students at USC than any other school in the country. It's really not about the rich and poor there. That's L.A., really. That's California."

The job at USC brought him to Southern California. He and his wife, Karen, and their three children settled in the San Fernando Valley's Woodland Hills. Now, beginning their tenth year in high-toned Montecito, they live in a house built by Frank Lloyd Wright in 1909. These days, Boyle is perhaps a little more like a character in his story "Achates McNeil" now than "Greasy Lake." Here, the narrator in "Achates McNeil" describes his father, a famous writer:

A skinny man in his late forties with kinky hair and a goatee who dressed like he was twenty-five and had a dead black morbid outlook on life and twisted everything into the kind of joke that made you squirm.

Sound familiar? It certainly sounds familiar to the waitress at Café del Sol, whom Boyle knows by name. She and Boyle talk briefly about the fire burning in Kern County, close to where they both have friends and vacation spots. Boyle has been going up to Kern County since 1978, and all his books have been completed there. He enjoys the calm, the change of scenery, and the chance to work without interruptions. "It's absolutely boring up there. All I do is write and walk around in the trees. It's great!"

For all his rebel looks and wild performances, Boyle is a workhorse who writes every morning, seven days a week. "I think it really gets under people's skin," he says. "I'm just happy, happy and successful. No huge problems, at least not visible ones." He has been married for over twenty-five years—and to the same woman, no less. He has a steady job that he loves. Beneath the raucous sense of humor and that crazy hairdo, he's an undercover Mr. Stability.

"He's actually one of the most disciplined writers I've ever met," says Alice K. Turner, the former fiction editor of *Playboy*. "He maps out his life, his career and his books in an extremely disciplined way. He's a neat freak. He runs around the house picking things up. This is not the image he likes to project."

He described one of his first book tours, driving around from bookstore to bookstore. Going into a shop in San Francisco, he saw two of his paperbacks on the shelf. When he offered to sign them, the store manager seemed reluctant, but finally allowed Boyle to sign, with a "sure, what the hell" shrug. Walking out of the bookstore, underwhelmed by his fame, Boyle looked at a bookshop across the street to see a huge line of people circling the store, all clutching hardbound copies of a huge, expensive book in their arms. Who were they waiting for? What great literary figure could attract such a crowd? he wondered. "Bette Midler," he says, still shaking his head twenty years later. "They lined up like that to buy Bette Midler." Ah, fame. It wasn't until the publication of his fifth book, *Water Music*, that he knew publishers had marketing departments. "Wow! What a revelation!" Suddenly, all America was reading this punk with the unpronounceable name.

Now, he publishes as T.C. Boyle, at least on the cover, so they can make each letter in his name bigger. His new novel, *Drop City*, about hippies who head to Alaska to homestead, will be out in 2003. A fiction anthology is in the works. Seven new stories are done and scheduled to appear in magazines like *Esquire* and *The New Yorker*. Life is good.

Boyle struts down the train tracks on his walk home, planning to do a little yard work before heading to Lucky's Bar for a stiff one. Meanwhile, across from the former wealth and squalor of one of an old Montecito mansion, seditious capybaras consider a swim in the slough. The sun shimmers with affluence and the Santa Barbara Cemetery waits just to the left, like something out of a T.C. Boyle novel.

August 2002

Playboy INTERVIEW
Ray Bradbury

A CANDID CONVERSATION WITH SCIENCE FICTION'S GRAND
MASTER ON THE FUTURE OF SPACE TRAVEL, COMPUTER FLIMFLAMS,
POLITICAL CORRECTNESS AND WHY HE'S ALWAYS RIGHT.

KEN KELLEY

Even at the age of seventy-five, there's something childlike about Ray
Bradbury. He bounces with enthusiasm, he nearly always wears shorts
and his homes are stocked with toys—from the statue of Bullwinkle
that presides over the basement of his Los Angeles home to the nine-
foot dinosaur that occupies its own bed at his desert hideaway.

Bradbury is fascinated with bigger toys, too. Like spaceships (real
ones) and Martians (imaginary ones). With his white hair and grin-
ning, ruddy face, he defies you to take him seriously. But then he
starts talking and you realize you're in the presence of a vast mind
whose interests span the galaxy. His writing has baffled people much
the same way. His early work was ignored—after all, it was science
fiction and was thus treated with the scorn often saved for comic books
and romance novels.

*The Martian Chronicles, Dandelion Wine, Fahrenheit 451, The Illus-
trated Man* and other Bradbury works came out at a time when science
fiction was deemed a refuge for hacks and would-be writers who droned
on in technical prose about gizmos and gadgets of their imaginations.
Bradbury, however, was no drone. His prose soared like literature, and
he populated his tales with appealing characters and inventive contrap-
tions. Beyond that, he introduced challenging themes and asked the
complex questions that had been the province of serious novelists. No
one in science fiction had asked them before.

Today, in this age of *Star Trek* and *The X Files*, it's hard to imagine
life without Bradbury's influence. In addition to his books, he has published more than five hundred short stories and hundreds of teleplays,

259

plus stage plays, operas, essays, nonfiction and the screenplay for John Huston's version of *Moby Dick*. He gives fifty lectures a year and is consulted by a variety of professions, from space science to municipal government. Having trouble getting the residents of your city to use mass transit? Bradbury can offer a quick fix. Are you the owner of a dying mall? Bradbury will tell you how to bring back the customers. Disney hired him to help design Epcot, and NASA flew him to Cape Canaveral to lecture astronauts.

Yet Bradbury seldom sees any of his work reviewed in *The New York Times*, *The New Yorker*, *The Atlantic* or any other house organs of the intelligentsia. Science fiction purists scoff at his attempts at poetry and metaphoric fancy. Undaunted, he rises each morning and heads to the typewriter (computers, he complains, are too quiet) to write, a habit that began when he was a teen in Los Angeles.

In 1934, Bradbury's father, made jobless by the Depression, moved his family from Waukegan, Illinois to Los Angeles, where he found a steady job and an apartment right in the middle of Hollywood. It was a magical summer for the fourteen-year-old Bradbury, who roller-skated to movie premieres, studio gates and the Brown Derby to badger movie stars for autographs.

He was determined to break into show business and nagged George Burns so persistently that Burns finally used some of Bradbury's writing in the vignettes that close the *Burns and Allen* radio show. With no money for college, he spent three years after high school selling newspapers and every free moment reading at the library and browsing local bookstores. He also took a writing class and sold his first story (for $13.75). At twenty-two, he found his writer's voice with the short story "The Lake," which gave him the confidence to write full-time. In another burst of confidence, he asked a young bookstore clerk out for coffee. Maggie is the only woman he has ever dated, and in 1947 he married her (they are still together and are the parents of four grown daughters). Over the next few years he eked out a living selling short stories to magazines until he his Martian pay dirt.

His first novel, *The Martian Chronicles*, was published in 1950 (it has remained in print ever since) and was hailed—in an influential review by literary heavyweight Christopher Isherwood—for eliminating the traditional technical exposition found in most science fiction and for invoking the power of metaphor.

Despite Isherwood's praise, *The Martian Chronicles* pigeonholed Bradbury as a science fiction writer—but it also put him in the company of Robert Heinlein, Isaac Asimov and Arthur C. Clarke, first-rate talents trying to bring creativity and respectability to the genre.

With his next book, he established his reputation as a generally popular writer: 1951's *The Illustrated Man* is an eerie portrayal of a man literally turned inside out. In 1953 he published what many believe is his most compelling novel: *Fahrenheit 451*. The title refers to the temperature at which books burst into flames, and the story is a neo-Orwellian tale of a totalitarian society in which books are forbidden. The book was timely warning against the anti-Communist hysteria that had gripped the country. (In the movie business the Hollywood Ten were sent to prison for refusing to testify before the House Un-American Activities Committee, and in the Screen Writers Guild, Bradbury was one of the lonely voices opposing the loyalty oath imposed on its members.)

Bradbury endured "the worst six months of my life" after agreeing to write the screenplay of *Moby Dick* for Huston. He recounts the ordeal in a memoir entitled *Green Shadows, White Whale*, released in 1992.

After Bradbury made a dismal attempt at adapting *Fahrenheit 451* into a stage play for Charles Laughton, Francois Truffaut turned it into a movie that proved to be an artless hodgepodge and box-office dud. Bradbury did, however, create an original screen treatment for what is considered one of the most influential science fiction movies ever made, *It Came From Outer Space*. *The October Country* is a chilling collection of short stories, while *Dandelion Wine* powerfully recalls Bradbury's boyhood awakenings.

With the science fiction boom in the aftermath of Sputnik, Bradbury's popularity soared; when NASA's Viking landed on Mars in 1976, he was hailed as a space-age prophet. These days he's busier than ever, with an output that now includes twenty-nine books, among them this year's *Quicker Than the Eye*, a collection of twenty new short stories (another five hundred await his fine-tuning for publication), and two volumes of essays. In addition, he writes most of the half-hour episodes for the weekly *Ray Bradbury Theater* on the Science Fiction Channel.

Playboy sent writer Ken Kelley, who interviewed Arthur C. Clarke for this magazine, to talk with Bradbury at his Los Angeles residence. Kelley reports:

"When I arrived at his modest home of forty years in an obscure Los Angeles neighborhood, Bradbury was standing on the front porch bellowing about one of his arch nemeses, the automobile—specifically, his wife's brand-new one, which had been stolen the night before, 'right in front of my own house!' Bradbury is one of the few Angelenos who has never driven a car. Maggie pointed out that they were insured, and when that failed to calm him she offered the first of many heaping bowls of popcorn. That did the trick, and he soon became the avuncular raconteur.

"Our week-long noon-to-dusk sessions were an emotional seesaw between laid-back reminiscences and sudden bursts of passion whenever we touched on any one of Bradbury's pet peeves—Los Angeles, politics, censorship, educators, bureaucrats, cars. He is always blunt and often politically incorrect and he rarely backs down, no matter how unpopular his views. When he raised the logical solutions he espouses in countless essays and on the lecture circuit, I could tell why he's so popular: His enthusiasm is so spontaneous he reminds you of an insistent child—a big, overgrown kid not unlike the one who roller-skated up to Oliver Hardy and asked for his autograph. He beamed as he signed the dog-eared copy of *Dandelion Wine* I've kept since I was ten years old."

Playboy: Many people don't take science fiction seriously, and yet you maintain that it is the essential literature of our age. Why is it so important?

Bradbury: In science fiction, we dream. In order to colonize in space, to rebuild our cities, which are so far out of whack, to tackle any number of problems, we must imagine the future, including the new technologies that are required.

Playboy: Yet most people don't consider science fiction to be part of mainstream literature.

Bradbury: It isn't part of the mainstream—science fiction is the mainstream. It has been since Sputnik. And it will be for the next 10,000 years.

Playboy: So how did Sputnik change things?

Bradbury: People, especially kids, went crazy over science fiction after Sputnik lit the sky. Overnight, instead of an apple on the teacher's desk, there was a book by Asimov. For the first time in history, education came from the bottom up as kids taught their teachers.

Playboy: Why do kids respond to science fiction more than adults?

Bradbury: Obviously, children's imaginations are piqued by the implications of science fiction. Also, as a child, did you want to have someone tying your shoes? Like hell you did. You tied your own as soon as you could. Science fiction acknowledges that we don't want to be lectured at, just shown enough so we can look it up ourselves. The way to teach in this world is to pretend you're not teaching. Science fiction offers the chance to pretend to look the other way while teaching. Science fiction is also a great way to pretend you are writing about the future when in reality you are attacking the recent past and the present. You can criticize communists, racists, fascists or any other clear and present danger, and they can't imagine you are writing about them. Unfortunately, so much old science fiction is too technical and dry.

Playboy: Beyond kids, science fiction is the purview of men, for the most part. Why aren't women as interested?

Bradbury: There are two races of people—men and women—no matter what women's libbers would have you pretend. The male is motivated by toys and science because men are born with no purpose in the universe except to procreate. There is lots of time to kill beyond that. They've got to find work. Men have no inherent center to themselves beyond procreating. Women, however, are born with a center. They can create the universe, mother it, teach it, nurture it. Men read science fiction to build the future. Women don't need to read it. They are the future.

Playboy: Some women don't like it when you make those distinctions. In fact, in People, you said that CD-ROMs are more for men than for women—and you were denounced as sexist on the letters-to-the-editors page shortly thereafter.

Bradbury: Oh well. Unscrew them.

Playboy: What does "unscrew them" mean?

Bradbury: That they'll never get any sex again. [Laughs] Listen, men are nuts. Young men are crazy. We all love toys. I'm toy oriented. I write about toys. I've got a lot of toys. Hundreds of things. But computers are toys, and men like to mess around with smart dumb things. They feel creative.

Playboy: But computers aren't just toys. They're tools for the future.

Bradbury: People are talking about the Internet as a creative tool for writers. I say, "B.S. Stay away from that. Stop talking to people around the world and get your work done." We are being flimflammed by Bill Gates and his partners. Look at Windows '95. That's a lot of flimflam, you know.

Playboy: Why is it flimflam?

Bradbury: Because it doesn't give most people anything more that want they already have. On top of that, when they buy it they have to buy other things to go with it. So you're talking about hundreds of dollars from people who cant afford it. The Windows thing isn't bought by women. I bet if you look at the sales figures, it's 80 percent men. Crazy young men or crazy older men who love toys.

Playboy: For a man who has built a career looking into the future, you seem skeptical of technology—CD-ROMs, the Internet, and multimedia—

Bradbury: It's all meaningless unless you teach reading and writing. It's not going to do a bit of good if you don't know how to read and write.

Playboy: But reading is involved—on computers, people can interact with works of fiction, choosing to move the plot any way they want to.

Bradbury: Don't tell me how to write my novel. Don't tell me you've got a better ending for it. I have no time for that.

Playboy: When you talk about the future, you tend to talk about space travel. Do you really think it's in our future?

Bradbury: It must be. First of all, it's a religious endeavor to be immortal. If the earth dies, we must be able to continue. Space travel will give us other planets to live on so we can continue to have children. It's that simple, that great and that exciting.

Playboy: Will we really be forced to escape earth? Will we be able to in time?

Bradbury: We are already on our way. We should back on the moon right now. And we should be going off to Mars immediately.

Playboy: Yet there doesn't seem to be a rush into space anymore. NASA's budget is being whittled away as we speak.

Bradbury: How come we're looking at our shoes instead of at the great nebula in Orion? Where did we mislay the moon and back off from Mars? The problem is, of course, our politicians, men who have no romance in their hearts or dreams in their heads. JFK, for a brief moment in his last year, challenged us to go to the moon. But even he wasn't motivated by astronomical love. He cried, "Watch my dust!" to the Russians, and we were off. But once we reached the moon, the romance started to fade. Without that, dreams don't last. That's no surprise—material rewards do last, so the history of exploration on earth is about harvesting rich lodes. If NASA's budgeters could be convinced that there are riches on Mars, we would explode overnight to stand on the rim of the Martian abyss. We need space for reasons we have not as yet discovered, and I don't mean Tupperware.

Playboy: Tupperware?

Bradbury: NASA feels it has to justify everything it does in practical terms. And Tupperware was one of the many practical products that came out of space travel. NASA feels it has got to flimflam you to get you to spend money on space. That's b.s. We don't need that. Space travel is life-enhancing, and anything that's life-enhancing is worth doing. It makes you want to live forever.

Playboy: How much is NASA to blame for the apathy about the space program?

Bradbury: The NASA bigwigs have been their own worst enemy. I've pleaded with them for twenty years to let me do a film for them. Most of the early films NASA made about the Mercury and Apollo projects were inept. I want to fuse poetry and fact in a way that, as my various presentations at world fairs did, leaves the audience in tears. But NASA never does transcendent, poetic or explosive things to sell itself—nobody cares about NASA in Congress except, notably enough, Bob Packwood.

Playboy: Do you still see Packwood as a visionary even though he was forced to resign in disgrace?

Bradbury: He's still a visionary. I wish he were still in Congress. I sent him a telegram a year ago and told him to stand firm because those women are jerks. They wait twenty years. They are offended twenty years later. Don't hand me that. There are very few other senators like him, and it's a shame he's gone.

Playboy: What's the biggest mistake NASA has made?

Bradbury: It should have done the space shuttle before the Apollo missions. The shuttle is a big mailbox, an expensive experimental lab. It's not nearly as exciting as it should be. It should have been launched first to circle the earth, which is all it's doing. After that, it should have been sent to the moon, and the program could have ended there. Then we could have built a colony on the moon and moved on to Mars. We need something larger than ourselves—that's a real religious activity. That's what space travel can be—relating ourselves to the universe.

Playboy: When the space program started, did you expect all that to occur?

Bradbury: Yes. But it didn't. NASA is to blame—the entire government is to blame—and the end of the Cold War really pulled the plug, draining any passion that remained. The odd thing to me is the extraordinary number of young people the world over who care about these things, who go to see science fiction films—*2001*, *Close Encounters* and *Star Wars*—who spend billions of dollars to watch the most popular films ever made. Yet the government pays absolutely no attention to this phenomenon. It's always the last to know.

Playboy: Do you think we will at least return to the moon?

Bradbury: I hope we do it while I'm still alive, which means within the next ten to fifteen years. But I think it is a forlorn hope. I hope we'll have a manned expedition to Mars, though the politicians put it way down on their list. But it would be so uplifting for the human spirit. It's hard to get the government to act the way it should.

Playboy: How did you feel when Viking landed on Mars?

Bradbury: There was this festive feeling, like a surprise party, at the CalTech Planetarium the night the Viking ship landed. Carl Sagan and I and a lot of others stayed up all night. Suddenly, the first photographs of Mars started coming back on the giant screen. We were all exhilarated—dancing, laughing and singing. Around nine in the morning, Roy Neal from NBC News came by and held this microphone in front of my face. He said, "Mr. Bradbury, you've been writing about Mars and its civilizations and cities for all these years. Now that we're there and we see that there's no life, how does it feel?" I took a deep breath—I'm so proud I said this out loud to him—and replied: "You idiot! You fool! There is life on Mars—look at us! Look at us! We are the Martians!"

Playboy: You must have felt much the same way when Galileo reached Jupiter last year.

Bradbury: These scientists are incredible. Every time I go to a place like the Jet Propulsion Lab and someone shows me a telescope, he says, "What do you mean?" I say, "You are wonderful. You invented this. You are genius."

Playboy: What is your motivation for writing?

Bradbury: I had decided to be a magician well before I decided to be a writer. I was the little boy who would get up on-stage and do magic wearing a fake mustache, which would fall off during the performance. I'm still trying to perform those tricks. Now I do it with writing. Also, writers write because of a need to be loved. I suppose that's greedy, isn't it? Writing has helped me in other ways. When I started writing seriously, I made the major discovery of my life—that I am right and everybody else is wrong if they disagree with me. What a great thing to learn: Don't listen to anyone else, and always go your own way.

Playboy: Do you admit that that's an unrepentant, egotistical view?

Bradbury: Unfortunately, I don't think I keep my ego in check very well. I try to remember that my voice is loud, which is an ego problem. But at least I don't suffer from self-deluding identity problem like, say, Carl Sagan does.

Playboy: What is the problem with Sagan?

Bradbury: With each passing year he grows stiffer because he goes around thinking he's Carl Sagan. Just as Norman Mailer thinks he's Norman Mailer and Gore Vidal thinks he's Gore Vidal. I don't think I'm Ray Bradbury. That's a big distinction. It doesn't matter who you are. You mustn't go around saying who you are, or else you get captured by the mask of false identity. It's the work that identifies you.

Playboy: Some critics say that you rely too much on fantasy and not enough on science to be a respected science fiction writer.

Bradbury: I don't care what the science fiction trade technicians say, either. They are furious that I get away with murder. I use a scientific idea as a platform to leap into the air and never come back. This keeps them angry at me. They still begrudge my putting an atmosphere on Mars in *The Martian Chronicles* more than forty years ago.

Playboy: A review by Christopher Isherwood launched *The Martian Chronicles*. Did you know him?

Bradbury: The entire scenario set in motion was a fluke. Summertime, 1950, I recognized Isherwood browsing in a Santa Monica bookstore. My book had just come out, so I grabbed a copy off the shelf, signed it and gave it to him. His face fell and my heart sank, but two days later he called and said, "Do you know what you've done?" I asked, "What?" And he simply told me to read his review in the *Times*. His rave turned my life around; the book immediately made the best-seller lists and has been in print ever since. He was very kind in introducing me to various people he thought I should know, like Aldous Huxley, who had been my literary hero since *Brave New World* came out.

Playboy: What was Huxley like?

Bradbury: He was very polite. Most Englishmen, most intellectual Englishmen, are very polite, and they treat you as if you're the genius, which is a sweet thing to do. Years after we met, I was a panelist along with Huxley discussing the future of American literature. However, I was disappointed when he refused to admit that science fiction is the only way for fiction to go.

Playboy: He was already extolling the virtues of psychedelics by then. We presume he offered you some.

Bradbury: I gave him the right answer: No, thank. I don't want anyone lifting the trapdoor on my head—it may not go down again.

Playboy: Who are the best new science fiction writers?

Bradbury: I'm so busy with a full agenda, I just don't have the time to hunt around for any. Do you realize that hundreds of novels come out every year now?

Playboy: Are you ducking the question?

Bradbury: OK—I admit I don't want to read in my own field.

Playboy: Why not?

Bradbury: Because it's incestuous, and you can't do that. You should read in your own field only when you're young. When I was eight, ten, twelve, sixteen, twenty-five, I read science fiction. But then I went on to Alexander Pope and John Donne and Molière to mix it up.

Playboy: What about some of the more famous science fiction names, such as Kurt Vonnegut?

Bradbury: I know him and we get on fine. We had a wonderful day together in New York a few years ago, and he had a nice sense of humor.

But I haven't read anything since Player Piano, and that was forty years ago. So I can't give you any comment.

Playboy: How about Robert Heinlein?

Bradbury: I met him at Clifton's cafeteria in downtown Los Angeles. I had just graduated from high school, and Heinlein was thirty-one years old. He was well-known, and he wrote humanistic science fiction, which influenced me to dare to be human instead of mechanical.

Playboy: What about those writers who popularize science in nonfiction books, such as Stephen Hawkings and his *Brief History of Time*?

Bradbury: We have his book, but I'm not going to kid you and say I read it. My wife claims she has, but I don't believe her. I don't believe anyone has read it. I'm positive the guy is a genius and it's wonderful he has done what he's done.

Playboy: You have also written nonfiction, such as *Green Shadows, White Whale*, about your attempt to adapt *Moby Dick* with director John Huston. Were you attempting to get even for a disastrous experience?

Bradbury: Writing that book was gloriously cathartic. What got me started was that Katherine Hepburn's bad book about the making of *The African Queen* excluded so much and was quite scant about Huston's character. Her skimpy failure made me furious and propelled me to begin my own book.

Playboy: Was it that she was too easy on Huston?

Bradbury: Yes, and that upset me.

Playboy: How did you get the job to adapt *Moby Dick* in the first place?

Bradbury: Huston invited my to his Beverly Hills Hotel suite, put a drink in my hand and flattered my with enough Irish charm that, before I knew it, I'd agreed to spend six months in Ireland writing the script. Acting ability runs in Huston's bloodline.

Playboy: So he was on good behavior.

Bradbury: And I was fooled. I should have just admitted that he embodied the monster I realized he was and then quit. What kept me going despite the merciless cruelty he showed toward me and everyone else near him were three things: the love I felt for Herman Melville and his whale; my awe of John Huston's genius, as proved in *The Maltese Falcon*—he had directed the perfect movie; and my deep appreciation of how very few people in the world are lucky enough to get that kind of opportunity. Now I'm left with the bittersweet knowledge that, thanks to him, I learned so much that I otherwise wouldn't know. Nobody else in Hollywood would have given an unproven newcomer the chance to write a major script.

Playboy: Did that experience influence your decision not to write the screenplay for the movie adaptation of your next hit novel, *Fahrenheit 451*?

Bradbury: No. In 1955, Charles Laughton got me thoroughly drunk before he told me how bad the stage play I'd adapted for him was and convinced my I should give it up. So years later I told Francois Truffaut, "You do it." I'd had it.

Playboy: Were you happy with Truffaut's effort?

Bradbury: It was very good, but he was a coward about doing certain things. He didn't put in the Mechanical Hound, which should be included, because it's a metaphoric adventure thing. The tactical stuff is really miserable. The flying men should be cut out. They're not flying anywhere except down. And the casting was a mistake. Not all of it. Oskar Werner I like very much.

Playboy: Who didn't you like?

Bradbury: Julie Christie playing the girl next-door. She couldn't play it. She was supposed to be sixteen. So Truffaut did the trick. He had Julie Christie play the wife and the girl next-door, which was confusing. Sometimes you weren't quite sure who was talking.

Playboy: How do you feel about having a second opportunity to turn the novel into a movie now that Mel Gibson is interested?

Bradbury: I've wanted to redo *Fahrenheit 451* ever since it came out in 1966, because Truffaut left out so much from the novel. I sat bolt upright when I was told that Warner Bros. wanted to make the new version with Mel Gibson.

Playboy: Along with Orwell's *1984* and Huxley's *Brave New World*, your book presents a bleak view of the future. Were you trying to write a cautionary story?

Bradbury: That's fatal. You must never do that. A lot of lousy novels come from people who want to do good. The do-gooder novel. The ecological novel. And if you tell me you're doing a novel or a film about how a woodsman spares a tree, I'm not going to go see it for a minute.

Playboy: It's hard to imagine that the man who wrote *Fahrenheit 451* was not trying to predict the future.

Bradbury: It's "prevent the future," that's the way I put it. Not predict it, prevent it. And with anger and attacking, yes. You have the fun of attacking the thing you think is stupid. But your motives are hidden from you at the time. It's like, "I'll be damned. I didn't know I was doing that." For instance, when a bright Sony inventor read about my seashell radios in that novel, he invented the Walkman. That was one good thing to emerge from that book—the banishment of most picnic-ruining ghetto blasters. But I had no idea I was doing it.

Playboy: *Fahrenheit 451* seems to have predicted the unpredictable for years.

Bradbury: Yes. When O.J. Simpson prowled the freeway pursued by cop cars and helicopters, Russell Baker wrote in his *New York Times* column words to the effect: This is the last act of *Fahrenheit 451*! I watched the reruns and thought, "My God, he's right." In the final pages of my novel, Montag is running ahead of the book burners and sees himself on TV screens in every home, through each window, as he flees. When he eludes the Mechanical Hound, the society he left behind gets frustrated and kills a proxy Montag on television to satisfy the panicked need. Even more depressing is that I foresaw political correctness forty-three years ago.

Playboy: In *Fahrenheit 451*, too?

Bradbury: Yes. [At one point, another character,] the fire chief, describes how the minorities, one by one, shut the mouths and minds of the public, suggesting a precedent: The Jews hated Fagin and Shylock—burn them both, or at least never mention them. The blacks didn't like Nigger Jim floating on Huck's raft with him—burn, or at least hide, him. Women's libbers hated Jane Austen as an awfully inconvenient woman in a dreadfully old-fashioned time—off with her head! Family-values groups detested Oscar Wilde—back in the closet, Oscar! Communists hated the bourgeoisie—shoot them! An on and on it goes. So whereas back then I wrote about the tyranny of the majority, today I'd combine that with the tyranny of the minorities. These days, you have to be careful of both. They both want to control you. The first group, by making you do the same thing over and over again. The second group is indicated by the letters I get from the Vassar girls who want me to put more women's lib in *The Martian Chronicles*, or from blacks who want more black people in *Dandelion Wine*.

Playboy: Do you respond to them?

Bradbury: I say to both bunches, Whether you're a majority or minority, bug off! To hell with anybody who wants to tell me what to write. Their society breaks down into subsections of minorities who then, in effect, burn books by banning them. All this political correctness that's rampant on campuses is b.s. You can't fool around with the dangerous notion of telling a university what to teach and what not to. If you don't like the curriculum, go to another school. Faculty members who toe the same line are sanctimonious nincompoops! It's time to stop the trend. Whenever it appears, you should yell, "Idiot!" and back them down. In the same vein, we should immediately bar all quotas, which politicize the process through lowered admission standards that accept less-qualified students. The terrible result is the priceless chance lost by all.

Playboy: So you disapprove of affirmative action?

Bradbury: The whole concept of higher education is negated unless the sole criterion used to determine if students qualify is the grades they score on standardized tests. Education is purely an issue of learning— we can no longer afford to have it polluted by damn politics. Leave pollution up to the politicians [laughs].P How did you feel being so prescient?

Bradbury: Thoroughly disgruntled.

Playboy: Is the public well-informed about these issues?

Bradbury: The news is all rapes and murders we didn't commit, funerals we don't attend, AIDS we don't want to catch. All crammed into a quarter of a minute! But at least we still have a hand with which to switch channels or turn off altogether. I tell my lecture audiences to never, ever watch local TV news.

Playboy: What about magazines? You have been an avid magazine reader since you were a kid. How would you rate the current crop?

Bradbury: Magazines today are almost all stupid and moronic to start with. And it makes me furious that I can't find any articles to read anymore. I used to enjoy *Forbes* and *Fortune*, but now the pages are completely cluttered with ads. That's what caused me to explode three years ago when I spoke to a gathering of the country's leading editors and publishers.

Playboy: Why did you explode?

Bradbury: Let's say the slow burn grew hotter the more I thought about what a chance I had. So I took along my props—copies of *Forbes*, *Fortune*, *Good Housekeeping*, *McCall's*, *Vogue* and *People*. I went up onstage and said, "Let's talk about the real problems with your magazines." I held up *Good Housekeeping*, flipped through the pages and said, "Find the articles—you can't." I held up *McCall's* and *Vogue* and said, "Look, the same thing." I held up *Forbes* and *Fortune*—"Look at this," I said. "You've got a half-page article here, you've got the start of an article on the left, then you look to the right and it's a full-page ad." I threw them off the podium. Then I held up an issue of *People* and said, "Do you really want to read a magazine like this? To hell with Time Inc.!" and threw it down. I paused and lowered the boom, saying, "The magazines of this country have to take over education—even more than the corporations—because you want readers in the future, don't you? Can you keep downgrading people's intelligence and insult them with the shit you're publishing? You should make sure the schools teach reading, or you're out on your ass in a couple of years. You won't have any readers— doesn't that scare you? It scares me. Change your product and invite me back to talk to you again." I stopped and waited, figuring that maybe they would do something if I managed to scare them enough.

Playboy: Did they?

Bradbury: I got a standing ovation. Afterward, Christie Hefner came over and congratulated me—I didn't even know *Playboy* would be there. *Playboy* is in fact one of the best magazines in history, simply because it has done more than any other magazine. It has published the works of most of the important short story writers of our time, as well as some of the most important novelists and essayists—and just about every important American artist. The interviews have included just about everyone in the world with something important to say. Nowhere else can you find such a complete spectrum, from the semi-vulgar to the highfalutin [laughs]. I have defended *Playboy* since the beginning. Its editors were brave enough to say, "The hell with what McCarthy thing" when they ran excerpts from *Fahrenheit 451*. I couldn't sell that to any other magazine because they were all running scared. And I must add another important point—one I'm sure that many other guys growing up in the sorry years before *Playboy* existed will agree with—which is that there would have been a lot fewer problems if *Playboy* had been around back then. I wish I'd had *Playboy* when I was fourteen.

Playboy: To sharpen your writing skills?

Bradbury: Come on! Those pictures are great. There was nothing when my generation was growing up. Like it or not, I rest my case, except to add that Hugh Hefner is one of the great sexual revolutionaries.

Playboy: Why do you shy away from eroticism in your own writing?

Bradbury: There is no reason to write pornography when your own sex life is good. Why waste time writing about it?

Playboy: It has always struck us as strange that most science fiction is relatively sexless.

Bradbury: There are certain kinds of people who write science fiction. I think a lot of us married late. A lot of us are mama's boys. I lived at home until I was twenty-seven. But most of the writers I know in any field, especially science fiction, grew up late. They're so interested in doing what they do and in their science, they don't think about other things.

Playboy: What is the most challenging literary form you have worked in?

Bradbury: I'm trying to write operas. I'm still learning. I'm writing a musical based on *Dandelion Wine*, which I've been working on for thirty years with various composers. I'm doing a new thing now with Jimmy Webb. We've been messing around with these things for eight years. Juggling the pieces, trying to figure out where you shut your mouth and let the song take over.

Playboy: What brought you to Hollywood in the first place?

Bradbury: The Depression brought me here from Waukegan, Illinois. The majority of people in the country were unemployed. My dad had been jobless in Waukegan for at least two years when in 1934 he announced to my mom, my brother and me that it was time to head West. I had just turned fourteen when we got to California with only forty dollars, which paid for our rent and bought our food until he finally found a job making wire at a cable company for fourteen dollars a week. That meant I could stay in Los Angeles, which was great. I was thrilled.

Playboy: With what aspect of it?

Bradbury: I was madly in love with Hollywood. We lived about four blocks from the Uptown Theater, which was the flagship theater for MGM and Fox. I learned how to sneak in. There were previews almost every week. I'd roller-skate over there—I skated all over town, hell-bent on getting autographs from glamorous stars. It was glorious. I saw big MGM stars such as Norma Shearer, Laurel and Hardy, Ronald Coleman. Or I'd spend all day in front of Paramount or Columbia, then zoom over to the Brown Derby to watch the stars coming or going. I'd see Cary Grant, Marlene Dietrich, Fred Allen, Burns and Allen—whoever was on the Coast. Mae West made her appearance—bodyguard in tow—every Friday night.

Playboy: The story is that you pestered George Burns to give you your first show business job. Is that true?

Bradbury: Yes. George was kind. He would read the scripts I'd write every week. They were dreadful, and I was so blindly and madly in love with the film and radio business in Hollywood that I didn't realize what a pest I was. George no doubt thought he could get me off his back by using my words for one of the eight-line vignettes he had Gracie close their broadcasts with. I wanted to live that special life forever. When that summer was over, I stopped my inner time clock at the age of fourteen. Another reason I became a writer was to escape the hopelessness and despair of the real world and enter the world of hope I could create with my imagination.

Playboy: Did your parents approve?

Bradbury: They were very permissive, thank God. And strangely enough, my parents never protested. They just figured I was crazy and that God would protect me. Of course back then you could go around town at night and never risk getting mugged or beaten up.

Playboy: What do you think of modern Los Angeles—earthquakes, riots, O.J., fires and all?

Bradbury: The earthquake actually renewed optimism throughout L.A.—it fused us, just as all the other calamities did. You pick up the first brick, then the second and so on. I've never seen so many people helping so many other people. A small boy cam to my door to tell me my chimney was about to collapse—I didn't know. The next day a stranger from up the street dropped in to give us the names of some really good builders and repairmen. They turned out to be superb—jolly, bright and inventive library people, readers! They lived with us for more than a month. They became family—we missed them when they left. I've heard similar things from everyone around us and in the San Fernando Valley, where things were twenty times worse.

Playboy: Were you surprised when, after the earthquake, the freeways were rebuilt within a few months?

Bradbury: And almost before anything else? No. Here a human without a car is a samurai without his sword. I would replace cars wherever possible with buses, monorails, rapid trains—whatever is takes to make pedestrians the center of our society again, and cities worthwhile enough for pedestrians to live in. I don't care what people do with their cars, as long as they give them up three quarters of the time—roughly the amount of time people spend every week superfluously driving places they don't want to go to visit people who don't want to see them.

Playboy: That's easy for you to say; you have never driven a car.

Bradbury: Not a day in my life.

Playboy: Why not?

Bradbury: When I was sixteen, I saw six people die horribly in an accident. I walked home holding on to walls and trees. It took me months to being to function again. So I don't drive. But whether I drive or not is irrelevant. The automobile is the most dangerous weapon in our society—cars kill more than wars do. More than 50,000 people will die this year because of them and nobody seems to notice.

Playboy: Until recently, you were the futurist afraid to fly in airplanes, never mind spaceships. What was it that cured your phobia?

Bradbury: A car breaking down in so many small Southern towns and the chauffeur taking three miserable days just to get through Florida. After the second tire blew, I got the word. In a loud and clear voice from the heavens above I heard the message: Fly, dummy, fly! [Laughs] I was afraid for forty years that I'd run around the plane yelling, "Stop! Let me off!" But I fly all the time now. I just sit back relaxed, occasionally peep out the window and peruse the magazines.

Playboy: Was your faith in law enforcement shaken because of Stacey Koon and Mark Fuhrman?

Bradbury: We've become what I call a Kleenex society—I saw the public's reaction as the symbolic chance to blow its collective nose on the whole police force of the United States, holding all cops responsible for incidents in Los Angeles. Of course I knew there was a problem in the LAPD. On the other hand, three of my daughters have been raped and robbed by black men, so I have a prejudice, too, don't I? And if I ever were to find the bastards, I'd kill them. I've seen violence used by police, and I've seen it used against white people, too.

Playboy: Did the Rodney King riots shock you?

Bradbury: I was more than shocked—I was terribly upset, and terribly angry at Mayor Bradley. The friend I've known for ten years was the man who went on television half an hour after the trial was over and used terrible language to say he was outraged. Boom!—next thing you know, the mobs burned the streets. Thus far I haven't had the guts to tell Tom Bradley, face-to-face, "You did it!"

Playboy: Did you have any idea there was so much rage in Los Angeles' black community?

Bradbury: I don't think anybody knew

Playboy: Did you feel any empathy for the rioters?

Bradbury: None. Why should I? I don't approve of any mob anywhere at any time. Had we not controlled it in L.A., all the big cities in this country would have gone up in flames.

Playboy: If Los Angeles is an indicator for the nation, what is the future of other big cities?

Bradbury: Along with man's return to the moon, my biggest hope is that L.A. will show the way for all of our cities to rebuild, because they've gone to hell and the crime rate has soared. When we can repopulate them, the crime rate will plunge.

Playboy: What will help?

Bradbury: We need enlightened corporations to do it; they're the only ones who can. All the great malls have been built by corporate enterprises. We have to rebuild cities with the same conceptual flair that the great malls have. We can turn any bad section of town into a vibrant new community.

Playboy: How do you convince corporate leaders and bureaucrats that you have the right approach?

Bradbury: They listen because they know my track record. The center of downtown San Diego was nonexistent until a concept of mine, the Horton Plaza, was built right in the middle of bleakest skid row. Civilization returned to San Diego upon its completion. It became the center of a thriving community. And the Glendale Galleria, based on my concept, changed downtown Glendale when it was built nearly twenty-five years ago. So if I live another ten years—please, God!—I'll be around to witness a lot of this in Los Angeles and inspire the same thing in big cities throughout the country.

Playboy: You have said that you want to influence children. Is that you most important audience?

Bradbury: I feel like I own all the kids in the world because, since I've never grown up myself, all my books are automatically for children.

Playboy: How does it feel to have an impact on children?

Bradbury: It's mutual delight and love made manifest. For one thing, kids love me because I write stories that tell them about their capacity for evil. I'm one of the few writers who lets you cleanse yourself that way.

Playboy: Would you say you're nostalgic for childhood?

Bradbury: Yeah. Once you let yourself begin to be grown-up, you face a world full of problems you can't solve. The politicians and specialists—adults, all—have a hard enough time trying to figure out where to look. It doesn't have to be that way. The greatest solutions in society are reached by corporate thinking, ruled by a motive to either make a profit or go out of business. There's great incentive to strive for excellence. On the other hand, bloated bureaucracies like city governments don't have to make a profit—they just raise people's taxes when they need more money. If you want to get anything done, it should be through a corporation. Disney is a prime example.

Playboy: Didn't the Eighties—the decade of Wall Street junk-bond scandals and bankrupt banks—establish that corporate chiefs can be little more than thieves?

Bradbury: I'm talking about top-flight people like those at IBM, Apple, AT&T. If corporations don't take over the educational system soon, we'll end up with all black-and-brown cities surrounded by white-flight small towns, which are under construction even as we speak. You can't blame whites for getting the hell out. City governments have neglected the biggest factor in our criminal environment—education. Kindergarten. First grade. If we don't change those immediately, we'll raise another generation of empty-headed dummies. If you let boys grow up as that, when they reach the age of ten they're bored, drop out, take dope, rob stores, rape—all that good stuff. Our jails overflow with illiterates who have been ignored by our city leaders. Jails should be run as schools, where kids are taught the basics, instead of spending a billion dollars a day just to keep them locked up. The government should stop sending schools money until they prove they are teaching reading and writing. We should fire half the teachers right now. This is an emergency—we're raising a criminal culture in all races and every walk of life by not teaching kids how to read and write. That scares me more than anything, yet I don't hear anyone else talking about the primary grades— where our future lies. The corporations I mention are getting involved more and more in magnet school relationships with local schools. The reasoning is hardly utopian—it's actually a selfish endeavor since they must educate the kids who grow up to be a part of their companies.

Playboy: A future when our children are taught to be useful employees of big companies? It sounds like a robotic race in some science fiction story.

Bradbury: You mean the way Japan-bashers portray that society? Listen, you can't turn really bright people into robots. You can turn dumb people into robots, but that's true in every society and system. I don't know what to do with dumb people, but we must try to educate them along with the sharp kids. You teach a kid to read and write by the second grade, and the rest will take care of itself. To solve the drug problem, we have to start at the root—first grade. If a boy has all the toys in his head that reading can give him, and you hook him into science fiction, then you've got the future secured.

Playboy: How does it feel to get older?

Bradbury: On my seventieth birthday, when I reflected that so many of my friends were dead or dying, it hit me that it was high time I got more work done. Ever since that time, I have done the active, smart thing by increasing my productivity. I'm not on the rocks or shoals yet, but the last few years have been a devastation of illnesses and deaths of many good friends. [*Star Trek* creator] Gene Roddenberry was a loss that deeply grieved me.

Playboy: How well did you know him?

Bradbury: Gene was an intimate friend. We'd been friends for many years when he asked me to write for *Star Trek* more than twenty-five years ago. But I've never had the ability to adapt other people's ideas into any sensible form.

Playboy: What did you think of Roddenberry's final flourish, when NASA honored his will's request and released his ashes into space on one of its missions? Sound tempting?

Bradbury: That was interesting. At one time, I had planned to have my ashes put into a Campbell's tomato soup can and then have it planted on Mars. [Laughs] But in recent years, I have come to realize that I have a lot of fans and lovers out there. So I plan to design a big, long, flat gravestone that will be inscribed with the names of my books and lots of dandelions, as a tribute to *Dandelion Wine*, because so many people love it. At the bottom of the slab there will be a sign saying PLACE DANDELIONS HERE—I hope people will, so a living yellow meadow can bloom in the spring and summertime.

Playboy: Do you believe in God?

Bradbury: I believe in Darwin and God together. It's all one. It's all mysterious. Look at the universe. It's been here forever. It's totally impossible. But, then, the size of the universe is impossible. It goes on forever, there's no end. That's impossible. We're impossible. And the fact that the sun gave birth to the planets, and the planets cooled, and the rain fell and we came out of the oceans as animals. How come dead matter decided to come alive? It just did. There is no explanation. There's no theory.

Playboy: You almost sound like a fundamentalist preacher. You say you believe in Darwinism, but you sometimes sound like a creationist.

Bradbury: Or a combination of both. Because nobody knows. Science and religion have to go hand in hand with the mystery, because there's a certain point beyond which you say, "There are no answers." Why does the sun burn? We don't know. It just does—that's the answer. Why were the planets created? We don't know. It happened. How come there's life on the earth? We don't know. It just happened. You accept that as a scientist and as a religious preacher. The scientist can teach us to survive by learning more about how the body works, what disease is, how to cure ourselves and how to work on longevity. The preacher then says, "Don't forget to pay attention to the fact that you're alive." Just the mere fact, the glory of getting up every morning and looking at the sunrise or a good rainfall or whatever, and saying, "That's wonderful." That's just wonderful. The Darwin theory can't be proved; it's a theory. We think it is true.

Playboy: Do you think it's true?

Bradbury: Nobody knows. I can't give you an opinion about it. It's only a theory, you see.

Playboy: Do you go to church?

Bradbury: No. I don't believe in the anthropomorphic God.

Playboy: Do you think our souls live on or do we cease to exist when we die?

Bradbury: Well. I have four daughters and eight grandchildren. My soul lives on in them. That's immortality. That's the only immortality I care about.

May 1996

CONTRIBUTORS' NOTES

BRENDAN BERNHARD is a staff writer at the *L.A. Weekly*, where he writes about the arts and also makes the occasional foray into sports and politics. He moved to Los Angeles in 1995. He is not related to the Mulhollands, though his half-brother is.

DAVID FINE is a recently-retired professor of English at California State Long Beach, where he has taught since 1968. His publications include the books, *The City, The Immigrant, and American Fiction, 1880–1920* and *Imagining Los Angeles: a City in Fiction*. He has also edited five collections of essays on California writing and has published a few dozen articles on literary topics.

KATE GALE is the author of four poetry books, a novel and a children's book. She teaches journalism at Loyola Marymount University. She is a Ph.D candidate in literature at Claremont Graduate University and the managing editor of Red Hen Press.

LYNELL GEORGE was born and raised in Los Angeles. She is the author of *No Crystal Stair: African Americans in the City of Angels* (Verso/Anchor), a collection of essays and reportage about the history and persistence of black Los Angeles. After graduating from Loyola Marymount University, she did post-graduate work in creative writing at San Francisco State University. Formerly a staff writer at *L.A. Weekly* covering culture and race, she now writes for the *Los Angeles Times*.

PETER GILSTRAP was born and raised in Pasadena. He graduated from John Muir High School, where he had the same philosophy teacher as noted Muir alumni David Lee Roth and Sirhan Sirhan. He took his diploma and moved to Washington D.C., where he immediately quit college and began playing in bands and waiting tables, ultimately writing for *The Washington Post*. He returned to L.A. for good in 1993, writing an award-winning column for the

L.A. New Times. He now writes for Hollywood, and eagerly waits each new dawn that finds him in the greatest city on earth.

LAURENCE GOLDSTEIN grew up in Culver City, the "Heart of Screenland," and received a B.A. from UCLA and a Ph.D. from Brown University. Since 1970 he has taught at the University of Michigan, where he has edited *Michigan Quarterly Review* since 1977. Poems about Los Angeles appear in his three volumes: *Altamira* (Abattoir), *The Three Gardens* (Copper Beech, 1987), and *Cold Reading* (Copper Beech, 1995). He is the author of *The American Poet at the Movies: A Critical History* (University of Michigan Press), and the editor or co-editor of seven books.

PICO IYER is the author of several books on the romance between cultures, including *Video Night in Kathmandu, The Lady and the Monk and The Global Soul.* His latest book, the novel *Abandon*, discusses the dialogue between Islam and southern California (where he has lived on and off since 1965).

KEN KELLEY was a San Francisco-based magazine writer and a regular contributor to the *Playboy* Interview.

DAVID KIPEN is a native Angeleno who bleeds Dodger blue—among Giant fans, sometimes literally—and the book critic for the *San Francisco Chronicle.* He tries to think of himself as a Californian.

SUSAN MOFFAT was a staff writer at the *Los Angeles Times* in the early '90s and has been based in Tokyo, Seoul, and Hong Kong for the Associated Press, *Fortune* magazine and other publications. She has also worked as communications director for Greenbelt Alliance, a San Francisco Bay Area land conservation and urban planning non-profit. Currently, she is a stay-at-home mom in the small town of Albany, near Berkeley, and goes to a lot of zoning and traffic meetings.

JOHN POWERS is deputy editor of the *L.A. Weekly*, for which he writes a media/culture column, "On." He is also film critic for National Public Radio's *Fresh Air* and *Gourmet*'s International Correspondent. After teaching at Georgetown University, he moved to Los Angeles in 1985, first becoming film editor at *L.A. Weekly* (where he worked from 1985–1993), then becoming the L.A.-based film critic for *Vogue*. He lives in Pasadena with his filmmaker wife Sandi Tan.

SARA SCRIBNER is a Los Angeles freelancer and native Angeleno who has written about music and books for *Rolling Stone*, the *Los Angeles Times*, *L.A. Weekly*, and *MOJO*.

PAUL SKENAZY teaches literature and writing at the University of California, Santa Cruz. He has written extensively on California detective fiction and L.A. noir literature and edited volumes of essays on Los Angeles and San Francisco fiction. His review columns on detective fiction appear regularly in *The Washington Post*. He is the editor of *Conversations with Maxine Hong Kingston* and *La Mollie and the King of Tears* a posthumous novel by Arturo Islas. He lives in Santa Cruz.

ARIEL SWARTLEY is the book columnist for *Los Angeles Magazine*. A former Bostonian, she emigrated to Los Angeles in 1988. Since then, her writings about varieties of popular culture including rock and roll, film and food have appeared in the *New York Times*, *Boston Globe* and *L.A. Weekly*.

DAVID L. ULIN is the editor of two collections of Southern California literature: *Another City: Writing from Los Angeles* (City Lights) and *Writing Los Angeles: A Literary Anthology* (The Library of America). His essays and criticism have appeared in *The Atlantic Monthly*, the *Los Angeles Times*, *The Nation*, *L.A. Weekly*, *The New York Times Book Review*, and on National Public Radio's *All Things Considered*.

MARCOS M. VILLATORO is a poet and novelist whose last book, *Minos: A Romilia Chacon Novel* will be published in the fall of 2003. He has won the Silver Medal in the *Foreword* Magazine Literary Awards and the Latino Literary Hall of Fame Prize. He holds the Fletcher Jones Endowed Chair in Writing at Mount St. Mary's College. He is also the host of *Shelf Life*, a weekly program on KPFK 90.7 fm, in which he interviews novelists and poets from all over the world.

CHRYSS YOST was born in San Diego and has lived in Santa Barbara since 1990, where she runs a poetry series and is a book columnist for the *Santa Barbara Independent*. She is the co-editor of two poetry anthologies, *California Poetry*, with Dana Gioia, and *Poetry Daily Unplugged*, with Diane Boller and Don Selby), editor of the literary magazine *Solo*, and author of two chapbooks, *La Jolla Boys* (Mille Grazie) and *Escaping from Autopia* (Oberon).

ABOUT THE EDITORS

SCOTT TIMBERG, a Palo Alto native, made the mistake of spending most of his first twenty-eight years on the East Coast. A graduate of Wesleyan University and the University of North Carolina at Chapel Hill, he worked for five years as an editor and writer for *New Times Los Angeles*. He currently covers the arts and culture for the *Los Angeles Times*.

DANA GIOIA was born in Los Angeles in 1950. He received his B.A. and M.B.A. degrees from Stanford University. He also has an M.A. in Comparative Literature from Harvard University. For fifteen years, he worked as a business executive in New York before quitting in 1992 to write full-time. He has published three collections of poetry—*Daily Horoscope* (Graywolf, 1986), *The Gods of Winter* (Graywolf, 1991), and *Interrogations at Noon* (Graywolf, 2001), which won the American Book Award. He has also written an opera libretto, *Nosferatu* (Graywolf, 2001). The first editions of *Can Poetry Matter?* (Graywolf, 1992) was a finalist for the National Book Critics Circle Award. A prolific essayist, reviewer, and translator, Gioia has also published nine anthologies of poetry and fiction. Dana Gioia was appointed Chairman of the National Endowment for the Arts in February 2003.